DEATH'S IMPERFE...

Death's Imperfect Witness

Pam Leonard

North Star Press of St. Cloud, Inc.
St. Cloud, Minnesota

ISBN-10: 0-87839-386-2
ISBN-13: 978-0-87839-386-2

First Edition, September 2010

Printed in the United States of America

Published by
North Star Press of St. Cloud, Inc.
P.O. Box 451
St. Cloud, Minnesota 56302

www.northstarpress.com

Dedication...

... For Bill

Acknowledgements

This absolutely must be said ... thanks Mom ... for sharing your love of mystery and suspense, and for always being in my corner. To Bill, Kati, David, and the rest of my enthusiastic clan ... thanks for believing. To my family of friends Cecie, Shelli, Pat, Vicki, Jeni, Eileen, Lori, Brenda, Judy, Janelle, Kris, Kirsten and Sharon ... thanks for giving of yourselves and your support so generously. A special thank you to Sylvia Crannell for the insightful and thoughtful feedback ... the answer to a writer's prayer. And finally, to the staff and patients of "Mother Hennepin" ... thank you for the lessons in humanity.

PROLOGUE

Should have brought bug dope.

A breeze tousled Lucy's hair and scattered the mosquitoes for a single blessed moment. She stayed alert at the treehouse window that didn't have a screen and figured the stupid-ass rich kid who'd built it must have moved from somewhere without bugs.

Dumb little dick-wad.

She briefly clicked on her flashlight and swept the room, noticing pot seeds on the floor. Wasting his parent's money on weed.

Yeah ... older maybe, but still dumb. And probably still a dick-wad.

Deciding that made her feel better.

Finally.

Lucy watched the sun disappear in a thin pink ribbon. Tonight all the smug, arrogant fucks on this block would be careless. She knew them well.

Watching while squatting in a foreclosure, she'd seen how they left garage doors open while driving off to run errands or visit with the neighbors, and she couldn't believe her luck. Place was like soap opera land ... every door left open a crack. She could come and go without knocking.

Lucy thought maybe they acted this way because they were life-stupid ... not getting how vulnerable they were, having what others needed. Still, it seemed like such a simple thing to figure out. Shouldn't have to come from poor to think it through.

But sometimes she also wondered if there was a different reason they lived this way, a reason that *she* didn't understand. Maybe you even had to grow up here to know it. After all, they did seem happy. She kicked at the pot seeds on the floor. Hell, maybe they *did* trust people. Maybe it even felt *good* to do that.

Yeah, stupid it is. She scratched harder at the bug bites.

But stupid or not ... this block had been tougher than the others. She hoped it was because these houses contained more items of value. But it was probably just

1

that these folks were home less often. Maybe traveled a lot for work. Because it was when they were home that they got really careless. After all, who would have the balls to walk right into a house when the owner was in the backyard? Lucy had to laugh. They sure as hell wouldn't figure *her* for it.

Balls.

She smiled thinking about it. Oh, yeah, sure, there was nerve involved . . . but mostly you just needed smarts. As a girl, she figured she had an advantage there.

She wiped down her sweaty forearms, leaving streaks of mosquito blood. It'd been fun thinking of this high-end Minneapolis neighborhood as hers, but she'd been working it for three months and knew she'd have to move on soon. The key was to leave a light footprint, then disappear into her jungle. The shadows of the city . . . the very places these people avoided.

She kind of puffed up at the thought. It made her feel tougher, better than them even. The fact that she wasn't afraid of the dark alleys and maze of buildings made her proud.

Surveying the backyards from her elevated vantage point the rush of adrenaline was getting ahead of her.

Hurry the fuck up, people!

Uncharacteristic. Maybe it was the mosquito hatch. Lucy's line of work not only required smarts, but patience. In this place, forcing things would put a predator like Lucy at a disadvantage. Instead, you had to observe their habits and wait for opportunities. Rule number one of the three she religiously adhered to . . . observe and plan. Then stick to it, or things could go wrong in a hurry. To do that, you had to be patient.

Yeah, it was brains, patience *and* discipline, Lucy told herself. That was why she could do this and others couldn't. It was also that she was so small. Fifteen years old on paper maybe, but she looked more like twelve. Still had to shoplift from the "kids" section. If she'd been born a boy, with size and muscle, she wouldn't have been forced to develop skills. The fast, lazy route to getting what she needed would have been available . . . beating the crap out of people, or flashing a gun. But hell, those that did were in jail or dead. And unlike them, she could actually take care of herself.

Yeah, beware of the little guy, she laughed. *Low expectations.*

Lucy thought back to when she still went to school. Junior high. She'd gotten a perfect score on a science test. The grade hadn't surprised her, hadn't even seemed hard to get, but the pond-scum teacher had hauled her ass up in front of the class and tried to embarrass her. Tried. Asked her whose paper she'd copied . . . figuring a goof-off girl like her *must* have cheated.

Funny thing was though, up until that very moment she'd never scammed anyone, let alone a teacher. So she asked . . . did anyone else get a perfect score? When he'd said no one had, she asked . . . then just who in the hell did I copy from? He didn't have an answer. F minus. It felt good to see *him* turn red instead. Yeah, low expectations. If they'd been higher, she might still be in school.

Too fucking bad. She preferred being on her own anyway. Working alone. She had skills and knowledge that she'd taken big risks to get. Nope, Lucy wasn't into sharing anything that had come that hard . . . except with Andi. She never bragged. Andi kept quiet too. It was one of the first things Lucy taught her. If you were a kid with money, or a way to get it . . . hell if you were a kid . . . you were a target.

And they stayed away from the other kids. Why attract hovering pimps and dealers, promising all kinds of shit, only so they could use you up? As smart as Lucy was, she was smart enough to know there would always be Someone more cunning than she, and Someone Else willing to do anything to get what he wanted. It was simple sense to avoid them.

Still all of it seemed kind of stupid to Lucy, at least not very efficient, that most of those cunning Someones chose to take from people who didn't have jack . . . each other. She guessed it was the same with white-collar crooks, they went after each other too, but at least *there* it made some kind of sense. Too easy, she shook her head, like the science test. Keep a low profile, and take from people who actually *have* shit.

One by one the lights finally went out. She watched her dimwitted herd emerge from their garages and file onto the street. They all headed in the same direction and kind of reminded her of cows in a field, taking well-worn paths.

Hell if I get these people. With all that money, I'd sure as hell figure out someone might be after it. Why not turn around and lock the damn door? Or engage the expensive security system? Should be easy. Why not do it?

Dumb fucks.

Small comfort. She tried not to like them. Problem was, they didn't seem all that bad, just stupid . . . as . . . hell. After all, they did keep her employed. Most of the runaway girls she knew were tits-up downtown, giving their money to Someone Else. But not Lucy. And while it kind of annoyed her, she had to admit that she owed it to the morons in this neighborhood.

So she had a soft spot for them, like you would some stupid animal that never fights back. Mules and cows and such. *Even teenage girls*, she thought. The dumb shits that just fucking take it. The ones who trust you.

She decided the people here could trust her far enough to keep this neighborhood a secret . . . and harvest sparingly. She'd do that much for them. Protect them a little. Then she decided not to think too hard on it. Something about it kind of bothered her, gave her a headache and made her breathe too fast.

She scratched and swatted at mosquitoes while the houses emptied. Many carried lawn chairs or blankets. In a few minutes all eyes would be looking out over Pearl Lake. The name made her smile.

They wouldn't think about all the easy entries they'd left behind. And they'd never imagine Someone like Lucy.

Making a mental map of which houses had gone dark, she put on gloves and grabbed her backpack . . . the week's take was already heavy . . . then climbed down as the fireworks began. The show would last no more than half an hour. Quick in-and-outs tonight, with small, easily carried valuables.

Usually the loss of a single item of jewelry wouldn't be noticed. And even if it were, they'd write it off as lost or misplaced. If suspicions were seriously raised, Lucy's pattern of theft would point to the domestic help. They all had maids and nannies and shit, and would find it easy to blame them. It was a convenient explanation that protected their sense of security.

Lucy liked that phrase, "sense of security." After all, it *was* only a sense, a *feeling*. Nothing real about it.

She just had to remember her third rule, about not getting too greedy, and she could farm an area for months. After all, she was the rabbit living securely *inside* the rabbit-proof fence.

Lucy casually approached the first house as if she lived there. The entry into the home from the open garage was unlocked. Always were. No alarm triggered with the opening of the door. They were never set. No surprises. She clicked on her flashlight and made directly for the stairs. It took her less than twenty seconds to locate the master bedroom. Lucy grinned at her reflection in the mirror. The dresser was ripe.

Remembering rule number three, Lucy left behind a jewelry box lighter by only one expensive and rarely used item. It was tucked down below everything else. Lady probably used it but once a year. And because Lucy wasn't a stoner and worked alone, it now belonged to *her*.

She exited as fast as she'd entered and made for the next target. Lights out two houses down. The closed garage door caused Lucy to hesitate as she moved to check the main entry. *Rule number one ... folks here rarely use their front doors, everything happens through the garages.*

Might not get another chance though.

She turned the knob. Once again, up the stairs and into the master bedroom. But this time what she saw pulled her to the open window, locking her gaze on the drama unfolding through the bedroom window next door.

The woman was clearly visible, struggling weakly against restraints at all four corners of the bed. All she could see of the man was his back. Her instincts told her to bolt ... but instead she waited a moment, and watched. He seemed to be playing with her. Teasing her sexually. He was also well dressed. And there didn't seem to be any serious fight in this chick. Wouldn't she be fighting harder if it were for real?

Yeah ... yeah she would. Must just be some sort of edgy sex game. After all, women don't get raped in this neighborhood ... but she was pretty sure they had their fun.

She shuddered a bit, thinking of her second rule ... never let yourself feel too safe ... but ignored the sudden insight and aimed her flashlight at the dresser. This was a work night. Eight drawers.

And no fucking jewelry! Who the hell lives here anyway?

The walk-in closet held items of value, but she knew they would all be missed. Electronic equipment. Several laptops, monitors, and hard drives all neatly arrayed. She guessed they were used frequently.

She'd been in too long ... hurry ... when she jumped at the sound. The firework sounded close. She turned to leave.

As she swung her flashlight back into the bedroom, her quick exit to normal was interrupted. It was all the blood. She froze, staring at it. Wasn't a game after all. Variant on rule number two . . . women are targets everywhere.

She forced her gaze away from the bloodstained wall. The man had moved to the window and was facing her. She stepped back . . . and, remembering the flashlight in her hand, clicked it off.

Whole neighborhood was blown now. She'd already ignored her rules, so she grabbed a laptop and ran. He *might* have seen her, but she sure as hell wasn't going to see him again, or this neighborhood. But there *was* going to be some money made off this shit-of-a-night.

Lucy tried to focus as she ran through the backyards.

When the guy had turned to face her he was backlit, his front in shadow. She hadn't seen him very well, so he probably hadn't seen her either.

Well now that's just stupid. In fact it's creepy how fucking stupid that is!

She hopped a short fence, and dashed in between two houses, leaving what she'd seen farther behind.

She couldn't possibly have been visible.

Well, why the hell not? There might have been street light shining in. Was there?

She ran the alleys, heading for the neighboring development; they had a good bolthole there. But . . .

He probably just noticed the flashlight beam, didn't see anything else.

Yeah, right. Why the hell am I thinking this way? Th'fuck's wrong with me?

Carefully avoiding the important question . . . the one that would have given her a headache . . . she tried to conjure explanations that preserved her sense of security. But really, she knew . . . she'd made a serious mistake. And hadn't even seen that the whole fucking neighborhood was built on quicksand.

Lucy kept running hard . . . toward safety . . . and looked over her shoulder. He'd seen her all right. And he was gaining. Rule number two; don't *ever* relax, don't ever feel safe. All women should be born knowing that. And so should punks like Lucy. Thinking it still mattered . . . *should probably move that up to number one.*

CHAPTER ONE
JULY 06

That figures. Now I'm sleepy.

The birdsong outside her window sounded the alarm, and she finally gave up. It had been a rough night. Some of them just were.

The noise of distant traffic and sirens had been of some comfort, reminding her that she wasn't alone. Others were up too. But enough of that shit now. Her own weakness had her pissed off.

Zoe inhaled deeply, filling her lungs with warm, wet air off the Mississippi. There was a faint hint of sewer gas. She was used to it. It surfaced off the river sometimes, and didn't even register as good or bad. She just noted that it *was*. Lying there, she pictured the long day ahead and the night she'd just wasted.

Collapsing in bed after a thirty-six-hour shift, it was one of those nights when she still couldn't fall asleep. She'd turned to alcohol first, stiff one with a beer chaser. Hadn't worked. Sometimes did, sometimes didn't.

Zoe turned her head to see the bottle on its side. Must have knocked it over during the night. Hadn't finished it either ... her bedside table was sticky. Place was really going to stink now. The sheets were already rank with July sweat and sex. How long had it been since she'd had time to do laundry? And just how the fuck did normal people manage to fit in shit like that when she couldn't? Or did they? *Fuck normal people.*

Back to last night. *Oh, yeah.* She'd tried not to ... thinking it was even more of a crutch than booze ... but she'd finally turned on the television. White noise might help. Stupid idea. And apparently the wrong channel.

The last thing she remembered hearing was the grim report from a crime scene. Some mention of the weapon used. Tensing, she'd turned away from the screen toward the flickering light on the wall and hit OFF on her remote. Too late. A phantom had already ridden in on the shifting blue-and-white waves. The weapon? A shotgun.

The damage? A vacant stare from one eye and unrecognizable mush in place of the other … something that had once been brain and bone … and shared DNA. Thoughts and memories painted the wall. They'd escaped in the blood spray off the exit wound and marked the violent moment in kinetic abstract art.

Rolling over to look out the window she was thankful for one thing though, at least she'd been home last night … and probably wound up with a couple hours of sleep. It was always harder in the call rooms at work where the doors had no locks, not even to the shared baths. Why didn't that bother anyone else?

Okay, rough night. Racing thoughts. What else is new? Nights like these were like sewer gas … they just surfaced sometimes. Shouldn't attach any importance to them either.

She threw on scrubs and hit the weights. Her gym … with its stationary bike, Russian Box and puck-shooting alley … took up the entire basement of her mid-century house on East River Road, a property she'd financed after selling her inherited farmstead and spraying gravel on the way out. She loved her new house as much as she could love anything, so much so that she had to remind herself not to feel too comfortable there.

She pushed off the sides of her Russian Box, simulating sprints down the ice in perfect form, and found herself involuntarily replaying the ghostly images that had kept her awake. Her workout was, as always, another way to forget.

Stages of healing? Waste of time. *Fucking therapists.*

She was responsible. It had been their love for her painting that wall in red, and that could never happen again.

It wouldn't. As she moved to the bike, the sheen on her skin combined in drops to soak the blue scrubs and roll down her arms. Avoiding attachments had become a reflex. A conditioned response, like Pavlov's dog. No … like *his* dog, *his bitch* he'd said.

Her stomach pitched. She let it settle, then stretched, and welcomed the pain in her muscles. It felt fucking good to be strong … and untouchable.

The attempts to "analyze" her lathering impulses hadn't worked out so well. Not for her, or for the therapist. He was dead. And no one would ever have that power over her again. *Fucking therapists.*

She toweled off. At age thirty-two, she'd sculpted her body into near perfect shape and enjoyed that her slim boyish hips and well-defined legs turned heads.

Yet no one would have described her as perfect, least of all Zoe. The raven hair that swept her broad muscular shoulders was always unruly, and she wasted no time on it. Nor did she make any attempt to sunbathe away the tan lines that betrayed her obsession with biking. She'd never even once considered hiding the jagged white line at her collarbone, a reminder of what was still missing from her life. It wasn't uninterrupted sleep or some childish notion of happiness. It was revenge; an impulse she would never pretend was good. Zoe didn't need it to be good. She wasn't that weak. And it certainly wasn't justice. She'd never fool herself in that way either.

So it was a lousy night. Don't make it so fucking important . . . and don't bring this shit to work.

By 6:00 a.m. Zoe heard the paper hit the front door. She grabbed a cup of coffee and sat outside to scan the headlines, reconnecting with the rest of the world. She could feel the heat and humidity building already. The air was thick, and it wasn't moving. And neither was the sweat off her skin. But at least the night was lifting.

Interesting, she thought, that the passing of the hospital administrator was front page and above the fold, yet there was no mention of how she'd died. Julia Nelson's failure to show up for work the day before had been the focus of "talk," always tolerated at a hospital as a diversion known to keep unhappy, whiny complainers entertained and docile. But the usual topics, sexual liaisons triggered by the long hours and intimacy of hospital work, had been largely ignored. Her unexplained absence fueled wild speculation of a different sort.

And Zoe would know before the paper did. Finishing the last of her coffee she looked out over the Mississippi and admired the lean bodies of two men running the path across the street. Shirtless. Ripped.

Dependable. On time, she smiled, having noticed them before. Nice view. She imagined making *them* forget that her sheets hadn't been washed.

Remembering to stuff the crossword puzzle in her backpack she selected the full-suspension Cannondale mountain bike, her favorite, for the daily commute to work. Another cup of coffee and a shower would be waiting for her there. Meanwhile, the image of the two men suddenly crowded out thoughts of her disturbing night. *Far better than talk therapy.*

9

KELLY LOOKED UP AT ZOE OVER HIS READING glasses. "You know she was murdered, don't you?"

"I figured. The paper held back. Hear anything?"

"Darling, despite being head of maintenance and my ranking status in the gossip chain, that's all I've heard. You'll have to get the details from your cop friends. And the minute you do, I expect a full report." He tilted his head back to look down through the glasses on the end of his nose. "They made a mistake."

"I just gave you that. How the hell are you so sure?"

"Because gorgeous, it's ridiculously easy. I'm nearly done ... would be if they hadn't screwed me up with the stupid mistake. Sundays provide the only occasional challenge."

Zoe reached down and grabbed the paper out of his hand. "Let me see that. Where is it? They never make mistakes."

"Three down ... 'true or false'? The answer should read 'too good to be', t-o-o, but they spelled it with a t-o. You shouldn't be so trusting." He smiled.

"Believe me, Kelly, I'm not. But it looks like you need a new hobby. Perhaps something more challenging?" she teased.

"I like Scrabble." His full-moon face tried for seriousness.

"Yeah, well I bet I can kick your ass at that too," she only grinned.

"Like you can kick my ass in general?" Rubbing the yellowing bruise on his jaw from the last time Zoe had checked him into the boards at the rink, he seemed to reconsider. "If so, it's only because I'm old. But I'm not conceding. When are you on call?"

"Tomorrow night. If I have free time I'll come down, and we'll duke it out." Thankful for an excuse to avoid the bed in the call room the next night, she positioned her bike in the corner of Kelly's basement office and grabbed a cup of the best coffee in the hospital. No, in the *world*, Zoe thought.

She peeked in the minifridge. "Looks like you're getting low on your supply of Peets. I've got some coming from California, freshly roasted. I'll bring it. Just make sure to keep our coffee a secret, old man. Anyone else tastes this liquid sunshine and our love affair with it's done. I can't afford to supply everyone on a residents salary."

"Trust me, darling Zoe, you're the only one to grace my office. It's you and me, kiddo. Anyway, notice how I've so cleverly hidden the coffeemaker behind the screen where my cot is. No one goes back there except you."

"The aroma, Einstein. People might follow their noses."

"Sugar, you and I could die down here and they wouldn't find us for weeks."

"Mm . . . .just think of *that* aroma. Might just prove my point too." She narrowed her eyes on him. "But it's certainly a comfort to know they won't find the coffee." She handed back the paper. "Gotta run. I need to find an open call room so I can get a shower. I start in the emergency room today. Hours should be a lot better."

IT WAS A STAT CALL TO THE STABILIZATION ROOM where the victim of a motor vehicle accident was expected to arrive by ambulance within minutes. She'd only just emerged from the quick shower when her beeper went off. After throwing on a fresh pair of scrubs and draping the stethoscope around her neck, she ran and jumped stairs to the ER.

"Hey, Zoe." Maleah, one of the ER nurses, struggled with scissors cutting tight leather pants off the unconscious victim. "Gonna be fun to have you around full time. Got us a mess here now though. Motorcycle versus utility pole."

"Yeah, Mal, looks like a party all right." Zoe hooked wet hair behind her ears, threw on a pair of gloves and took her place across the head of the table from the others.

The source of the patient's deteriorating respiratory status was being evaluated with an intern making his case to the other senior resident. He wanted to treat a suspected tension pneumothorax, arguing that a broken rib must have pierced the lung, letting air leak into the surrounding space with each inspiration. And without creating a way for that air to escape, the lung would collapse under the pressure. Serious shit, the intern had said as he looked across the patient at Zoe. And Zoe was indeed paying very close attention . . . to just how proud he looked. Kid actually thinks he's a fucking hero.

They'd already inserted a needle through the chest wall, expecting it to relieve the pressure around the lung so it could re-expand. But it hadn't improved the patient's hemodynamic or respiratory status. Dr. Shepard, the intern, was now arguing for a chest wall incision through which to insert a larger catheter. He stood poised with a scalpel. It was time for an intervention.

"Wait." Zoe listened to the breath sounds over both lungs. "I think we've got bowel in there. It's not a tension pneumothorax; it's a ruptured diaphragm." She only hoped they hadn't perforated bowel . . . because that would be a serious shit screw-up.

The attending physician walked into the room as a digital image of the portable chest x-ray filled the screen. Where there should have been air-filled lung, bowel had crowded it out on the left side, unmistakably confirming the diagnosis.

By now Maleah had inserted the urinary catheter and red-tinged liquid was flowing into a bag. Zoe felt the tense abdomen. "Blunt abdominal trauma, primarily on the left side. I'm guessing kidney and spleen."

The other resident agreed. "Let's get the ultrasound and confirm this while we pack him up."

The hand-off went smoothly. Zoe looked up as the patient was being transported, and was met by the attending physician's eyes. Dr. Parker stripped off his gloves and reached out a hand. "Glad to meet you, Dr. Lawrence. I've heard a lot about you." His smile broadened. "All good. Welcome to my ER. Kaj Parker."

If it weren't for the dark hair, she might have mistaken him for some sort of Nordic warrior. "Dr. Parker, I've been looking forward to working with you." As he gripped her hand his eyes held hers just a moment too long, and Zoe felt the sharp intake of air as she realized she'd forgotten to breathe.

Parker abruptly broke their gaze and took his own deep breath. "I'll let *you* deal with the intern for now. But keep a close eye on him. The nurses tell me he's a cowboy."

"I'll see to it. He won't be a problem," Zoe found it hard to say through gritted teeth. She had no intention of letting an underling on her team threaten any of her patients with arrogance.

"Good. We've got a full board and it's backing up. Let's hit it."

Chapter Two
July 20

EVEN WITH THE DETERIORATED CONDITION of the corpse, it took the responding officer no time at all to call it in as a homicide. Manner of death was obvious. But everything else was a guess, lost in a writhing, crackling blanket of maggots. The body was small and the ripped clothing on the floor was of the unisex type, so the working theory was very young female victim.

The killer had done considerable damage before the bugs took over . . . and in the July heat and humidity the insects had all but finished the job. Everyone agreed there must have been one hell of a struggle, accounting for all the blood sprays. It seemed the victim had eventually been subdued on top of the kitchen table and only God, the killer, and maybe a forensic pathologist could know what happened after that.

"Holy shit. Pathologist may have trouble with this one."

"Yeah, Goldy isn't exactly the guy I'd want to be right now." Detective Ray Perry surveyed the room, seeing where the locksmith had tossed his lunch, and was thankful he'd come on an empty stomach.

"Did the guys find anything else . . . other than the obvious shit in here?" Detective Jack Reynolds swatted at flies, driving them back to coat the walls.

"Sure doesn't look to have been a robbery, eh?" Ray did a slow 360 of the trashed surroundings.

"I'd say being a tad angry played a big role here." Jack grimaced, drew in a deep breath, and continued. "Yeah, well."

"Yeah . . . real cute . . . anyway . . . there *was* a backpack found in another room. Contained some high-end jewelry. Believe it or not, something of actual value to take from this dump. Would've said we've got ourselves a homeless dispute here, but why leave the jewelry? The zipper was closed, but it was in plain site."

"Probably just means we've got a sex crime gone way off the rails." Jack paused. "Still . . . why leave the goods? Think of the bottom-feeders camping out in these empties. Not one would ever leave that shit behind, no matter why they killed."

"Looks like he broke every chair over her." Ray stared past the carnage through a window onto the backyard. A tree swing swayed. Normal was just that far away. He wondered about her last minutes trying to reach it. Nodding toward the small, bloodied handprint on the back door, "Probably hers. Smeared though. Might have trouble IDing her if the body's too decomposed and she's had no dental history. Assuming she's even been in the system that is."

Both men drew in close to the corpse, inspecting what was left of the small hands. Not only decomposed, they also appeared to have been nibbled on. Jack pivoted quickly and looked toward the floor at the periphery of the room. "I hate rats."

"I hate this fucking smell. You think the death molecules get in your veins after you breathe them in?" Ray actually pictured them traveling to his brain.

"Hadn't thought of that. Wish you hadn't brought it up either." Jack started taking shallow breaths.

Ray clapped his gloved hands.

Jack jumped a little at the sound.

"Okay. It's a helluva mess, but let's quit putting it off." Ray added an extra layer of gloves and began inspecting more closely.

The photographer documented as they moved through the rooms. Evidence markers cluttered the kitchen, but only a few sat next to items elsewhere in the house.

In one room a mattress was found askew on the floor. They examined it for signs of semen, hoping for DNA that might be in the system, but the bed appeared to have been used only for slumber. On it were two sleeping bags. One was a drab green, the other pink and adorned with Barbie imagery. Both were threadbare and filthy.

In the same room with the mattress, they found rodent droppings surrounding a bag from the Dairy Queen. There was very little else to reveal that anyone had even been staying there.

"Whoever these two were, they sure as hell didn't have much."

"Except for a fucking bag of jewelry." Jack's eyebrows shot up.

"Two sleeping bags, and only one body . . . a body that I'd guess belongs to the pink one."

"And a … fucking … bag … of jewelry."

"Yeah, fucking bag of jewelry. Makes no sense." Ray shook his head.

"Maybe we'll get a match on some prints."

"Maybe. I'm guessing that whoever belongs to that green bag might be our killer. But a fucking bag of jewelry … ?"

They moved back to the kitchen, leaving the photographer to document the makeshift bedroom.

"This had to be a guy, a strong one, unless we had a zoned victim. Ever seen this much damage done to one person?"

"Nope, I'm glad to say that I haven't." Ray looked around. "There's probably not a fucking thing in this kitchen that he didn't use on her. Blood's everywhere … on every potential weapon."

Jack gestured toward an iron on the floor. Still plugged in. "Good thing for her the power'd been shut off."

"Yeah, Jack, that's real funny." Ray just shrugged. "I've never seen anything this bad though. Takes it to a whole new level for me. And why? Who in the hell would need to kill like this? Let's just hope she wasn't awake to feel it."

Jack laughed loudly. "You fuckin' serious? That actually is funny. Look at the blood spray patterns. She was on the move through this."

"Yeah … I know. Just don't like thinking about it is all. The shit we have to look at is way worse on our brains than those fucking death molecules."

Jack seemed to think about that.

Ray added quietly, "Kid must have had spine to fight so hard. I think I might bring Zoe in on this one Jack. Just so you know."

"Aw, Christ."

Chapter Three
July 26 (Midday)

WHERE'S MY GOLD TOOTH? I HAD it when I walked in the bar!" He rammed a hand into his mouth, his fingers coming back bloody . . . and empty. After rotating them a few inches from his eyes, he erupted, "Those cocksuckers! They stole my gold tooth!"

"Yeah, well you should see the other guy. Let me take a look there, friend." Zoe drew in close and inserted a gloved hand around the inside of his mouth. "Open wide now. Yep, it's gone. But maybe you swallowed it, eh?" The "other guy" had only been the beer glass his face tipped into when he'd passed out. The tooth had either fallen in or around the glass, or was indeed on a journey through his intestines.

His eyes got big as he worked to focus on Zoe. "Oh, no, you don't doc!"

"Don't worry, pal. We have ways of collecting your stool."

RAY LEANED AGAINST THE WALL OUTSIDE the cubicle where Zoe was finishing up her evaluation of a drunk hauled in by a squad. Waiting his turn to talk to her, he could hear the nonsensical exchange behind the curtain and couldn't help but chuckle.

"Got a minute when you're done, Zoe?" Ray poked his head around the curtain. "Got a favor to ask."

"Anything for you, Ray. Just give me a second. I need to get some restraints on here so he doesn't take a tumble off the gurney." Zoe, distracted by Ray, never did see the roundhouse to her head.

Ray did . . . but a moment too late. As Zoe hit the wall, he was on the drunk. "Need some help in here! Zoe, you all right?"

"I'm fine, just stupid is all. I misread him." Zoe pulled herself up from the floor and fastened leather restraints at all four limbs while Ray and two orderlies held the patient down.

"Thanks guys. Ray, I've gotta put in a quick call to detox and reserve him a bed. Meet you in the break room." Zoe strode down to the triage area with the shouts and oaths of the drunk following her down the hall.

RAY HELPED HIMSELF TO THE COFFEE and leaned a hip on the table. Zoe paused to kiss him on her way past him to the coffeemaker. A slow weary smile followed her back. "You sure you're okay?"

She leaned against the wall and snorted through a wince. "The old sot got me good. He's stronger than he looks. Too bad . . . I kinda liked the guy before he hit me." She met his eyes with a comfortable look that spoke of their long history. "But it's good to see *you*, handsome. And thanks for helping in there." She smiled. "What's up? What can I do for you?"

"Zoe, we've got ourselves a found body in one of the empties on the south side. Homicide. We think it was a kid named Lucy Franklin. Doubt that's her real name though. Came through the system as a runaway a couple years back. Never found any relatives. Apparently Lucy didn't want them found. She was put in foster care but blew first chance. Been flying under the radar till now. Thing is, she ties to the murder of Julia Nelson, your administrator, from a few weeks back."

"Finally got a lead, eh?"

"That's just it, I'm not really sure. I've got a theory about how it might play, but that's all." He blew on his coffee and took a sip. "See, we found a jewelry stash with the kid. Turns out they were items stolen from the same neighborhood Nelson lived in. The body was too decomposed, and we got no usable prints in the blood, but partial prints on the jewelry match our file prints from Franklin. In fact her prints were in every room of the foreclosed house.

"Funny thing is though, no one in Nelson's neighborhood noticed anything was missing until one of them was getting ready for her funeral and couldn't find some piece of jewelry. Of course that created a buzz. Then everyone else started looking around and found half the neighborhood had been ripped off. Clever kid. Must have taken her awhile.

"I was thinking about calling you on the kid anyway, but then when we figured out the tie to Nelson, it made even more sense. Besides, we're not getting anywhere on Nelson."

Zoe raised her eyebrows asking the obvious question without a sound.

"No, robbery doesn't fit. Why leave the jewelry? Besides, when you see the crime scene photos you'll understand. There was a lot of emotion behind the girl's murder. That's where you come in. I'd like you to help us profile the killer. You were good, Zoe, and I want you back on this one. You promised to stick around as a consultant, so here it is … your first case as an independent contractor." He reached out to touch her face.

"You want me back or you need me back?" She smirked.

"Doesn't matter. But both." He looked serious.

Zoe smiled. "Just stick to the facts of the case, Ray, and you know me, I won't be able to say no."

He smiled back. "Gotcha. I do happen to know how you get. Anyway, we're pretty sure this is a guy, but other than that, we've got very little to go on. And we're not even sure of that. Despite the sexual nature of the assaults, there was no semen left at either scene."

"Seriously Ray? No good physical evidence? Prints, DNA?"

"Oh we've got prints all right. More than one set from both scenes. But other than Franklin's, they're all virgin. No matches. We're tracking down the previous owners of the foreclosure. But otherwise, we got nothing."

"So you're guessing the kid saw something, was a witness? The same guy who did Julia had to shut her up? Or there were two of them working the neighborhood and one of them is a killer?"

"That's about it, Zoe. And when you see the photos, you'll want him as bad as I do."

"Suspecting a sexual deviant then? Unfortunately, my kind of case."

"Afraid so. Sorry."

"No worries, it's what I do best. Anyway, the witness thing sounds good. That plays. Time of death on the kid?"

"It was a mess. The heat and humidity did a number on her. But taking it into account, Goldy tells me it works that she could have been killed that same night. You can picture two July weeks in a stuffy boarded up house without AC, can't you?"

"Yeah," Zoe gulped down two aspirins with the last of her coffee, "dead or alive it'd be hell." They both winced.

"We found some other kids who knew her...sort of...apparently she liked to work alone. But anyway, they place her at the McDonalds downtown at about eight the evening of July 4th. No one reports seeing her or the other girl she'd been sharing space with since then."

"So it fits. You guys have any luck with the other girl? Where were they squatting?"

"We only know about the one empty. Got a description of the other girl, but haven't found her yet. Real young kid they say."

"Any chance she could be our killer?"

"The other kids say no. Said she was a little bigger, but not by much. And anyway, they say it was Lucy who was the badass. Real tough. If anyone would have won a fight between the two girls, it would have been Lucy, and I quote...hands down. Besides, when you see the photos...well...I keep thinking it was a guy."

"Listen, Zoe, can I put you on payroll for this one?"

"Yeah, you've got me interested, I'm in. If it was the same guy and both killings happened on the same night without any disconnect, you can obviously view both killings as the same event."

"Yeah, and I'm hoping that means less chance of a repeat. Listen, I know you're busy as hell these days, but can we meet when you're done here? Dinner's on me."

"Sure, Ray. Back booth at Humphreys. Six o'clock. It's private. We can talk. Bring the photos."

Ray reached out a hand to touch the developing bruise on her temple. "You ever miss the force, Zoe?"

"Part-time consulting will be good enough." She grabbed his hand and pulled it away from her face, "I like what I'm doing here, Ray. Can't say it's any less dangerous though," she admitted through a half-grin. "But I do miss seeing your face every day," she added, answering the real question.

He squeezed her hand, kissed her wound, and smiled. "Ain't that the truth," he leaned close and whispered, "that I miss the hell out of you, Zoe."

She pulled back to give him a warning look, and he smiled, putting his hands up in mock surrender. "Okay, okay." He turned to leave. "See you tonight."

Kaj waited as Zoe watched Ray exit, then continued into the room. She jerked her thoughts out of the past and apologized. "Sorry Dr. Parker, were you looking for me?"

HE'D WITNESSED THE EXCHANGE and stirred at the kiss, the touch, and the easy, effortless connection. There was something about what he'd just seen ... and about this woman he'd been working with for the past few weeks ... that tugged at him in a way he hadn't expected. And if he hadn't thought it impossible, he might have considered that he was jealous.

He found himself having to refocus. "I heard what happened with the patient in cube two ..."

INTERRUPTING HIM, ZOE AMAZED herself by apologizing a second time. "I'm sorry about that. I'll never let that happen again. Did you have something you wanted me to take care of?"

"Actually, yes. I was thinking we could take care of you." He nodded toward the expanding bruise near the corner of her eye.

As his head tilted, she witnessed the full force of the most seductive smile she'd ever seen. He wasn't making this easy.

"Let me take a look, and then we can get some ice on it."

Of course she'd felt the attraction from day one, and knew better. But what was with this guy? Didn't he know better? And what was with all the apologizing? She reminded herself of his rather mysterious reputation as a player. The kind where sexual tension was effortless, just how he carried himself. She knew the type. Had slept with the type. And she couldn't trust herself with the type. *So get a fucking grip.*

"I'm okay, really. But thanks. I just feel stupid I let that happen. I'll get back to work." She gave an involuntary wince as she touched a hand to her face.

"You obviously haven't seen yourself yet." He chuckled and took a step toward her, stopping as she stepped back, her retreat interrupted by the wall behind her. His smile was replaced by a look of concern. "Did something else happen in that cube? What else did he do?"

Zoe felt a jolt at the familiar look ... and the assumption. She'd seen it before, from people who wouldn't make that same mistake twice. "Nothing. It's fine. Really."

He grabbed her shoulders as she tried to get by him, his face now more than merely concerned. "Dr. Lawrence, you're obviously not all right."

Zoe knew he could feel her forcing slow deep breaths under his hands.

"Listen, I'm responsible for everyone in this ER. Just let me take a look."

He felt good. Smelled good. Looked good. And he was making her angry.

Although she'd often traded on the easy access to men at work . . . and it was always tempting, even now . . . as her supervisor, this guy was clearly off limits. Why wasn't there a demeaning word for a guy who was a tease? Aw, fuck . . . it wasn't him. She knew it. Once again, it was really herself she was so off-the-charts angry with.

No good option but to play along. She had more than enough experience in that. "Okay, if you think it looks that bad. Knock yourself out. But don't confuse me with something fragile. I certainly don't need rescuing."

He lifted an eyebrow. "Clearly." Studying her face, he smiled broadly again. "I'll never confuse you with anything delicate. I swear. Now let me take a look."

Carefully, he ran his hands over the side of her temple and cheek, pressing gently on the orbital bones, looking for any sign of a fracture.

Zoe struggled to stay angry as his hands caressed her face. But she felt herself lean into his hand, its warmth, and jumped.

"Is that area especially tender?" he asked, drawing closer to inspect it. "I don't feel an edge there, but if it's that painful perhaps we should get some films."

"No, really, it's not that bad. I've had hits to the head far worse than that." She shrugged at his look of surprise. "Hey, this doesn't even warrant a write-up. I'd know if there was something wrong." She looked away as he seemed to take measure of her honesty, and to consider what she'd said.

"You're probably right, just a bad bruise. Here's what you'll do. Take twenty minutes and get some ice on it. After that, there's a bone that needs setting in the cast room."

He combed his hands through long locks of thick dark hair, pulling it away from his eyes, and turned to leave. At the door he seemed to hesitate, and swung back to face her. "Who was the man that just left?"

"Someone I used to work with." *Stay the fuck out of my life.*

He held her gaze for several long moments with a piercing stare before releasing her. She felt his command of her physically. *Holy shit. In another life maybe.* She finally blinked.

CHAPTER FOUR
JULY 26 (EVENING)

ZOE KEPT MOVING HER FEET SO THEY wouldn't stick to the floor. There was something slimy on the seat too, but they'd been forced to take this booth. As Humphrey's was a block from the hospital, and a medical crowd hangout, they poured over notes and photos in privacy at the rear.

"July 4th, eh? Ray, I know these two murders must connect somehow, but I'm guessing you're as struck as I am by the differences."

"Yeah, no kidding. We've got one murder that appears cold and calculated, more like an execution, and another that looks like a bloodbath unleashed in some kind of nuclear reaction of sex and violence." The two of them stared at the photos. "Nelson was shot, and the girl beaten to a literal bloody pulp. Never thought I'd actually describe someone in that way, but it's the goddamn truth here. And I grant you, it *is* a little hard to picture these as being the same guy."

"But there's sexual violence in both cases." Zoe stared at the photos some more. "If you go with your instinct that Franklin interrupted a murder, it still might work. He may have been planning on a lot more with Nelson, but having been discovered had to kill her prematurely and go for the witness. Perhaps he took it all out on the kid."

Ray finished his beer and signaled for another. He turned the photos upside down on the table while he waited. "Other thing is, Zoe, the jewelry was left there. It seems to me that no matter what the motive was, any killer I've ever known would have taken that stuff. It was worth a lot."

She'd been working that over in her head too. "We know the kid didn't die so quickly, Ray. I hate to think of it, but it sure looks like she was tortured."

Ray tipped his head back and squeezed his eyes shut in a grimace. "I know Z. Either the guy got off on it, he wanted something from her, or both."

"My guess is both, but he needed *something* from her. Maybe it was nothing more than information. Wanting to make sure there were no other loose ends. The fact that he didn't take the jewelry makes sense if there was a reason that it might incriminate him. It does suggest that he's not from Lucy's crowd, and not like most killers you've seen. He must not need the money. Because you're right, anyone else would have taken it and simply ignored the risk." Zoe finished off the last of her beer and grabbed at the popcorn basket. "But either way, makes me think there might be a loose end out there he didn't find."

"Yeah, but I'm still troubled by the jewelry thing. What wound up happening is that it *does* tie the two murders. And Zoe," he leveled a serious look at her, "without that there is *no way* I would have made them as related."

Zoe looked again at the photos and blew out a long, slow breath. Ray was right. "Could the guy not have anticipated that? No, it's too stupid. Maybe he knew that any attempt to move the jewelry would put him at even greater risk, as there'd be an interaction with a witness. If he didn't desperately need the money, why chance it?"

"All right, I'm good with that. But why not take the jewelry and at least get *rid* of it? Bury it somewhere even. That still bugs me."

"You're right of course. It doesn't fit. It could be that we've got a psychotic killer here, rather than a psychopathic one. The Nelson murder appears to be the work of an organized personality. Planned. The kid on the other hand, could be anything. Might be two different people. If a psychotic killed the kid, he might not have noticed the jewelry. Simple as that. The lack of physical evidence left behind could be purely dumb luck. However it plays out, let's just hope he, or they, made mistakes. If there's a mistake, we'll find it." She paused, thinking. "Maybe the jewelry *was* his mistake. Maybe that's why it doesn't make sense."

"There were drugs in her system. Enough to make it hard for her to resist in any meaningful way."

"Lucy?"

"Ah . . . no, actually I'm talking about Nelson."

"What kind of drugs? That doesn't seem right. I'd be very surprised if Nelson was a user. But it *could* explain an association with the wrong crowd I suppose."

"Naw, it's not what you're thinking. Her wine was spiked . . . date rape drug. Another reason I figured the kid interrupted something."

"No forced entry into the house?"

"No, but even with all the stolen goods from the neighborhood, not one person reported any forced entry or anything suspicious at all. These people seem pretty lax about security. I'm not sure it proves one way or the other whether Nelson knew her attacker."

"Apparently she was a pretty private person too. Few people knew much about her personal life, or chose not to admit to it. We canvassed everyone in that neighborhood and not one person noticed anything out of the ordinary on the night in question. Most people were watching the fireworks."

Zoe considered the fateful intersection of lives on that night. "Seems a clever, resourceful young girl and a very devious man had similar notions about the cover that would provide. That, and the drug, tells me we have an organized personality at work in the Nelson murder and leaves open the possibility that the Franklin kill might have involved someone else. Pure coincidence. But then again neither of us like coincidences."

Ray noticed Zoe working on her neck. "I'm sorry Zoe, you're tired. Probably starving too. Let's put this away for now and order our food." He signaled for the server and reached out to rub her shoulders. "Let me take care of that for you. How's the face feeling by the way?"

"Not too bad. It's my neck's that killing me."

"Tell you what, let's get the food to go. We can throw your bike in the back of my truck and head over to your house." He pulled her toward him and let his hands wander down her back, flirting with the sides of her breasts.

Say no.

"We can eat while we finish this, and then I'll tuck you in." He released the irresistibly confident smile of an insider, a man in charge. He knew what Zoe needed. And she knew *that.*

Although she'd already quit on Ray, and since moved on to Rex, she warned herself that this thing was about to happen. Because whatever it was ... this thing ... it felt too good at the moment.

"Ray, this isn't a good idea. We ought to leave things alone. Between us it should just be work ..."

Zoe stopped talking and moaned when she felt the unmistakable addition of sensuality to his efforts as he moved onto her lower back. Possessing the rugged good looks and confidence that should have belonged to a New York cop, Zoe found both qualities hard to resist. His Mediterranean color would have fit in better there too. But he was here, and available to her. Not being known for her self-control, she didn't even give Rex a thought as she leaned into his touch and closed her eyes. "Let's."

T HE REST OF THE EVENING THEY SPENT eating, drinking and discussing the case. There was some preliminary profiling, tossing around the timeworn terms . . . sociopath, sexual sadist . . . the usual suspect when Zoe was involved. But teasing something of practical use out of the whole thing was eluding them.

While he could be assumed to be of above average size and build, it wouldn't have taken much to overpower the diminutive Lucy. And the presence of drugs in Nelson's body could mean that he, or she, knew the victim and only proceeded after rendering her relatively helpless. There was little to work from.

And no gun. Again, squat.

They circled back around to the uncomfortable possibility that Ray's initial assumption was wrong, and that there may in fact have been two different killers. A lack of prints didn't actually prove anything. They even discussed the possibility that Lucy worked with an accomplice, who'd killed both she and Nelson.

After exhausting what little information they had, Zoe pulled on her fourth beer of the night and then poured the rest in the houseplant she was trying to keep alive.

"I wish I'd seen the crime scenes first hand. It's hard to get a feel for them from photos." She paused, and then laughed. "But Ray, the idea that Lucy had an accomplice who panicked and killed Nelson, then did Lucy later in another panic to eliminate any witnesses . . . we'd have to be idiots to buy into that theory. We're over-thinking things." The booze was helping to simplify her thoughts. "Yeah, sure, he could have left the jewelry in a panic. Problem is, the Nelson murder wasn't a panic killing."

"Yeah, I agree. It's the same guy, and two different motives. The first killing had nothing to do with jewelry. And neither did the second. I like your idea that the jewelry might have been his mistake in all this. A big one too, since it ties the two murders."

Zoe looked again at the images. "What about the Dairy Queen bag?"

"What about it?"

"I thought you said Lucy was seen at McDonalds that night. Why the DQ bag?"

"Maybe belonged to the other kid."

"Exactly. Why don't you take that description you got of the missing kid from her street associates over to the Dairy Queen nearest to that empty? Start there anyway."

"Good idea." He smiled and leaned in close, "It's late." He took the empty bottle from her hand and set it down, and then took her mouth in his.

Zoe found herself being lifted and carried into bed. She'd almost forgotten how much she welcomed the chance to surrender to someone who knew how to take care of her needs. He required no coaching. With Ray, it was effortless, and he was as close to a real lover as she'd ever had. And that was the problem... the reason she'd broken it off. He was too close. But tonight, Zoe was weak.

THE AROMAS OF BACON AND COFFEE competed with air off the Mississippi muscling in through the window. The river breeze took advantage of her bare skin, making her want Ray back in bed. She threw on Ray's shirt, breathing in his scent too, and found him in the kitchen.

"Ray, you didn't have to do this. But thanks." Zoe walked up to him, opening the shirt, and pressed herself against his firm, bare chest. "Did you sleep okay?" She kissed the dark shadow over his jaw.

Ray grabbed her hips pulling her tighter... and then talked when he should have acted. "Do you really have to ask me that? Of course I did. I sleep like a baby next to you Zoe. I love you after all."

She stiffened.

"Oh yeah... but I forgot, you're not supposed to care, right?"

The surprising sarcasm slapped at her. She'd always made it clear... they were casual, nothing more. Why couldn't he just deal with it? And what exactly was it that she didn't understand?

Zoe pushed away. But he held on, and kept talking. "I'm sorry, Zoe. I didn't mean it like that."

He paused, then moved to pin her against the counter, keeping her close.

"Well . . . I meant some of it. But I get it. You don't have to say anything. The wisecrack about 'not caring' was way out of line. I'm sorry."

He wrapped her in his arms, and Zoe worried that he could feel the catch in her breath. She didn't trust herself yet to speak.

"I just wish you'd let me love you."

Finally she did. "I wish I could, Ray." But as she said it, she wondered what he . . . or any other man . . . saw that was good in her.

CHAPTER FIVE
JULY 27 (MORNING)

ZOE POSITIONED HER BIKE IN THE corner of the room. She was sweaty and out of breath.

"What route did you take today, sugar?"

Zoe smiled weakly. "The back alley trail."

It was one of several pathways she followed between home and work. This one kept her away from people and traffic, leading her through warehouse lots, train yards, and alleys, with plenty of stairs to jump. The double track next to the rails was winding and full of dirt moguls built by industrious kids. It matched her mood, offering her physical release.

"Rough night, eh?"

Zoe smiled at his comforting Canadian accent. It reminded her of home...in a surprisingly good way. She'd come to view the stocky man with his unique blend of Cree features and Irish color as something like family, or as close as she'd accept.

It was such a gentle query. Disarming even. Like he already knew, and that it was okay. "Night was beautiful, it was the morning that sucked. Ray stayed over. I don't know what I was thinking. I just needed . . . I don't know, something. Just needed I guess." She laughed. "Maybe I'm needy, eh?"

"Need *me* to break his legs?" Kelly smiled. "There's an answer to every problem, sunshine, and I . . . am . . . yours."

Zoe laughed heartily this time. "Naw, I can always take care of that at the rink. Perfect cover." She sobered. "It's not that, Kell. It's that he's right."

Zoe walked over to fill her mug with coffee. She took a seat on the couch and stared at the Edward Hopper print on the wall, "Nighthawks." Zoe had given it to him.

"Right about what, darling?"

"He told me I didn't care, Kell, and on some level, that's probably true. There's just a whole lot that I don't give a shit about." She blew out a long breath over the coffee, and took a sip.

"Come on, Zoe, you care. You'd do anything for your patients. And you love your friends. You don't even realize it, do you? You're bound to them whether you want to admit it or not."

Zoe had to set down her coffee, it threatened to spill. "But, Kelly, that's just it ... I don't want anyone tied to me. And, come on, I don't love anyone. If that were true, wouldn't I feel the joy in it?"

She'd said way too much, and felt the familiar sway of shaky ground. Images intruded. Random snapshots. Blood pooling, stains on a couch, even the fucking therapist. At the merciful image of a gun in her hand, she took control ... steadied, and stared at nothing.

"I just have to accept who I am. And there's no room for lovers or promises that I can't keep."

She wanted to stop there, hadn't meant for this conversation to take place at all, let alone go in this direction ... but inexplicably, she heard herself keep talking.

"There's a hell of a lot I don't know, Kell, but I'm pretty sure of one thing ... I'm not a very good person." Noticing him lean in toward her, she stopped him, and looked down. "Don't. I'm not looking for an argument here. It's how I feel. How it is."

How could anyone who thought what she thought and wanted what she wanted actually be a good person? She couldn't imagine what kept her friends hanging around.

"Zoe, you and I both know that good, nice people are way too boring."

She laughed ... and nodded. But still wouldn't look at him.

"Anything you want to share with me? My shoulders are broad, sweetheart."

She felt him willing her to look squarely at his eyes, but knew that if she spent even one more minute here, she might keep talking. And that just wasn't an option. She rolled her eyes at his grin. "You *are* built like a gorilla. Maybe another time, Kell. I've got to get up to the ER. Here's the crossword. Thanks for the coffee."

She reached over and squeezed his big shoulder as she rose to leave. "And, Kelly, if you absolutely insist on a nickname for me, would it be too much to ask that you decide on one? I'm getting a little confused here."

He smiled, but she didn't see it in his eyes. "I'll work on it, Zoe."

As she rose to leave he added, "How about dinner tonight, at my place?"

"Kelly! Well, I'm honored! Of course! What can I bring?"

"Just your tired, exhausted, adorable self. I imagine you'll be fried after your shift."

"It's a date then. Only, Kell, not even *I* know where you live."

"That *is* a problem." This time everything smiled. "Meet me down here at six. If you promise not to tell anyone I won't have to lead you there blindfolded."

It left her laughing as she walked out. Zoe usually misinterpreted genuine concern ... it always felt too close to pity. But from him, she'd never sensed it. In a strange way she felt understood. It was why she liked him. He accepted all of her repellant emotions, without judging, and never pressed for explanations. She thought about what she'd just confessed. She never shared stuff like that with *anyone*. How was he able to pull it out of her ... without even trying ... when others couldn't? She'd have to be more careful.

EVERY CHAIR IN THE WAITING ROOM WAS occupied. The influx from the night before hadn't been cleared, and with new people spilling in, it was looking to be a chaotic day. Zoe had Maleah shoving a chart in her hands the minute she walked through the door.

"Zoe, Stabilization room 2 is priority right now. Can you take it? Parker's finishing up with a bad one in Stab 1. He's got the other resident with him. Gonna have to spread you guys thin today."

"Sure, Mal, no problem." Zoe scanned the chart. "Talk to me. What's the story?"

"Guy cut off his penis." Seeing Zoe's raised eyebrows she added emphasis. "No shit!"

"Where is it?"

"I told you, Stab 2."

"I mean the penis, Mal."

"Oh, they dug it out of a drain. Guy apparently didn't want to make a mess and did it over a utility sink. Really, imagine worrying more about the mess than the self-mutilation." She shook her head in disbelief. "Medics brought it on ice."

"Has surgery been called?"

"Yeah, Parker put the calls in before the guy even hit the door. Plastics, urology, and vascular are all aware and communicating. One of them will be here shortly.

Your intern is packing him for transfer. Shouldn't be too complicated, but Parker
wants you in there."

Crap, not again. She bolted into the Stab room. What she saw on the EKG
monitor brought her up short. She asked the nurse for vitals and laid her stethoscope on his chest.

Directing her questions to the intern, she took charge. "How's his mental status?"

"Better, Dr. Lawrence. He started out combative and hallucinatory. But he's
calmed down quite a bit."

"You call this better? Have you done a full neurologic exam on him? And
have you noticed the EKG monitor?"

"What? I don't understand? He's undergone a traumatic event. I'd expect his
heart rate to be up."

Zoe turned her attention to the nurse. "Has a tox screen been sent?"

"Yes, Dr. Lawrence. Dr. Parker requested it verbally for us while he was attending to a critical in Stab 1. He hasn't been able to step away yet."

"Change the bed request from Surgical to Coronary Care. Page the internist
and neurology resident on call right away."

As the beepers went off upstairs, Zoe conducted a quick neurologic exam
and ordered a full EKG. She shoved the EKG into the intern's hand and asked him
what he saw.

Not wanting to wait for the delayed response, she launched into him. "As hard
as it may be for you to believe, his missing dick is the least of this guy's problems
right now. Did anyone wonder *why* he cut it off? It's not exactly something we see
every day is it?"

The intern seemed ready for that question. "Well, he's crazy as a loon, that's
why. He was hallucinating!"

"And why would that be? Does he have a history of that? A psych condition
maybe? Or did it just happen out of the blue?" she asked sarcastically, losing patience.

"Well, I didn't exactly look."

"Right, of course not. If you had, you'd have noticed that he has no history of
mental illness, but rather a long record of stimulant abuse. If you'd bothered to look

past his missing cock, you'd have seen a twenty-four-year-old man in the process of both a heart attack and an ischemic insult to his brain. His tox screen *will* come back positive for stimulants, the reason for everything... the heart attack, the psychotic episode, and the self-mutilation. Now he's losing consciousness secondary to ischemia that you misinterpreted as an improving mental status. We can only hope that, as a young man, he's strong enough to withstand the insults."

On cue, the residents arrived and the hand-off was accomplished without incident. He was escorted to the CCU with a crash cart at hand. When she didn't hear the overhead speaker barking "code blue" she allowed herself a deep breath. The surgery teams were redirected to the CCU to consult there.

By MID-AFTERNOON KAJ SAT in the break room with Zoe for a quick update on the outstanding patients. He was glad he'd made the right call and sent her to run the show on the self-mutilation case. He still didn't trust the intern. It appeared that Zoe didn't either.

He watched her as she made her way down the punch list. He was always watching her. He listened to her voice as she spoke. There was something about it. He loved hearing her speak, watching her full lips form around the words. Wandering... not at all like him. And though he recognized it, he didn't fight it.

She could sometimes appear exhausted, even upon arriving for a shift. Yet she always managed to function without impairment. In fact there was both a competence and confidence about her actions that he found himself drawn to. It was attractive.

And they were smooth together, anticipated each other. She eliminated distractions and focused when it counted, but contributed mischief and light-hearted banter during the lulls. Just the right mix in a stressful ER. She made things fun. She made others successful. The nurses loved her, and the doctors trusted her.

He watched her eyes as they swept up across his face, then back down to her notes. They never stayed with him long. He wanted to look into them, but she wouldn't give him that. Did she know she was depriving him? He didn't think so.

Still, he worried; this attraction ran deeper than a desire to get her on her back. *That* he could fight. Common impulse after all. But with her, he couldn't seem to redirect himself. There was so much he felt drawn to, and couldn't quit thinking about. That she had no apparent interest in him didn't help.

RAY POPPED IN, AS THEY WERE FINISHING. He startled Zoe, whose back was to the door. "Sorry to interrupt, Zoe, but they told me I could find you here. I just hauled in an arrest. Guy managed to get himself a little banged up in the process." He chuckled. "Imagine that?"

Zoe swung her head around. "Ray, now's not the time. I'm swamped." She looked back toward the papers in front of her on the table, waiting for him to leave.

Ray looked over Zoe's shoulder at Parker, and felt a jolt, as the look that was returned seemed as annoyed and protective as his own. He made a point of reaching out to touch her hair and give her a shoulder a squeeze, never breaking his gaze with Parker.

"I'll call you later, Z."

"Make it tomorrow, unless it's about work. I'm eating with Kelly tonight. Now we're pretty busy here." She waited only a beat before raising her voice. "Go!"

Despite the unresolved stare-down, Ray was forced to break it off first and leave.

"APPARENTLY MORE THAN JUST SOMEONE you used to work with?"

"Yes, more. More than *used to* that is, I'm working with him now. On the side, it never interferes with my work here." If all the bad-asses she'd collared while on the force had taught her one thing, it was to never admit to more than you had to. It generally worked for them.

When the uncomfortable silence that followed the snippy and incomplete reply brought her gaze up from the notes, his anger was unmistakable. He also looked hurt, the perpetual smile gone. She noticed the tension in his body and felt oddly guilty.

"If there's nothing else, I'd better get back out there."

"GO." THE WORD RODE A LONG EXHALE. Kaj leaned back against the chair, running both hands through his hair, and resisted the bizarre urge to run after her.

He hadn't been turned down since he was a pimply kid, and it had him wanting her even more. She was a resident, for God's sake. He *thought* he knew better, even though there'd never been one he'd found to be all that desirable anyway. They were always too young, too inexperienced, and definitely too insecure. Never mature enough to deal with uncomplicated coupling.

But there was no denying what he felt. Rising, he shoved the chair back in disgust. Could be her judgment was better than his. She wasn't exactly leading him on; in fact she was giving him nothing.

ZOE STRODE QUICKLY TO THE NURSES STATION where the head of pharmacy, Mal, and two other residents were clearly having a good laugh. "What'd I miss?"

"Well, Zoe, Carmen's back in." Martin, the head of Pharmacy, was smirking. "She sure keeps things interesting down here doesn't she?"

"I'm afraid I haven't had the pleasure of meeting Ms. Carmen yet."

"Oh . . . my . . . God." Mal looked at Zoe in disbelief. "Then you should absolutely take her." She shoved the chart in Zoe's hand as the rest of them exchanged looks that made Zoe nervous. "Cube three."

ZOE FINISHED HER ASSESSMENT and brought her stunned look out into the hallway.

"Says she's a superhero." Zoe looked at the crowd gathered around a table in the triage area. "What the hell am I supposed to do with that? Comes in here with nothing but minor cuts and scrapes, and says she's exhausted and hungry from saving a young man's life today."

"Yeah, so what? Send out for lunch. Feed her. What else?" Mal choked on her laugh.

Zoe laughed too, but nervously. Something wasn't right. It didn't sound like Mal was entirely joking. "Well, it's not what *else,* so much as *what.* What she tells me happened sounds suspiciously like it was actually the other way around, the young man saved *her* life. Acts like she and I are sharing a laugh about something. And it's definitely not in the chart. All I see here are multiple admits for observation following minor mishaps that probably wouldn't even warrant a trip to the ER. I'm guessing her age has made everyone cautious about letting her go right away. Is that it?"

"Yeah, Zoe, that's it. Except that she *is* a superhero and she *did* save a life today." No one could hold back any longer. They laughed so hard even the guy in the waiting room wearing five coats actually quit his hour-long monologue in curiosity.

"Guys, have a heart." Kaj joined the group. "Come with me, Dr. Lawrence. I'll fill you in."

They walked to a quiet corner of the ER. "I don't get it, Dr. Parker. What in the hell am I supposed to do with this lady? I mean given her age, it's reasonable to keep her overnight for observation like they usually seem to do. But no one's asking the obvious question. Why does she keep getting herself into these situations? Should we think about vulnerable adult status?"

Kaj grabbed her hand in his and got serious. "If you were *ever* to do that ... it might just kill her." Without letting go he pulled her down into a chair and sat next to her.

"It wasn't fair of them to throw you in there without a little warning, because you'll never find it in the chart. And she won't make sense to you, even though she's telling you the God's honest truth."

"And that would be that she's a superhero?" Zoe chuckled and shook her head.

She wasn't expecting an actual answer to the rhetorical question, but he gave her one anyway. "Oh, yes, Dr. Lawrence, she is indeed." He held the poker face. "And we are ... let's see, how can I put this?" He paused, "The 'Bat Cave'. From here she transitions into anonymity."

She took a full half-minute to stare at him in disbelief. This was a highly educated professional. Then her eyes narrowed on him.

"Okay, I get it. I'm the brunt of some joke. What do you want me to do with the old gal?" She said impatiently, "I've got others to see out there."

Still holding her hand, he pulled her closer. "No, you don't understand. I'm completely serious. You'll write it up concluding that it's best she stay a night or two for observation, and there'll be no mention of any concern regarding vulnerable adult status. When you're done with her disposition, we'll talk. And don't talk to any member of the press until we've discussed things. Okay?"

"Yeah, sure." *Anything to get my hand back.*

ZOE MADE ANOTHER FORAY INTO CARMEN'S CUBE, this time armed with a partial truth. She found the elderly woman to be charming, but was still left with questions.

After she finished, Kaj received her in the break room with another apology. "Again, it wasn't fair to spring that on you. But go easy on your pals. They thought they were doing you a favor. Everyone loves Carmen."

At Zoe's skeptical look he beamed his perfect smile. "*Really.*"

"Well, I'm not exactly feeling it, but, okay, I'll buy it. They want me in on the love fest. Now what am I supposed to do with the two reporters? What exactly *is* the truth?"

"Okay, here it is…but you won't tell them. We *do* consider her to be a superhero. But she's completely flipped it…the idea of being a hero, that is. She told me once that with age she'd disappeared, and only felt noticed as a burden. So she decided to turn her increasing physical dependence on people into something worthwhile."

"You're losing me here. Disappeared? Her dependence, worthwhile?"

Kaj signaled for her to take a seat and walked to the coffee pot. He came back with two cups. Handing her one, he sat down and continued. "She notices a young person at risk. You know, someone feeling the pull of gangs, drugs, or prostitution …on the edge. They're easy to spot. She lives in one of those assisted-living high-rises for the elderly a few blocks from here. Downtown is her backyard, so she's familiar with the type.

"Then she gives that young person an opportunity to become a hero. Faking some kind of 'event' that requires a rescue, and making sure to do it in such a way so that the young person in question has the first opportunity to help her."

At the dawning on Zoe's face he leaned in with a conspiratorial smile. "You're beginning to see it aren't you? Some kid does a genuinely good deed and gets attention that should have been there all along. They view themselves differently afterward. They've done something to be proud of. Others are proud of them. People take an interest. It's quite amazing really."

"And the secrecy?"

"We have to provide patient privacy." He grinned. "But really, think about it . . . the same woman over and over? Social Services might have the same reaction you had. The press might even get wind and portray her as eccentric, or crazy. And then the kids might view their good deeds as somehow tainted, even though it wouldn't really change the essence of their heroic acts.

"So we talk to the press, indicating that the elderly lady in question is grateful beyond measure but wishes to have her privacy respected. We give them her account of the events and then redirect their attention to the new hero . . . the one she's created."

Zoe's smile followed his. Suddenly this guy was more complicated than she'd given him credit for. And it was no longer just his body she felt annoyingly drawn to. *Never gonna happen though.*

He looked at her quizzically for a moment, and went on. "So . . . we keep her a day or two while things cool down. My only real concern is that one of these days she might put herself in some situation, not recognizing real danger, at the same time that one of her chosen heroes disappoints her."

"How often does that happen?"

"She's never been forthcoming about that. But I do know one thing. Those who respond seem to make the most of it. Maybe the act of helping in and of itself is the ultimate selection process.

"But I think it's largely that people start expecting more from them, and they feel it. They're viewed as good, and trusted. They feel that too. Trust is a powerful thing. Most people don't ever want to lose it."

He started to lean toward her, stopping as she reflexively stiffened, and they studied each other for a few moments. Then he simply smiled, and raised his cup of coffee in a toast.

"To Carmen."

Zoe's cup met his. "To Carmen." They both swallowed down the last of their coffee, and she paused on her way out. "One more thing. What did Carmen used to do . . . for a living? What was it she'd had to give up as she'd aged?"

"You know, that's a good question. Come to think of it, I don't think she's ever told me."

"Thanks, Dr. Parker."

"My pleasure, Dr. Lawrence." And to Zoe, it looked like he meant it.

"MAL! I COULD AND SHOULD STUFF this chart up your tight ass."

The others looked uncomfortable, until Zoe laughed. Mal's relief spilled out. "I'm sorry Zoe. I should have thought that through a little better. You can shove it up the new one Parker just gave me. But please don't hate me."

"Too late." Her eyes narrowed on Mal. "Parker reamed you a new one, eh?" Zoe nodded in appreciation. "Short of witnessing it myself, I guess that'll have to do."

Martin's coffee shot out his nose.

CHAPTER SIX
JULY 27 (EVENING)

I T WAS A BREAD DELIVERY TRUCK PARKED behind the artist's lofts a block from the hospital. The building used to be a bakery. When it was sold and renovated, Kelly paid cash for the large truck and worked out an agreement to receive electric service from the artist's cooperative in exchange for maintenance duties. She didn't even want to think about all the laws he was breaking with his water and sewer arrangement, hidden by the accumulation of junk around the truck. Going by it every day, she'd paid no attention, not even to the orange cable tying it to the building.

The interior was comfortable, fully insulated, and private. There were no traditional windows, and Kelly had completely sealed off the front seats from his living area. He'd also divided the back of the truck into a bedroom and bath, with the living, dining and kitchen occupying the remainder. It felt surprisingly large, and despite the rusted exterior, it was clean and modern inside.

Camouflaged, Zoe thought, in the middle of the city. You could walk right by it and have no idea that anyone was inside. No light would shine out. It was an expected sight in this area, an old abandoned truck. You wouldn't even *see* it.

She sat at the table while Kelly worked at the stove and noticed the small slats that would, if slid horizontally, provide a small portal from which to look out onto the street. They were strategically located so as to provide a view in every direction. Like a fortress.

"Kell, I don't know of anyone who lives more off the grid than you do except for the homeless in squatter's hollow. This is *amazing*. I always just sort of assumed you lived in the lofts." She was still awed.

"Good thing is it's all paid for. No debt. Don't own a credit card, have no bank account, no permanent address, just a post office box. And I get health care through the program at the hospital.

"Of course as I *am* gainfully employed I'm required to contribute to Social

Security, and of course I do pay taxes. But considering my salary, it's not surprising that I pay very little." He chuckled.

"Why, Kell? Why worry about your footprint?" It was the cop in her talking now.

Zoe noticed Kelly stiffen and was quick to correct herself. She'd intruded, and added enthusiastically, "It does seem like a simpler, less complicated way to live though. I can actually see the attraction to it."

Kelly seemed to relax. "That's exactly the point, sweetheart. I like things simple. I like my privacy. And since I'm pretty much broke . . . I like things cheap!" He smiled again.

He grabbed two beers out of the fridge bringing them down hard in front of her, "Here, open these for me, darling, and set up the Scrabble game," then walked into the living room to turn on his stereo. It was a Canadian group.

The haunting blend of whistling First Nation sounds combined with Celtic fiddles was intoxicating. When she added the booze, Zoe felt her entire body give in to it. She closed her eyes to focus on the sound.

"You've got a good life here, Kell." She raised her beer in a toast, the second of the day, and clinked Kelly's outstretched bottle.

"To having been here, Zoe."

"To having been here." It created an itch in the back of her mind, wondering if she'd actually made a difference.

She felt guilty that Kelly had splurged on the bacon-wrapped tenderloins. He'd broiled them to medium rare perfection, practically melting in her mouth. And the sides of asparagus and garlic-mashed potatoes had her over the top.

"You know, we used to pick wild asparagus. We lived close to the border and it grew wild there." Shocked that she was speaking of home, she quickly stuffed her mouth with another bite.

"We did too." He tilted his head toward the ceiling, like he was looking for the images. "Remember the wild berries? Huge." He spoke as if they were reliving the same benign memories.

"Yeah, blueberry pancakes. And raspberry jam, with dense, sweet, homemade bread. God, I wish I'd learned how to make that bread." She felt the sudden need for a mother she could barely remember, except in death. Despite the piece of meat in her mouth, she found herself reaching into her pocket for a jellybean. Then put it back.

Kelly's eyes had followed the path of her hand, and Zoe wondered for a moment what he must think.

"Whenever I smell wood smoke I think of the warming house down by the rink. It's one of my favorite aromas," he continued.

"Yeah, I miss that in winter. Not enough outdoor rinks here in the city." She paused, remembering. "And the odor of creosote from the mission bridge! I actually find myself missing that caustic smell. Amazing isn't it? We used to jump off that bridge into the river. Dad would get so mad at Dan and me. He worried about all the boat traffic. Probably right too. If I had kids I'd never let 'em do that. Foolish of us really."

Zoe thought she saw him erase and reset his expression, and then noticed her own hand traveling back toward her pocket.

"Yes, Zoe. I do remember that bridge. Fun though, eh?"

Once again, she replaced the candy in her pocket. "To this day, when I smell creosote, that's what I think of. Dan and I had so many good memories there. My brother was my best friend you know."

"Your Dan, he'd have been a couple years younger than you, right?"

"Yeah, and he was the absolute best." It started to swamp her. She'd failed to protect him after all.

Her forehead knotted in confusion, subsequent events were intruding.

Kelly announced loudly, "Voila! I'm laying all seven letters. Give me the fifty-point bonus! C. H. I. M. N. E. Y. S." He tied it to an S at the end of another word. "What do you think of that, Zoe girl?"

"Kelly, you just wait till I get you on the rink again. I can reliably kick your ass at hockey. How come it's never even close in Scrabble?"

"You wouldn't be giving up would you? That would seriously disappoint me."

"You know me, Kell. I fight to the finish. Let's keep going."

"That's what I'm counting on kiddo."

HE'D LOGGED CLOSE TO 500 POINTS by the end, laid all his letters twice and left Zoe shaking her head. "I keep playing this and I will beat you one day, right?"

"It's bound to happen." He smiled.

"Well, that was fun." She squinted suspiciously at him. "Sort of. I'd better get home before it gets too dark. I didn't bring my bike light with me today. Didn't think I'd need it."

"I'd drive you but, as you can see, I don't own a car." Palms up, he smiled apologetically.

She laughed. "I ride all year, in all kinds of weather, day or night. I'm fine. I'd tell you I would call when I get home to let you know I'd arrived safely, but ... I'm guessing you don't own a phone either?" she teased.

"In that ... you'd be right." He held his fisted hands out together as if to welcome the handcuffs. "Promise me you'll be careful."

"I will."

"See you in the morning. I'll have coffee ready."

Zoe reached out in an embrace and thanked him for dinner, promising to host him at her place soon.

HER RIDE HOME TOOK HER ALONG HER "architectural" path. It exposed her to traffic, which was a bit of a hazard at twilight, but it was the perfect time for this route.

As she made her way toward the River Road, she had the uncomfortable feeling that she'd missed something. She didn't think it involved work. It felt like it was at Kelly's. Something he'd said? She'd been so completely disarmed by the lovely evening. Yet by the time she'd reached the River Road her concerns seemed trivial.

She loved this route because of the variety of homes lining the Mississippi. The Craftsman bungalows, Frank Lloyd Wright knock-offs, and mid-century moderns like hers, were favorites.

It seemed odd, growing up in a rural area, that she would feel so passionate about architecture. Yet city scenes inspired all the prints and paintings on her walls at home. She collected abstracts of urban landscapes ... and Edward Hopper prints. She particularly liked his views through windows.

At dusk, the lights in the houses that lined this road were being turned on, but no one would have thought yet about closing their blinds. The window vignettes would have reminded her of Hopper prints, but in this case she wasn't looking in on isolation and unanswered questions. Instead she saw families at dining tables, kids crawling up on kitchen counters, and televisions glowing neon. She deliberately slowed her pace to enjoy them.

By the time she got home, she was caught up in her usual tug-of-war.

Happiness? Perfect families in perfect houses? *Overrated,* she thought.

Aloneness? Probably safer . . . but then she thought of the sculpted runners she kept noticing on the path across the street. Men she thought about as she grabbed a beer, shed her clothes, and headed for the shower.

If only she had a man in her bed tonight.

CHAPTER SEVEN

JULY 28 (4:00 AM)

S HE STARTLED AT THE POUNDING on the door, followed quickly by Ray's reassurance, "It's only me! Wake up, Zoe!"

Naked, Zoe grabbed her sheet, wrapping it around her as she raced to the door. She thought of her last wish before bed . . . *there is a God* . . . but scolded him in a hushed, forceful tone. "Quiet. You'll wake the neighbors."

Seeing his carnal grin at her hasty attempt at covering up she added, "And you can ditch the look on your face. Could that be why you didn't bother to call first?"

"Busted," he grinned and stepped inside, then sobered. "We've got another one, Zoe. I want you to see the scene now, before you have to be at work."

"Shit. All right." Looking at the clock, "If I'm going to make it in time I'd better take my car. I can't expect you to drive me around. Hang on while I get dressed."

"You can get dressed, but you won't need your car." He called at her back as she headed for the bedroom.

She reappeared in blue jeans and a sweatshirt. "What were you saying, Ray? I didn't hear you."

"I said you wouldn't need your car. It's only a few blocks from here. Woman named Hanover. Just on the Minneapolis side of the line."

"And you're sure this is the same guy? What's he doing way over here?"

"Not one hundred percent, but pretty sure. You'll see. Let's get going."

THIS HOUSE WAS ONE OF THE FEW HOMES on the street with some actual woods around it. While the others were visible from the road, this homeowner had apparently liked her privacy. The structure was shielded by trees and appeared to sit on a double lot with extra room between it and the neighbors.

There were two cement gargoyles guarding the front steps, intermittently washed by blue and red. With the exception of the gaping black voids of the attic windows, light spilled out through almost every other fenestration, painting distorted amber rectangles on the lawn.

Zoe and Ray booted, gloved, and gave their names to the officer with the clipboard by the door. Zoe corrected his spelling and followed Ray inside.

The familiar metallic odor of blood hit her immediately. She paused to take in the living room scene. No obvious struggle here. The television was on and muted. There were remnants of dinner for two on the coffee table, but it appeared that only one plate had been eaten from, with one wine glass empty, the other full.

"Was that the way you found it?" She nodded toward the television.

"Yeah. Some adult pay-per-view channel. S and M shit."

"Were all these lights on? Shades up?" Zoe walked over to the fireplace mantel, and looked at pictures of the woman in life. A few were posed, but most were candid shots, some with other people about her age.

"Yes and no. Shades were all up as you see them, even in the kitchen where we found her. We shut those to block the view. But the only lights that were on when we got here were the television and all the lights in the kitchen."

"Focused your attention, eh?"

"Yeah, you couldn't miss it if you tried. Come see the body."

Ray led her across the hall into the kitchen. Zoe steadied herself as she tried first for a detached clinical assessment of what had transpired. It seemed on the surface that Hanover had shown some degree of resistance here. The chairs had been overturned, and there was a large tuft of hair on the floor that matched that of the victim in color and length. But it looked like the sexual assault and kill had both taken place where he'd left her laying.

"Nothing's been disturbed?"

"No. Just marking and documenting. Nothing's been moved."

"Looks like she was posed, either for purposes of the assault, or immediately post-mortem. But I don't think she was moved. How was this called in? Who found her?"

"Get this, some poor slob of a paper boy saw her through the kitchen window."

"Ouch. Yeah, he wanted her found like this, wanted us all shocked. But he wanted her like this too."

She now allowed herself to "feel" the scene, from both perspectives, victim and attacker. Always an exhausting process. The victim, naked except for the dishtowel across her face, was spread out on the kitchen table. The pattern of bleeding indicating a violent sexual assault probably in the position she was found. Zoe sensed that the attacker had intimidated this woman into cooperating at least to a degree. She wasn't bound and there was evidence of only token resistance. He'd probably wanted *some* fight from her . . . it would have increased his pleasure, but how much did he require?

Zoe decided that this woman must have thought he was going to rape her, and then let her live. There would be no drugs found in her. But the victim would have had no idea of the actual danger she was in until it was too late. She'd have fought harder had she known.

Zoe looked at the wooden block that held the kitchen knives. The missing knife was lodged at an upward angle in her left side, just below the rib cage. It was left in the final stab wound, but it looked as though she'd suffered as many as four other wounds to the same area. It was driven in to the hilt. The guy had to be strong, as she'd have started resisting in earnest by that point. But there was no blood trail, only a large pool below her. She'd been subdued and attacked where she lay.

"Guy knew what he was going for. Her spleen must be in shreds. Would have bled out fast."

"Yeah, but look at her neck." Ray lifted a corner of the dishtowel.

"Maybe not quite fast enough. Looks like he helped her along."

"That's the way I see it too. We'll find out on autopsy, but I'm guessing the terminal event will be strangulation."

Zoe carefully examined the entire body. Outside of the traumatic vaginal and stab wounds and marks at the neck, there were a few defensive bruises on her arms and thighs. The only other obvious and severe marks were signs of breast mutilation. Zoe looked at the nails. "Doesn't look like she got him with these."

The victim's hand rested on the handle of a knife. Zoe pictured her trying to grab it and pull it out, maybe to use on him as he'd strangled her. Good idea, just too late.

"Rest of the house?"

"I think we've got some small traces of blood on the couch. Found her clothes neatly folded in the living room, nothing ripped. That's it. Let's do a walk-through and see what you think."

He'd gotten her cooperation in some way. She'd stripped for him. The television had probably been used as a prop during his direction of her, and she'd submitted, hoping to escape with her life. Zoe understood that. Really understood it.

Hanover's surrender, the defeat, was suddenly replaced by the attacker's power. Zoe now sensed his sexual appetites. And although she hated this part, it *always* helped her do her job. There was no fighting it anyway; she'd already tried.

"You okay, Zoe?"

"Yeah." She looked away from him; trying to calm her breathing and slow her heart...a picture emerging.

NOTHING ELSE LOOKED DISTURBED. Anywhere. And missing was the yeasty smell of sex. "Guy's not stupid. Bet he only had to worry about leaving evidence in two rooms. Any sign of forced entry?"

"Once again, yes and no. There were some trampled bushes outside of the living room and bedroom windows. No clear shoe prints. From the look of the shrubs, there may have been someone messing around there very recently, but it also looks like it wasn't the first time.

"Windows weren't locked. Hard to say if he knew her and walked right in, invited or not. Or he could have crawled in through a window. But there was no sign of anything haven been broken to gain entry."

Zoe paused for a moment, lost in thought. "I *do* think this is the same guy, Ray. You want my take? This is just the start. If he's in crisis, he may act at a faster pace, and that *could* make him careless. But right now, I sense that he's confident. And it looks like he deserves to be."

She paused as Ray stiffened at the comment.

"Eventually he'll become over-confident, and want to taunt us. But we've got to piece it together now." She pictured the attack. He'd not gotten the resistance he'd wanted. She *knew* it. He'd have to make them suffer even more, and this could get *far* worse.

"We're canvassing the neighborhood. I know you have to get to the hospital. I'll find you there later. We can meet tonight."

"The kid fought."

"Yeah, so?"

Zoe considered what her gut was telling her. "He might have slipped through. Any promising witnesses?"

"I think the paper boy is the extent of our wits. We're going to scour the neighborhood though."

"Good. Maybe someone remembers a car or something. One other thing, either he wore a condom or he doesn't get off at the scene. I'd bet on it. You won't find anything on or in her. In fact he may use some tool on her by the looks of the damage. You'll want to check the grounds very thoroughly though, especially below those windows. I'll bet at some point in time he left something. Probably degraded by now though . . . unless." Zoe still didn't have a complete feel for what motivated this guy, but she allowed for the possibility that he'd stayed long enough to see the paperboy's reaction. *Maybe that's when he shot his wad.*

"Unless what, Zoe?"

"Unless . . . just tell them to take a special interest in the area around those windows, and anywhere he might have hidden and seen the paperboy. Also, get me everything you can on the victim. That may be our best shot at him."

"Already on it. I'll fill you in tonight."

ZOE BIKED IN AFTER ALL. BY THE TIME SHE got there she couldn't remember her ride, but had developed a startling picture of the attacker. It brought back why she'd elected to back off on police work. And it didn't help that she'd gotten only a few hours of sleep.

Kelly looked at his watch when she came running in with her bike on her shoulder.

"Sorry, Kell, no time to talk." She parked her bike, grabbed a cup of coffee and ran for the door. Her words trailed her out. "Going to be a very long day."

She slammed down her coffee and darted toward the ER call room, grabbing a fresh pair of scrubs from the shelf on her way in. She caught Mal's irritated look.

"Mal! Please! Unless you're holding someone's brain matter in over a gunshot wound like the Little Dutch Boy, just give me a few minutes to shower before you shove a chart in my face. Just a *literal* few minutes." She needed to wash off the crime scene and bike ride, and wished she'd taken her car after all.

"Whatever, I guess. There's nothing that critical, it's just getting royally backed up, and Parker's off about it."

KAJ WAS CASUALLY LEANING against the doorjamb as she emerged from the shower. He threw her a towel. "What's with the late entrance?"

Caught between the surprisingly frequent need to apologize and justifiable anger, she wrapped herself in the towel and pushed past him into the call room.

"What in the hell are you doing coming in here like this?" Zoe stood next to the bed, waiting. For him to leave . . . or an answer . . . whichever came first.

Kaj waited too, silent and staring, then reached for her scrubs on the bed. He tossed them to her, maintaining his position between her and the door, as she trapped them out of mid-air against her chest.

"Well, do you need anything else?" He didn't move.

Neither did Zoe.

"You can shove me aside again if you want, but you're going to want to put those on first."

He'd said it so smoothly, like this shouldn't bother her. She even thought she saw a slight grin.

"Listen, I'm sorry I was late." *Oh God.* She turned her back defiantly, dropped the towel and threw on her scrubs. Kaj's eyes were still on her ass when she turned around.

"Yeah, that's right . . . it's round and it's tight . . . seen enough?" She looked up to find one eyebrow lifted over a wry smile. "What? You find this amusing?"

"Amusing? Somewhat. Arousing?" He looked her up and down. "Definitely."

With that, she tried to shove past him, but he grabbed her arm. Stopping abruptly at the power in his grip, there was no mistaking what she saw in his eyes. As he pulled her to him, she felt herself weaken, and grow warm. She hadn't shaken the crime scene yet. The submission, the lust, the power were still convoluted with her own desires. They all gave form to one non-specific impulse.

And her sharp intake of breath betrayed it. He smiled and let go.

She walked out, and slammed the door behind her . . . on him and his fucking, enticing smile. Asshole player.

But she still couldn't catch her breath, and leaned against the door. What the hell just happened?

"Okay, Zoe, what gives?" Mal cornered Zoe in the hallway. "I'm sensing a little tension between you and Parker. Everyone is. Spill it, what happened? And don't tell me you screwed up. Cuz right now it's so thick that everyone thinks you're about to get kicked out of the residency program. Girl, it's only been a few weeks down here, what did you go and do to get yourself in trouble?"

The tension was real, and Zoe *had* been avoiding Parker for two reasons. She didn't trust him . . . and she didn't trust herself. The other part, about screwing up and getting kicked out of the program . . . maybe, she didn't know.

"Sorry, Mal. I'm not sure if I'm in or out. Guess I'll just have to keep working and find out." Quickly changing the subject, "Still having that party?"

"Yeah, you're coming, aren't you?"

"Gonna try. I could use a little mind-numbing fun. Is this party going to be good for that?"

"Nothing but the best, Zoe." She smiled conspiratorially.

Zoe's intern slid to a stop in front of her, catching his breath. "Dr. Lawrence, I need you to come and see my guy in cube seven."

"What's the story?"

He started walking toward the cube as he talked, trying to hurry her along. Zoe thought that if he could have grabbed her by the arm and pulled her, he would have. His narrative came out in breathless fragments.

"Came in with severe back pain. Sixty-year-old guy. Out pumping gas into his car when he goes down in a heap. Winds up driving in himself. He's lucid and all, but it's weird."

Oh, Lord, save me from interns. She had to remind herself that she *was* one once. "What's *weird* about it? Think. Be specific, Dr. Shepard . . . focus."

"Okay. Okay." The panic in his voice was starting to make Zoe a little worried. "He comes in, main complaint is pain. No history of back problems whatsoever. Says he has high blood pressure. No other medical problems. Doesn't take his meds regularly though. History is negative otherwise. Complete neurological exam is negative. Just says this sudden pain floored him.

"Okay. Okay. So then I notice that he's really perspiring, but I'm still thinking routine back pain at this point, and that maybe he's getting a little vagal from it . . . maybe even referred pain from something else. But it turns out he's not vagal, his heart rate is high and here's the thing . . . his blood pressure, which should be through the roof in a hypertensive guy with pain . . . it's bottoming out."

Zoe didn't have to be guided in the direction of the cube any longer. She was jogging toward it as the intern finished his account. "So I put oxygen on him and order a flat plate of his abdomen while I get an IV in, thinking maybe it's renal stones. But the blood pressure still doesn't fit. Now I'm thinking maybe a coronary event. I mean what else can it be, right? So I get an EKG, and it's normal except for the tachycardia. Then the flat plate comes back. Look at it. *That's* what's weird."

"No shit." They'd come to a stop at the computer image of the man's abdomen. She caught herself, and readjusted her language and demeanor as the lucid and frightened patient looked toward her for reassurance.

"Lower extremity pulses?"

"Can't find 'em."

"Page the vascular surgery resident on call right away. Set up for a CT scan. Let's wheel this gentleman into Stab one where we're better equipped to deal with his situation. I'll explain as I move him."

WHEN THEY ARRIVED, SHE BROUGHT the x-ray image up again as a prop.

"See this, Mr. Logan? This has probably been developing for quite some time. Look at the irregular whitish lines in the shape of a circle, about the size of a small soccer ball. As you follow them around, you kind of lose them right here, but you can easily make out how big the circle is. See it?"

He nodded.

"Well, we can't be sure yet, but what Dr. Shepard and I suspect is that your pain is related to an abdominal aortic aneurysm. It's an out-pouching of the main artery that leaves your heart and supplies your abdomen and lower extremities. The white lines are calcifications within the aortic wall. It can continue to grow over a long period of time, often silently. What happens when it grows too large is that it can rupture. Basically, we think you might be springing a leak."

At his long, slow exhale; she could see it was sinking in. "Okay, we're going to work fast and transfer you to the surgical team and they'll take it from there. I'm going to get some fluid running and a second line in before they come. We'll draw some blood to type and cross. Any allergies?" He shook his head. "We'll also be arranging for an abdominal CT scan. Anyone you'd like me to call?"

When Zoe had finished the transfer, spoken with Mr. Logan's wife and dictated her notes, she called her intern aside. "Shep, I think I could kiss you right now." Looking like he thought she meant it, the redness crept up his face. "That wasn't all by the book, and you definitely could have handled it better, but you did a *very* good thing today."

"Thanks, Dr. Lawrence … I think. I feel like I bumbled my way through it."

"Well, you sort of did that too, like we all do at times. But you kept at it. You trusted the evidence in front of you. A lot of new interns would have been so focused on the back pain, they'd have missed the incongruities. But things didn't fit, and you kept going until it made sense. So, yeah, maybe you stumbled a bit, but you were smart to question things.

"If you'd have simply treated this as a routine back strain and medicated him for pain, leaving this undiagnosed much longer, his chances of survival would have gone way down. Worst case … he could have died suddenly, sitting in that cube. Instead, we've got things under control. I'm pretty sure you're going to be right on this one. And if so, you'll have very directly saved his life. *You* will have."

The intern validated her growing faith in him with a reluctant smile. It was a look she knew all too well. In it there was gratitude for not having blown it. After all there were far more pathways to messing up than there were to success.

He'd finally lost the cowboy swagger and discovered the one thing you had to know as a physician … your own limitations. All *good* doctors understood that. Coming to her, hat in hand, meant that he did too. She felt like maybe she could trust him now.

"Now I'm going to tell you what comes next. Whenever you dodge some bullet and save a patient, maybe even think you're some kind of hero and want to look in the mirror and start grinning … don't. That's exactly when you damned well better ask yourself if you could have done it better. Just because it was good enough … don't be satisfied with that."

He nodded, and she smiled, reaching out to take him by the shoulders, looking him squarely in the eyes. "But on the other hand, you won't save every patient, even when you've done everything *perfectly*. People die. And you'll have been the last one to touch them. When that day comes ... and it will ... remember to ask yourself if you did the best you could. If the answer is yes, then you *have* done enough."

ZOE HAD DONE HER OWN GOOD JOB of avoiding Parker, but eventually he cornered her. "I heard what you said to Shepard, and I want to thank you. You've supervised him through the opportunities he's needed to learn things first-hand. Even when you and I both know it would have been far easier for you to do them yourself." He smiled knowingly. "I appreciate what you've done with him."

"All that matters is that the patients appreciate it." Zoe looked down the hallway, wanting to keep moving.

"We all do. You've earned a lot of respect down here. If he hadn't felt comfortable enough to lay himself out there and risk looking stupid even, we all could have been regretting this day and planning a trip to the morbidity and mortality conference." He maneuvered, to force her gaze to his. "Listen, although a lot of residents are ace doctors, mentoring is one thing most never really get the hang of. I expected all kinds of drama with that kid, and it never happened. Thanks to you."

The conversation seemed to indicate she wasn't about to be thrown out of the program. She felt so relieved that inexplicably, she apologized again. "Sorry about earlier. I won't be late again."

"No, I doubt you will." He grinned just slightly. "Listen, about the predicament I put you in ... well ... it was an ill-conceived ... anyway ... I'm the one who's sorry ... can we both just leave it at that?"

Ray came jogging down the hallway, his pace slowing as all three locked eyes.

Kaj answered his own question. "Unless something else has come up that will take your attention away from work, where it belongs?"

Zoe waved Ray off. "Meet me here at six." Turning back to Parker she reassured him. "You've got my full attention here. There'll be no problem."

She looked at them both, and then walked toward her next patient, hissing under her breath as she walked past Ray, "You couldn't have picked a worse time. My career could be in a slipknot here."

CHAPTER EIGHT
JULY 28 (EVENING)

Zoe finally broke away from the chaotic ER. No one else had gotten out on time either, and they would all quickly repopulate the cafeteria tables.

"God Ray, I thought I'd pass out there at the end. Didn't have time for anything more than a piss break all day. And Parker was really riding me. Didn't like that I was late I guess."

Her uncomfortable encounter with Parker that morning had her looking away from Ray. Somehow she'd managed to feel guilty about it. How in the hell did he do that? She winced.

"Did I cause trouble for you with Parker? Cuz I don't like the guy you know."

"No," she lied. "What else did you find?"

"Okay. It's more like what we didn't find. No obvious DNA source on or in the victim. Nor was there anything outside the house. No foreign object found that could account for the violent sexual assault. And it was violent. Caused a lot of damage. Nothing to account for the mutilation either. Makes me think he might use a murder kit. There were no drugs in this one, nothing except alcohol, consistent with the empty wine glass on the coffee table. And although there were prints . . . none matched any from the other crime scenes."

"That's what I figured. And I'd have been surprised to learn she was zoned. He'd want her painfully aware . . . and resisting to at least some degree."

"You're talking like you know the guy."

"I'm getting there. I've given it a lot of thought." She chewed at another mouthful of hamburger then washed it down with hot coffee. "Here's how I see it."

Zoe laid it all out.

"If Nelson was his first kill, it would have functioned like an experiment. He went in there with the cover of fireworks, and the drug, to help him work out the logistics. It made things easier. My guess is that the gun was meant to serve as both the primary method of intimidation and control as well as the back-up murder weapon if needed. With the use of the drug, he wouldn't have had to use it for either purpose if the kid hadn't interrupted him. But then he had to act quickly. So he shot her and went for the kid."

"So he doesn't trust his skills?"

"Well...yes and no. He's confident, but he was trying things out. Settling on a method. My guess is he's smart enough to know that what he *thinks* may happen based on his fantasies, may not be how his victim actually responds. When he had to chase down the kid and do her, it could have scared him out of trying it again, for maybe a long while. But the second event last night confirms what I was sensing. He actually gained confidence out of the whole fiasco. That's why he had the nerve to repeat so soon."

"Yeah, just under a month apart."

Zoe watched Ray glance at Parker as he took a seat across the cafeteria with a few other attending physicians.

"What are you thinking Ray? Got any other ideas?"

"Yeah, I've got other ideas all right," he mumbled and reached out to caress Zoe's face, making a purposeful show out of it, Zoe thought. "Naw, I'm with you. Keep going. The way you get in these guys heads though...I don't know how you do it."

"Come on Ray. It's my job." How she did it? He didn't really want to know. "Anyway, I'm thinking this guy plans carefully. He probably stalked this victim for some time. But why her, that's what I can't figure. I've got no handle whatsoever on how he picks them.

"Nelson and the kill last night resemble each other in their attractiveness, but we need to find other similarities. I want everything there is on the victims, to help us determine how he culls them out. Hopefully that will tell us something about *him*. He's left us nothing otherwise. We may need to depend on the victims to introduce him to us.

"The other thing is, I picture him coming in and using the gun to threaten and intimidate the victim into cooperating. Perhaps reassuring her that if she goes along, she won't be hurt. He probably even had Hanover strip for him in the living room. Remember the carefully folded pile of clothes? She cooperated, at least up to that point. But he ditched the idea of using the drug. It takes the edge off his pleasure. He needs his victims to suffer. It's what he gets off on." *That and other things.* She wasn't ready to share those ideas with Ray just yet. They were still a little unformed.

"But aside from how he picks them, how does he gain entry? If he knows them personally, does he smooth-talk his way in? Does he show the gun right away? Does he climb in a window and surprise them? I'm hoping that unanswered question is a clue in and of itself."

"How so?"

"Both neighborhoods are considered relatively safe and many people don't lock everything up at night. I know I don't." She noticed Ray open his mouth to speak, but then just shake his head. "They could be unwittingly handing themselves over to him. And if he stalked them, he'd know all of this ahead of time.

"Or did it happen differently in each case? I'm thinking it might have. Often times, the first case is closer to the killer's neighborhood. It's a crime of convenience in a way. Maybe Nelson was someone he knew or saw every day and developed a fantasy about. She could easily have invited him in. We'll need to look at that too. But after the first, all bets are off. He could strike anywhere."

Zoe noticed Ray, looking across the room . . . at Parker. Other people were filing in now too, but for Ray, it seemed he was the only one that mattered. She saw that Parker's attention, while pleasantly directed toward the others seated at his table, was also clearly divided. The uncomfortable intersecting glances made her want to leave.

"Let's finish this somewhere else. My place or yours?"

"I'm *very* good with that idea." Ray seemed ready to go to.

As they stood to leave, Rex strode in, tired but wired. "Hey Zoe, you here tonight?" He grinned suggestively and claimed her mouth with his.

Kaj felt himself tense.

Zoe pushed Rex away, and holding him at a distance with both arms, looked him up and down.

"No, I'm going home. You look spent, and you've got 24 hours yet to go. What's been happening?"

"It was crazy for a while. Had cardiac cases crashing all over the place. I personally ran three codes today already, and helped with others. It was pretty cool actually. But you're probably right." He stretched and yawned. "I should try to catch some sleep now while I can, in case it doesn't let up tonight. I'm zonked already."

"Sounds like a good idea Rex. Rain check, eh?"

"What, forget that you owe me? Not a chance." Rex looked pointedly at Ray, who responded by rolling his eyes as you would with a child.

Rex grabbed Zoe one more time and went back for more. "Just a goodbye kiss," but he groped her this time.

Kaj watched Zoe shoot Ray a warning glance and then free herself from Rex. Kaj let himself drop back into his seat.

"Bye Rex. Make sure you get up to a call room and catch some zees while you still can. Promise me?"

"Yeah, Zoe. A quick bite and I'm all over it. Man it was awesome today!"

Zoe and Ray made for the door before Rex had a chance to further embarrass himself.

"You know Zoe, he doesn't get it. He thinks he has a claim on you."

"Naw, he's just tired and loopy. I've been that way many times myself. You really don't think straight sometimes with the hours they make us work. And sometimes you get all revved up in more ways than one. Cut him some slack. Besides, I know what you were about to do, and it's not your place."

"Sorry if it's hard to watch another man pawing you. I know my place Zoe, but that doesn't mean I like it, and I certainly don't want to have to watch this shit."

"Do *not* lay that on me again. I don't hear you complaining when we make love. You got too possessive before, and I'll call everything off if you get weird on me again."

But they paused at the exit, and he reached out to sear his own brand over her mouth. Zoe found herself leaning into him.

Finally separating, they each drew back to look into each other's eyes. Zoe simply shook her head. "Let's go get my bike."

CHAPTER NINE
JULY 29 (7:00 AM)

D<small>R. VINCENT OPENED HER OFFICE</small> door at the knock, still taking her jacket off.

"Good morning Camilla. I know you've a habit of starting your days early, but would you happen to have a moment for me? You're listed as a reference in this resident's file and I wondered if you could fill me in on a few things."

"Dr. Parker, what a pleasure." She reached for the folder and seeing the name on it allowed a trace of worry to show. "Is there a problem? Is she all right?"

"Listen, there's hardly anything in this file. It's as though she materialized out of nowhere when she started college at the U of M. And there's almost nothing in here except the essentials. It's a name, rank and serial number kind of resume. Nothing else."

"Well, perhaps if you can explain your interest in her background I'll know where to start. Why the need to know? What's happened? I'd be very surprised if she wasn't performing well."

"She's performing fine, but ... " He seemed to struggle for a way to put it. "I'm a little worried for her."

"Worried about what exactly? What have you noticed?" Camilla remembered the first time she'd met Kaj. Recalling the handshake and the look in his eyes as he'd reached across the table suddenly had her worried for Zoe too. His eyes had virtually undressed her. Camilla remembered it as more than disarming. Despite her happy marriage, it had attracted her.

She needed a chance to pull her thoughts together before she went any further with the conversation. "Excuse me for just a moment while I get a cup of coffee from the waiting room. Would you like one?"

"No, thank you."

"I'll be right back then." She took the time alone to quickly gauge the situation. There wasn't anyone who wasn't aware of Dr. Parker's arcane reputation. Yet it was also true that a trail of angry, bitter women simply didn't exist. You'd be hard-pressed to find anyone who'd speak ill of him.

She thought of his conquests, the ones she was aware of anyway. They weren't the kind to need public acknowledgement of their affairs. They were as discrete as he. All independent, confident women … no one too needy. Her psychiatrist mind wandered to question whether that simply made him a mature, thoughtful man who didn't want complications, or something closer to a testosterone-laden adolescent ill-equipped to deal with real life needs.

As she picked up the coffee and turned back toward her office she also recalled another detail of her first encounter with Dr. Parker … the quick shift in his demeanor when he'd noticed the wedding ring on her finger. If he'd been ready to make a move, it had ended abruptly with that. She'd never felt the slightest bit uncomfortable with him since then. Up until now.

So what *was* his interest in Zoe? An intimate interest didn't fit. She didn't seem his type by any stretch. Although Zoe was confident, both in her skills at work and in her own ability to attract, she could tend toward abrasiveness. She was certainly independent enough, but too much so for most men … almost defiantly so. Genuinely unconcerned with her own beauty, it would also take a man with his own brand of confidence to ignore conventional expectations. And although Zoe would never admit to it, she had the most frustrating of all needs … the kind that no one seemed able to satisfy. Camilla had been through too much with Zoe not to realize that.

She was left to trust that Kaj's interest must be professional and warranted. Deciding to cooperate, she walked back in and waved him into a chair.

"Okay, I'll do my best. What exactly is it you need to know?"

"Listen, I've watched her work now for weeks. She's highly competent. But I've noticed she's often showing up exhausted and late. She's also mixing in some sort of outside work. I'm concerned that it may be getting in the way of her duties here."

"You can't possibly have anything to back that up with. I *know* her. She'd never let anything interfere."

She now viewed Kaj with skepticism. If this was some sort of evidence-building exercise aimed at shoving Zoe out the door, she wanted no part of it.

"I think very highly of her, Dr. Vincent. This isn't a witch hunt."

"Well then, what exactly is it?" She didn't even try to hide the protective edge in her voice.

"It's genuine concern. No more, but certainly no less." He spoke with a measured and convincing calm. "I consider her to be the single best resident to come through this training program ... ever. I've no intention of losing her. But I think she may be juggling a lot right now. I only want to make sure that if there's any way I can help, I'm equipped to do it." He looked past Camilla's shoulder, "I'd hate to see a collision between competing areas of her life."

Camilla reconsidered. When she worried about Zoe, that's exactly what she pictured, but had never understood. Internal collisions. Conflicting impulses.

She knew that Zoe, not being one to talk, purposefully chose hobbies that allowed her to release that tension physically. And as her friend, she'd witnessed Zoe's sometimes-reckless behavior firsthand. But that's all Camilla was to her ... a friend, not her shrink. And she'd never considered Zoe's behavior to be self-destructive as many would, indeed as most psychiatrists would, but rather a reasonable coping mechanism. After all, Zoe functioned at a very high level, and needed her outlets. But they *could*, she supposed, put Zoe at risk. She decided to talk, but guardedly.

"All right Dr. Parker. I'll trust you to use this information only for Zoe's benefit. But I must warn you. I'm not sure there's much I can add to what you see in that file."

"It's just that the words in that file really don't give me a complete picture. And as I'm responsible for her in this program, I'd rather talk with someone who knows her well. She used you as a reference, I'm only requesting information that she trusted you to give."

With mention of trust, she reminded herself to be careful.

"Well as I said, I don't know if I can be all that helpful, but I'll start with when I first met her. As I'm sure you've seen, aside from being five or six years older than most of her peers, Zoe is not a traditional trauma surgery resident."

She paused as she recalled encouraging Zoe to pursue a career in medicine. If Zoe were now in trouble over that decision, she would feel partly responsible.

"She was on a completely different track before medical school. She'd graduated from the U of M with a degree in criminal psychology, and after joining the

Minneapolis Police Department, rapidly worked her way up to a niche profiling. It had been quickly discovered to be something she was very good at it."

Camilla kept to herself that some of Zoe's colleagues on the force found her competence at profiling a little unnerving.

"I first met her during a trial. You see, my patients and her suspects were one in the same on occasion."

"So you've only had a professional relationship with her?"

"I met her under those circumstances, yes, but we quickly became friends. After that we'd discuss hypothetical cases, but tried to reserve our time together for fun and relaxation. We both had stressful jobs and liked to escape together socially. So in that respect, I know her very well.

"I also know that she's a very complicated person Kaj; it's part of why I find her both interesting and challenging as a friend. But if you're asking about her more remote past, before her arrival at the U of M, I'm not of much help there. She never talks about that. I can honestly know nothing of that period in her life. I have some guesses of course, but would rather keep those possibilities to myself."

"Fair enough, but don't you find it odd? That she refuses to speak of her past?"

"Well yes of course. But I have a deep affection for Zoe, as I think all of her friends do. And my selfish desire to keep her in my life is far greater than my need to know everything about her. It doesn't threaten me not to know.

"I've also reached the obvious conclusion that her past is painful. She doesn't want to be reminded of it. I may be wrong, but it's certainly not unheard of, is it? Many people have pasts they'd like to forget. Pasts they may have had no control over. And even if so, she's clearly risen above whatever it was, to make a tremendous success of her life.

"All of her friends will tell you the same thing. That's the deal with Zoe. And through experience, we all know better than to push it. I think I can safely say that if you want to know specifics about what came before, you won't get it from her friends. It's that we simply don't know. Nor will you get it from her. You'll have to find another way. Are you really so sure it's relevant?"

Kaj pushed back in his seat and let out a sharp breath. "I'm not sure at all. I'm just trying to get an impression about her life outside of work. I *am* convinced that somehow it's getting in her way right now."

"Perhaps you can be more specific. What exactly have you witnessed in the way of concerning behavior?"

"As I mentioned before, she sometimes appears completely exhausted, and she's interrupted frequently while working. I think it's somehow tied to her relationship with a detective who's been tracking her down in the ER lately."

Camilla didn't try to hide the smirk. "Dr. Parker, if this is about her personal relationships with men, well, good luck, and ... should I say get in line?"

Kaj shook his head, but leaned forward.

"And if you're referring to Detective Perry, yes, he's one of them. A special one, as it appears you've already noticed. I have no idea if she's currently involved with him intimately or not, but she may be involved with him professionally.

"She agreed to part-time consulting for the MPD, but I know she would never allow it to interfere with her work here. She's very protective of her responsibilities in both realms."

He seemed to go cold. Camilla saw the sheen form in his eyes and something pull down at his shoulders.

"Is she working on Julia Nelson's case?"

"I heard from a friend over at Justice that she might be. It certainly wouldn't surprise me, she's got a great track record with the MPD and I can assure you they wouldn't hesitate to involve her if they thought it might help."

He paused, but then continued. "I also witnessed a confrontation with another man, a resident here. He seemed to be an unwelcome but insistent intrusion. I almost moved to intervene, but she managed to disengage from the situation."

Camilla suddenly felt worried again. Perhaps there really was cause for concern. He seemed genuine. Either he knew something about Zoe that she didn't, or was a very good actor. As a psychiatrist, she was sensitive to being manipulated, but she couldn't read this guy. The tug of war between worry over Zoe and skepticism at Kaj's motives pulled in the cynical direction.

"If you're concerned about her male companions, you needn't be. Yes, she's had ... probably *has* ... more than one. You of all people shouldn't find that alarming. The ones I've met, while perhaps not as discrete as you might be, are first rate. In fact I think I'm safe in saying that most would prefer long-term, committed relationships ... if she'd only let them. Frankly, I've liked them all. But she's not the type for commitment."

Kaj looked interested . . . and Camilla worried that she may have just overstepped her bounds by saying too much.

"Listen, believe me, Zoe can handle herself. Her time on the force put her in conditions that were demanding both mentally and physically. About all I can say is Lord help anyone she feels truly threatened by. Now, if you have reason to think she's in danger from someone *because* of her work here, then as the attending physician, by all means do whatever you have to do. But with that, I think I've said enough. If you have any other specific complaint or concern, I would encourage you to let me know. I'd be happy to talk with Zoe if you want, as a friend. Otherwise, I think our conversation is over."

"No need. I'm not trying to make any trouble. I can ask her if she wants her vacation moved up. She's due for one soon. If there's a temporary work conflict, I'll offer her a way to work it out. Believe me, I don't want to lose her to exhaustion or the pull of competing jobs. I'll do whatever I can to help."

He grabbed for a deep breath, blowing it out slowly through pursed lips. "Thank you very much Dr. Vincent. You've been a great help. And don't worry, I'll be certain to do what's best." He rose to leave, but paused.

"Camilla, on a personal note if you don't mind me asking . . . how do you remain loyal to someone who keeps you so completely in the dark?" He smiled warmly.

Disarmed once again, Camilla thought, by that smile. She refocused. "I don't honestly know."

His grin broadened. "Neither do I."

Chapter Ten
July 30 (4:00 AM)

SHE COULD SMELL THE BOOZE . . . AND something else, garlic maybe? His breath warmed her neck as he stood behind her, a knife held at her throat. Blood spilled from the jagged wound, dividing to paint several paths over her breasts. They were done for the day.

She caught a glimpse down through a window framing normal. It was so close. But there was no way out. This wasn't even his place. The man who lived here was dead. She knew that because she'd killed him. And eventually this guy was going to kill *her*. She knew *that* because he didn't care that she saw his face. The only question was when.

Not today, she thought, as he reattached her other wrist to the shackle. He forced the gag into her mouth and shoved her onto a gray, stained couch, the chain bringing her to an abrupt stop. Not enough chain to come close to an attic window. No, he wasn't going to kill her today, and she wasn't even sure if that was good.

Although he'd let her see him, she was careful not to look more than she had to. That it gave him a chance to change his mind was the one ridiculous hope she clung to. But today she found herself thinking hard about death. Maybe she was even wishing for it.

He could never just leave when he was done. He'd always stay a while, and make her listen. *He* was her world now. She was alive only because he allowed it . . . and *maybe*, if she were good, he'd take pity and let her go. Not mercy, pity. He was careful to say it that way. It always stung, and yet she wanted to believe it. By now she hated herself anyway, seeing through his eyes . . . she was weak, vulnerable . . . pitiful . . . and it seemed no one was looking for her. How could they? They were all dead. He was her world.

She soon learned to do what he wanted. Things that went against everything she was. Things that *should* have been good enough.

But they weren't. He always found some fault, some excuse for punishing her. Then just as quickly, he'd do something to make her wonder. Things like emptying the bucket and replacing it within the perimeter of her chain. Carefully and gently cleaning her with his own hands and allowing her to eat before he replaced and locked the gag. For that, she loved him foolishly. Felt actual gratitude, and finally became convinced of her debt . . . she owed her life to him.

Early on, she *had* tried to fight, but that hadn't turned out so well. He'd liked it . . . and the idea of helping him feel good in that way by fighting back made her sick. It had also set her up . . . and he'd known it. He'd planned on her conflicted feelings. She'd come to prefer beatings . . . somehow that seemed better than rape. And as he'd created a new set of choices for her, she hadn't even seen it coming.

There were no longer yes or no options when it came to being violated. Instead it had become a non-choice . . . which kind of brutality would she 'like'? He told her it had to be her decision. Survival in this new world, with its new laws, required asking for what she *wanted*.

He always stressed that word. And of course he made her beg for it. A good day had her pleading to be beaten, and happy to get it. On a bad day, nursing broken ribs, she'd get practical, and ask for rape. Had even cooperated.

Unable to resist the physical violation, she'd invented mind games, trying at least for distance between their thoughts. But after a while she had trouble recognizing where her mind ended and his began. She even started to think like him, predicting things he would say or do. And in the end . . . her knowledge of him turned out to be worthless, it had never helped with anything.

She started to surface. Wanted to surface, but struggled against hands pinning her down. There was cold, hard floor beneath her bare skin and a warm weight on top of her. Then she heard her own screams, muffled, as if under water. And another voice, someone . . . not her . . . saying wake up. Then there was crying. Was that her?

She pushed up . . . against Ray. She was on her own kitchen floor.

As she started to relax, realizing where she was, he let his head fall into her neck, but still held tight to her wrist. They were both slippery with sweat.

"Zoe, it's okay! You're with me. You're safe. Wake up now, all the way hon."

She felt the knife in her hand. "Oh God! How did I get this?" She quickly let it drop.

"It was pretty bad Zoe. How much do you remember?'

Zoe sent the knife skidding across the floor, out of reach, and then went flaccid. She remembered everything, but spoke with an eerie calm, "What did I say? Could you make anything out?"

"Not really Zoe." He released his grip and brought his hands to her face, wiping at the tears.

"Ray, don't. I'm just sorry you had to see this. I don't know what happened. I don't sleepwalk you know. And the knife…oh my God. Please tell me I didn't hurt you."

Ray rolled to the side and stared at the ceiling. "Zoe, I'm okay. But you're not. Please tell me what's going on. You shouldn't keep this to yourself anymore."

He couldn't look at her. Not while he was saying something he wasn't even sure was true. And he was tired of seeing Thor's hammer come down in her eyes. Truly tired.

"Ray, it's *never* like this. I don't have nightmares. In fact I rarely dream at all. I don't know where this came from. Maybe it's the case. It's been a while since I worked crime scenes like these. Probably just got to me. You know, a cleansing dream. Something like that?"

He could tell by her tone that she'd also heard just how lame that sounded, but he didn't argue. Ray thought about what he'd heard her say, and could never talk about. He would also never tell her how close she'd come. Maybe it *was* the case…but it just didn't feel that way. "Want to go back to bed? It's only four AM."

"Think I'll go work out. The adrenaline has me awake now, you know? I don't think I could fall asleep."

Ray wondered how she ever slept with shit like that going on in her head. And how do you help someone who doesn't want it? Made him feel completely impotent. "Sure Zoe. You want company?"

"No Ray. You go ahead and get some sleep. Or take off whenever you want. Whatever. I'm…I'm just sorry. I don't know what else to say. I need to get down to the gym right now. Gotta work some of this zip off. I'm too wired."

He sat up and reached for her hand.

She felt a panic surge through her. This *was* different. She usually didn't sleep well enough to dream, and rarely had nightmares about anything. She had no recollection of *ever* sleepwalking. Yes, this was different.

Could she have been sleepwalking all along? After all, she might not have had any awareness of it. What could happen at work? She tried to slow her breathing, to steady herself. And still, Ray was there.

"I'll stay if you want me to. I feel responsible. After all it was me who brought you in. If it's too much for you, I'll take you off Zoe. No questions asked."

She needed him to go. "Absolutely not Ray, you're worrying for nothing. I still want in on the case, nothing's changed. I just had a bad nightmare, that's all. I can't believe we're talking about it like it's some big crisis." She tried not to look at the knife, but it was there. "Why don't you head home? Everything's fine."

She was already leaving him. He could feel it in her hand, trying to let go. She used to seem so strong, so sure of herself. Now, her hand in his felt fragile and flighty. It was like trying to hold onto a butterfly without crushing it ... something so beautiful, wanting more than anything to be gone from him.

Should he ... or not? He let go ... and heard her quick intake of breath. Was it relief ... or regret? He wasn't sure. He didn't even know how he felt.

They both headed for their clothes. They both wondered about the knife, about what could have happened. They both smiled silently at each other as they sorted through their communal thoughts. Then they went their separate ways, still joined by the same shocking memory. Ray closed the door gently while Zoe pounded down the steps to her gym. It felt like a good time to work on her slap shot.

CHAPTER ELEVEN
JULY 30TH (6:00 AM)

WHEN ZOE FINISHED HER WORKOUT, she jumped the stairs to her kitchen, moving every knife off the counter and into the pantry. Then she ran to the window and leaned out, sucking for air.

Watching the runners and bikers on the River Road, she envied their lives . . . *whatever* lives they had. It was a good bet they could sleep at night. Could have relationships and not worry about stabbing anyone for Christ's sake. Probably even thought the world was a good place . . . *stupid fucks* . . . happy not knowing the truth.

Somehow this had to end. She dared to consider that she might actually need help. But at the thought, she barely managed to make it to the sink before her stomach heaved.

After all, it wasn't only about what had happened to her . . . she might even have been able to recount that dispassionately. It was what she'd become as a result. That she now wanted and needed terrible things. She could never tell *anyone* that.

She recalled the last time she'd spoken of these things, and the look of concern he'd shown. It had been an easy and slippery slide into a look of torment. She felt the bile in her mouth again. *Fucking therapists.*

There was no one to trust, not even herself anymore. It was as she'd always feared, he'd damaged her . . . her soul, if there was such a thing. It felt like he could still reach out now, after all this time, and control her. And there was a bizarre, soothing familiarity in that, a comfort she occasionally felt because of it. Like the warmth she craved on those cold, early summer nights . . . unclothed and shackled . . . even though it came from the man who promised pain whenever he drew near. She barely even allowed that to register in *her* own mind. It made no sense, and to Zoe . . . it only seemed like a weak excuse. No, she didn't even trust herself.

The idea that Ray, having had to wrestle her down while she wielded a knife, might not trust her again as a partner had her head throbbing. Zoe squeezed her eyes shut, trying to stave off the migraine that was rapidly developing. She popped two aspirin, knowing it would upset her stomach, then went for the paper and set off for work.

SHE RODE HARD AND RECKLESSLY, LIKE SHE did whenever she felt this way. It was her back alley route again. She jumped stairs and slid around the twisting turns of the double track. The trail narrowed and detoured into some woods behind the rail yard. Not slowing, she attacked the slalom of bifurcating tree trunks and jumped downed logs that lay across the only passage through thick trees and underbrush. There were six-inch wide planks crossing some wetlands that she didn't decelerate for. She knew that to hesitate there would mean an accident.

But it happened anyway. There was no warning, and she hadn't hesitated. If anything she would have increased her speed, knowing it was the best way to navigate a tight spot. But instead of flying down the trail she suddenly found herself tattooed to a tree.

The searing pain with each breath had her feeling her own ribs. They didn't seem fractured, but the bruises were rapidly developing. The aspirin she'd taken would make that worse. Her blood would resist clotting.

Pieces of bark clung to her on one side. Her helmet had cracked and the headache was now far worse.

At least her bike was okay. She limped back to the spot where she'd launched. The reflection from the wire caught her eyes right away. It was purposefully wrapped taut between two trees she'd had to go between.

She quickly looked around. There were no laughing kids peering from behind the bushes. In fact, there weren't even any houses visible from this spot. Nothing, no vantage points to view the area from. No businesses, no railroad buildings or sheds. She'd never paused long enough to notice this spot before. But obviously someone had.

She unwound the wire and tossed it angrily into the woods. It was her bad luck to be the first one to come along after some punk had set this up. The little butt-wipe imp was probably sitting at a desk in school laughing about how clever he was.

Well, he'd gotten *her* hadn't he? The picture she was creating of the devil's little minion was pissing her off. She'd never liked kids much anyway. *Fucking kids.*

And she was going to be late for work again. At least she'd have an excuse this time. She climbed painfully onto her bike and detoured to a street at the nearest opportunity, finding the quickest, most direct route. With the exertion, her head clouded. She didn't even notice the shocked looks as she biked by. Tattered and bloody, unsteady... it was bad.

KELLY WASN'T IN HIS OFFICE, but the coffee was fresh and waiting for her. She grabbed a cup and headed upstairs. On autopilot, she planned on cleaning up and changing there. Her clothes were ripped on one side, with pieces of bark still embedded along the torn edges. Yet her head threatened to trump it all. It was pounding to the point of distraction. Maleah saw her push unsteadily through the ER doors and recognized someone in need of a cube immediately.

"Zoe, cube two is open. Let's take a look at you."

"Yeah thanks, I might need help getting this bark out. I can't maneuver to see all of it, and what's left is in there pretty good."

Mal could only shake her head. As Zoe ducked into the cube, Kaj held Maleah back and took her place following Zoe into the room. "Late again. What is it this time?" As she turned to look at him, the answer was obvious. It brought him to her quickly. "Okay, What happened? Who did this?"

Zoe was in too much pain to argue, but tried anyway. It felt like her brain was about to herniate out through her eyes. She squeezed them shut, grimacing. "What makes you think *someone* did this to me. It was a tree for God's sake. I had a bike accident."

Recalling that someone *had* indeed done this to her, with the wire, she backed off a bit. "But anyway, it held me up. Sorry I'm late again."

Kaj patted the exam table and waited for her to sit down. "What were you doing on a bike?" He carefully palpated the wounds that traced from the side of her head down to her hip, "That's a long ride in here, isn't it?"

"I bike to work every day. Nothing out of the ordinary except that today I had a fucking accident. I suppose you could say *that* hardly ever happens. Some punk rigged a booby trap. Fucking clever kid, eh?" She felt herself getting sleepy.

Kaj moved quickly to lay her down. "Head hurt?"

She was vaguely aware of becoming disoriented. "It hurts like hell. I've got a migraine."

She began to get combative. Speaking in abbreviated, exhausted phrases. "Just let me go! I need to sleep. Let me go home."

Her neurological exam was non-focal; there were no obvious deficits. But the deterioration in her level of consciousness was alarming.

"Mal! Get in here! Get her clothes off and clean up these wounds while I call and arrange for a scan. She's got some mental status changes. Says she's got a migraine, but there's this pesky little detail of the head trauma," he said sarcastically.

When he returned, Mal hadn't made much progress. Zoe was still fighting it. "Here, let me help you." He held Zoe down while Mal cut off her clothing. Zoe didn't appear to have much fight left in her, but somehow managed to make it hard for them. As Kaj restrained her, Mal gently washed the wounds and dug the bark out. Kaj felt her ribs for any sign of a fracture, and listened to her lungs. "Badly bruised, but I doubt she's broken anything. I'm more worried about her head."

As they were finishing, Kaj's cell rang. Radiology was ready. "Mal, get Dr. Thomas to take over for me while I accompany her."

Zoe surfaced briefly to feel herself being held down for the second time that morning, the third time if you counted the nightmare. The panic in her eyes was reflected back at her from his worried face, and the pressure, holding her down, belied his reassuring words. Something like ... *it'll be okay. You're doing fine. Don't worry. I'll take care of you. Just relax ...*

Yeah right, easy to say. His voice though, something about it, got her through the scan. She relaxed long enough for them to get the images. They were negative. So was her chest x-ray. No freshly broken bones. No intracranial bleed. No intracerebral swelling.

WHEN SHE WOKE AGAIN SHE WAS IN A hospital bed, and he was at her side.

"How long have I been out?"

He reached for her hand. "Bad head bonk Dr. Lawrence. Apparently bike versus tree from what you told me when you came in. You've sustained more than just a mild concussion. You tirelessly made the case that it was only a migraine. But trust me, it was far more than that. Your somnolence had me worried for a while."

It was coming back to her. "Oh yeah ... I did have a migraine before I left the house. I remember that."

"You also said something about a booby trap. Was that the concussion talking or did you really run into someone's sick idea of a joke?"

"It's all still a little fuzzy. Ow! What the hell?" She tightened up with pain trying to shift positions in bed.

"You'll find that you're essentially one big bruise on that side of your body Dr. Lawrence. We got all the bark out. It should heal without any significant scarring."

She chuckled. "Do I really look like someone who cares about a few scars?"

Recalling the absurd tan lines and the fairly large scar at her collarbone, among others, he guessed not.

"No, I suppose not. Nor am I someone who is unaccustomed to or put off by the sight of scars. Just wanted you to know that we did our best to prevent it."

She smiled, squeezed his hand and then pulled away. "Thank you."

Reaching out to gently touch the scar at her neck, "Another bike accident? Or was that hockey? I seem to recall you mentioning something about hockey the other day. You've got some old healed rib fractures on your chest x-ray too."

He watched the life drain out of her. It started with her face, paling as if by a switch. Then she closed her eyes at an involuntarily release of strength. Her muscles went flaccid. It seemed to take enormous effort to inhale deeply, followed by a pressured exhale, as if a great weight was on her chest. He'd seen this before in patients and it was never a good sign.

"Can you ask them to get me something for sleep? I really need it."

He'd caught himself holding his breath at the dramatic change in her demeanor, until she'd spoken again. "Absolutely Zoe. I'll see to it right away. We're keeping you here at least overnight for observation." He rose to leave.

She reached out to grab his arm in a sudden panic, "Tell them ... *please* tell them ... I don't sleep very well. They'll really have to knock me out." Releasing him, she added softly, "I desperately need to sleep." Then she closed her eyes to signal the end of the conversation.

She doesn't sleep well. That fits. Might explain the frequent exhaustion. But why so panicked about it? Without thinking, he reflexively bent down and kissed her on the forehead. Her eyes snapped open. He froze, and then recovered.

"I only mentioned hockey because you'll have to take two or three weeks off from any contact sport. You may want to move your week of vacation up too. I can arrange it. We'll talk tomorrow. I'll go see about those meds." Angry with himself, he left the room.

CHAPTER TWELVE
JULY 31 (EVENING)

S LEEPING A FULL NIGHT HAD HELPED. Her headache was better and she'd recovered a partial memory of the accident. Kelly sat in the one oversized chair while Camilla, Rex, Martin and Mal sat in smaller chairs or perched on the edge of the bed. Given her improvement Zoe had argued to be cut loose. One more night they'd said.

She recounted what she could piece together of her encounter with the wire on the trail. "There would have been no way around it there. I had to go through those two trees and even if I'd seen it, it would have been impossible to stop in time. Could have maybe slowed maybe, but I'd have still launched."

"How fast do you think you were going Zoe?"

"Christ Rex, I don't know. I accelerate there because it's so narrow and I don't want to have to turn my handlebars. They might catch on a tree. The best way to avoid that is actually to speed up. It makes it easier to keep straight. You know, he who hesitates... and all that?"

The six-year age difference between the two of them suddenly seemed like too much. She'd have to deal with that soon too, and end it. His kind of stamina, while definitely pleasurable, wasn't enough to maintain even the most superficial relationship.

"But how fast Zoe? Just take a guess."

"Rex?"

"Yeah?"

"Why did you choose Internal Medicine to specialize in?"

"Well, I guess it's because as a medical student, it always seemed to me that the Internists were the ones who knew the most. And I wanted to know everything..."

"Stop! Stop right there," Zoe interrupted him, "I rest my case." Everyone laughed, and Rex shut up.

THE SOUND OF DR. PARKER'S VOICE on the evening news pulled all their eyes to the television. He was handsomely dressed, with a woman of matching elegance clinging to his arm. It was some formal function.

His confident stride and slow sweep of the ballroom as he entered looked natural, not practiced. He seemed as comfortable in that environment as he did in the hospital. It caught them all off guard, as most had never seen him in anything other than scrubs.

"Will you get a load of that? He's got a life after all." Rex, as the only resident in the room other than Zoe, seemed genuinely surprised.

Camilla chuckled. Why was it so hard for young people to picture anyone older with a life, let alone a life far more interesting than theirs? "Yeah. Well. If you only knew." Camilla's raised eyebrows pretty much said it all.

Zoe eyes were locked on the screen. "Cleans up well, doesn't he? What's the big gala about? Do you know Camilla?"

"It's a fundraiser in honor of Julia Nelson's service to the hospital and the community. She was very active in arranging free care for the homeless, particularly teenagers. This is about creating an endowment that will keep her vision alive."

Camilla watched the close-up of Kaj's face as he and his date walked up to Nelson's mother on screen. There were real tears rising to his eyes.

"Did Parker know Nelson very well?"

"I'm not sure Zoe. He certainly knew her as a colleague here at the hospital. How close that brought them, I don't know. Of course they could have been close socially, personally even. Knowing him that wouldn't be at all surprising."

Camilla's playful smirk sobered instantly as all at once she read the meaning behind the question. She caught Zoe's eyes and simply shook her head, hoping it would communicate her reluctance to believe there could be any connection.

Zoe nodded at the unspoken sentiment. "Yeah, I agree." She smiled at Camilla, "God, I wish it was Stoli in that IV bag."

ZOE HELD KELLY BACK WHEN EVERYONE else left, and whispered, "My gun. It's in the pack on my bike, down in your office. Will you to take it and keep it for me? Just for a while."

"Zoe, you *have* to tell me what's going on. You have a permit to carry right? After what happened to you in the woods, I suggest you *carry*."

"Kell, don't ask me why. Just know that I don't trust myself with it right now."

Kelly forced his jaw back up.

"I understand Zoe. Please don't do anything to harm yourself. Whatever it is, we can work it out. I *promise* you."

She chose not to correct his false impression, as long as he would take the gun without argument. "I know Kell. We'll work it out. I'm counting on it."

He agreed to keep it.

"One last thing Kell. When I sleep in your office, have you ever heard me talk in my sleep, or sleepwalk?"

He seemed to consider this. "You've done some mumbling. Nothing coherent. Sleepwalking? I don't know about that. Not that I've seen anyway."

She squeezed his hand and smiled. Relieved.

"Thanks Kell." Tired, the words rode an exhausted exhale.

"You okay hon?"

"Better now. We'll talk more when they spring me."

CHAPTER THIRTEEN
AUGUST 02 (EVENING)

MAL'S HOUSE WAS VIBRATING WITH a pulsating bass, the main room lit by a bloody wash of ruby light. No wonder the pounding beat reminded Zoe of an amplified human heart.

Anonymously pinned together in a dense weave of bodies . . . hands, hips, even lips found their way from one to another. Some still stood, only because of the press of people around them. Their exchanges looked almost viral. Give it a little time, Zoe thought, and they probably would be infectious. Yet this was exactly where she wanted to be. Didn't feel dangerous at all, only therapeutic.

Tonight, all Zoe wanted was a mindless escape surrounded by a lot of hospital friends. She tried to picture Kelly here and it made her smile. He'd make a great addition. Camilla too. Zoe really missed hanging with her. They'd had some great times. Ray? Too many drugs going on . . . wouldn't be good for his career. Then she tried to picture Parker here. Somehow that didn't compute after what she'd seen of him on television. While there was obviously more to the guy than she'd given him credit for, this wouldn't be his thing. She looked at some of the other staff physicians in the crowd, letting loose, but him? No, she thought, he wouldn't fit in. And why had she even wondered?

SHE SHOULD HAVE KNOWN. He seemed to be everywhere lately. His entrance caught her attention from across the room. He didn't have to look around long to find her either.

Without hesitating he made his way in her direction. Zoe leaned back against the wall, raised her eyes to the ceiling and shook her head. *Busted.*

And there was really nowhere to hide. But there was more than one way to escape. "Hey! How about another drink here? Stoli. A double!" The guy tending Mal's makeshift bar nodded and poured. The drink disappeared into the crowd while it traveled from hand to hand, until it reached her.

She looked back to find Parker effortlessly navigating the writhing bodies, stopping to flash his charismatic smile at women who seemed more than anxious for him to stay and dance. She hoped he would give in, but it was clear he had a destination in mind. He graciously disengaged from pawing hands and pouting faces without disrupting the smooth flow of his path toward her.

"Break me off a piece of that!" A nurse from the Neurological Intensive Care Unit was looking in the same direction as Zoe.

Zoe rolled her eyes, but invited her to try. "Please, take him off my hands. I know he's gonna bust my butt for partying when I'm supposed to be at home resting."

As he neared, she returned his gaze by downing the entire drink in one pull. A little courage for the impending clash of wills.

He drew in close, face to face, pressed against her by the push of bodies. "Dr. Lawrence." He nodded at the glass in her hand. "You're not driving home are you?"

"No." Nothing more. While it was rude, she owed him no explanations. But she did look at him with a question in her eyes.

"Your intern Shep asked to be cut loose early today. Said he was heading for Mal's. And he looked pretty excited about you being here."

Zoe smiled. "We're on good terms now. Must have been slow in the ER, for you to let him go."

"Excruciatingly slow." His hand went around to the small of her back and she felt the pressure as it began. She set down her empty glass.

"How about biking? You're not biking home?" He smiled, and Zoe could actually hear the nurse moan. *Good God.* But his hand pressed, bringing them closer.

"No, of course not. I'd planned on a taxi."

His hand drifted down just slightly. She wanted it to keep going, and noticed that her own hands were now flat on his chest. She held his eyes with hers and raised an eyebrow as she felt the pressure grow at the front of her waist too.

And suddenly, she felt off... *must be really drunk* ... like she was watching herself in a movie. Was she about to push him away... ?

Apparently not. She watched her own hands slip down over his stomach ... a rock-hard stomach ... and at that moment, she wanted nothing more than to simply give her hands permission to roam. Managing to stop just before reaching for his belt . . . . *dangerously drunk* . . . she quickly pulled her hands away, and directed his attention toward the nurse.

"I'd like you to meet Heather. She's from the NICU. Heather, this is Dr. Parker." Her own words sounded funny to her, and she wondered if they sounded strange to the others.

"Good evening Heather. It's a pleasure."

"How do you pronounce your first name Dr. Parker?"

Heather obviously didn't waste any time, Zoe thought. Good girl, and good luck.

"It's pronounced like sky without the 's'. It's Nordic."

Then Zoe laughed for some reason. Maybe it was because she was picturing him as a Viking. But she didn't really know, and anyway . . . the room was starting to swim.

"Sooo . . . why don't you two get acquainted while I go dance. I *might* be back."

Parker seemed to think that was funny, because then he laughed.

THE MUSIC SHIFTED TO A LESS COMPLEX BEAT, connecting with all that was left of Zoe's brain . . . its reptilian core. Yet her gray matter managed a brief moment of panic when she realized it wasn't only music and booze that she felt. And then there were hands, pulling at her, but she couldn't tell her own hands what to do. Nothing worked. Except for Rex.

In fact he was doing *all* the work. Her legs weren't moving and he was all but carrying her. He kissed her, but she didn't kiss back, or fight it. She was incapable of anything. He managed to get her outside, saying something about cool fresh air, and then the last thing Zoe remembered was managing a weak protest as Rex scooped her up and carried her he rest of the way to his car.

HE POSITIONED HER IN THE PASSENGER seat and ran around to the other side. As he reached for the driver's door he found himself spun and shoved hard against the side of the car.

"What the hell?"

"I could ask the same thing of you. What do you think you're doing with her? She's obviously in no condition . . . " Kaj shoved hard in disgust at Rex's shoulders before letting go.

"Listen! Take it easy man! I know who you are. But hey, I'm no threat. Zoe and I, we go way back. We're friends. She must have had a little too much. I'll make sure she's all right."

"You're not taking her anywhere. I've got her from here."

"Okay, okay!" Rex put his hands up in surrender. "No problem."

Kaj went to the passenger door, opened it and caught her as she spilled out. She was so flaccid he had to put her over his shoulder to keep her from slipping out of his arms. Watching Kaj carry her to his car, Rex wondered.

"Hey! Do you know where she lives?"

Chapter Fourteen
August 03 (Morning)

Zoe was trying to surface again, but from where this time? Her eyes wouldn't focus yet, there was only a suggestion of sound from somewhere, and she couldn't seem to make herself move. When trying to sit up, the throbbing in her head pulled her down. It was a helpless in-between state, and reminded her of waking after anesthesia. Finally, a loud moan was all she could manage, and she rolled over in resignation.

"Good morning Dr. Lawrence. I see that you're up." He sat down. "Some after-party."

Shit. She knew that voice, and now knew where she was. The tangle of twisted sheets explained why she couldn't move. "What in the hell are you doing here?"

He waited a moment before answering, looking at her from behind a slowly developing smile. "I brought you home last night, but as your legs didn't seem to want to work, I was forced to carry you inside, undress you and then tuck you into bed."

"Undress me?"

"If you'd have preferred, I could have left you in the same clothes you'd thrown up on, but I elected to remove them and prop you up in the shower for a quick hose-down. And then rather than leave you in that state I thought it best to remain here in case you had any more episodes of a similar nature."

"You didn't do anything else?" She wasn't sure if she was relieved or disappointed. Her nakedness had her wishing he'd do something now. The hands she'd admired expertly work on patients, were resting not six inches from her. *They* could ease the ache in her head, she was sure of it.

He smiled at her uncomfortable tug on the sheets. Way ahead of her, she thought, refusing to touch her in any way. Then he got up very matter-of-factly.

"Well, it seems that you've recovered sufficiently. I've work to do and you have a vacation to enjoy."

"You're leaving? Just like that?" *What the hell, Zoe. Do you know how that sounded?*

"Unless you need me for anything else?" He sat back down, smiling.

"No! You've done enough. Thank you ... I guess." Zoe pulled out of the tailspin she'd been in. Searching for altitude, self-respect.

"You can thank me after the drug screen comes back. Your intern, Dr. Shepard, flagged me down before we left the party and suggested I test you. He thinks someone might have put something in your drink. From what I saw last night, that wouldn't surprise me. You won't remember, but we swung by the ER on the way here. You probably *should* thank him. I'm pretty confident the test will come back positive. You took a dramatic turn after your last drink."

Zoe rolled over to bury her face in the pillow and moaned. "Nooo." Pinching off the end of the word in an angry staccato, she rolled back over to face him.

"Do you remember anything about the party?"

"Actually ... very little." Knowing they were probably right, she tried to focus. She was well versed in the use of alcohol, and what she'd consumed would have lit her up good, but it shouldn't have had *this* effect on her. She now felt even more vulnerable not remembering what had transpired. "I want to know what happened."

"I told you."

"What else?" She raised her voice. "What else happened?"

"Other than your inability to walk or talk, the vomiting and the stop at the ER, there was some dancing with that Internal Medicine resident, Rex, if you can call it dancing. It looked more like Rex was making out with a rag doll. Then there was his attempt to put you in his car. An effort I interrupted, as I don't know Rex very well and your condition seemed to preclude any consensual recreational activities."

"What happened *here*?"

"Once again, I told you. To recap, I undressed you, washed you, put you to bed, and you slept. I stayed and slept in the living room to make sure you'd be all right. Do I need to say it again? I hoped I wouldn't have to spell it out, that I was afraid you might throw up again and choke on your own vomit. Nice image isn't it?"

It quieted her. And he waited.

"No, you needn't say anymore." Wishing she hadn't asked, "I'm sorry you had to do all this . . . and see me that way."

"You seem to be very fond of apologizing," he grinned.

She had to laugh. "Actually I'm not at all fond of apologizing. And why I've been doing so much of it lately is really quite inexplicable."

"I told you, someone might have spiked your drink. How is that something *you* need to apologize for? I would keep a closer eye on my drinks though. We've both knowledge of how easily this sort of thing can happen."

"Yeah. No argument there. Normally I'd know better. I must have relaxed because it was Mal's." She now recalled the urgent need for a drink when she'd seen Parker.

"Well, I've got a car to clean out before I get to work." Still his hands remained close, refusing to touch her. He was talking about cleaning her vomit out of his car and still managed to radiate sensuality. At that moment, headache and all, she felt warm, weak, and very ready.

But he was the one who refused. No one ever did that. How could she be so attracted and angry all at once? He rose to leave. No gentle pat, no kiss . . . just his smile. He left her in agony.

CHAPTER FIFTEEN
AUGUST 03 (MIDDAY)

THROWING UP IN HIS CAR FOR CHRIST'S sake. Sleepwalking. Thank God for the vacation.

Ray had delivered everything he had on the victims. There had to be some commonality. After pulling up a chair, she spread the documents out on her kitchen table. Nelson had been thirty-six, Hanover twenty-eight. Both were white and attractive, having well-maintained, athletic bodies. Zoe made a mental note to check their gym records.

Each was highly educated, Nelson having a Ph.D. in hospital administration from Harvard and Hanover a Masters in English from the U of M. She worked as a freelance technical writer in a small downtown office.

She grabbed a handful of Swedish Fish. It kept her away from her nails.

Both women had good, solid reputations among their friends, family, and coworkers. These sources of information also seemed reliable, no questionable characters among them. All verified that both women were heterosexual; neither had expressed any recent fears or worries about safety, and as far as they knew, had no enemies.

Neither had large families, but Nelson had a list of friends that was almost too large to track down. Hanover, on the other hand, had a small, tight circle of coworkers, gourmet cooking class acquaintances and curling league teammates.

The Swedish Fish were gone. Zoe went to the fridge for a beer. Neither victim had a history of alcohol or drug abuse, and no criminal record other than speeding tickets. Nor was there evidence at autopsy of any chronic physical or sexual abuse. Neither had ever been married. Hanover had a steady boyfriend of many years with a solid alibi and Nelson had a long list of casual relationships.

Zoe sat back down to find the fitness club records. They both belonged to neighborhood gyms. Each was independently owned and neither affiliated with a chain. As far as she could see, there was no link. Ray had already cross-referenced the personal trainers and none overlapped.

The kid, Lucy Franklin, was another story entirely. Zoe was convinced she was collateral damage. The killer had never intended to target her. The few homeless teens that could be tracked down all painted the same picture of a reclusive kid who got by on her wits. They verified that she was a thief who preferred working alone, and had a habit of squatting in foreclosed houses that often provided both left-behind food and shelter. While there was another girl who shared space with her, the kids didn't think they worked together. And none, not one, had ever seen her using. Unusual among that crowd, where drugs were ubiquitous and often used as both currency and a means of control. Most importantly for Zoe, they were all quite sure she wasn't being pimped.

The techs had gone through both Nelson's and Hanover's computers. They had numerous intersecting points, but they were the same sites everyone used ... E-shopping, downloading music, getting driving directions and maps. Nelson frequently used the Internet to purchase tickets and make reservations. Nothing suspicious.

Likewise, there were no pornographic magazines or videos found in either home and the channel playing on Hanover's television was found by inspecting her purchase records to have been a one-time event. Zoe had assumed this would be the case.

The photos and personal belongings revealed nothing that would conflict with the pictures that were emerging. No saved correspondence stashed away to reveal a secret relationship. The photos were a mixture of professional sittings with family, and a few candid shots, either alone or with known associates.

She looked through the file of digital photos they'd found in the computers. Most of the displayed non-professional photos were there, but not all. There were also numerous photos that hadn't been framed or displayed.

Zoe's head started to swim for some reason and she tipped it. The beer maybe? More likely too much useless information. She stood and stretched, then rested her hands on the table and leaned forward over the documents. Cell-phone records, texts and emails had all been scoured for unusual, threatening or intersecting activity. Clean, and separate ... almost.

Nelson's phone contacts included half the staff from Minneapolis General. Given her job, no surprise there. But Hanover also had a link. Her call to the ER.

They'd obtained the notes from her visit on that day. She'd seen an intern for an upper respiratory infection, received a chest x-ray, and had been prescribed antibiotics and cough medicine for bronchitis, which she'd filled in the hospital pharmacy. The intern's name was illegible, but the attending physician who signed off on the visit was Parker. That had been about three weeks before her murder.

It seemed far-fetched to think it would amount to anything, given the volume of people who came and went through that ER. But as they had so little in common, it *had* caught her attention.

Finally she reconsidered the neighborhoods. Nelson's was high-end. Hanover's, while not as exclusive, had a solid mixture of expensive to mid-value homes. What the two neighborhoods had in common was safety. Crime statistics supported that. Zoe always pictured neighborhoods like these as oases within the city. They seemed to go unnoticed by the criminal element. Made her wonder why.

While they hadn't come to any definite conclusions about how the killer gained entry, there was unanimous agreement that he'd scoped out Hanover's place from at least one window. Actually, the foliage outside of two windows had been disturbed, and it appeared that it had occurred at more than one point in time, at least once remote to the night of the murder given the state of decay of the trampled shrubbery.

It was time to meet with Ray again.

She opened the pantry, there had to be more candy somewhere.

CHAPTER SIXTEEN
AUGUST 04 (LATE AFTERNOON)

THEY ARRANGED TO MEET AT MPD headquarters. Neutral territory, Zoe thought. No knives either.

"I've been through everything we've got on the victims and there's nothing to link them. The main commonalities are the neighborhoods. They're safe. People get careless. Makes me think he uses that to his advantage when scoping and entering. I'm guessing he comes in through an unlocked window or door. At both the Nelson and Hanover scenes there were unlocked entries. Besides, look at the kid, and what she was able to accomplish. She'd been inside half the houses in Nelson's area and no one had a literal clue."

"Well sure, I agree. But I don't think we can ignore the potential link to the hospital. Nelson worked there and Hanover was seen there. It would put both their names and personal information in the computer, and put them there physically."

"Yeah, but both you and I are in that system as well as half the inhabitants of the metro area. It doesn't really tell us anything."

"Zoe, Parker knew Nelson well enough to attend the fundraiser. Well enough to speak directly with her mother. He also saw Hanover in the ER. You sure you're clear on this? Got distance?"

"But that's not how it works Ray. The intern of record would have handled something as simple as a visit for bronchitis. If Parker had been involved, it would only have been to listen to the intern and sign off on the management plan. He probably never even laid eyes on her."

Ray's teeth visibly clenched, and she considered that he might be right.

"I shouldn't be there for the interview, what with the work relationship and all."

"I know." There was an unspoken accusation in there somewhere, Zoe thought.

"Listen, I know what you're thinking. But you can't just haul him in and accuse him of anything other than doing his job. There's really nothing more than would be expected here. When interviewed after Nelson's murder he readily admitted to knowing her, both at work and socially. Lots of people did. He cooperated and provided any information he could that might be helpful. Even provided some contacts we were able to track down."

"Yeah, right. Good for him. And he seemed pretty broken up about it according to the interviewing officer. What else is new? He didn't have an alibi. Says he was home *alone* on the night of the murder."

"So were many of her acquaintances. It proves nothing." Hearing herself, she added, "But of course you're right Ray, you still have to take a run at him. Still, I think we need to consider another angle. I keep coming back to the neighborhoods. Unless he's done this before, I still think the first victim, Nelson, was chosen either out of convenience or because she was someone who the killer saw often and developed a real or imagined relationship with. I think we have to look more closely at the contacts in her neighborhood.

"In fact, I say we take a second look at any neighbor from either area with a connection to the hospital. That hospital link is the direction you're going with Parker anyway.

"Any neighbor with ties to the hospital, puts even more weight on them. They would've had the opportunity to intersect with both victims and lived in proximity to at least one. I'm guessing it's Nelson's neighborhood that matters here. The first kill."

He let out a held breath. "Okay. Let's go through the lists. Names, addresses, and employment history." He handed her a stack and took one for himself.

AFTER ABOUT THIRTY MINUTES they'd gone through all the contacts. It was, as predicted a fairly long list. It included Zoe herself because of her proximity to Hanover. There were two other physicians, an x-ray technician and another administrator living within a mile of Hanover. Eleven physicians, two pharmacists, three nurses, two administrators and the Chief of Staff lived within a mile of Nelson.

"We'll add these names to the second interview list. And this'll take a while. I'll be in touch when we're done."

She rose to leave.

"Hey Zoe?"

She stopped. "Yeah?"

"Why didn't you report the spiked drink the other night? Or even tell me about it? I had to hear about it from Mal. Wish I'd been there."

Zoe watched the tic at the corner of his eye come to life. But she smiled. "Trust me, you wouldn't have wanted to be there. And really, I didn't know for sure until the drug screen came back. By then it was too late anyway. I knew a lot of the people, but there were far more I didn't know. It happens. I didn't make the report because there was nothing that could be done by then anyway. And I was okay. Nothing happened."

"Still, after what happened with you in the woods, I don't like it."

"Yeah, that's what Kelly said. I think you guys have overactive imaginations. The wire was just random, rotten luck. The drink *could* have been someone who had targeted me specifically at the party, but more than likely my drink was just the one that happened to pass through his hands. Convenient, that's all. If it hadn't been for Rex copping free feels and trying to take me home the guy might have succeeded. But he didn't. So it's okay. Rex got in the way."

She didn't mention how she actually *had* gotten home and hoped Rex hadn't spilled it, but Ray's skeptical look had her doubting that. Whatever he knew, he was kind enough not to say. "Hey, don't worry, I'll be careful. But I think you guys are overreacting."

"Just be careful. Of *everyone*."

Yeah, she got it.

"One more thing Ray. The Dairy Queen. You never told me what happened with that."

"Oh, yeah. It wound up being a dead end. They knew her there all right. In fact she actually worked there."

"So why the dead end?"

"She never showed again. They haven't seen her in a month, not since July 4th."

"No sign of her?"

"None."

"That's no dead end Ray. We need to find her."

"We're working on it."

"Hmm." Zoe continued toward the door, and then turned once more before leaving. "Let's hope she's okay."

CHAPTER SEVENTEEN

THREE MONTHS LATER...A DAY OFF FOR ZOE

ZOE WAVED THE BAG OF HOAGIES IN front of Kelly's nose as she cruised in.

"Hell yes! Let me get some drinks out of the fridge. Coke alright?"

"Perfect. I need a some caffeine."

Zoe unwrapped the food while Kelly set them up with drinks.

"I plan on hiding out here at the hospital tonight so I won't have to deal with children in Halloween costumes begging for candy. I hate that."

Zoe tried not to laugh, and only stared at him for a few moments. "My sentiments exactly, I don't much like kids either, under any circumstances, but Kelly... you're as hidden as you can possibly get in that truck of yours."

He smiled. "Aw, it'll be noisy on the streets tonight. Quieter down here."

"Lame...try again."

His smile disappeared. "So I get lonely sometimes...especially holidays. That's when I like to be around people. There are always people here, day and night. Awake people."

Zoe nodded, and looked away. "Yeah. And a lot of people with way worse problems than ours," she looked back at him and smiled.

They were both quiet for a few moments, until Zoe cleared her throat. "Scary movie or Scrabble?"

"Is there really a choice? Scrabble!"

He readied the board to play while they ate.

"So no progress on the murder cases you were working on?"

"No. Not much activity for a while now. I haven't even seen Ray in weeks. He called a few times, just to keep me up to speed, but ... maybe I was wrong about the guy. I hope so. It would be a good thing, because I'd predicted an escalation in his activities."

"That's too bad...I mean that you haven't found him yet. But I guess it's good he hasn't killed anyone else." Kelly laid his tiles, spelling adytum.

90

"Damn nice lay Kelly."

"Thank you."

"It's given me some free time too. Gotta admit, it was hard there for a while, balancing both jobs."

"You don't have to, you know. Forget the police work."

"Yeah, but I like it."

"How about what happened to you in the woods, and at that party. Any luck there?"

"What? You're still worried about that? Ancient history Kelly. Nothing to figure out there."

"Oh I don't know. It all happened when you were neck deep investigating three murders. So think practically ... who could be benefiting from it?"

He held her gun out to her. "I think you should take this back."

CHAPTER EIGHTEEN
OCTOBER 31 (EVENING)

THE SPIKED DRINK HADN'T ALARMED her all that much. That sort of thing happened, and she was the dumb one there. The incident in the woods was probably just teenagers pulling pranks. Some of them were stupid, and enough of them were mean ... a dangerous combination.

It was odd though ... what Kelly had said.

He'd even decided to buy a cell phone and let her leave only after she memorized the number. And the gun ... insisting that she take it.

In truth, it probably was time. She'd let no one into her bed since that awful night with Ray, and there'd been no evidence of any sleepwalking. For a while she'd even put giveaways around the house ... trapped paper in closed doors and set objects on the floor ... things she would disrupt by walking out of her bedroom. All were undisturbed through every occasion, whether her work schedule forced her to sleep nights or days, no matter how tired she was or wasn't. Apparently she wasn't wandering.

But what was with him anyway? Kelly seemed to *want* her upset. He also wanted her armed. It felt odd that he could be reassured by the image of her with a gun in her hand. Just who in the hell did he picture her using it on? These things were nothing but pranks, mischief. Needing a gun? What was he thinking?

But she did consider what he'd asked ... who might be benefiting from this? If these *were* targeted acts, it was an interesting question. Someone trying to throw her off? Distract her from the case maybe? Now *that* actually made some sense. Unfortunately it was a question she didn't have time to consider.

ZOE DROVE HER CAR THIS TIME.

It was a madhouse, both figuratively and literally. Cops were still fighting back onlookers, the media, and hysterical parents. They wouldn't be able to keep a lid on this one, and the killer would undoubtedly be enjoying the attention.

Walking through the crowd, she overheard fragments of conversation that had her preparing for what she was about to walk into. *I think I just threw up in my mouth . . . she looked so real . . . well, duh, she was real . . . but they all look real . . . the kids will never get over this . . . I feel like I need a shower . . .* Zoe knew *that* feeling, and decided against the jellybeans she'd started to reach for.

Ray and Jack waved her past the tape.

Ray lifted it for her to scoot under. "Let's not talk out here. We're in the spotlight."

Zoe booted and gloved, following the two detectives inside. It was a Halloween "funhouse," set up in an old neighborhood of winding streets. Many of the homes were listed in the national historic register. This area was again considered safe, with stately homes either on or near the famed lakes of Minneapolis.

The owners of this property were well known within the community and graciously donated the carriage house in back every year for the Halloween fundraiser. They owned quite a bit of the surrounding land, Zoe guessed the equivalent of four lots, and the carriage house was well concealed by trees. One reason for the killer's choice of it was obvious.

As Zoe listened to the cacophony around her, she appreciated his timing too. It was reminiscent of the July Fourth fireworks. Good cover. But this time covering the desperate pleas of a dying woman, instead of a gun he was now too clever to have need of. There would have been clamorous children everywhere. Speakers artificially piping in loud wails and screams. Volunteer actors, playing roles that required shrieks and howls. He would have been able to encourage her screams, and enjoy them, without fear of discovery.

And of course everyone was "bloody." He could leave the scene, covered in the victim's blood, only to fit right in on the street among all the costumed people.

"Let me guess, the perfect pose?"

Jack nodded. "But don't think for one minute you can guess what you're about to see. Something like this is beyond a normal imagination."

At the comment, Zoe caught Ray's eyes, and saw what she'd expected . . . worry over the depths to which her imagination could dive. She looked back toward Jack. Jack-ass wasn't going to make this easy. He rarely missed a chance to accuse her of treating Ray like shit . . . and never hid his dislike.

"So far, anything off here that you can see?" Ray was the first to speak after the thinly veiled insult.

"Not at all. Fits perfectly. Let's get in there and see what we're dealing with." Almost with admiration, she added, "This guy is unbelievably clever."

Both Ray and Jack stopped. She only shrugged, and pushed past them. "He's a fucking mad genius. What can I say? You both know it. And if you don't, you should."

SHE WAS PREPARED THIS TIME. It was repulsive and maddening, but certainly not surprising.

There were different vignettes set up in each of the eight rooms within the two-story carriage house. Two of the lower rooms had direct access to the outside. Each room was assigned at least one actor to play a scary role, and they were all being held in their own rooms for questioning.

The one with the metallic smell of real blood was set up to be an operating room. A surgical table and a variety of rusty surgical instruments sat at its center. Frightening…yes, but what it couldn't be this time was lewd. It would have tipped off the very first visitor.

"How was this thing set up, you know, before the visitors arrived?"

"Initial interviews revealed that the actors were in charge of staging their own rooms. There'd be a cash prize for the winner. The theater department at the U of M had arranged it, as well as provided the actors. In addition, each actor had been given a small stipend with which to purchase the necessary supplies. Turns out the prize money was fairly substantial. Also appears they didn't trust each other.

"They were pretty protective of their ideas. Guarded them closely enough to have the doors to their rooms closed while they prepared. They stayed that way until the shout-out came that they were opening the house to the public."

"Anything like you *guessed*?" Jack chided.

"Yeah, actually I wouldn't have expected anything less. Had to keep the pose within the bounds of expectations here, straight up violent for the reactions to unfold slowly and have the biggest impact. When we look, we'll find that he had his sexual fun, but he couldn't pose her that way. What did *you* think we'd find?" She looked toward Jack and kept the stare going until he looked away.

"Jesus, Ray! Th'hell are you doing with her anyway?" Jack looked like he'd swallowed a wasp.

That was only one tactic in Zoe's arsenal, for deflecting unwanted personal attention. Even Ray had faced it before and Zoe remembered him saying that as beautiful as she was, she could still make it damn uncomfortable to look at her. He'd said it was like an alpha-dog stare, and that it was lucky her hobbies didn't include demolition derby. He'd actually disarmed her at the time, even made her laugh. Not so with Jack.

Zoe resumed working after Jack looked away.

The scene was at first frightening, but that was expected, desired even. It's what everyone paid to see. In fact there were more than a few attendees who came and went without realizing what they'd witnessed. It wasn't until later, after they'd heard, that it really hit them.

It was a doctor, with her kid, who went through and knew right away. She was familiar with the smell of real blood. She was also well versed in anatomy, and if that was a real person ... well, it wasn't possible to fake.

The victim was dressed in a mini-skirted nurse's outfit. While there were trails of blood down the insides of her legs, her skirt had been carefully repositioned, with the pose designed to draw initial attention elsewhere. She was lying on the surgical table, her blouse pulled up just short of her breasts, and the waistband of her skirt rolled down to her pubis. The area in between had been fully exposed.

It looked as though the abdomen had been surgically opened; an incision ran from breastbone to pubis. Her intestines had then been pulled out to drape off the table.

Zoe pictured parents and children coming by this room and fixing their eyes on the woman ... expectantly. When nothing happened they might get a little uncomfortable. Meanwhile they'd have gotten a good look at her, fixed it in their minds, and then hurried along to the next vignette.

The other rooms had actors who were moving and actively scaring people. But this actor wasn't even breathing. And the doctor new what real blood and guts both looked and smelled like. Still, it was too late. There were probably two-dozen or more families that came through first.

Zoe looked around. Had he been watching from somewhere? He would have had to be quick. *Or not.* "Ray, how long had the piped-in screams been going on?"

"Yep, you got it. All day. They were creating anticipation. Also thought it was good advertising. Got people to notice."

"Holy shit. He could have had considerable time to do the sexual assault as well as the posing." She glanced at both doors. They each had locks from inside the room. "He could have gained entry from the outside door, then locked both and taken his time. No fear of discovery."

"Yeah, the outside door was unlocked when we got here. Presumably exited that way." Ray kept filling in the information as Zoe let her imagination wander.

"The curtains, were they open or closed?"

"Partially closed when we found her, but as secretive as everyone was, we figure they were closed tight right up until the last moment."

"Why would she have felt the need to open the curtains, even partially? Should have been enough to just open the door, don't you think? That's where the paying customers were."

"Yeah, I suppose. Why?"

She had an uncomfortable feeling this killer may have been watching the reactions from the crowd as they'd filed past the doorway. "He could easily have been watching and stayed until someone caught on."

She stared at the window, and then her eyes got big. "In fact, he *had* to stay until someone connected the dots. A *little* risky perhaps, but their reactions would have been the real payoff here."

She walked to the window and looked out into the blackness. "It would have been an easy trot into the trees and away." She turned back to look at the victim.

All three backed away while the photographer snapped some more pictures. Something stirred in the back of her brain, a ghostly image that she couldn't seem to get hold of. She closed her eyes to refresh her mind then opened them again, focusing on the same spot. But it was gone. The image didn't do the same thing for her this time. They all moved back toward the body.

"All the pictures done here?" Ray called after the photographer as he was walking out.

"Yeah, for now. I was going to get some outside, but I'll stay if you're going to roll the vic."

"Naw, go ahead. Come back in five." Ray eyed Zoe, watching her struggle.

Her eyes closed against any other input, and then reopened trying to bring back the trail of thought, until finally her forehead knotted in frustration.

It felt important. What had changed? She closed her eyes again, paused, and then opened them. But this time she squinted and purposely kept everything out of focus. Sometimes that helped. Just an overall blurry image was better than focusing too hard on one thing. Still nothing.

"No luck?" Ray looked discouraged.

Jack, watching the whole thing, turned away with "Whatever."

Zoe ignored him. "I'm afraid not. When it gets like this, I need to relax my mind for a while and try again later. I'll have the photos to work from. But take a look." Zoe carefully lifted one edge of the blouse. "Goldy can tell us for sure, but the bleeding associated with the vaginal and breast wounds make them look pre-mortem, and the abdominal wound looks to be post. There are also strangulation wounds to the neck. All as we would expect." She smiled at Jack as if bragging about her honor student child, "It's our guy."

Ray laughed, and elbowed Jack. "You're back to your old self, Zoe. It's good to see."

Zoe preferred spooky and strong to weak and vulnerable, and knew that Ray did too. She smiled . . . at both of them.

Jack called for the photographer.

CHAPTER NINETEEN
OCTOBER 31 (NIGHT)

THE ACTRESS WAS IDENTIFIED AS Kayla Mickman, twenty-one years old and a senior in the BFA acting program at the U of M. Mickman was well known within the Minneapolis theater scene, having already landed two highly prized lead roles in productions at the Guthrie Theater. She was a popular young woman with a huge circle of friends, and the addition of a public following this time. Zoe knew the killer would be feeling a very satisfied buzz at the very moment they were now getting to know Kayla.

And it pissed her off. With the selection of both victim and crime scene, he'd created a media stir. She was just glad it wasn't up to her to manage that anymore.

Mickman's apartment was located in the university area's West Bank. It was in a building approximately equidistant between the U of M's Rarig Theater and the Guthrie. She'd moved there as a freshman. Zoe thought about the confidence evident in that decision and admired it. Mickman knew full well what she was capable of, and had planned for it.

The apartment was spotless. The overall impression appealed to Zoe...loft-like design, modern furnishings, and a balcony overlooking the Mississippi from the fourteenth floor. The abstract art, some looking to have been quite an investment for a college student, fit the surroundings perfectly. *She had quite an eye.*

Zoe noticed the collection of "head shots" on the bookcase. There was a new promotional photo from each of the four years Mickman had been here. In the shot from her freshman year she could have been mistaken for a fourteen-year old. But the transformation into an alluring young woman wasn't gradual at all. It was the final photo that seduced. Zoe turned it over to read the resume.

Mickman had grown up in Little Falls, Minnesota. Her theater chops went all the way back to third grade when she'd started performing both in school and at the Flying Aces Community Theater. After arriving at the University of Minnesota, her star status was sealed, when she'd been cast in lead roles without an apparent break. All the BFA students had an automatic link to the Guthrie, but she landed the choice roles. It got her the attention.

"What do you think, Zoe?" Ray was looking through the closet.

Zoe took one glove off and popped some candy in her mouth. "I think it might have been fun to know this Mickman ... great life ... promising future. Fuckin' shame is what it is. That's what I think."

"From the looks of these clothes, she knew how to party."

"Yeah. She'd have been fun to hang with. Her looks would have brought a steady stream of eligibles by her table at the clubs. A girl could easily draft off that."

"Yeah, well I've never known you to eat anyone's dust, Z." He laughed.

She smiled sadly, "No. I guess I'm just trying to find a way to say how much I like this kid ... a kid I've never even met ... without crying about the whole mess. Sucks like a fucking quasar."

Zoe walked out to the balcony. None of them connected. There were a few other buildings that might provide views into her apartment, but it would require a powerful telescope, as they were across the river. She doubted that the apartment was a direct link to the killer, unless he lived in the building, or was welcomed in as an acquaintance. There would be no other access or vantage point from which to easily observe her.

"Ray, the tenant list. Any matches?"

"No, but we're still tracking down her circles. List is a mile long. Gonna take forever to talk to them all."

"How are the follow up interviews going?"

"We're pretty much done. Couple stragglers who've been out of the country, but they're due back soon. Nothing's come of it though."

She looked at him, not wanting to ask.

"Yeah, I did talk with Parker though."

"And?" Her hand went to her pocket for another piece of candy.

"He was less than cooperative. I don't think the guy thinks much of me either. But he did agree to talk, *out of concern for Julia and her family* he said. Nothing new. He did seem a little broken up about her death. I guess I *think* it was real. He seemed like he was struggling not to show it. Could have been acting the part, but it'd be hard, I've got to admit."

"What's your next move with that?"

"Well, I can't exactly haul him in without something to go on. I was hoping for a break, some inconsistency I could pursue till it led me to cause. But it's not there yet. Right now he's just one of about forty people we could look at with links from either her neighborhood or the hospital who don't have verifiable alibis. And I don't want to put blinders on any more than you do, right?"

"Yeah, Ray. Don't worry, I'm clear on this." Zoe wandered over to the desk. "We have the U of M connection with Hanover here. I think the commonalities, if there are any, will exist between Hanover and Mickman. I'm sticking to my theory that Nelson, as the first, was special. And of course I don't think Franklin was ever intended as a target. I can't escape that thinking either. It's pretty solid for me."

Ray cocked his head and raised his eyebrows in a silent question.

"It fits, that's all." Still nothing from Ray, except a smirk. "I know, I know. I'll keep an open mind. I *can* walk and chew at the same time." To prove it she pointed at her open mouth. An atomic fireball had painted her tongue red. He laughed.

"We'll look at Mickman's health records. She probably got her care through the U of M. But we'll go back the full four years she's been here for any link to Minneapolis General."

Zoe wondered whether she wanted them to find it or not. "Let me know what they get." She put a fresh glove on and paged through bills, receipts, phone numbers, and calendar notations. "Probably used the gym at the U. Did some serving. Look here. Pay stub from Lorna's Table. Good God, can the crowd around her get any bigger?"

"I don't think we're going to find anything in this apartment. I'll wager dinner at Cosmos that the prints here won't match any from the other scenes. I don't think the guy was ever in here."

"I agree, but there's a feeling I got from the crime scene. We're missing something."

"Let me help work it."

Zoe winced in frustration. "That's just it. It's nagging at me. It *seems* important, but I really don't have *any* idea what it is. I might talk to Camilla. I've never had to resort to hypnosis before, but if we've got nothing else it might be worth a try. Camilla's good with that technique." Zoe still hoped she wouldn't have to find out first-hand though.

"Why don't we get the gloves off and let the troops go through her computer and phone records here."

"Let me know if anything shows up. I'm at work tomorrow, so just call my cell."

"Sounds good Zoe. Likewise."

ZOE SAT IN HER CAR for a few minutes looking up at Mickman's high-rise. This was a great kid, who'd grown into a beautiful and talented young woman with a host of loving family and friends. If the killer didn't know it going in, he sure as hell did now. It was all over the news. The media vans were still at the crime scene, but eventually they would descend on the tenants of this building.

She decided to try and watch some of the coverage. Every once in a while, a "witness," eager for a little attention knew something he shouldn't, and let it slip. Turned out to be a killer going off script.

Zoe recalled a memorable rush of adrenaline. It happened while watching the news one night. A little slip of the tongue and she knew she had him. Just had to reel him in. There wasn't even a word for the thrill that followed. She'd confronted him again in interview, watching it play across his face as he felt the hook. Pleasurable for her, but the instantaneous panic in his eyes betrayed the exact moment he'd felt the barb set. She remembered smiling at him, her trademark sinister smile, while she imagined the grins and high-fives from her guys behind the glass.

He'd twisted and yanked, setting it deeper with every frantic attempt to get away. The lies kept getting bigger and making less and less sense. Eventually he'd looked at her across the table, ignoring his lawyer, and admitted his guilt. It was one of those times when they'd had little to go on, and it was looking like he'd get away clean. Instead it helped cement Zoe's reputation on the force. She was both scary and good.

Her instincts were sharp ... about killers *and* victims. As she sat in her car, she reminded herself to trust them. They were hard-won, insightful, and rarely wrong, having developed while traveling in and out of the mind of a killer.

Somehow she'd managed to survive the indistinct boundaries separating her thoughts from his. But that lack of definition still damned her to question her own goodness, even now. And it sickened her to know that she didn't *always* try to fight it, occasionally she accepted him in her life. She told herself she was "using" him, for work. And while that was true, deep inside, it was far more complicated. He'd become so intertwined that it occasionally comforted her to submit. Her desire for revenge was even a form of submission . . . she knew that . . . and it was one of the things she didn't fight.

She wasn't afraid of him . . . that was true, but neither was it a comfort. Hatred and anger left no room for that. And fear was still present, in thinking of what she'd become at his hands. It haunted her every time she slipped into the mind of a killer a little too easily, or felt the final terror of a victim as if living through it. Whenever she pulled back from a relationship, she knew who was commanding her. And with each passing year, she worried she'd never get her chance to confront him. So those were the things she feared, the damage done . . . and not getting her hate on with him.

But Zoe still had to live . . . by avenging death and tending the wounded, her only ways to fight back . . . and get up every fucking morning. Logically, they were *good* ways to fight. Appropriate even. They just weren't good *enough*.

She pulled her head up off the steering wheel and started the car.

Chapter Twenty
November 06 (Midday)

ANYTHING THAT WASN'T LIFE THREATENING was mercilessly backing up, thanks to the disaster drill they were obligated to run. It was required, and *good*, but it left the ER in disarray. Follow-up on their performance had taken many of the attending physicians away from patient duties, and left the residents swamped.

With the theatrics over, Zoe dove into the pile of charts. She was about to grab the next chart in line when Mal held a different one up to her face.

"Kid says she wants to see you . . . or rather she'll only see you. Knows your name and all."

Zoe looked at the name on the chart. Lory Justus. "Funny way to spell it. Doesn't ring any bells. Have I seen her before?"

"Doesn't look like it. But the kid acts like she's seen you. Says she trusts you. But Zoe . . . I gotta say . . . she's really skittish. Won't even tell me why she's here. And, well . . . do you want me to call Psych?"

"Is that your assessment?"

"Yeah, it is. Looks like she hasn't bathed in a month, probably not eating either. And she's acting real paranoid. Made me take her right back into a cube and pull the curtains. Said she didn't want any male doctors to come near her."

"Poor kid. Wonder what that's all about. Let's just trust your instincts on this. I'll go see her. Put a call in to psych."

"Psych's already down here. They just finished up with another patient. You want her to see the kid now, or after your done?"

"Let me get in there first. Tell Psych to stay. I'll be quick. Who is it?"

"Camilla."

"Yes! Definitely tell her to wait if she can." It would be good to see Camilla again. It'd been too long.

ZOE PULLED BACK THE CURTAINS on the cube only to find the girl gone. All that was left was a computer disc, sitting prominently on the examination table.

Zoe grabbed it and found Mal. "Where'd she go?"

"Who?"

"The kid?"

"She's not in there?"

"Nope. Only this." She tossed it to Mal. "Figure out what it is. And try to find the kid before Camilla has to leave. Wish I knew why this kid singled me out."

"Well, she did kind of mention something about seeing you on television. But I just figured you'd seen her at some point in time."

"Oh, for crying out loud. Let me know when you find her."

ZOE MADE QUICK WORK of another patient, an elderly male with congestive heart failure requiring frequent hospitalizations, and then went looking for Mal. She'd hoped to find her with both the girl and Camilla, but as there was no sign of any of them, so she veered toward the break room only to find it locked.

She knocked and someone opened the door slightly.

"Get in here quick and shut it!" It was Mal.

"What's going on in here?" She noticed Camilla sitting at the table. "Oh, hi, Camilla. You did stay. No sign of the kid?"

"No, but look what she left us." Mal sat back down in front of a computer screen.

"Mal, there's no time for screwing around today. We've still got a waiting room full of people out there you know."

"Girl, get over here. You are not going to believe this." Mal made room for Zoe.

"Are you sure you want to do this, Zoe?" Camilla's eyes got big.

Zoe hesitated. "Do what?"

"Oh, no. We're not shutting this off until we've seen every last bit. Zoe too." Mal looked eagerly at the screen.

"Come on. Have a peek. I guarantee you'll never look at him the same way again." She laughed, but quickly added, "This doesn't leave the room though. I like my job too much. For our eyes only."

"I repeat, if you don't want this to leave the room . . . are you sure *you* want to see this, Zoe?" Camilla now looked equal parts disgusted and earnest.

Zoe tried to read the hidden meaning, but she was curious now, and drew up next to Mal. The image was a little grainy, but there was no doubt about who she was looking at. She recognized Nelson's bedroom from the crime scene photos. There were two lovers locked in the most intimate of embraces. Parker. This would be the "cause" Ray had been hoping for. Her muscles tightened. Zoe said nothing for a while, and just stared at the performance playing itself out on screen.

"I've got to get this to Ray."

"Whoa! You can't do that!" Mal seemed to be enjoying the show.

"Mal, don't you get it? She can't *not* do that," but added, "Zoe, I know it's what you have to do, but look at the screen. Those aren't the actions of a homicidal man."

Camilla made sense, and Zoe hadn't taken her eyes off the screen. She'd witnessed the tenderness evolve into a passion that left her longing. Whatever else you might call it, this was lovemaking done right. No, this was not what you'd expect from the kind of monster they were dealing with. But it *was* evidence. And how in the hell had the kid gotten hold of it?

She was now in a very uncomfortable position. He held power over her at work. He was also a suspect in a crime she was helping to investigate. And she was squarely in the middle. His secrets were no longer his.

Thank God for rules. She put a call in to Ray, and planned on handing the whole mess off to him. Preserving the evidence in a sterile surgical towel, she waited.

You've already got my prints and Mal has agreed to give you hers. Wonder if the kid left any."

"If she's even the slightest bit streetwise, I'd say that's a no. But it looks like we found our missing kid."

"Yep. But it's more like she found us."

"Ouch."

"Yeah, don't we look good?"

"She'll be on the security tapes here, but they may not help. Mal says she was wearing a hoodie over a baseball cap. Mal got a good look though, she can give you a description."

"Christ, Zoe. I was starting to think he was off the hook, and now this. I knew there was something about the guy."

"Yeah, well after you've seen it, let me know if you still feel that way. I'm honestly not sure what to think." Zoe fell back into a chair. "Mal's pissed. Afraid's more like it. Parker carries a lot of weight around here."

"Her problem. She was the one getting such a kick out of watching it."

"Yeah, everyone except Camilla. She had the right instincts. No one would listen to her though."

"What about you?"

Zoe considered lying, but there was really no point in it. "Yeah, well, I basically couldn't look away either." She watched his eyes grow dark.

"It should stand up to a warrant request. I'll want him in interview, his prints and his DNA. I also plan on tearing his house apart."

"You know it doesn't prove anything. So he had a relationship with her, is that so far-fetched? They worked together. They're attractive, single, and social. It might be more surprising if they hadn't hooked up at some point."

"Go ahead, Zoe, keep blowin' smoke if you want, but it's weak. Two interviews so far and no mention of it. Makes me think the guy's got something to hide."

"He could have been protecting her." She looked at the floor again as soon as she'd said it.

"Zoe! Do you hear yourself? This is a video of a man making love to a woman who is now dead! What kind of man is that? The kind of man who would worry about protecting her? Seriously Zoe! Get a grip here."

She *was* off. The idea that Parker would even participate in this sort of video was repulsive. Why would she feel like protecting him?

And Mal was right too. She'd never look at him the same way again.

CHAPTER TWENTY-ONE
NOVEMBER 06 (6:00 PM)

ZOE'S LAST CASE OF THE DAY CAUGHT everyone leaning. A young gangster, stabbed just outside the ER doors, had run in unannounced. He'd surprised the slow and overweight security guard by shouldering past him, leaving the man in uniform on the floor checking to see whose blood he was covered in.

The boy charged past the triage area at a dead run and pushed through the double doors, racing down the hall of the patient exam area. Arterial blood pumped from the injured arm, trailing behind him as if he was running away from it. Zoe followed the slippery trail at a sprint and tackled him just before he was about to burst through the curtain of a cube with a cardiac patient on the other side.

She wrapped her hand up into his armpit, applying direct pressure to the artery just above the spurting end. It wasn't easy . . . the wound was high in the arm and it was barely possible to reach the artery before it disappeared into his chest. It took all her strength to hold him down. She straddled him, while simultaneously keeping direct pressure on the artery, and telling him . . . yelling at him really . . . that it was going to be fine, he just had to keep still.

She wasn't sure if it was her words or the fact that she'd stopped the blood fountain, but he finally calmed. Flat on his back, his eyes looked into hers. "Go fuck yourself."

She smiled. "Well, now . . . that would be a little difficult without letting go of you, wouldn't it?"

He looked away, and she didn't let go . . . but added, "You came to the right place."

MAINTENANCE WAS CLEANING the bloodied floor and Zoe was dictating her notes when she noticed Parker. She'd hoped to get out of there without having to interact.

Kaj stopped abruptly, taking it all in. Spotting Zoe, he hurried toward her. Her scrubs were still covered in blood. Grabbing hold of her arm, he spun her around to examine her face. "Tell me none of this blood is yours."

She tried to jerk away from his grip, an effort he wouldn't allow.

"*None* of this is my blood. It all happened too fast to glove and gown. The patient presented unannounced and bleeding out. He wouldn't stop and allow us to help him without being physically restrained." She paused and looked at his hand wrapped around her arm.

He let go, but quickly grabbed hold of both hands. Turning them over, he inspected everything . . . her arms, neck and face, anywhere there was blood, as she tried to look away. "There's a blood spray near your eye. Do you have any open wounds anywhere?"

The urgency in his voice, the worry, didn't correspond to the monster she was imagining him to be. "The patient is being tested. I'll be sure to follow up and take any necessary steps."

"You shouldn't have put yourself in that position. Do you have any idea what it could mean? The HIV risk alone . . . for God's sake!" His voice was now angry. "I won't allow any harm to come to you. It can't happen."

Zoe found herself squinting slightly as she cocked her head to look at him. *What?* This was a man always in control, of himself and his surroundings. And this was the first time she'd seen him lose his cool, let alone become irrational. And that's exactly what he was at the moment . . . irrational. Had Ray already spoken with him? Maybe that was it. But if so, he should be angry with her, not worried.

"First of all, I'm not sure it's within your *power* to prevent any harm from coming to me, and secondly, just what would you have had me do? I was the closest, the one with an opportunity to stop him before he rushed another patient's cube. You *know* I couldn't let that happen. You'd have done the same thing. He needed to be subdued for his own good, as well as the safety of others."

"And what about your safety?"

"Listen, my shift is over, and I need to clean up. I have no open wounds and I'll be sure to follow up in Employee Health. I need to go. By the way, the patient did fine."

She shouldered her way past him toward the call room shower, pausing long enough to look over her shoulder and ask, "Has Detective Perry contacted you yet?"

"There's a message to call him, but I haven't had time. Why?"

Zoe didn't answer the question. "Call him."

CHAPTER TWENTY-TWO
NOVEMBER 06 (EVENING)

AWARRANT HADN'T BEEN NECESSARY. Kaj agreed to everything voluntarily. Zoe watched through the glass of the mirrored wall as he waived his right to a lawyer. Either he was innocent or very confident in his ability to handle the situation. Arrogant maybe?

Ray looked pleased.

"Doctor Parker, it's come to our attention that you and the deceased, Julia Nelson, were more than colleagues or casual acquaintances. That in fact you had a much more intimate relationship with her."

"Yes. That's true. I never denied it."

"In our two previous interviews there was no mention of it."

"You didn't ask. If asked I would have confirmed it. But as it has no bearing on her murder, I didn't feel it was necessary to drag the personal details of our relationship into the public record."

"This isn't a game, Parker. And it's not up to you to determine what is or is not pertinent to the investigation. If you do, as you've said, have an interest in the apprehension of her killer, we'll expect full cooperation from you. To begin with you can quit censoring yourself and give us everything you know."

He looked at the glass, at her. She knew he couldn't see her, but it didn't feel that way. Though he would have no way of knowing she was there, he could have guessed at her presence. She felt uncomfortable. What was *he* feeling?

He continued to stare at the glass as he spoke. "We were intimately involved for several months. It ended last spring. There isn't much more to tell you. I knew her as a lover, as a companion, but we weren't on track for anything more serious than that by mutual agreement. We had a solid friendship and respected each other."

He stopped and shifted his gaze to Ray, allowing Zoe to breathe.

"Respecting and fulfilling a woman's needs and desires is something I'm more than familiar with." Ray had Parker on his turf now. Zoe rolled her eyes. *Careful, Ray.*

Stay on the rails. And don't pretend for even one minute this is a pissing match that has any-thing at all to do with me. Unless . . . it threw Parker off and made him say something careless.

"You claim your relationship with her was built on mutual respect?"

He didn't get careless. "Yes. We had a relationship based on mutual respect. And we fulfilled each other's expectations." A little dig Zoe supposed. But said with an icy calm.

"Would you say that your relationship with her, the one built on respect, in-cluded complete trust between the two of you?"

Again, Parker directed his gaze to the glass. Zoe felt herself step back a little. "Detective, we trusted each other. But that doesn't mean we knew everything about each other's lives. In fact, *because* we trusted each other, it wasn't necessary to know everything." He half smiled at the glass as he continued. "Some people have secrets. I only knew what she chose to share with me." Returning his attention to Ray, he leaned back in his chair. "And I only did what I was invited to do."

Ray seemed impatient. "And just what did she *choose* to share with you?"

"She never expressed any concern over her safety, if that's what you're getting at. Never mentioned any fear of anyone, or even appeared upset. I've told you all of that before. Perhaps it's more meaningful now that you know of our close relationship?"

Ignoring the question, "Did she *choose* to give you anything to remember her by? In pictures or discs maybe?"

For a moment, Parker looked confused, and then calmly answered the ques-tion. "No detective. I have nothing but very fond memories of her." He now looked down at his own hands on the table. "She was a remarkable woman. I continued to consider her a dear friend after we'd parted ways romantically. I'd have done any-thing for her, given anything, to have prevented this. Believe me. Don't you think I've gone over it all in my head a thousand times? I've tried to think of anything that might shed light on it. It's just not there."

Zoe wondered if his look of confusion was a recalibration of the direction his answers should take. Suddenly he was offering more. People tend to get chatty when they're nervous.

Ray cut to it. "Are you willing to give us a sample of your fingerprints, Doctor Parker?"

He didn't hesitate. "Absolutely. However I can tell you right now that you'll find them in her bedroom. In fact my prints will likely be all over her house. But if you still require them, I've nothing to hide."

Ray signaled for the tech to come in and take the prints. "We have it on record that you are offering your prints voluntarily then? And DNA?"

"Of course."

Zoe knew the last act was yet to play out. Ray was taking it one step at a time, getting everything he could before Parker changed his mind about the lawyer.

The tech finished with the prints and as Parker rose to leave, Ray sat him back down with the PLAY button on the video remote.

The screen filled with the image of Parker thrusting hard and deep into Nelson. Ray had cued it to the most intimate of moments. As Parker increased his pace, Nelson arched up, tensed, and Parker threw his head back in release.

Zoe felt herself pulled closer to the glass again. She was torn between watching the video monitor and Parker's reaction to it. She saw the Parker on tape lower his head to kiss Nelson's neck, to caress her, to bring her back to him gently. The Parker in the interview room looked at the glass. At Zoe. His eyes betrayed first surprise, then worry.

"I'd call this quite a memento, wouldn't you Parker?"

He recovered quickly to offer a response that was both measured and calm. "I'd no idea she'd taken this. I'd never noticed a camera, and she hadn't shared this with me." He said nothing else. The surprise, the worry... all gone.

Zoe wondered about the surprise. Was he truly shocked that the disc existed at all, or just that they had it? Whatever it was, it was gone. He'd walled it up in an instant. Protective of Nelson or of himself, Zoe wondered?

"How did it wind up in the ER then, Parker? *She* definitely didn't put it there."

"You found this in the ER? Where? That's not possible. I had no knowledge of this. Whatever her reasons for taking it, I'll not question, but ..." His voice trailed off as his eyes darkened. "Was she being blackmailed? Is that what you suspect?"

This time it was Ray who seemed thrown off. None of them had thought of that, or of the possibility that a blackmailer had now planned on turning his attention toward Parker. "We're not making any assumptions here Parker."

Zoe shook her head at the lie.

"Well, I'll tell you right now, I've never seen that disc before, and had no knowledge of its existence. You'll find no fingerprints of mine on it. It only serves to verify what I've told you of our relationship. If she had need of such a video, it was one of the secrets she chose not to tell me. And if someone was blackmailing her, and using our relationship to do it, you damn well better find him before I do."

THE REST OF THE INTERVIEW consisted of dates and alibis, or rather lack thereof. The time frames of the other murders were checked against Parker's schedule and of course he couldn't offer independent verification of his whereabouts during any of them. Having his prints wasn't going to help either. Even if guilty, the idea that he would leave his prints in any of those places was ridiculous.

Then there was the whole matter of the girl. They'd been assuming that she was the missing kid, but maybe she was some random street kid paid to drop the disc and leave. Or, maybe she was this Andi kid, and having taken the disc from Nelson's house while robbing her, now wanted to come forward with it as evidence. But why leave it at the ER? Suppose if she didn't trust cops ...

Another problem was that the girl's description from her street associates didn't match the one Mal provided. All the more reason to find her.

Then again, it might have been someone else entirely who'd left the disc. They hadn't had eyes on the cube at all times.

Zoe began down another train of thought. What if it was Parker himself who was being blackmailed? If so, he'd played this perfectly. We would expect his prints to be in Nelson's bedroom. A relationship with her wasn't even such a surprise. And the lack of prints in the other cases would be expected as well. He could plant his copy of the disc with the police, rendering whatever copy the blackmailer had as useless. But it would still make him a killer. And that still didn't feel right.

Besides, hadn't he been occupied all day with the disaster drill? It would have been hard to slip into the ER unnoticed.

Maybe there'd never been any blackmail at all. Had mention of it been a last minute decision by Parker because the disc had surfaced?

There was also another possibility. She had the uncomfortable feeling that they were trying to fit a square peg in a round hole. Working too hard at trying to make the facts fit their own assumptions and failing to treat them dispassionately. Suddenly there was this disc, hard to ignore, but it proved nothing.

She was lost in thought when Ray entered the room. "Damn it! We've still got nothing more than when we started except a big flashing arrow pointing at Parker with nothing solid to back it up. The guy is slick. At least we have the opportunity to search his house now."

"I don't know, Ray. I really don't. I agree we've got nothing more than when we started. We knew he had no alibis, along with a few dozen other people. The presence of the disc proves a close relationship, which isn't entirely unexpected. You and I both know we'll find no prints of his at the other crime scenes or on the disc. Again, proves nothing either way does it?

"I know. It could point to guilt *or* innocence. But the disc is just too big to ignore." Ray's frustration was felt by the chair he kicked across the room.

Zoe set it upright. "I agree, but there's something else. We've got to run the possibility that he's innocent, that he's actually telling the truth." Waving off Ray's attempt to interrupt her, "*If* that's the case, who should we be looking at here?"

"Oh, Mother of God, I know. It hit me too when he started talking about blackmail. But then I figured he was smart enough to pre-empt our suspicion that Nelson or someone else might blackmail him by switching it up on us. That she was the one being blackmailed by someone who'd had a showdown with her. He's always one fucking step ahead."

"You're still missing the point Ray. I said we have to follow the line of thinking that he might actually be *innocent*. You keep inserting the assumption that he's not. You've got to be able to put that aside for the sake of the intellectual exercise here. The Parker that I've come to know from work doesn't match up with the monster we're after. But he is a bit of a puzzle to me. Did you notice that in the end he didn't seem as concerned with the existence of the disc so much as its implications regarding Nelson? I'm not sure anyone *could* blackmail this guy." She snorted. "And what *that* tells us I just don't know either."

Zoe fell into the chair that was now closer to her than before the kick. "I am going down that path, Ray, with or without you. We owe it to the victims to get this right. Let me know if they find anything at his house." She looked back through the glass. "But they won't."

Zoe reached for her malted milk balls.

CHAPTER TWENTY-THREE
NOVEMBER 08 (MORNING)

ZOE'S RIDE IN WOULD BE COLD, through November winds and twenty-degree temperatures. It bothered her that she hadn't faced her route through the woods since the accident. The idea of limitations on her activities pissed her off. It was also a path that would take her down and out of the wind. It made sense to go that way.

REFLECTIONS OFF SHARDS OF GLASS caught her eye at the last second. In this area she had room to veer off the path to avoid them. Was it paranoid thinking that they'd been placed for maximum effect? Probably. Had she hit them though, she would have been stopped for several minutes while she repaired a tire.

Zoe quickly looked around at the surroundings. Once again, a spot that wasn't visible from any obvious vantage point. She swallowed down the caustic taste of fear, but let it take her back fourteen years. It really didn't matter who'd put the glass there, or even if it was meant for her, which it almost certainly wasn't.

She carefully pulled the glass shards out of the ground and tossed them into the bushes, taking control. She wouldn't let him, *or anyone*, dictate her actions. But as she pushed off, she still felt his breath on her neck…and she couldn't ride fast enough.

KELLY WELCOMED ZOE with fresh coffee, and she reciprocated with the crossword puzzle, electing not to mention the glass on the trail. Logically, there was no reason to suspect it was meant for her. It was probably just the remnants of a teenage drinking party. Any alarm was irrational, so why needlessly fuel Kelly's paranoia?

"How was your ride in this morning, Zoe? Cold I bet. Funny it hasn't snowed yet."

"Yeah, but I was dressed for it. Didn't really bother me."

"What route today?" He looked at her over his reading glasses. She always felt like she was in the principal's office when he did that.

Zoe thought about lying, but chose not to . . . something she occasionally did, a small act of rebellion against the ease with which she *could* lie . . . and wanted to believe that it really was her choice.

"The back alley trail." But she'd said it too matter-of-factly. The way in which she'd said it *was* a lie, and she could see that he'd noticed. Zoe couldn't help but smile . . . at her own idiocy . . . that she actually thought she wasn't lying to the old man.

"And?"

"And what?"

"Did it go okay? Were you able to get through it without any trouble?"

"Well, I was a little nervous at first, but it was fine. Made it all the way." Zoe thought she saw surprise register on his face. "Didn't think I could do it, eh?"

This time when he looked at her, she had the uncomfortable feeling she'd been caught in the very lie she *wasn't* telling . . . and she almost laughed.

"No Zoe, I believe *in* you, I just don't *believe* you."

He'd cheered her up anyway. The smile was for real now. *Far too amusing.* Maybe just telling the truth was easier. But instead, Zoe changed the subject.

"Thanksgiving at my place this year? I've never had you over. I think it's about time." Time to reclaim some holidays too, some sense of normalcy, she thought.

"I'd love that, Zoe. What can I bring?"

"How about a guest?" The old guy needed to make other friends. "Invite someone to come with you. I think I'll invite Mal too. She's single, no family in town, and I've got some bridges to repair there. I'll tell her to bring a friend as well. Maybe Shep too. He doesn't have anyone either. Came here for his internship from Montana."

"Sounds great, Zoe." He smiled warmly. "I know exactly who I'll invite."

CHAPTER TWENTY-FOUR
NOVEMBER 20 (MIDDAY)

THE BUZZ IN THE MEDIA WAS TRAILING OFF. With no arrests and no suspect sketches, there was little more to cover. They'd exhausted their interviews with grieving family and publicly dissected every aspect of Mickman's life, speaking with the long list of friends and classmates. Everyone "adored" her.

Zoe had watched and listened at every opportunity, but nothing ever caught her attention. No obvious slips. Not even guilty body language except from a few female classmates secretly embarrassed by their relief that, as competition, Mickman was out of the way. They weren't even good enough actors to be able to hide it. Zoe found herself unimpressed with the whole adoring crowd, and figured Mickman deserved better friends.

She wondered if, as the limelight dimmed, the killer would be ramping up for another attack. Actually, she didn't really wonder, she was sure of it now and decided to devote her day off to the intellectual exercise she'd spoken to Ray about. The only premise ... Parker's innocence. Where would that lead?

First she spread out the crime scene photos, hoping they'd shake loose the detail she'd been missing. While it might be nothing, she still had to try.

Starting from square one. Nelson. The enlargements of the bedroom *did* itch. There was something there. Again, out of her conscious reach. She felt it most strongly as she looked at the room from Nelson's point of view. As she would have been seeing her attacker.

There was a photo from Nelson's living room that had a similar effect. It was nothing more than a wall with two windows and a bookcase containing books, portraits, bric-a-brac, and DVDs. It offered some small insight into Nelson's personality, but other than that, Zoe couldn't figure out the connection.

One framed photo on the shelf caught her attention though. She rummaged for the enlargement of the area. In the close-up she could see that the photo was a candid shot of Nelson sitting on her bed, laughing. She was looking to the side of the camera, presumably *at* someone. It seemed to Zoe like an odd photo, but she couldn't consciously identify why. She moved on.

As she looked at the Franklin scene, she quickly shifted to remembering the Hanover house. Zoe felt that thinking about the kid right now was actually a distraction. It had been for the killer too. There was something there though . . . at Hanover's.

She dug out the Hanover and Mickman photos again. What was it about the two places? Again, she ignored Mickman's apartment, intuitively going for the photos of the crime scene. She was onto something. It felt close. Straining to bring it to the surface, she closed her eyes and pictured the various views that had caught her attention almost as if superimposed. Searching for a commonality. The tension finally erupted in an oath. "Damn it! Why the fuck can't I see it?"

She pushed up hard from the table, telling herself she hadn't really meant to send the chair flying into the corner, chipping off a piece of the drywall . . . but felt better afterwards.

Forcing it wasn't working. She had to consider that the reason she couldn't retrieve it was that it wasn't there in the first place. She did, however, decide to try Camilla at the next opportunity. She felt both better and worried after having finally made the decision, and still hoped she wouldn't need to do it. The idea of someone inside her head like that . . . well, what might happen? *Worry about it later.* She popped a chocolate-covered marshmallow.

On to the next exercise. This time she would re-rack all the theories, but at every juncture, leave Parker out, and see what happens. She dressed for a bike ride along Summit Avenue.

SUMMIT STRETCHED FROM THE College of St. Thomas, several blocks from her house on the river, to downtown St. Paul, passing two universities, a college of law, the governor's residence, and countless other mansions along the way. Architectural variety, carefully maintained . . . this road was always a treat for her.

For much of the route there was a grassy central boulevard separating the traffic in both directions. It was wide, lined with trees, and had a well-worn dirt path down its center that runners continually padded down. Plenty of eye candy there too.

Zoe biked the miles to Cathedral Hill, overlooking downtown St. Paul. She paused only briefly to take in the view of both city and river. She didn't dare stop long in the cold.

Riding cleared her mind, and as expected, it worked. Her most creative thinking happened while biking. The exercise of removing Parker as a suspect seemed to tidy things up for her. She still couldn't trust that it was real, or maybe what Parker had intended all along, but it *did* make things neater. It fit with both her knowledge of serial killers and her instincts about them.

The first kill was close to home, convenient, and perhaps the most personal of all. The kid was unintended but necessary. Subsequent murders were working their way into a pattern. A signature the killer felt comfortable with, and that she thought made sense. She drifted into his vantage point, an easy slide.

She let herself fill with his power, and imagined him as he was now. Successful, at this anyway, but probably more. He was clever, intelligent. But she tested his confident swagger, and dared him into the past. *What made you?*

She thought of the crime scenes. There was an imprint from his past at work there. Reenactments meant not only to satisfy him, but staged for others as well. *Why?*

The posing of Mickman was carefully designed for that effect. There would be young children there. A lot of them. *They would have to witness what he had done.*

She pictured the trauma that had disfigured the man inside.

He'd have been powerless when these claws had raked across his brain, probably very young. She pictured wounds, which as they'd "healed" had scarred in such a way as to pull and twist his mind into an unstable collection of deevolutionary neuronal connections. There were bridges and shortcuts where there shouldn't be. A new cause and effect.

Zoe considered his distorted view of the world as akin to a funhouse mirror. One he'd been looking in his entire life, and he had accounted for it. It reflected a reality that to him . . . made sense.

She guessed at the new control he felt over his world. Others now had to conform to his way of thinking. He probably was, at least for the time being, as close to happiness as he'd ever been. Happiness . . . nothing more than a fucking shiny lure.

CHAPTER TWENTY-FIVE
THANKSGIVING DAY

AKE THE PASS! SOMEONE'S GOTTA be freakin' open! How many times has he been sacked anyway?"

"Sheez Marty, take it easy. It's only a game." Mal gave Marty's shoulder a punch.

"Only a game?" He tackled Mal and pinned her to the couch. "The whole world is watching, and we're getting our asses handed to us." He let Mal go.

"Okay, okay." She tackled him this time. "Game's not over, Marty."

Zoe cocked an eyebrow at the horseplay. A budding romance? "Anybody want pie?"

Out of the chorus of "yeses" came an "I'll help you, Dr. Lawrence" from Shep. He followed her into the kitchen.

"Thanks for inviting me today. It was really nice of you. I'm sure I've been a pain in the ass to work with and all, but doing this? It's great, really. It means a lot to me."

"My pleasure, Shep. I know how it is, being alone in a new city. And yes, you have been a pain in the ass at times, I'm not gonna lie." She smiled at him. "But you've come a long way, don't you think?"

They'd formed an assembly line of pie, ice cream, and whipped cream.

"No shit, Zoe, I mean Dr. Lawrence. It's been unbelievable."

"It's okay, call me Zoe. Anyone who would let me call him Shep deserves the right to call me by my first name. Just *don't* tell me you had a dog once named Zoe."

He missed the joke. Good, Zoe thought. Probably wasn't funny.

"And I think you're gonna be an ace doctor by the way."

She noticed the surprise spread red over his face, and she laughed. "I mean it, Shep." She was feeling good. It was a beautiful day. Good company. If the Vikes would play better, Marty might even leave happy.

They passed out the pie and coffee. Kelly and Carmen were locked in a Scrabble battle. The board had filled in nicely. There was no over-concentration of tiles in any one corner. Instead they spread out evenly in long-word plays. Kelly looked focused. He obviously appreciated having a worthy adversary. Zoe glanced at the score sheet. *Close.* She might have to watch this instead of the football game.

"Great pie, Zoe!" Mal seemed especially upbeat today. Zoe was glad that the embarrassment of the whole disc thing was wearing off and Mal hadn't gotten into any trouble over it. She probably could have, but Parker didn't seem to hold it against her. In fact he himself didn't seem at all embarrassed by it. The other ramifications appeared to be his only concern.

"It was nothing, Mal." She winked at Shep, for whom it didn't take much and he reddened again.

She joined Kelly and Carmen at the Scrabble game. "Carmen, you might just be able to kick his ass at this, and it's about time someone did!"

"Take it easy there, Zoe, don't encourage her." His eyes laughed as he held Carmen's gaze over the table.

"God, it's nice to know I can still kick someone's ass at my age." Carmen returned with a ruthless stare, then as if on cue laid all seven letters. "That would be sixty-two points plus the plural to me. S-E-I-S-M-I-C. I hate using up two S tiles, but the situation calls for it. An elegant lay, don't you think?"

She might have been seventy, but her coquettish smile could have played across the face of a sixteen-year old. Carmen was happy too. And Zoe was feeling uncharacteristically good about this day.

"Halftime! How about a picture? I brought my camera." Marty was a little more upbeat now that the Vikings had scored.

"Why Marty that's a great idea! I hadn't thought of it. This *is* a good day to remember with a picture." Zoe looked at Marty with a new appreciation. He'd always been the "hanger on" of the group. Usually following someone else's lead, just kind of "there."

Obviously Mal saw a lot more in him. He certainly was handsome, built even. Yeah, she could see how Mal would be attracted. It explained why Marty spent so much time in the ER lately when he should have been in the Pharmacy. And here he was, actually initiating something.

"How about in front of the fireplace?" He was already getting the tripod out. They all gathered.

Marty looked through the lens, directing their movements. Everyone jockeyed around, inching this way and that, until Marty was satisfied that they could all be seen and there was a spot left for him.

"Three, two, one, here I come!" He pushed the button and dove into the scene. "Smile, everyone!"

It flashed and everyone breathed. The digital image of the picture was perfect. A second attempt wasn't required. Everyone was smiling, no closed eyes. Marty looked appreciatively at his subjects. "That hardly ever happens. You guys are naturals."

"Game's back on. Better get over here Marty." Mal called from the couch.

"And I still haven't given up on this game, my dear." Kelly called to Carmen from his seat at the Scrabble table.

"Looks like that leaves you and me to clean up?" Shep looked hopefully at Zoe.

"Guess so."

The two of them gathered the dishes and loaded the dishwasher.

"I love your house, Dr. Lawrence. It's awesome."

"Thanks, Shep. But really, call me Zoe. I bought it when I first moved here. I love the neighborhood. Right next to the Mississippi and the Grand Rounds Bike Trail, it's perfect for me. But it was the house itself that finally convinced me in the end. You interested in architecture?"

"Well, I know what I like. This place is like a New York City loft. Nothing ornate or froufrou about it. The structural elements are exposed and featured as part of the design itself. You've used neutral colors but with splashes of boldness in just the right doses.

"The choice of natural materials . . . the wood, stone, and leather . . . add warmth to an environment some might consider too spare. But I like that there's nothing 'extra,' you know, nothing you don't need here. It fits you.

"And of course the art is great. But the house *itself* is art . . . I can see how it might have taken shape in the architect's mind. It's because of the site. There are parameters, obstacles that would have forced a creative solution. Art doesn't just come from nothing. It requires seeding, to crystallize, you know? I can see how the slope, the trees, and the amazing view would have started that process. In fact the surroundings are brought right in to your home. It's all the glass."

Zoe thought she might have to pick her jaw up off the floor. And he hadn't once used the timeworn, meaningless phrase "warm and inviting." "Keep going, Shep. Don't let me stop you." She looked at him with undisguised shock. It was seductive language to an architecture buff. Everyone was surprising her today.

"Okay. The only thing you could use more of is greenery. A house like this . . . it needs plants, Zoe." He looked at her with an earnestness she thought just might be for real.

"Yeah, I know. I've been trying to keep that plant in the living room alive, but it doesn't seem to like the last few sips of martinis or day-old beer. I'm not quite sure why. I figured, if it's good enough for me . . ." Her words trailed off as she smiled at him.

"Seriously?" He looked shocked.

"Sadly, yes. I decided to cut back on my drinking and the plant seems to be the beneficiary of that decision."

"You need help." At her raised eyebrows he started stammering. "No! Wait! It wasn't supposed to sound like that. I mean, I *didn't* mean . . . not about drinking, not like it sounded! Oh, shit. All I meant was that you need help with your plants. I know a lot about plants. I can fix you up with some." He was sweating now. "I blew it. I'm sorry."

Zoe thought about messing with him some more, it was just too easy, but waved off the impulse . . . as well as his apology. She was still back at his description of her house. "Shep, I'm impressed, and I want you to know, I don't impress easily. You really understand this place don't you?"

"Well, yeah, I guess so. I like it. One probably doesn't have to know a lot about architecture to appreciate it as both habitat and art. A good architect captures the imagination of everyday people, not just architecture critics. After all, architect-designed homes are meant to be lived in. They're designed *for* someone, to *please* someone. Once again, like the site, parameters that force creativity . . . clients."

"You're a very observant, intelligent, and thoughtful young man, Shep. I do love the efficiency of the design as you've noticed. The structure is art. Nothing's hidden or camouflaged. It is what it is. No pretense. It's not 'added to' to give a false impression. I guess what I'm trying to say is that it's *honest*. A person can like it, or not . . . but it's honest design. Then again, you seem to know all of that."

SHE MAY HAVE CALLED HIM a "young man," but he had her attention. He smiled warmly at her. He really did like it, for all the reasons he'd said. And he liked her, for other reasons.

"You must have *some* background in architecture though, Shep. Or art?"

"No, biology. It was my major in college. But I've always admired art and architecture. Perhaps as you have?" *Careful, Shep.*

"Yes, as I have. No formal training, just an admiration."

"Well then, I think you owe me a complete tour of the place after we finish cleaning up here." *I can't believe I just said that.*

"You're on! Just wait until you see what I've done with the basement!"

Wow.

The others were still engrossed in either football or Scrabble, so Zoe and Shep excused themselves to take the tour. They started with her basement gym.

"So, you play hockey then?"

"Yes. It's one of my favorite pastimes. Hockey, and biking. It's pretty obvious from the equipment, isn't it?"

Shep was enjoying the tour, but more than anything he was enjoying what he could learn about Zoe. He felt closer to her somehow, and a little bolder. If nothing else, his fantasies wouldn't seem quite as far-fetched.

They walked back upstairs, and he thought he would explode when she let him see her bedroom and master bath. She seemed so matter-of-fact about it. Didn't she see what it was doing to him? He pictured the two of them there. *Down, Shep.*

The bath, with its shades of white and gray, the marble and subway tile, reminded him of a mid-century Washington, D.C., hotel. Elegant and sophisticated, but not ornate.

The bedroom was entirely different. Still a mid-century economy of design, but in this room the mood was dark and sensual. The smoky gray of the walls and ceiling *was* a sophisticated color, but he didn't think that was why she'd chosen it. It didn't fit as her motivation.

It occurred to him that it was the gray color of a menswear suit. He pictured how she might feel as her lover, noticing a chill in the air, draped his jacket over her shoulders. Yeah, that's what the color of this room made him think of. In fact the headboard seemed to be upholstered in that same kind of material.

Had she felt that when she picked it? What made *her* choose this color, that fabric?

He didn't ask.

"SHEP? YOU OKAY? Where'd you go? Lost in thought?" It was the first time Zoe wondered if maybe she'd missed something or given off the wrong signals herself. "We'd better join the others, don't you think?"

"Uh, yeah, I guess."

There he was, Zoe told herself, the old Shep … a little unsure. Probably nothing to worry about. "Okay, I'll mix up a cocktail for everyone before the football game ends. What's your poison? I've got my favorites, but if you've got a preference, chances are I can make it."

"I'll trust you to choose, Zoe."

"Okay, why don't you take orders from the others and meet me in the kitchen. I'll get things together."

THE MOJITO, KEY-LIME PIE MARTINI, and four Summit Ales were history. They'd even fixed sandwiches with leftover turkey and had seconds of pie with Peet's coffee. Everyone was sated and moving toward disbanding for the night. The Vikings had won. Kelly and Carmen had traded wins at Scrabble and were already making plans for a rubber match. And Zoe had tasted sweetness in this day.

These friends of hers were happy. She'd learned things too. Marty, Shep, and Carmen had all surprised her, even Mal, who hadn't bothered to mention her attraction to Marty. Maybe she should do stuff like this more often. Or maybe she should just pay better attention.

The wail came from the back steps. Marty and Mal had just left, and Shep had volunteered to take the garbage out.

All three ran toward him. It was a no-nonsense howl that had ended abruptly, with the hollow thud of a pumpkin hurled at pavement. They expected something bad.

Although only one step separated the threshold from the cement walkway, it had apparently been the cause of Shep's fall. That, and the layer of ball bearings scattered on top of it.

Zoe rushed to his side, checking his breathing and pulse. Both okay. No outward signs of trauma, not even a head laceration. She stabilized his neck and tried to wake him. Not okay.

"Kelly, call 911. Tell them head and possible neck injury. I'll stay here with him. We can't let him move. Hurry. Then bring a blanket to cover him with."

"THEY'RE ON THEIR WAY, ZOE. Carmen is waiting out front. She'll direct them back here. Is he all right?" Kelly dropped next to Zoe.

"I don't know, Kelly. He seems to be out cold. I can't do much of an evaluation right now. I need to keep his neck absolutely still. At this point we need to wait until the medics get here to immobilize it. Then I'll be able to tell more. Right now, he's breathing fine, he's got a good pulse, and if there's any spinal cord damage, I'm preventing it from getting any worse."

"Zoe, the ball bearings…"

"Don't say it, Kelly. Not now!" The sound of the approaching siren slowed her breathing. Her world, not his, she reminded herself. "We'll talk at the hospital after I know how bad this is. I can't think about that now."

"I understand, Zoe. We'll talk there. I'll call a cab and meet you."

"No! My keys are on the table. You do know *how* to drive don't you, Kell?" Zoe knew better than to ask if he had a license.

"Yes, Zoe. I can drive just fine."

"Okay, take Carmen home and meet me at the hospital." She heard Carmen ushering the medics around back. "Kelly, I couldn't bear it if someone else got hurt because of me again."

"*Again?*"

Zoe didn't hear him. The medics were there, and her attention was focused on communicating with them.

CHAPTER TWENTY-SIX
THANKSGIVING EVENING

ZOE WAS GRATEFUL TO SEE PARKER, AND found that she thought of him more generously under these circumstances. She permitted herself a step back, watching Parker take over. Shep had finally moved spontaneously, but not until they'd obtained C-spine films. He was opening his eyes, speaking in a slightly confused manner and following commands. They would get a CT scan, but it was looking like everything would probably be okay.

"HAH! NOW YOU'RE THE ONE held captive for observation. My only advice ... sleep through it ... ask for meds." Zoe reached out to hold Shep's hand. "But seriously, Shep, I'm so *very* sorry." Zoe looked toward Kelly, and shook her head slightly.

Kaj noticed. He'd gotten precious little information about what happened. Just a bad fall was all they'd said. Slipped on something. Marty and Mal had gotten word and come in, but had nothing to offer.

Kaj finally stepped out to take care of the paperwork and leave the group to worry over young Dr. Shepard. He seemed to be enjoying the attention.

The photo Marty had brought in with him was tacked to the bulletin board, and as Kaj was finishing his notes, it caught his eye. He rose to get a closer look at the charming and cheerful group. Clearly the day had been a good one, up until the mishap. Marty and Mal, close and apparently familiar, Carmen looking as radiant as he'd ever seen her, Dr. Shepard leaning in toward Zoe, his hand resting gently on an area of bare skin, and the maintenance guy, Kelly. He was smiling, but looking more at Zoe than the camera.

Then there was Zoe. The camera had caught something. He'd seen her in all kinds of situations over the past several months, from edgy and alert with adrenaline, to drunk and doped, but he had yet to see her look intoxicated in this way. There was actual pleasure in her eyes. Missing was the "I dare you to cross me" stare, her full lips open slightly in flirtatious amusement.

The tile and steel running around the fireplace mirrored her hard edges, the ones he was used to running into. But the art above the mantel was what really reflected her contrasts ... fiery reds and oranges tempered by shades of gray and steel blue. Her warmth ... no, heat ... un-shadowed, but balanced by cool smoky phantoms. She was made of extremes. It was on her walls, in her face, beckoning him.

As he remembered what he'd seen of Zoe's house, he heard hushed but insistent voices in the hallway. They continually pressed down on the volume, trying to keep their conversation private, but it was impossible not to hear them. Clearly audible was the note of urgency.

"Kelly, I *know* it was meant for me. What the hell do you want me to say? What can I even do about it right now? And what good will it do for Shep to know?"

"You owe it to him. Tell him exactly what happened. At least you'll thrill the poor boy into thinking he saved you from a similar fate. He probably *did* you know. You'd have gone down behind your house with no one to notice. If you'd been knocked unconscious as he was, you'd have frozen out there."

"What in God's name are you talking about?"

"What, that he has eyes for you, or that you might have been dead by morning?"

"Kelly, you're so full of shit right now ..." She threw her back up hard against the wall with her arms crossed over her chest. "Don't make this any harder. It's bad enough already. Listen, back to the point. It was purposeful, there's no mistaking it this time, and it was meant for me. I've *got* that."

"You should have gotten that with the booby trap in the woods and the drug at the party, Zoe. You're slipping here. You've got to protect yourself. Someone's messing with you."

"Yeah, Kell, I *see* that. When I get home I'll take a good look around. But I don't like someone thinking they can make me look over my shoulder. I won't live like that again."

He grabbed her by both shoulders and pulled her toward him roughly. "Okay, Zoe, out with it. Back at the house you said you couldn't bear it if someone was hurt because of you *again*. Now you're talking about looking over your shoulder *again*. What is this 'again' stuff?"

"Let go of me, Kell!"

"Quiet, Zoe."

The last exchange had Kaj up and out of his chair. He pulled up short at the doorway, but made no attempt to hide. Zoe pushed Kelly away, as the nurse appeared with word that they were ready in CT.

"I'm going with him. This is all my fault and I won't leave him until I know he's okay."

"Go then, but we'll talk later. You're worried about him? Well you should be. And you owe him, at least enough to be honest about this. We *will* talk."

Zoe looked hard at Kelly as she turned to leave. "Whoever this is, Kell, he's messing with my head. He wants me scared, paranoid. He wants me thinking about *him*."

She'd started down the hall toward Shep's cubicle when she spun towards Kelly, "But I won't. Right now I'm thinking about Shep. No one will *ever* control me in that way again. Not even you."

Kaj flinched. And *there* was the "I dare you to cross me look." As well as the use of "again," something Kelly seemed to think was important.

Kaj noticed something else. He'd first become consciously aware of it with the Kelly character. There was a Canadian accent to his speech. It was hard to pick up on at first because in Minnesota nearly everyone shared speech patterns to some degree with their neighbors to the north. But this was slightly different, and blended with First Nation inflections.

He'd also noticed it in Zoe as she'd ramped up and gotten angry. Her accent was unmistakably French Canadian. He'd always found her voice, her way of speaking, attractive. But the "why" of it had never occurred to him before.

Kaj wondered if Canada held any memories of Zoe. He also wondered about her relationship with the old man. What was Kelly to her? Was it a shared homeland, nothing more? They were clearly friends, but how had that come about? They weren't even close in age. Kelly must be in his late fifties.

The overhead speakers announcing a code in radiology interrupted his thoughts. It was the CT room. He bolted, arriving there at a run.

Flying into the room and sliding to a stop, he saw Zoe giving Shep mouth-to-mouth while Dr. Carter, the radiologist, was breaking out the crash cart containing the ambu bag for Zoe to fit over Shep's face. It would provide more effective assisted breathing until they could intubate him, if that became necessary.

Zoe flushed and sweating, covered his mouth with her own, breathing for him, all the while keeping one eye on the cardiac monitor. It revealed an elevated but normal heart rhythm. Just as Zoe was handed the ambu bag and released her lips from Shep's mouth, he coughed and came around... an innocent, bewildered smile on his face.

"What's going on? Is it over? I must have fallen asleep."

Zoe leaned over at the waist, panting, and propped herself up with her hands on her knees. "God, Shep, you scared me. You just flat out quit breathing."

She struggled to catch her breath. "The respiratory monitor... it alarmed... and when I got in here you had no inspiratory efforts at all. Had me flying in here at a dead run."

"Uh yeah, that would be an understatement." Carter looked at Parker. "She vaulted over the console and nearly punched a hole in the door as she went through. It was a sight that I won't soon forget." He shook his head and smiled.

"Dr. Lawrence, could you give me a moment alone with Dr. Shepard before we resume the CT scan? I want to take a look at him first." Kaj fixed his gaze on Shep while talking to Zoe. Shep, on the other hand, seemed to be looking somewhere else.

"All right, I'll be in the control room." Both she and the radiologist went back to sit down at the console, still watching Shep through the glass. Carter began to make adjustments to reset for a second try at the CT scan.

Kaj grabbed his stethoscope from around his neck, pretending to listen to Shep's heart. He leaned in close and whispered, "That must have taken quite a bit of self-control, holding your breath that long, Shepard."

Shep looked up at Kaj, who loomed inches from his face, and smiled tentatively. "It didn't take long actually, she pretty much flew in here."

"Enjoyed yourself then, eh?"

"Uh, yeah, I guess you could say that."

He pressed down hard through the stethoscope on Shep's chest, and the heart monitor showed a rising heart rate again. Kaj saw Zoe stand for a better look.

He kept his voice down, "Listen carefully, Shepard, I know what you were up to. In any other situation I might have said "well played." But here and now, with her, there will be no games. Do you understand me?"

Kaj felt Shep's heart ramming against his chest, barely having time to fill before emptying again. Remembering that Shep had just been knocked unconscious only a couple of hours ago, he added, "She obviously cares a great deal about you . . . Lord only knows why . . . and I don't think she can take much more right now."

That seemed to calm Shep slightly, and he managed a nod.

Kaj stood and said in a normal tone, knowing there was an audio feed into the control room, "You'll be fine, Shep. Now I want you to hold still for another try at the CT."

He leaned in close again to quietly threaten, just inches from Shep's ear, "And you will remain awake and breathing. Understood?"

Again, Shep managed only a nod.

Chapter Twenty-Seven
December 02 (Evening)

Zoe's search of the grounds surrounding her house had revealed nothing. She'd managed to clean up all the ball bearings before a light snow started to fall. Now if someone made another foray into her yard, there'd be a give-away.

Ray had come over with videos of the follow-up interviews. Most of Nelson's neighbors had an alibi of sorts, but in many cases, it couldn't be confirmed. They all claimed to be out watching the fireworks.

"I've racked up the discs for you, and I can tell you right now, there's not a lot here. A couple of the interviews though, I thought you should see them. It's the first two. Take a real close look at them. The rest . . . just look when you have a chance. Not much more there."

"Let's look at the first two right now then. Can you stay that long?"

"Yeah. I was hoping you'd have time."

"Okay, let's go." They both sat down on the couch as Zoe pushed PLAY.

The image on screen was of a relatively handsome, distinguished looking man, graying at the temples. Well dressed, and clearly angry. She recognized him as a radiologist from the hospital.

"How long will this take? I've a full schedule and I was told this would be a quick affair." Wow, gravelly voice didn't match his looks. His leg jumped up and down.

"Shouldn't take long at all, Doctor Mayhew. We appreciate you taking the time to stop by on your way to work, and we'll do our best to respect your busy schedule. Can we begin by going over your actions and observations on the night in question? July 4th of this year. First, exactly what did you do that evening?"

"As I've said before, I enjoyed a rare day of rest and relaxation, then wandered out briefly to view the fireworks. I was back in the house by ten-thirty, had a well-deserved nightcap and went to bed."

"Have you given any more thought to having seen someone who might have recognized you at the fireworks?"

"As before, there were many people gathered around the lake. It was dark and all eyes were watching the sky. I certainly couldn't tell you who was next to me, and I doubt any of them would have noticed me either."

"You're right about that Doctor Mayhew. No one we've interviewed who was lakeside during the fireworks can remember seeing you at *all* that night. I was just hoping you might have thought of someone who could verify your whereabouts."

He shrugged dismissively. "It doesn't surprise me. Not only was everyone paying attention to the sky, but I'm not exactly a recognizable fixture in the neighborhood. I keep long and late hours, I live alone, I don't entertain and rarely stand about chatting with neighbors. I don't particularly care to know my neighbors and even if I did, I haven't the time. I hadn't even been aware that Julia Nelson lived near me until she was murdered." Palms on pants, he made a wiping motion. "Last I checked none of those things qualify as crimes."

Zoe wasn't at all surprised by his impatience or his anger. He wasn't used to having his agenda disrupted or questioned. But Ray was right, that there was something about the guy.

"Of course they're not crimes. We aren't questioning that, Doctor Mayhew. Just tying up loose ends. We like to have a verifiable alibi where possible before we close the file on someone as a potential suspect. We were only hoping you might have thought of someone who could provide that for us."

Zoe saw it now. The wheels turning, the moisture forming on his upper lip. Thinking of a way to lie? Ray was dangling it in front of him, a simple way to get off the radar screen.

Ray pushed it further. "Being a loner is certainly no crime, but it sure as hell is inconvenient at a time like this, isn't it?" Ray smiled and chuckled. "Would have been nice to have had contact with someone that night, eh?"

Zoe wondered if the doctor knew anyone well enough that they'd lie for him. She saw him tense at the thinly veiled insult.

Zoe paused the disc. "Trying to catch him in a lie, Ray?"

"Yeah, I was hoping he'd bite. Give me cause to take it to the next level with him. But that's about the end of the interview. He clammed up after that."

"Well, with a guy like that, lying about an alibi might have seemed no worse than swatting at a mosquito. Getting rid of a pest ... you. It still wouldn't make him guilty. Would have given you cause though, which is what you were after."

Zoe grinned at Ray. "But I think you might have accomplished your objective anyway. He got pissed off and chatty just long enough to say he hadn't known Nelson lived in his neighborhood prior to her murder. I'd follow up on that. Could be easy to disprove."

Ray nodded in agreement.

It was hard to believe Mayhew didn't know Nelson, unless he really was a hermit.

"Who's the other one?"

"Well, this is a weird one. She's a cardiologist at the hospital and ... I'm a little embarrassed to show it to you." Ray inserted the second disc.

This had Zoe leaning forward. "Why?"

"Just push PLAY Zoe, you'll see."

The image this time was of an elegantly dressed woman, probably mid-thirties. She was leaning back confidently in her chair.

"She's beautiful isn't she?" Ray stared at the woman on screen.

Watching Ray ogle, Zoe was pretty sure he had his own copy of this particular disc at home. Then it got even better. Zoe couldn't help but laugh, spoiling Ray's fantasy.

"Look at her! Did you see that?"

"How could I *not* notice that, Zoe?" He said flatly.

"Ray, it's like right out of that Sharon Stone movie! Oh ... my ... God."

Dr. Warren had carelessly crossed her legs, offering Ray a good, long look. The result of her action was now a dress that had ridden up dangerously high, barely covering the essentials.

Zoe watched as Ray, his back to the camera, shifted uncomfortably in his seat. He got up to get a glass of water and offered her one. Her move had accomplished the desired effect ... no matter what it was. If she had something to hide, she'd thrown him off his game. He was the nervous one now. And if she were truly coming on to him, that had clearly worked too. But the lady was only getting started.

Ray walked back toward her with the water. As she leaned across the table reaching for the water, her breasts brushed up against the wood, threatening to spill out. Zoe marveled at the multi-functional and versatile dress worn by the good doctor ... and her mastery of it. She seemed very experienced in its limitations. And Zoe could easily read the fun she was having at Ray's expense. "You didn't actually fall for this did you?"

"Of course not, Zoe! Shut up and listen. It's what she *says* that has me wondering."

Zoe watched as Ray went through the night of July 4th with her in detail. There were no red flags. She'd been out watching the fireworks and no one had seen her. It was the same story as so many others. There were a number of single professionals with no one at home to confirm an alibi. But it seemed like it would be hard not to notice *this* woman. Zoe couldn't help but punctuate the disc with a laugh track as the dress crept up higher and the breasts made occasional trips to the precipice, never quite going over the edge.

"Shut up, Zoe. Here it is!"

"Doctor Warner, how well did you know Julia Nelson?"

"We partied ... and shared an appreciation for strong, powerful men." Her lips parted slightly as she lazily looked Ray up and down, bringing her eyes to rest on his face.

"Oh, my God, how could you keep a straight face? She's having so much fun playing you. I bet she'd like a copy of this disc too!" She looked quickly at Ray and seeing exactly what she'd expected, shook her head. "You didn't, Ray. It's not right."

"Shut up! You're just jealous that another woman finds me attractive."

Zoe rolled her eyes. "Trust me, Ray. You're *very* attractive, but she's messing with you. And as far as jealousy goes, I'll be the first to congratulate you when you meet the future Mrs. Perry."

"Here, listen ... this is the weird part."

"*The* weird part? What *hasn't* been weird?" She shut up when he cast her a warning glance.

"Julia and I were confidantes of sorts. I was aware that she had relationships with a number of very prominent men. It was an interest we shared." She smiled seductively at Ray, who again adjusted himself in his chair. Warner's eyes were clearly laughing.

"Can you tell me again who she'd admitted to having affairs with?"

And this *was* the weird part. Warner recounted the same men she'd offered up during her previous interview, all having alibis, but this time she added Parker's name.

Zoe paused the disc, closed her eyes, and took a deep breath. "This is too . . . much . . . shit. Just too much." She turned on the couch to face Ray directly. "Did this interview take place before or after the sex tape surfaced?"

"After."

"Okay, first of all, she's lying . . . about a lot of things. Problem is they're not the kind of lies you can catch her in. And then there's the question of why. I looked into Nelson's personal life in great detail. She wasn't the kind to talk about her sexual adventures. That's Warner's first lie. Even those who were far closer to Nelson attested to that fact.

"I pick up on the gossip at work too, Ray, and trust me, Nelson was discrete. There weren't any details floating around about her love life. And from the looks of this manipulative bitch, Nelson wouldn't have 'partied' or done anything with her."

Ray leaned back against the couch, blowing out a long breath. Zoe kept at him. "The men Warner gave you the first time were all men that Nelson had been seen with in highly public places. There was never any mystery there. The addition of Parker to that list is her second lie. I can almost guarantee she had no first-hand knowledge of that. She heard about the disc at work and felt safe throwing you that bone.

"She may be guilty of nothing more than having a good time with you, Ray, that may be the only reason she lied, but she *did* lie. And here's what I think. She's either having fun, has something against Parker and or Nelson, or she's involved and wants to throw you off, but nothing she said should add any weight to your liking Parker for all of this. Nothing."

"You think *she* could have anything to do with these kills?"

"Honest opinion? No. Not even tangentially." Ray visibly relaxed. What was it about the effect some women had on men?

"But she's sick, Ray, honest to God. Watch out with her. My guess? She likes this sport and plays it all the time . . . looks right at home in the role. But she *is* messing with you."

135

Zoe paused and stared at the frozen images on screen. "I'll see what I can dig up on her at work. I doubt she knows I'm working the case. We have very little interaction.

"I will say this, both these discs you've shown me are evidence of fringe people, maybe nothing more. But they do deserve another a look. I'll get what I can on both Warren and Mayhew at work."

She angrily tossed back a handful of jellybeans, chewing until she could wash them down with beer. She saw Ray wince. He'd never understood her candy jones.

Chapter Twenty-Eight
December 10 (Evening)

IT WAS AS BAD AS IT GETS, AND STILL working its way into a blizzard. As the first significant snowfall of the season, Minnesotans seemed to forget how to drive in it. Local weather was even making national news. Of course the ER was swamped.

Motor vehicle accidents dominated the board, many involving minor injuries, but there were enough serious collisions that the Stabilization rooms were never completely empty. If it wasn't a crash victim, it was an older male found down while shoveling snow. They'd sent up so many of the old guys with heart attacks that the Coronary Care Unit had filled, and MI cases were rerouted to the Respiratory Intensive Care Unit.

Everyone had stayed past shift's end, exhausted. Zoe and Mal chose to bypass the cafeteria and head straight for Humphrey's. It would be their first meal in fourteen hours. They'd functioned on cup after cup of coffee, swallowed on the run, nothing more.

"I need food in my stomach before I have any more of this beer. I'll puke if I don't." Mal looked longingly at the beer in front of her, "I want it, but I don't trust it. I'm not kidding. I don't feel so good."

"Here, have some of this. The food shouldn't be much longer." Zoe shoved the basket of popcorn at Mal. "God, what a day. I'm just flat out beat. I could fall asleep right here."

"Too tired to whine?" Rex pulled up a chair to join them.

"Rex, I'm always too tired to whine. But you go right ahead."

"You guys think you had it bad? Try being on the receiving end of all the MIs you sent up. We overflowed the CCU by mid-day. It was fun for a while, but jeez, after a dozen heart attacks in sixty-year-old men shoveling snow, you've seen 'em all."

"Not true, Rex. We didn't send you anyone who was shoveling snow off his roof when it happened. Those guys fall off you know. No, you haven't seen that one yet. But you will... trust me... after a little more snow."

"That one MVA was *nasty* though." Mal really did look like she was going to hurl now. "I've never seen a face caved in that bad."

"Oh for God's sake Mal, don't think about it now. Wait till your stomach settles."

They all slumped in their seats.

PARKER WALKED INTO THE BAR and made his way toward them.

"Mind if I join you?" He actually waited for a response.

Finally Zoe spoke up. "Of course not, Dr. Parker, have a seat. We're all too tired to complain about anything anyway." She cast a dubious look at Mal and kicked Rex in warning under the table.

Kaj noticed Rex jump and managed a tired smile. He couldn't remember the last time he'd felt so dead on his feet, and assumed they were in no better shape. It really *had* been a bad day, no exaggeration.

"Dr. Parker, this is Rex Collins, he's an internal medicine resident." Zoe made the introduction.

"It's Kaj here. But I believe we met at a party a while back. Came down a number of times to collect patients today didn't you? They all do okay?"

"Yes, Dr. Parker, um … I mean Kaj. Hadn't lost anyone when I left." He looked away while his hand went to the shoulder Kaj had previously maimed in a vice grip.

ZOE THOUGHT BACK to the aftermath of the party too and suddenly wondered how Parker had propped her up in the shower and washed her off without getting his clothes wet. Only one way she could see that happening. Feeling a little buzzed, she suddenly wished she'd been awake for that.

"Then it looks as though we all did good work today." Kaj's smile swept over the group, landing on Zoe.

"Has it just been one day? Feels like three." One of Zoe's hands propped up her head, while the other lifted her second beer. She let herself stare at Kaj, imagining a lot of things. He only smiled back, seeming to welcome her gaze.

And then she wondered just how in the hell she'd managed to keep her distance? As she finished a second beer, she decided that it must have had to do with his discipline, not hers.

THE FOOD FINALLY ARRIVED, along with a glass for Kaj, who sat back to stretch out his legs in Zoe's direction, making do with a watery beer. He watched, both amused and annoyed, as Rex's hand repeatedly went for Zoe's leg and she kept forcefully redirecting it to his own lap. It looked like she might be in a mood to give in though, as she left it there a little longer each time.

Meanwhile Mal hadn't said much of anything, and after making her apologies, she was out the door.

Kaj, Zoe, and Rex remained to finish off the third pitcher of beer, while Kaj gauged what it would take to rid Zoe of the apparently unwanted companion. Then her phone rang.

"Yeah, hi, Ray. What's up?"

Her eyes closed.

"When? ... Where? ... Okay, I'll meet you there. I'm going to need twenty minutes before I leave here." She hung up.

"Zoe, you can't be serious!" It was Rex who spoke up first.

"Rex and I are in agreement there. You're in no condition to ..."

"Back off ... both of you. I'll be fine. Hey, Carl, pot of coffee here please? Strong."

"How far?" Kaj cut to the heart of the matter. He was worried about her driving, especially in this snow. A pot of coffee wasn't going to make all those beers disappear, and she damn well knew it. She was a doctor for Christ's sake. "At least let me drive you. I've only had a couple, but you've had quite a head start."

He saw her begin to dismiss him, but then look through the window at the swirling whiteout and seem to reconsider. "Okay. Thanks. You can drop me off on your way home and I'll get a ride back here from Ray."

AFTER ZOE HAD DOWNED THREE CUPS of coffee she climbed into Kaj's ride. The one she'd been in before, but had no recollection of. There was no trace of the vomit, and she found that really, she no longer cared. After watching him in a sex tape for Christ's sake, it wasn't Zoe who should be embarrassed.

"So where to?" Kaj climbed in after brushing the snow off the windows, mirrors, and lights.

"It's over by Lake Nokomis. Couple blocks south, and a few blocks east of Cedar Avenue. Thanks for the ride by the way. This was the last thing I expected tonight."

"I know the area. Is this connected to Julia and the others?"

"Ray seems to think so." Gradually sobering, Zoe decided to take advantage of the casual talk. "Say, you know Doctor Warren, don't you?"

"Yes, I do." He offered nothing.

"Well, she lives in Nelson's neighborhood. What can you tell me about her? Did she know Nelson very well? Did Nelson say anything to you about her?"

"Although I've no particular admiration for Dr. Warren personally, I'm also not inclined to go into any details as to the why of it. Professionally, she's competent. And no, I don't think they were particularly close. Julia never spoke of her to me."

"That's pretty much what I figured."

She looked at him, and he smiled, still watching the road. They traveled in silence for a while. The roads were slippery, and it was taking great concentration on Kaj's part. Zoe, normally would be tensing with every slip and slide, not used to giving up control, but felt unexpectedly safe with him at the wheel. He drove expertly through the rapidly accumulating powder. She was glad she'd let him drive.

"Now I've got a question for you." She noticed him chance a quick look away from the road, toward her. "Shepard's accidental fall at your place, your bike accident, the doping incident at the party... what's going on? Are you in some sort of danger? I couldn't help but overhear you and Kelly discussing the fact that you were being targeted in some way."

Zoe stared straight ahead into the white. Still a little loose from fatigue and beer, she was alarmed at the uncharacteristic urge to open a vein about it. But stopping herself, out of habit as much as anything, she dismissed the query. "It's nothing really. It's something I can take care of."

"Wait, it's *nothing* but it's *something*. Something you can take care of? Which is it?"

Zoe knew she'd have to sober quickly. If she couldn't handle this little conversation, how could she be ready for the crime scene? "It's a *minor* thing, okay?"

"That's not how it sounded."

"Listen, I was sick with worry over Shep. I'd invited him over for Thanksgiving. He's got no family in town, and look what happens. I felt it was both my fault and my responsibility to act as family for him. I'm not exactly used to that role."

"You have no family in town either, Zoe?"

She stiffened. Taking one hand off the wheel, he rested it over hers.

Zoe closed her eyes, saying nothing. She resented the intrusion, but imagined what it might actually be like to tell him. Picturing the horrified reaction, she stuffed the impulse, yet relaxed at his touch and sunk deeper into the seat. Leaning her head back, she kept her eyes closed to other distractions.

"I'm with you, Zoe."

It was all he said. Zoe felt a heat wash through her, and with it the tension eased. Her awareness of his touch heightened. Releasing her hand, he reached up to run his fingers through her hair, pulling it away from her face. He touched her cheek, confirming the tears that Zoe hadn't even realized were there, and then carefully wiped them away. She kept her eyes shut and leaned into his hand, saying nothing.

She sensed his breathing quicken, along with hers, and imagined *not now* winning in his inner struggle. *Not ever* she told herself. But the silence between them bridged a distance . . . and he couldn't possibly know how grateful she was for his restraint.

He squeezed her shoulder gently as he returned his hand to the wheel. "We're getting close . . ." Zoe opened her eyes as his words trailed off, wondering if *close* meant something else. They could both see the red and blue lights bouncing off the cottage up the street.

"No. God no." He punched the accelerator, racing the last block to the police tape. They came skidding to a stop perilously close to one of the cruisers.

He was out of the car and at a dead run toward the house. It took three uniforms and Zoe to stop him. "I know her!"

The uniforms were about to cuff him, when Zoe intervened. She held him in a bear hug while convincing him to wait for her. Suddenly it was Zoe comforting, and calming.

Kaj shoved his hands into his pockets and nodded in agreement through a long slow breath. "Hurry." He turned to lean against one of the cruisers, pulling his collar up around his neck. The wind was building and temperatures dropping. Vapor off each breath disappeared at thirty miles per hour, along with any warmth that wasn't trapped by down or wool.

Zoe raced into the house, met by a blast of heat and stink. Ray shot out a hand to stop her before she went any further. "You ready? Got your wits about you?"

"Yeah, Ray. Don't worry, I'm fine."

"Then boot, glove and tell me what in the hell that was all about out there?"

"It's Parker ... he knows her." Zoe looked at Ray with dead eyes, waiting for the accusations. It didn't look good for Parker. Zoe had to wonder herself. And she was so *fucking* tired.

"We'll have to talk to him. He's waiting?"

"Yeah. He won't go anywhere, trust me. He's pretty shook up."

"Damn thoughtful to deliver himself on a platter. Two of our other neighborhood interviews suddenly have mutually verifiable alibis."

Zoe opted not to get into it over Parker. "What? Did that Mayhew guy get someone to lie for him?"

"No, Warner and Marty suddenly remember seeing each other at the fireworks."

"Well, I'll bet that was an easy play. Marty wouldn't be hard to convince. I bet he really believes it too, after she described it to him. Like it really happened. She's good. What did they say?"

Ray laughed. "You're probably right, Zoe. Identical stories. And they were sure to keep it simple. Just forgot, that's all. Happened to be talking and it came back to them. She was flat-out reckless during that taped interview. I bet she worried it was too careless. How well do you know Marty? Any chance he's lying?"

"I don't think so, but I don't really know him all that well. I've just always pictured him as being kind of pliable, you know? It fits that he could be easily convinced to agree with her. Or maybe they really did remember. Whatever. I never seriously thought she was involved. Let's keep her in mind though, we might have lies piling up here."

"So are the bodies."

"Bodies? As in more than one?"

"Yeah, Zoe. Brace yourself."

He led her by the elbow into the bedroom. "We're estimating they were killed sometime between midnight and 4:00 a.m. last night."

In Zoe's darker moments she'd wondered how the murderer could possibly outdo the Halloween murder. That had been genius. It revealed a lot about the guy too. He wanted people to see what he'd done. Wanted them to watch. Wanted them as scarred as he was, Zoe had thought. And the kids who'd seen it, the effect in them would be hard-wired. She guessed he'd known all that first-hand, probably having suffered considerable trauma himself as a child. He'd seen things no one, let alone a kid, should ever have to witness. And now she was certain of it.

"Aw, Ray." She grabbed onto him for support. The mixture of beer and coffee threatened.

"I know, hon."

The roaring in Zoe's ears finally stopped after she leaned down, letting blood fill the emptying recesses of her brain. Deep breaths weren't possible through the stench. It only made her feel worse. She pivoted slowly to absorb a full sweep of the room and thought this was about as bad as it got. But hadn't she felt that way at the Mickman murder?

She knew with an absolute certainty how this had played out. And she knew, somehow, where he was taking this. It was going to get far more destructive if they didn't stop him. Her imagination was closing in.

"We've got a thirty-eight-year-old female, name is Liv Anders. The girl is her daughter, Hannah. Kid's only sixteen years old. Apparently the parents married in college and divorced when the kid was two. Mom never remarried. Shared custody. Jack's on his way over to notify the ex."

"We got all this from a neighbor who reported the bodies. The lights were on in the bedroom and all the shades up. Neighbor happened to be in the backyard with his dog and saw the display through a small opening in the trees."

"Did the neighbor have anything else to offer?"

"Yeah, but no opinion on the quality of the relationship between the parents. Never noticed any dispute though."

"Jack's telling the ex? He'd better make that conversation count."

"Yeah. But, Zoe, it's you I'm counting on here."

She knew that. She felt it. It was heavy on her every day.

Zoe and Ray carefully made their way through the room, avoiding the evidence team busy documenting and photographing. The mother had been restrained on the bed, resembling the scene at Nelson's. But this time she hadn't been shot. *No hurry here,* Zoe thought. She been stripped and sexually assaulted, premortem from the looks of the damage. She'd also suffered the same breast mutilation they'd seen in the Hanover and Mickman murders. The bleeding seemed to indicate those wounds were pre-mortem too. Cause of death had yet to be determined, but the strangulation wound, including an apparent fracture of her larynx, left little doubt in Zoe's mind. He'd come at her from the front. There was a gag in the victim's mouth that looked to have been fashioned from the victim's own undergarments. A corner of the sheet had been drawn down over her eyes. No surprises here.

The daughter had been positioned to have a front row seat for the tragic show. She'd been gagged and restrained against a pillar that framed the opening to the master bath, having been tied so tightly that even in death she was still erect. Her eyes, bloodied from hemorrhaging as he'd choked the life out of her, were still open and aimed at the stage. She'd been stripped and mutilated, but there appeared not to have been the first-degree sexual assault. At least not pre-mortem. She did appear to have been strangled, Zoe guessed from behind this time. Nothing covered her eyes, as he'd have wanted her mother to be the last thing she saw.

Zoe fought off the corrosive mix making it's way up. The restraints were identical to the ones used at the hospital, where drunks or demented patients were often bound for their own safety. They could be found all over the hospital, and were easily accessible in the ER.

She made a careful inventory of the personal items on display in the bedroom. Photos documented what had been important to the woman . . . mostly her daughter. There were photos of Hannah as a mop-haired toddler, caught in a candid moment hugging a puppy, delighted. Hannah as a child, probably about eight years old, hand in hand with her mother at the beach. Hannah in school colors, playing soccer. Caught in the act of shooting. Zoe guessed the ball had found its mark. This was a moment they were proud of. Finally, as the teenage Hannah, it was obvious she had inherited her mother's beauty. Striking in her prom dress, an equally attractive young man supported her at the waist.

While Zoe couldn't even imagine what it would be like to have a child, her heart ached at the loss in this room. It wasn't only the loss of two lives; it was what had been lost in the moments leading up to it. She *knew* what had happened, and sickened, wondering if that knowledge even had any value. A mother unable to protect her daughter. It would have been all she'd thought about as she'd been brutalized. The pain would have been trumped by the roaring, desperate need to free her child. To spare her this. She would have welcomed death in exchange for her daughter's safety. But she couldn't even make *that* bargain.

A young woman having to watch her mother die, and at sixteen, old enough to know she'd be next. She may have felt anger, at both her attacker and at her mother's inability to save her. Certainly panic. Zoe wondered how long it had taken this to play out. Had she had time to think? To wonder what had brought this man into their lives? And why?

There were other restless ghosts now, circling Zoe. She wondered about her own mother's final moments.

Zoe squatted, resting her elbows on her knees as she dipped her head again. She felt her brain darken at the edges. Ray was quick to support her.

"You okay?"

"Yeah. I'm all right."

The photographers were working their way through the living room when Zoe joined in. She went straight to the photos on the bookcase. Similar scenes. A candid photo of Anders caught raking leaves in her yard revealed an unadorned beauty. One photo showed the daughter with a man, probably her father, at some kind of ceremony. No other men in the photos. Hannah was clearly the priority in this household.

Zoe made her way around the rest of the house, crossing paths with the photographers, on alert for the same feeling she'd gotten at the Hanover and Mickman sites. This time she hoped to be ready for it. If it was relevant, it had to be here too . . . but she didn't sense it. Too tired maybe? Still, something was off. Maybe it concerned the selection of the victims. She hoped so. If not, Parker had some explaining to do.

"Ray, look at these windows."

"Unlocked. Yeah we know."

"Careless. And very weird in winter."

Zoe pictured again, the possibility of an unforeseen witness to Nelson's murder. The kid. Had it prompted the acting out of this need to make people watch? Had he enjoyed that fateful first night even more with the kid having seen it? If so, it would have played into his fixation perfectly.

But maybe the kid had even more to offer . . . an education. "He may have gotten inside here without her knowing it. Just like the kid."

Ray looked outside at the snow. "We looked. If there were any tracks around her windows . . . their gone now."

CHAPTER TWENTY-NINE
DECEMBER 11 (1:00 AM)

NOTHING BUT A THIN LINE OF police tape kept the media swarm back. The neighbor must have talked.

Ray ventured out to make a brief statement, offering little. The victim's identities were not confirmed, pending notification of relatives. Nor did he confirm that these murders were related to the previous high-profile killings. Ray allowed only for "a possible connection" and "a number of similarities."

Zoe kept mulling the implications of this scene. Everything was consistent with the profile. Working his way toward the ultimate goal, he wasn't there yet. She'd realized it tonight. It'd been foolish to think the Halloween kill would be hard to outdo. Even this was a lame second-best. He couldn't have been completely satisfied with it.

He would have had a temporary rush, forcing the girl to watch her own mother being brutally assaulted and murdered. But then he'd had to kill her. It would have been necessary, but not what he'd have preferred. What he really wanted was for her to *live* with the knowledge, and the scars. He'd rather she become someone who sees the world as he does.

Zoe pictured him experimenting with a desire to have others struggle with his same sadistic need for violence, distorted image of sex, and vacated conscience . . . fooling themselves with new rules, more easily obeyed . . . and governed by the same branding experience.

The Mickman murder, and now this, could each be viewed as half of what he desired. With Mickman he'd sent children home with the image, but he hadn't displayed the sexual violence and they hadn't actually watched her being killed. They might not even understand what they'd seen. And some might be young enough to forget, or allow their parents to remold the memory for them. With Anders, he'd forced the daughter to watch, but having seen him, she'd then had to die.

She thought back to the Hanover scene . . . and her suspicion about the paperboy, and the Mickman display, she'd been right from the start. This wasn't only about killing . . . it was about recruiting.

Parker couldn't possibly be capable of this, she thought, even with the mounting evidence. It was too convenient. And whenever she *tried* to make him fit as the killer, the facts never slid neatly into place. They always required force. Her profile was pointing to someone else.

But he was involved on some level, as his name kept coming up. There could be no coincidences. And tonight it finally made sense. He was a Plan B, a distraction for the cops. They must have brushed up against the killer recently. The repeat interviews, she thought. But why Parker? She had a theory that unfortunately had only to do with Parker having been in the wrong place at the wrong time. Of course Parker wouldn't see it that way, just as she never had. He would feel responsible.

THE FORMALITIES OF THE INTERVIEW were underway. Parker had dismissed the idea of having a lawyer present, and it seemed he'd pushed his personal animosity for Ray aside as well, eager to help. And he wanted Zoe in the room.

"Describe your relationship with both victims, Dr. Parker. Ms. Anders and her daughter, Hannah." Ray sounded impatient. Zoe knew he liked Parker for this.

"I'll be direct. We were lovers, then friends. Our relationship began several years ago when I met her at the Rosalux Gallery. We shared an appreciation for one of the artists on exhibit and struck up a conversation. Things progressed from there." He paused, waiting out the emotion clearly threatening his voice. "But I'm afraid I didn't know her daughter at all. Liv was adamant about not bringing another man into the household while Hannah was still living there."

"And why was that, Dr. Parker?" Ray sounded too eager.

"You have to understand about Liv, that Hannah was her whole world. She was protective. Having worked as a therapist, she was familiar with the damage caused by predators who seek out divorcees and widows with children. It's often the children they're really after. She'd also witnessed the upheaval that any man can cause in the life of a child asked to welcome him into the home. She vowed not to risk that, and put her own needs on hold when it came to protecting Hannah. She was selfless in that respect."

"Not so selfless she didn't want you around though?"

"It's not what you're thinking, about her, or our relationship. Hannah was with her father half the time. Those were the only occasions when I was invited into her home. Even then, we mainly met at my place. It was simpler that way. She never complicated things by having Hannah meet me. She didn't want her daughter to spend even one minute worrying or wondering about a second marriage."

"So it seems she might not have trusted you then."

"You can think that if you like. Your opinion of me really doesn't matter. And, yes, she did say once that the home of a single mother with children was like summer camp. It attracted both the worst and the best of men. I can assure you that she viewed me as well intentioned, but she also knew that even a well-meaning suitor would disrupt her daughter's life. I certainly respected that."

Kaj drew in a deep breath, and his eyes softened on Zoe. "But she had needs. I don't know how else to say this . . . I helped her with those needs, and she with mine. I reminded her that she was a desirable, beautiful woman, not just a mother. The soundness of our relationship is evident in the fact that we remained good friends after ending our intimacy."

"And why did she break it off with you? What happened?"

He looked back toward Ray. "It was by mutual agreement. We'd been seen at various places in public. I have a relatively high profile in this town, and she'd been worried about what her daughter might overhear. It also concerned her that her ex-husband might use it against her, with their daughter."

Ray leaned back and kicked out his legs, taking up space in the room, claiming territory. "You know what I think? I'll bet you just broke it off when she wouldn't let you weasel your way into their lives. My guess? You decided to cut your losses and move on to the next one."

"Dr. Parker, do you mind if I ask a few questions?" Zoe moved in quickly as Kaj's eyes flashed at Ray.

"Go ahead. Let's move on to something you can use. Otherwise, I'm of no value here. This is a waste of time."

"Can you tell me anything about the father?" She leaned toward him as she said it, hoping to calm with a close physical presence.

"Liv was discrete. And the devotion to her daughter she extended to her ex, whether he deserved that loyalty or not. I can't overemphasize the degree to which she wanted to shield her daughter from something she viewed as her own failure. It was always her policy never to speak ill of him, even when it may have been tempting, to preserve a good father-daughter relationship.

"The only time she suggested in my presence that there might have been tension between them was when we worried together about his using knowledge of our relationship to diminish her in the eyes of her daughter. If that was a possibility, I didn't want to be used by anyone to cause trouble for her.

"I used to think that maybe she could have given Hannah a little more credit for wanting her to be happy, for understanding, but, of course, it wasn't my call. I had no choice but to respect her decisions."

Another deep breath, "So, no, I'm afraid I can't offer much in regard to her ex. I'm sorry. I thought I'd have more. Maybe this was a mistake, I'm beginning to wonder if this is helping at all or just wasting precious time. Time you could be using to track down her killer."

Zoe jumped in again, separating Ray from his wisecrack. "Actually, this is very helpful, Dr. Parker. Do you know of any *other* men in her life?"

Kaj's eyes looked through Zoe this time. He winced as if in physical pain. Ray and Zoe waited patiently for an answer. It looked to Zoe as though he was trying to think, to remember whom she might have been seeing.

He finally spoke. "There was no one else. I'm sure of it."

In his eyes, Zoe saw that instead of remembering, he'd been trying to forget. . . the further tragedy in Liv Anders's life. She'd forced herself to give up the one man she'd wanted more than anything to be with. She saw it, but still questioned it.

"How can you be so sure? There *must* have been others." Zoe couldn't imagine denying herself that.

"You still don't understand her, do you? She was devoted *and* disciplined."

His image of Anders matched the impression Zoe had gotten from inside the home. But Zoe wasn't sure what kind of woman could live that way. Zoe knew nothing of having children, or of committed relationships for that matter. He was right . . . she didn't understand Anders. But she was curious.

"And what was your reaction?"

"I did my part not to make things difficult for her. Essentially, I backed off. But my *reaction*? What do you think? I loved her." Zoe could see his eyes fill. He looked quickly away from Zoe. "It was unbearably hard to keep my distance. And if I hadn't, she and her daughter would be alive today."

"What in the hell do you mean by that, Parker? She'd be alive if she hadn't dumped you? Pissed you off?"

Zoe quickly placed a hand on Kaj's arm, and squeezed, as he leaned in toward Ray, "You fucking piece of shit! I mean that had she been with me I could have protected her. What else? Wouldn't you wonder the same thing? Wouldn't you regret that?"

Ray sat up nervously in his chair, seeming to look at Zoe to keep going. She hoped he *was* beginning to wonder, and that he could feel her admonishing him to at least consider the possibility of Parker's innocence.

At the onset of the interview, they'd immediately established that Dr. Parker claimed to have been home in bed the night of the murder. There'd been no one with him to verify that, and given her theory, that was exactly what she'd expected. Zoe decided to venture back to the first murder. There was another angle, and tonight she felt even more confident about it.

"I want you to think carefully about something else. It's about Julia Nelson's neighborhood. Did you know anyone other than Nelson from that neighborhood? Think especially of people you would also have intersected with at work, but don't limit it to that. Anyone who could have knowledge of your schedule, or access to it, would be especially important."

"Well, I suppose I probably know a lot of people from that area. You know it's often referred to as 'pill hill' because of all the physicians who live there. But I don't know where most of the people I see at work every day actually live. I'm sure I can find out though."

"One more thing. When you think about the names, make note of anyone who might have known of your relationship with Nelson in particular, and perhaps Anders too."

All three silently considered the implications of what Zoe was saying. She was pointing in a direction away from Parker, but it didn't exactly soften things. Of course Parker already blamed himself for not having been there to protect Anders, but Zoe knew the further idea of being causally related to her death would be a tremendous burden. That he might in any way be responsible, even if tangentially, in the selection of these victims would be almost too much.

It was clear in his pained expression and slow, deliberate movements. The simple things . . . rising out of a chair, walking toward the door . . . were suddenly things he had to concentrate on. There was no effortless "autopilot." Everything required thought. Everything was hard. Zoe thought it best to help *him* home this time.

When they'd reached his car, Zoe made the offer. "Why don't you let me drive this time? I'd like to see you home."

He managed a tired smile. "Thank you, Zoe. But I assure you; I'm no worse off than you must be right now. I would, however, be concerned about you driving home after I drop you off at the hospital. You're tired and the road conditions are terrible."

"What time do you work tomorrow? Same as me?"

"Yes, 7:00 a.m., but I'd understand if you need to call in sick."

Oh, Christ, Zoe thought. Worrying about me again. She had to figure out a way to keep him from driving home alone.

"How about you let me drive to the hospital and we can sack out there? We'll both catch more sleep that way, maybe even three whole hours."

He gave her the keys.

CHAPTER THIRTY
DECEMBER 11 (3:00 A.M.)

THE RIDE WAS SLIPPERY AND TENSE FROM Zoe's perspective, but Parker didn't seem to notice. He'd fallen easily into a sleep . . . or trance . . . or something . . . almost immediately after settling back in his seat.

He'd laid a hand on Zoe's thigh, and left it there. If he was nervous about Zoe's ability to drive in the conditions, it didn't show. His hand twitched occasionally, squeezed. What was he thinking? Dreaming? His hand on her was distracting, but felt good, even if only forgotten there in his sleep.

It was 3:00 a.m. when Zoe pulled into the ramp and gently placed her hand over his, the hand that had remained on her thigh. Her heart breaking, right along with his, she understood the loss, the guilt, and the urgent need to act.

"Dr. Parker? We're here. Are you okay?" She was starting to wonder if maybe he wasn't.

"Please. Call me Kaj. We've been through too much tonight to pretend formalities. And, yes, I'm okay. Let's find a call room and get some rest. Tomorrow the roads will still be icy. There'll be even more snow, and a killer still on the loose. Too many ways to fill an ER."

They searched to the fourth floor before finding an empty call room. Apparently others had decided to ride the blizzard out at work.

"Choose your bunk, top or bottom, then get some rest. I need to wash the crime scene off first." Zoe grabbed a pair of fresh scrubs and headed straight for the shower.

She turned the temperature up as high as her skin would tolerate. Leaning her head forward against the wall, the warm stream ran over her head and back, washing away the cold and the acrid odor of death. Lifting her face to the spray, she closed her eyes and let the tears merge with the soothing water. She shuddered at his tug on her . . . and had to admit that it had been there all along, since the first day they'd met.

She should be thinking about Anders. Instead, the lazy vulnerability she felt with him infuriated her. *He* infuriated her. His pull, the promise of him, was so seductive, so enticing, and so *damn* distracting. Why couldn't it be uncomplicated, like she was used to? Like he was probably used to? But instead it felt *very* complicated.

In fact it was only a shared pain they had in common now. Nothing to build off. Confusing everything would be a huge mistake.

Her breath left her in a sudden rush as his hands found her hips. He pulled in close behind her, his mouth finding the nape of her neck. Water, slippery and warm, was the only thing between them. She found only a weak voice, as she fought for air, "No."

"Yes." His mouth worked its way slowly down her back, falling to his knees as he spun her around. "Oh, yes."

She found herself pushed up against the wall, as he focused everything on her, bringing her to the edge. Her legs buckled, and he lifted her, pressing even harder against the wall. His mouth met hers with a conquering force as she led him in, and with each thrust her lungs emptied. She wrapped her legs around his waist and fell into his slow, deep rhythm, shuddering as the release feathered over her in waves.

Suffocating steam met her lungs, as she pulled hard for air. Holding tight to him, gasping, she opened her eyes to find him moving them onto the cool sheets of a small bed that barely contained their rolling tangle of limbs. Her body rose to meet his hands as they explored her hips, and the small of her back… searching for every inch of flesh that responded. His mouth teased around her eyes, until he stopped, and lifted to look at her.

She met his eyes, and seeing nothing more than a wild, reckless, insane danger, she didn't look away. Neither did she search them for promises, as he paused for what seemed an eternity to Zoe. His breath quickened as he touched the scar at her collarbone. His fingers moved up the arch of her neck and then traced her full lips. She stayed with his eyes, sensing the war within. She felt it too. Blood spilled in death, merging with their own… alive with craving. Blending as one undeniable impulse.

"Zoe, I need you." He leaned down to kiss her gently, reassuringly, then plunged forcefully. Her scream escaped into his shoulder as she rode his pounding

crescendo. Pain and pleasure were now indistinguishable in either of them. His sti-
fled moan followed by quick hard breaths matched hers in a synchronous release.
He fell into her, and then quickly shifted off to the side, allowing her to breathe. The
beasts were tamed, in both of them ... at least for now, and they silently fell into a
deep sleep.

ZOE WOKE FIRST, hearing the shared bathroom being used by the occupant next
door. It yanked her out of the illusion of their night together and into the reality of
their impossible relationship. Trying to quietly pull away, she felt his hand grab her
wrist.

"Not yet."

"Listen, this was a mistake," Zoe countered, and gave him the same look she'd
given him so long ago, when he'd tried to tend to her bruised face.

He held tight, and Zoe thought she saw a look of recognition on his face, as
if he'd just now come to understand something. "This was no mistake, Zoe. What
are you afraid of? It can't be me."

"You told me last night that you needed me. Hey, I get that. I do. I understand
soothing pain in this way. But let's get something straight. You didn't need *me*. You
needed what we *did*. It was nothing more than a shower shimmy, and we can't let
it happen again."

It was a low blow, but one she was sure would separate them. Stinging insults
usually had a way of doing that. And if she didn't have the resolve, she'd push him
into saying no.

She pulled harder, but he only responded by dragging her down on top of
him, his eyes inches from hers. "It was far more than that."

Good, she'd hurt him.

"And what about you, Zoe? What is it that *you* need? To be honest, it surprises
me. *You* surprise me. I'm not used to needing anyone in this way. But as much as it
confounds me, and as much as I've resisted, I know that I need *you*. I now know
that much."

The look in his eyes ... and her reaction to it ... caught her off guard. She even
made a lame attempt to soften things. "Okay, maybe I needed it too. But that still
doesn't make it right ... between us. This can't happen again."

She felt his grip loosen, and jerked free. His eyes were all that held her now. Zoe shook her head and looked away.

When the water started she reached into the bathroom for her scrubs, hoping to slip in and out undetected. But the shower's occupant noticed and didn't seem to mind. He leaned out and greeted Zoe.

"Hi, Zoe. Sleep good?" He grinned.

Apparently they'd not been as quiet as she thought.

"Yeah, Alan, it was great. You?"

"Can't complain." He made no attempt to cover himself, and didn't hide his pleasure at getting an eyeful of Zoe either. The medical crowd, she shook her head, a different breed.

"Well, uh, sorry to jump in here, but I needed some fresh scrubs. Probably see you at lunch, eh?"

He took another long look at her and raised his eyebrows. "I certainly hope so."

She backed out of the bathroom and found Kaj standing, dressed only in a pair of scrub pants that hung loosely at his hips. His taut muscles were clearly outlined, and his skin damp with her scent. She needed to punch a wall … and it looked like he felt the same way.

CHAPTER THIRTY-ONE
DECEMBER 11 (MIDDAY)

T HE ER FILLED QUICKLY, AGAIN PRIMARILY weather-related injury and illness. MIs, MVAs, and, of course, just for Rex... an elderly man falling from his roof after suffering an MI while shoveling snow.

Zoe was just glad to be busy. It didn't help that every time they came within six feet of each other, she found herself breathing in his scent, their mix, the aroma of what they'd made last night. How could she think that was a mistake?

It just was. And so was the tension between them with every interaction. It told her that he was asking his own questions. But there was only one answer... no.

Zoe needed to refocus. Even while hating the whole idea, she decided on hypnosis. But there was something else... and if she were right, the latest murders had another purpose, one the killer would have to wait for. There'd be time to turn his plan against him. While it would be risky, it might also work. And she was feeling desperate to give Ray *something*. Probably shouldn't tell him though.

She managed to put in a call to Camilla during a brief moment of calm in between patients, finding her at her rural home, unable to get to work.

"Completely snowed in. Nothing's moving out here except snowmobiles."

"You call that an excuse? Dr. Peterson, you know... from Neurology? He made it in on cross-country skis."

"He lives near you, Zoe. I'd call that do-able on skis. I live twenty miles out."

"Camilla, why in the hell did you move anyway? I miss you." It was said through a teasing pout.

"Oh, I don't know, Zoe, other than this beautiful lake I'm looking at right now, the unbelievable sunsets, the privacy, and the beauty of the woods? Gee, I don't know."

"Come on, Camilla, we've got lakes right here *in* Minneapolis, not to mention *the* River. You make enough to pay for privacy. And hell, sunsets? They're great all over."

"Well, there is the outstanding school district here, and safe neighborhood. Great place to raise a kid."

There was a long stunned silence before Zoe finally found her voice.

"Are we talking theoretically here, Camilla?"

Camilla chuckled, apparently proud of having caught her completely guard.

"Oh, wow, really?" Zoe didn't know what to say. She didn't have any close friends with kids. Didn't much like kids either.

"Yes, really. Due the last week in April."

Zoe knew she was supposed to be happy for her, and *was* happy, but the words weren't there. "That's great, I guess." *Change the subject Zoe.* "How are you feeling?" Health issues during pregnancy... something she could handle.

"I'm feeling just fine, Zoe. But you're talking to a psychiatrist here. Take your time getting used to the idea," she laughed. "Meanwhile, I'm thrilled about it. We both are."

"Am I that transparent? Or just that predictable?"

"Both."

Zoe rolled her eyes and laughed. "That I am. Sorry Camilla. This is really great news. I'm just surprised. I guess it's been a while since we've had a chance to talk. We've both been so busy."

"Yes, and you with the added burden of your MPD work. I've been trying to follow it through the media, but it rises then dies just as quickly. How have you managed that?"

"Ray and Jack have been doing a good job of putting a lid on things. The string of arsons helped distract the media too. Quite frankly, we don't have much to go on. Or have too much, depending on how you look at it.

"The way I see it, the killer has probably been hiding in plain site, smack in the middle of too many suspects. But we must have brushed up against him in some way, and now he's taking cover by directing attention toward someone else, someone specific. I think he chose his last victim primarily for that purpose. At this point, I need your help if you're willing."

"What have you got in mind, Zoe?"

"I'd like to try hypnosis in review of the crime scenes. It's as if I've felt a predator... or prey... I'm not even sure which. But he's given me opportunities, little glimpses, maybe even teased me, and yet I can't seem to find his trail."

Zoe paused, thinking back to the crime scenes, and tried to explain what she'd felt. "Camilla, imagine a scent from somewhere close. It's faint, but it teases you, and when you turn to locate it, it's gone. Poof. As though it only exists if you try not to look for it. And any tracks left fill in as quickly as they're made. He's there Camilla, waiting for me. I need you to help me catch him."

"Zoe … have you had much sleep?"

Zoe exhaled through a reluctant laugh. "No. Not much for the past two days. It shows, eh?"

"Yeah, a little bit, sweetie."

Zoe cringed. First Kelly, now Camilla. What were with all the endearments and nicknames? She let it go. "I am tired. I'm going to try for some major sleep tonight. Can we meet tomorrow? Name the time, and I'll get an okay for an hour away. I suddenly find that I have 'connections.'"

"I'll call you first thing in the morning. I'll have to see what they did with my schedule, now that I've missed a day. But don't worry, we can always stay late and do it then."

"Thanks, Cam."

"Now get some sleep, sweetie. I'll see you tomorrow."

Zoe hung up the phone, still connected by their warm friendship. A rare and fragile thing for her.

CHAPTER THIRTY-TWO
DECEMBER 11 (EVENING)

ZOE ENJOYED HER RIDE HOME THROUGH the deserted streets, letting her Jeep fishtail around turns and plow through snowdrifts. She drove under a full vanilla moon, hanging low and large against the matte surface of the evening's gunmetal sky. The clouds had finally been carried away by the unnerving wind. Left behind was an absolute calm. Every noise echoed sharply off the cavernous downtown buildings, and the hollow sound of snow under her wheels made the temperature at well below zero.

Zoe gunned the Jeep until her warm house welcomed her. Shoveling could wait till morning. She took a run at the snowdrift and made it into the garage…an official end to her day. No dinner. No booze. No shower. Just bed. Her last foggy thought before falling asleep was that maybe this time she should just throw her sheets out and buy new ones. Might be simpler all around.

KAJ'S TASK KEPT HIM AT WORK, and it wasn't an easy one. There were a few references in the local paper, pertaining to her time on the force. She'd been involved in several high profile cases; at least one requiring the discharge of her weapon and the resulting "paid administrative leave" that routinely followed an officer-involved shooting.

Kaj skipped those, searching for what came before. It was the French-Canadian accent that finally produced results. He thought to check newspaper archives from Ontario and Manitoba. Several small papers referenced a Zoe Lawrence. None contained good news.

Children hide in attic while mother killed

Clearwater Bay – Genevieve Lawrence was murdered in a home invasion yesterday. The daughter, Zoe Lawrence, reported hearing at least one man struggle with the victim, as she and her brother hid in the home's attic. Authorities have verified the account but are reporting few leads.

Genevieve Lawrence is survived by her husband Roland, and children Zoe and Daniel Lawrence.

As Zoe slept soundly, the phantoms circled Kaj instead. What kind of vivid memories did Zoe wrestle with? She understood, as he did. Yet she'd revealed nothing. And he'd used her.

Another brief follow-up article reported that police were frustrated at having no further leads or suspects. There was nothing more until six years later.

Father and son murdered, daughter abducted

Clearwater Bay – In what police are describing as more than a coincidence, a local family has been hit by tragedy again. The Lawrence family, having lost the mother in a shocking murder six years ago, suffered yet another violent intrusion. Both the father, Roland Lawrence, and his son, Daniel, were brutally murdered during a home invasion at their rural farmhouse. Anonymous sources describe the scene as "a bloodbath." Police confirm that the daughter is missing but is not considered a suspect. They say evidence at the scene points to the girl having been abducted after the slayings. There is currently an APB out for the daughter, identified as Zoe Lawrence. Anyone with information is asked to call the Clearwater Bay authorities.

Police do not believe the daughter was a willing participant. Authorities are not revealing what ties this episode may have to the previous murder, but say they have reason to believe the two are linked.

The victims were discovered quickly after a neighbor called police reporting the sound of shotgun blasts from the house. Authorities say the crime scene might not have been discovered for days had a neighbor not alerted the police. The abduction took place on the night of the daughter's graduation from high school. Authorities indicate there are no surviving relatives. Zoe Lawrence is the last in her family.

The last in her family. Zoe's picture was a grainy graduation photo. What had they meant by referencing Zoe as not a willing participant? Had she been living under a cloud of suspicion? Kaj thought of Zoe now, of her distrust and distance, of the sharp elbows and toughness, but also her choice of careers. Who she was, had been forged in a fiery childhood crucible. She could easily have gone down a far more destructive path, but had chosen not to.

No wonder she'd buried her past. He wasn't sure anyone but the murderers could possibly know what she'd gone through. And perhaps that was a big part of the problem for Zoe.

The same edition of the paper included another article referring to Zoe's abduction and to an accident occurring that same night.

Policeman's family killed in car crash

Clearwater Bay – Local policeman, Scott Whitehorse, suffered the loss of his wife and three children in a tragic car accident Saturday night. While Whitehorse responded to a homicide call at the Lawrence family farm, his own family traveled in a vehicle that was clipped by a speeding car and sent flying into deep water off the Mission Bridge. According to witnesses, a dark sedan sped to pass the family on the narrow bridge, cutting them off when an oncoming car forced it over. The dead are identified as Vivienne Whitehorse and her three children, Lance, Tom, and Marcy. Authorities have suggested that the speeding car may be linked to the abduction of Zoe Lawrence and are hopeful the connection will produce information leading to her safe recovery. The vehicle is described as an older model sedan, dark in color, blue or black, and would have damage to the right rear fender area. Anyone with information is asked to call the Clearwater Bay authorities.

As Kaj knew the outcome, Zoe survived. He assumed the crash had generated leads. Though it had taken the loss of more people, at least they'd gotten the description of a car. He also knew that the involvement of a police officer's family would highly motivate the authorities to make this a priority.

The next article ran a month later. A whole month. He read on.

Lawrence found alive!

Firestrike – In what was described as a torture chamber, Zoe Lawrence was discovered along with the body of the homeowner, her longtime therapist, John Pender. Her condition is described as fair by hospital spokesman Walter Kennedy. Police are refusing to release further details on the girl's condition but indicate that she identified another unknown assailant as participating in her abduction. Lawrence had been forced from her nearby rural Clearwater Bay home a month prior. Her father and brother were murdered during the abduction. Police believe this event is linked to the murder of the mother six years earlier, but are refusing to reveal what evidence connects the two home invasions. An astute neighbor observed unusual activity at the rural home, and recalled the description of a car thought to be involved. Police credit her with saving the girls life. When asked to comment on the role of the therapist in the abduction, police simply discounted any link between Pender and the previous murder six years ago. Pender's family was notified of his death at their cabin near Minaki, where they had gone for an extended vacation the day before the abduction. They have refused all calls for interviews. A college fund is being set up for Lawrence through the Clearwater Bay bank.

Was her therapist involved all along? And if so, how many sessions had she sat through, only to be manipulated… and at such an impressionable age. What had he filled her head with?

The conversation between Zoe and Kelly now made sense. He didn't have to read on to know the second kidnapper was never found. But he continued. It was a Canadian paper with a Minneapolis source.

Lawrence successful in her new life

Minneapolis, Minnesota – Zoe Lawrence, the tragic victim of a kidnapping and survivor of the murder of her entire family at the hands of two assailants, one now dead, is currently living in the United States. At this time she is a successful doctor in the Twin Cities area of Minnesota. An exhaustive nationwide search for the remaining suspect failed to yield any trace of the man. The suspect is also believed to have been responsible for the tragic deaths of the family of former Clearwater Bay policeman Scott Whitehorse. Whitehorse could not be reached for comment. Local authorities report that his wallet was found recently at the edge of the Mission Bridge, the site of his family's death.

He is believed to have drowned in an apparent suicide. In an ironic twist, another peripherally associated person, the wife of John Pender, one of the abductors, was also involved in a home invasion incident about two months after the death of her husband. Authorities report that Mrs. Pender was attacked and held against her will for several hours while her children were away but refused to cooperate with police in the investigation. While the file remains open and police would like to make the identification and apprehension of her abductor a priority, authorities admit that the case has grown cold, and Lawrence's survival may be the best they can hope for now.

Okay, so that was odd. The article offered no new information other than Zoe having overcome her ordeal to lead a successful life. But there were no feel-good details to make it even worth writing about. Not even mention of Zoe's years as a police officer, an aspect that might have actually been of interest. What was the point? And why a year ago? Who were the sources? Did she have relatives she didn't know about?

That was the end of it. No further articles containing any reference to a Zoe Lawrence. He now had knowledge he wasn't supposed to have, information that she didn't trust to even her closest friends. He had to be patient, and careful.

He walked to the window and leaned his forehead against the cold glass. Closing his eyes against the pounding behind them, the glass clouded at his long exhale. When he finally opened his eyes, he wrote a name in the frost.

The gravity of Zoe and Kelly's discussion sunk in. They were referring to the kidnapper, and had reason to believe he was coming for her again.

Kaj jumped the stairs down to Kelly's office and was met with a locked door. He summoned a night janitor to the administrative offices, and gaining entry there instead, pulled Kelly's file.

The full name he got, Kelly Dumonceau, but the address he didn't. The only means of contacting him outside of work seemed to be a post office box. He ran the halls back to his office, and began his search. He'd call in chips if he had to. He had connections.

Chapter Thirty-Three
December 12 (Early Morning)

ZOE WOKE IN THE SAME POSITION SHE'D fallen asleep in . . . still smelling of hospital, sweat, and sex. Relieved that she'd been able to sleep so soundly, she stumbled into the shower and stripped her thoughts down to their essentials.

She was still convinced that the killer was someone from Nelson's neighborhood with ties to the hospital. Part of choosing his latest victim also involved deflecting suspicion toward Parker. She was sure of it. And she made the decision to use it, use Parker even, to bring the killers attention toward her. She was sure Parker wouldn't question her actions or even care why she was suddenly willing to accept his attention. He wanted her, that's all that mattered. She could only hope that it would make her the next target. Meanwhile, there was Camilla.

She threw the paper and an energy bar into her Jeep and then grabbed a shovel to dig her way out. That would have to be her morning workout.

KAJ HAD NEVER LEFT THE HOSPITAL, and was waiting for Kelly outside his office. The two exchanged wary looks as Kaj pushed off from the wall, waiting for Kelly to unlock the door. Kelly ushered him in.

"What can I do for you, Dr. Parker? It's not often that doctors find their way down to my office. Is it a maintenance complaint? I have good staff, but some of my custodians are still new and in need of further training. So I'm always glad to have things brought to my attention."

"No complaint. But I'm not the only doctor who's been spending time down here, am I?"

He watched Kelly's face harden briefly, and then brighten.

"Are you referring to my friend Zoe? Yes, she and I enjoy some coffee and Scrabble now and then. Can I offer you a cup? I was just about to get it going." He went behind the screen to fill the coffee pot.

Kaj moved to keep Kelly in his line of sight, and noticed the cot along with all the makings of a small apartment. "Sure, I've heard rumors of the coffee down here. How far back do you and Dr. Lawrence go?"

"Oh, I guess it's been at least several years now. When she used to come here for her medical school rotations, I offered her a place to safely store her bike. There'd been a rash of bike thefts, and she owns a fairly expensive one. I didn't want to see it stolen." Kelly turned to face Kaj and his next question.

"So that would be about when you were hired on here as head of maintenance? The same time Dr. Lawrence started here?"

"Why, I guess it probably would. We did start here at about the same time. I was acquainted with her before that though. I worked briefly in maintenance at the police department while Zoe was there, but only for a about a year. At that time Zoe and I weren't really what you'd call friends, just knew each other well enough to say hello to. It *is* where I noticed her bike though." Kelly moved to pour two cups. He handed one to Kaj.

Too convenient. Kaj breathed in the aroma, and then sampled the coffee. "Good." He took another swig. "I like to think I'm Zoe's friend too, Kelly. I worry about her just as you do. And I'm especially concerned after overhearing the conversation between the two of you when Shep was brought in." He set down his coffee. "Is she in any danger?" He watched Kelly's breathing deepen.

"You know just about as much as I do then. I admit, recent events have me a little worried about her safety, but you heard Zoe. She's not interested in thinking about it."

Kelly sat down on the sofa. "Take a chair if you like."

Kaj pulled a chair from the table. "You seemed quite worried. Why?"

"Listen, Doctor Parker, I care about her, that's all. She's like a daughter."

Kaj had two theories about Kelly. He decided to test one of them, the one he hoped was correct. "When did you come to the U.S.?"

"About ten years ago."

"You followed Zoe about four years after she moved here then?" Kaj watched Kelly for any sign of surprise. He got none. Only a matter-of-fact response.

"Well, let's see now. I know that she came here to attend the U of M as an undergraduate student. She told me about that. Then there was her brief time on the force, followed by med school and now the residency . . . so," he did the math on his fingers, "that would be about right."

"Did you know her in Canada?"

"No, but I think that finding out we were both transplants brought us closer. It's a comfort you know, and she has no family here."

Kaj decided on the direct approach. Kelly was good at bullshitting . . . a quick lie followed by a lot of chitchat. "I looked at the records. The Kelly Dumonceau who came here from Canada ten years ago would be a thirty-five-year-old woman right now. I'm not looking at a woman here, Kelly. And you're certainly not thirty-five." He saw the surprise now, albeit brief.

"I don't know what records you looked at, but you've got it all wrong. Beats me how, but there must be some mistake."

"You sure about that? Somehow, you knew her in Canada didn't you?"

"I don't know what in the hell you're talking about here, Parker, but I met her here, in Minneapolis. This is starting to piss me off. If you share a concern for Zoe, that's one thing, but if you've got some wild-ass crazy idea about me, that's another. You've got it all wrong. And I've got work to do."

He stood to usher Kaj out, but then seemed to reconsider.

"Listen, if you want to know about Zoe, all I can tell you is that she's had a few mishaps lately, on her bike and at a party, that I found to be a little too convenient if you know what I mean. When that Shep kid went down at her place, I knew for sure *that* wasn't a random coincidence. There were ball bearings strewn all over her back step. It had to have been meant for her. Shep just happened to walk out that door instead. They've all been things that I doubt were intended to seriously hurt her, more like pranks, but she *could* have been seriously hurt.

"Of course she's minimizing everything. Now if *you* have any idea what might be going on, I'd love to hear it, because she's not talking."

Kaj knew, and he wouldn't be talking either. All three of them knew, but no one could talk. Not yet.

Zoe cruised in and pulled up short as she handed Kelly the paper. "What are *you* doing down here, Kaj?"

Surprised, he rose to greet her with a kiss and was even more surprised when she didn't pull away. He lifted an eyebrow and pulled her close. "Just heard the rumors about your friend's coffee and thought I'd bum a cup. It's good."

"Did he actually tell you it was *his* coffee?" She swung around. "Kelly! I'm the supplier here. Now that makes three of us who have to keep the secret, or I'll go broke."

Kelly and Kaj traded uncomfortable smiles as Zoe went for a cup. As Zoe led him out the door, Kaj looked back to see Kelly throw the newspaper at the wall.

CHAPTER THIRTY-FOUR
DECEMBER 12 (7:00 AM)

AS THEY MADE THEIR WAY TOWARD THE ER, Zoe slowed and slipped her arm around his waist. She felt him tense, and then he steered them into an empty conference room.

"Are you sure you want to do this?" He tilted her chin up to face him squarely.

Zoe shrugged, and smiled. "We're consenting adults. Doesn't bother me. Are *you* worried? Think it might not look good for you?"

"Zoe, what do you take me for? You can't possibly believe I don't see through this. And I won't let you do it. It's too dangerous."

"Listen, Parker, you can enjoy the ride if you want, but either way we're now officially an item. Kelly saw it. Others suspect it. And even if you choose not to cooperate, they'll still be talk of it. I'll make sure. Besides, people always believe what they want to believe."

He seemed to be struggling. "After what happened the other night, you have every right to use me now. But to deliberately put your life in jeopardy? No. I won't be used so that you can insert yourself into a madman's fantasy."

Her stance widened, ready for a fight. She was all cop now.

"You seem to think you have some kind of say over what I do. Not true, Parker. And I don't need your cooperation to make this play. Got it?" She stepped toward him, but softened. "I've only got three leads, and I'll do this, with or without you."

"Three? What are the others?"

"I can't talk specifics with you. Besides, you must realize that you're still considered a suspect by my colleagues. And be warned, I'm sure the killer wants it that way. The less you're involved, the better."

Kaj paced toward the door and back, then roughly grabbed her toward him. "You don't want me involved. but you're willing to use me to precipitate an attack on you? Listen, now it's time for you to get something straight. I'll cooperate with you, but ..."

She smirked, and he looked even angrier.

"Yes...I'll cooperate...but not because I want to bed you. I won't be manipulated in that way either. I'll cooperate only so that I can remain close. If we're an *item*, as you say, it'll be expected of me. And I don't intend to let any harm come to you."

Oh, Christ. Zoe knew she'd been used by him, and didn't really care, it had been mutual... but she hadn't counted on this. "Maybe it's best that we just call ourselves an item, and I'll take it from there. I don't want to complicate things here. And anyway..."

He interrupted what she knew to be bullshit. "I don't think you've thought this through well enough Dr. Lawrence. There are several ways I can bring your little game to an end...and you know it. I'm not completely powerless in this situation. You want this to happen? Then here's the deal...you accept my presence in your life, and I *will* hear the specifics. Start now."

Zoe drew in a deep breath and considered her choices. At least he was open to it, and wouldn't pull the rug out from under her plan. He could, and she *did* know it.

"Okay...for now. It's all I've got. First, I plan to see Camilla about hypnosis. There's something about the crime scenes that I can't seem to shake loose. I'm hoping she can help. Second, your mention of the Rosalux Gallery rang a bell. One of the victims served part time at Lorna's Table. It's near the Gallery, isn't it?"

"Yes, so?"

"I want the wait-staff to get a look at Hanover's picture. I can't figure out how he chose either Mickman or Hanover, but if there's a link there, it could prove important.

"I already think that Nelson was chosen because the killer lived near her, knew quite a lot about her, maybe also worked with her. It's proximity and convenience. He may have developed fantasies involving her."

Zoe paused and debated saying it, "I'm sorry, but the fact that you happened to be her lover provided an emergency escape hatch for the guy. He realized he could deflect attention on you if we got too close.

"The disc is the strange part though. One theory is that the girl in that cube before it was discovered was the missing kid. She and Lucy might have taken it while robbing Nelson, and she wanted to come clean with it ... as evidence. Another theory is that the killer may have found the disc at the time of Nelson's murder and held on to it in order to frame you if need be, then found a way to plant it in the ER so that I'd find it. The fact that it didn't surface until the second round of interviews makes me think he's on that list. But it's a long list. And there's no physical evidence of anyone's involvement except you.

"He's also got connections to the hospital too, I'm sure of it. Somehow, he has access to a lot of information about you. I think he knows your schedule, and he's tapped into the rumor mill here. Knows the women you date. I'm even confident he chose his times for the other murders to coincide with the likelihood of your not having alibis for them ... to keep that option open. But regardless of who left that disc, I think you were a plan B for him from day one."

She reached a hand to his. "As hard as it may be for you to accept, Anders was chosen to make sure the attention was still on you."

She saw the pained expression she'd expected, and added quickly, "But it wasn't your fault. You could never have seen this coming and shouldn't even think of blaming yourself. Now it's my job to turn it against him. Make him think we're looking at you, yet need more convincing. Our new relationship should lend credibility to an ambivalence surrounding you as a suspect, and provide him with a new target ... me.

"Dead, I'd no longer be a threat. And we'd have you as the killer, leaving him to move on and kill elsewhere."

"Who else is going to know about this reckless scheme of yours?"

"I haven't decided yet. I thought about telling Ray, but he's already convinced that I'm soft on you. It won't surprise him to see we're an item. I might just leave it at that. The fewer people who know the truth, the greater likelihood it'll work."

"Be careful, Zoe. You might just be surprised by what the truth really is." He drew in close, lifting her face to his and took her mouth in a violent kiss.

Zoe yielded, but there was something else, more than passion in it. Another time and place, it might have felt right. But it didn't just then. She pushed away, uncomfortable with the image of a dog marking its territory. Looking at him, questioning, she began to doubt her plan.

"You made the deal. You're mine now." He went back for more. But this time it was tender, and she fell into it. They were late getting to the ER.

CHAPTER THIRTY-FIVE
DECEMBER 12 (MIDDAY)

INCOMINGS TO THE ER HAD SLOWED to a trickle, leaving everyone amazed . . . but bored. They'd even borrowed Kelly's Scrabble game to pass some time in between admits. Zoe couldn't remember a time, ever, when it had been this relaxed in the ER. If only Camilla were available. But she was still too swamped with patients she'd had to reschedule because of the blizzard, so they'd decided to meet after dinner. Wishing she could do something productive with her unexpected free time, Zoe went to work anyway.

"Hey, Marty. What's this I hear about you remembering someone at the fireworks? Got yourself an alibi, eh?" Zoe teased, but almost wished she hadn't when she saw him look uncomfortably toward Mal. Busted.

"Uh, yeah. Hey, I should get back to the pharmacy now. It's slow in there too, but I should still be a presence. Don't want them slacking off like we are." He smiled.

"Wait. You live near Nelson's place, right?"

"Yeah. That's why I was so glad I remembered seeing her at the fireworks."

Her. Hmmm. He wasn't giving up a name with Mal there. Maybe it *was* for real. Had he actually hooked up with that siren and didn't want Mal to know? Marty continued to surprise her. "How's that?"

"Well, living so close to her and all, it made me really uncomfortable not being able to account for that evening. And when we remembered seeing each other, or when she remembered seeing me anyway, it was a great relief."

"Yeah, I can imagine." Zoe smirked just a little, imagining that if it *was* true, they'd done far more than bump into each other at the fireworks. And if it wasn't true, Warren was using him. "So, Marty, got any theories about who did her?"

He looked momentarily confused. "Did? Oh, you mean killed. Julia? Uh, same guy who did the others I suppose. You'd know more about that than I would. I gotta say though, it creeped me out but good. I'm even thinking about moving. After all the crap that went down in that neighborhood, I don't know. I used to like the area, but it's just not the same."

"Hey Marty, did what's-her-name, your alibi lady, did she know Nelson very well?" Zoe was careful to play along. No names.

"I wouldn't know, Zoe. I don't really know *her* very well." He looked at Mal.

"How about that creepy radiologist. Aw shit. Now I can't remember his name either. You know the guy. Kind of reminds you of Popeye when he talks?"

Everyone laughed. They all knew the guy. "Him? Yeah, what about him?"

"He lives near you, doesn't he? You know him?"

"He lives near, but I don't really know him. I see him driving in and out. Talked to him once at a neighborhood association meeting and a few times out on the street. He's kind of a complainer, likes to bring his grievances to the attention of the board. Persnickety. You know the type."

"Yeah, I kind of figured him for that. Loner too, right?"

"I guess you could say that. He only shows up at the meetings to complain, but he never comes to the barbecues or block parties. I used to like that about the area, all the get-togethers and shit. It was nice. Now everyone's paranoid. It's creepy there. I'm pretty sure I'm going to move."

"So," bringing him back to the radiologist, "he must not have even known Nelson lived in the neighborhood then?"

He looked at her blankly. Zoe figured he'd gone way off track already.

"You know, Popeye, being a loner and all?"

"Oh! Him. Sorry. Well, no. That would be impossible since he complained to me once about her shrubs overtaking his lawn. He knew who she was."

"You mean he lives right next door to her?"

"Well, yeah, we each live next to her. He's on one side and I'm on the other. You can see why I'm creeped out. Popeye and a murdered lady for neighbors? Guy had a point though. She was pretty careless with her lawn. Didn't really matter to me, but I can see where it might bother someone who was real particular. He was pretty mad though. Way out of proportion if you ask me.

"You know her house hasn't sold yet. The family on the other side of me, they moved right away. Reduced the price and its still sitting there empty. Mine'll be hard to move too. Market's for shit now anyway. Throw in an unsolved murder, and there you go. You're done for. Oh, hell. Maybe I won't move. Unless Popeye buys me out so he can have the neighborhood to himself." He grinned and got up to leave, kissing Mal as he stood. "Maybe I'll just spend more time with you."

Mal beamed. "Yeah, well, my neighborhood sucks worse, babe. Where I live the garages are bigger than the houses, and people still can't seem to get their cars off the lawns. Probably meth labs in those garages, cuz there sure ain't no cars. Do you really have to get back to the pharmacy? Stay awhile. This is fun," she pouted.

"I like my job too much, hon. Gotta go. Here, put my tiles back in the bag. Hang on to your U's everyone . . . I just dumped a Q," he tempted. "Let me know who wins."

Well now. Zoe had known who lived in Nelson's neighborhood, but hadn't worried about how close they'd lived to her. Didn't seem to matter, as long as they were part of the same social circle. But Popeye had just been caught in a lie. Slow day in the ER hadn't been a complete waste of time after all. She snuck away for a minute to let Ray know. Time to follow up on Creepy Radiologist.

THE RADIO BARKED WHILE MAL was drooling over her chance to lay all seven letters. Dr. Weston fielded the call, and announced an incoming Stab case.

Parker joined the team in Stab one as they heard the siren approach. The day's lull had allowed him to catch up on paperwork, and he'd been sequestered in his office for most of it.

"Glad there's finally something meaningful to do. If I have to look at one more administrative document, I'll snap. So what's the story here, Weston?"

Weston, the other resident, was point man on this one. "It's a domestic. Some guy went ballistic on his wife. The daughter's coming in with her. Mom's real bad. Blunt force trauma. They've run through everything. Nothing's working. Been without a pulse since they got there. Started compressions in the field. From what they described, my guess is we'll be calling it. She's been fixed and dilated the whole time. Crew said the kid's gone off the deep end though. At first she was hysterical, like you'd expect. But now they say you can't even talk to her. They're describing her as catatonic."

"Mal, put in a call to Psych. Get someone down here right away." He'd noticed Zoe pale and pulled up close.

Cold air came in ahead of them. The violent compressions and bagged respirations continued as they rolled the gurney in from the ambulance. They'd decided to let the girl hang on to her mom, but not because they'd wanted to. Their efforts to pry her away had only made things worse. Not wanting to waste any more time getting the woman in, they'd given up and transported the whole mess the way they'd found it. Bloodied, essentially dead mom, with an obviously broken arm held in a vice-like grip by the little girl shuffling along beside her.

IT HIT ZOE HARD. THIS WAS AN ER where anything could and would come in. You had to be ready. But this? *Christ.* Zoe drew up close to the girl, hoping to redirect her attention away from her mother and from what they were doing to her. Sable eyes looked out at Zoe, following her movements through sweaty, matted bangs. But it wasn't the vacant, catatonic stare she'd expected...it was a feral, savage threat. In an instant, Zoe saw through those eyes. Recognizing danger, she quickly broke the connection and looked toward the two small hands, clinging to a lifeless wrist. She remembered what it felt like to embrace death. The room started to swim and her vision tunneled.

HE CAUGHT HER BEFORE SHE HIT THE FLOOR.
"Weston! Can you handle the room? Looks like we've got a situation here."
"Sure, Dr. Parker. No problem."
He scooped Zoe up. "I'll send Dr. Anderson in to give you a hand."
"Okay, but don't worry, I've got it under control. As long as Psych gets here pronto."
Mal looked out the door of the Stab room. "He's coming down the hall now!" She stepped out to meet the jogging psychiatry resident. "Sure am glad to see you. It's a whole lot easier dealing with delusional adults gone off their meds. Or even suicide attempts. Your basic 'protect them from themselves' protocol, you know...physical and medical restraints, then a chip shot up to psych. But this? What are we supposed to do with the kid? None of us wants to make it worse."
"Of course. Let's go in."

KAJ LAID ZOE DOWN ON A GURNEY in an empty cube. She was coming around.
"What happened?" She looked around, trying to remember. "Wait, the girl. Is she okay?" Her eyes threatened to spill. Kaj thought the expression on her face would haunt him forever.

"She's being taken care of, Zoe, don't worry. Psych got here right away. They'll see to it." He brushed damp hair away from her eyes and felt the cold sweat on her skin. In his caress, he measured the strengthening pulse at her carotid artery. The synaptic storm that had overtaken her heart and blood vessels was over.

Zoe sat up too quickly and said with a shaky voice, "I've got to make sure Camilla knows. I trust her to take care of the kid."

"Not so fast, Zoe, take it easy." He brought himself close to her, cradling her head on his shoulder. "You're not ready to stand yet. Do you know the girl, Zoe? Did you recognize her from somewhere?"

With the weary emptying of her lungs he drew her tight and kissed the dampness on her forehead. He felt her tense in his arms... and leave him.

"No," came out in a helpless whisper. It wasn't the Zoe he knew, or thought he knew. And it wasn't an answer, but more like a hopeless plea. It came from a little girl, one who'd lost control, lost her mother, lost the sense that life could be good. Lost the belief that she was good. That much he did understand. Perhaps the little girl in Stab 1 understood far more.

"It just got to me is all. I thought I'd seen everything, but that one was especially sad." He felt her relax a bit in his arms. "I'm sorry that happened. I hope it didn't cause too much of a problem."

"Ahhh, don't let it bother you, Zoe. Weston's fine. There's plenty of help today, and the ER's slow."

He tilted her head up to face his and felt her shift uncomfortably in his arms. She resisted that kind of connection. He'd seen it from her when they'd first met. At least it told him she'd sensed something between them from the start, something she needed to resist even then. Strangely, that realization comforted him.

He held her gaze, taking her mouth in his. This was a language she understood, and he felt her sink into him. They both gave in to the raw physical connection and cleared their minds, until Mal roughly pushed the curtain aside.

"Is she okay?" Mal pulled up short at interrupting the embrace. "Oh, I'm sorry. I didn't... I didn't know. I thought maybe you needed help in here. I'm sorry..."

Zoe interrupted. "No worries, Mal. I'm okay. Sorry I didn't tell you. Just figured it best to keep personal and professional separate, you know. Like you and Marty did for a while. But I guess you can only do that for so long, eh?" She grinned.

Mal smiled warmly. "Zoe, I'm happy for you. No problems. So, you're okay? What happened?"

"I caught her just as she was going down. She got a little light headed in there … what with the kid and all." Kaj stepped in to help.

"God, I know. I was never so glad to see Psych show up. I don't give them enough credit sometimes, but I'll never forget this. He had to dope her up on the spot before we could get her away from her mom. I don't know what's going to happen when she comes around. I don't think I've ever seen anything so sad."

Kaj felt the catch in Zoe's breath. "So, let's get you to a call room where you can lie down for a while. You're a little unsteady yet. Come on, take my arm." She didn't resist.

Kaj laid her down on the bed, and joined her. "What is it, Zoe?"

"Just hold me." She curled into him, filling the voids between them.

"I am, Zoe. But there's something wrong, and it's not just the girl."

"What are you talking about? So I flipped a little. I'm not made of stone, you know. It got to me."

"What else, Zoe?"

"She looked away as she spoke, "I saw her alone and hating herself for not being able to save her mother. And the guy who did this, she'll feel alternately terrified of and homicidal toward. No way out for her, I guess. No escape … unless that's why she went catatonic. Could be she knows something the rest of us don't."

"Children are very resilient, Zoe. She'll be scarred, no doubt. And you're right, of course, about what she'll be feeling. But with help, she'll overcome it." He propped himself up on one elbow, to better see her face.

"Sometimes that kind of help is worse than none at all." He felt a shiver run thorough her. "I'd trust Camilla to work with her though."

"As would I. We'll talk to her. I'm sure she'd want to take a personal interest in this case. Especially if you're the one asking."

Zoe smiled. "Yes, Camilla is that way. Hold me. Let's stop talking."

They remained that way for half an hour. No one bothered them. The ER seemed to function without them. Kaj didn't want to leave her sleeping only to wake and find him gone. So he stayed, until finally Zoe spoke. "Why don't you go ahead now. They'll be needing you soon, I expect. Do you mind if I stay here just a little longer? I need to clear my mind before I go back out."

"All right, Zoe. If you're sure you're okay. Take your time. I'll be close by." He gently pulled the door shut behind him and listened for a moment, hearing the sobs. She didn't even trust him enough to cry in his presence. He forced himself down the hallway, passing eyes that tracked his reappearance after the brief absence. All the while, Mal had been on the loose with information.

Kaj involuntarily smiled as it hit him. He wanted to believe she'd really needed him. Nevertheless, the two of them disappearing into a call room and spending half an hour alone … an embarrassingly short amount of time for the rumors that would spring from this, he thought … so much for his reputation as a slow, generous, and satisfying lover.

His wry smile only made the onlookers more curious, and further fed the rumors. Zoe had a way of getting things done.

Chapter Thirty-Six
December 12 (Evening)

GNORING CAMILLA'S SURPRISED LOOK, Kaj wasted no time with explanations.
"Zoe wants me present during the session. Where would you like me?" It wasn't really a question.

"I'd prefer that you wait outside. Are you sure about this, Zoe? Sometimes things come up during hypnosis that may be easily misinterpreted. There's no predicting what you might say."

Zoe hesitated, looking at Kaj.

"Zoe's committed to this. And to my involvement."

"It's okay, Camilla. I trust him," she lied. "I need him," she corrected. He was, in fact, now essential to her plans.

"All right then, if you're sure. Why don't you make yourself comfortable in that chair, Zoe," she pointed to an ergonomically designed recliner, "and you can have a seat over in the corner," she directed Kaj to a seat behind Zoe, out of her line of sight. "Just be sure to keep your mouth shut, no matter what. It's like you're not even here. But I warn you, you might not like what you hear."

BEFORE STARTING, CAMILLA WENT through a series of questions with Zoe, about her goals in undergoing hypnosis, and any specifics she wanted to explore. Zoe explained the crime scenes, describing the mysterious sense she kept having about missing something important.

Camilla then started the session, finding Zoe unusually challenging. It was obvious that Zoe didn't relax easily, and deep down probably didn't trust the process of hypnosis. Camilla finally broke through with comforting images of Zoe's house. It was one of her few vulnerabilities, and she seemed to yield to it.

The process continued as Zoe led them through the crime scenes in subconscious detail. Camilla took written notes of everything, hoping for images that might have eluded Zoe to surface in the free-flowing, uncensored hypnotic state. They were all counting on the unacknowledged details pushing their way up. But the difficulty she'd had in initiating the hypnotic state also made Zoe hard to steer.

She seemed fixed on photographs of the victims. She saw them as superimposed on images of windows. Camilla initially allowed Zoe free rein to focus on them, thinking it might be important. Finally, after repeating the same things over and over, important or not, they needed to move on or risk overlooking some other crucial detail. But Zoe still wouldn't cooperate, and couldn't be pulled out of Nelson's bedroom. She started to describe the room from the perspective of the victim.

As Camilla had seen the sex tape of Parker and Nelson, she recognized Zoe's description of being made love to by him. Zoe seemed lost in her own interpretation of what that must have felt like. The session was turning personal. Looking uncomfortably past Zoe's shoulder at Kaj, she shook her head. It seemed that Zoe was confusing things.

The description of lovemaking then drifted to a different scenario. One Camilla could only guess had actually occurred between Zoe and Kaj. Soon, Camilla found herself privy to the night of sex in the call room.

KAJ PRESSED THE HEELS OF HIS HANDS over his eyes. This was going nowhere. He'd become a distraction to her, but at least it appeared he was an important one. Small comforts.

They both visibly jumped at what Zoe said next. "He's coming for me again." Thinking she might be on the verge of a breakthrough, they leaned in. Zoe's uncanny ability to inhabit the minds of both predator and prey might have produced images too painful to consciously acknowledge.

"I can hear him downstairs. He's mad. I can tell. Something's made him mad. He'll be rough with me tonight." She started to cry softly. "I don't think I can take it anymore. He should just kill me."

Camilla and Kaj locked eyes. Camilla's confused; Kaj's terrified. He wanted to tell her. It broke his heart to picture an eighteen-year-old Zoe, wishing for death. He readied himself to say something, to help Camilla understand that Zoe wasn't talking about Nelson, or *this* killer, but found Camilla shaking her head.

She put a finger to her lips, signaling quiet. Kaj grimaced; realizing that Camilla still thought Zoe was speaking of the crime scenes. Could this be harmful?

There was a pause … and then a shriek that brought them both to their feet. "It hurts! … What? … I promise! … Please don't!" She cringed, and then jumped in the chair. "Please, I'm still bleeding from yesterday. I'm hurt." Zoe was suddenly curled up in a ball. "Please, no! … Not that way! … Just beat me! … Please! … Beat me." It was followed by a long pause. "I want you to," finally came out in a whimper, sounding resigned and hopeless. "I want you to."

Camilla broke in, frantically trying to bring her back, while Kaj rushed to Zoe's side and tried holding her, only to make things worse. She screamed and recoiled violently. He found himself having to restrain her from getting up. She was a lot stronger than he'd counted on.

"Okay, okay. Whatever you want," she spewed in a panicked rush. Her muscles relaxed almost imperceptibly, and although maintaining his grip, Kaj winced at his role in this. "Thank you," she choked on the words. " … I know. … You *should've* killed me. … I deserve it. … They'd be alive, wouldn't they? … Yes, it's my fault. … Just please don't …"

Kaj waited out her brief silence, hoping the storm was over.

"What? … Yes," she whimpered, "I want you." But tensing again, she hurried with, "No! Beat me instead! Please! Just beat me!"

Kaj could almost hear the invisible man laugh, taunting her. And the scream that followed held *nothing* back. It was like a war cry. "No! Now *I'm* the one with the gun!"

Camilla lost her composure, and shouted at Zoe to come back, to wake up, and then ran to the nurse's station for a hypodermic.

Zoe continued struggling against Kaj, reliving a horror he was only now coming even close to understanding. But this time she wasn't cringing as if fending off blows; she was on the attack. And then, just as suddenly as it had started, it was all over. She relaxed. Exhausted. "That's right you steaming pile of shit … I'm the one with the gun *now.*" There was a long silence. "Asshole. You bleed red like everyone else."

WHEN CAMILLA RETURNED TO THE ROOM, she found Zoe sleeping in Kaj's arms. The two of them exchanged the spent look of boxers after a fight, bound by a shared pain. Camilla quietly approached Zoe, but rather than risk waking her, she took Kaj's face in her hands instead, allowing him to see her cry. She kissed him on the forehead as his eyes closed against his own tears. He welcomed her warmth, but it threatened his control.

Camilla whispered, "I don't know what that was, Kaj, but it wasn't hypnosis. She's exhausted now, and may sleep a while. I'm just not sure how we ought to handle this when she wakes. I'm really not. Whatever this was, wherever this came from, it's clearly dangerous to her. That's about the only thing I *am* sure of right now. If any part of this actually happened, it threatens everything that I know her to be."

Camilla stared at Zoe, asleep and apparently peaceful. "Lets hope she's no longer in the past, and that we've caused her no damage." She turned to search his eyes.

Kaj was willing to give her that much at least, nodding in agreement. Telling her that, yes, this *was* Zoe's past. It *had* happened. And he was left feeling equally unsure of how to proceed. He resigned himself to letting Camilla make the call. She had the expertise. But he would say nothing more about what he knew. That was still up to Zoe. Besides, Camilla was already getting the picture.

THEY REMAINED IN THE OFFICE FOR SEVERAL HOURS. Zoe sleeping in Kaj's arms, unmoving, while Camilla did the worrying. She left only once to retrieve some coffee, and then once again to call her husband, letting him know that she might spend the night at the hospital.

At Zoe's stirring, Camilla thought she'd never felt so unsure of herself, of her abilities and her knowledge. Kaj's calm demeanor was all that kept her from losing control entirely.

The baby kicked. Camilla was instantly overwhelmed by horrible images of what could befall her child. The baby was real, a fact, and so was evil in the world. A tripwire ... one false move, she thought. Always threatening. Not just what would happen, but what *could* happen. Those possibilities would always contaminate the joy, as she supposed was true of all loving parents. But why hadn't she understood that before?

Kaj spoke first. "Zoe, you okay? You've been sleeping for quite a while." His voice was soft, smooth, and matter-of-fact.

It was now Camilla who took her cues from Kaj. He'd been right all along, and she softened toward him. His concern had been genuine.

He also seemed far less shocked by what he'd heard. It was time to accept that he knew her friend better than she did, and her expertise was no match for that knowledge. Standing back, she let him take over.

HE BRUSHED HIS FACE AGAINST ZOE'S, kissing her softly.

"Hey! When was the last time you shaved?" She laughed, but he recognized she was holding on by a thread to the safety of his eyes, afraid to look away.

"Well, it's been what, two or three days now? The last time I slept at home I guess." He smiled back, his eyes never leaving hers. "Suddenly I seem to have lost track."

He could see the fear. He was holding a child now, trying to ignore the black void behind the closet door. She would never be truly free until she faced it. Squarely. He knew that much. But when and how, those were the questions. His eyes asked her that ... he couldn't hide it .... and Zoe's face seemed unable to decide between a reluctant smile and grimace. Not now.

"It's okay, Zoe. You were exhausted by the effort. You slept quite a while, but you'll need more." He tried his best to look reassuring. "It's been a rough stretch lately, hasn't it Zoe?"

"Yes ... yes, it has." She kept looking at him, and seemed to relax.

Zoe took a deep breath and finally faced Camilla. He knew that she fully expected the terrified look, and seemed afraid to ask, but he heard the cop in her ask anyway. She'd be hoping for *something* productive out of all this, he knew. "I say anything useful?"

Camilla's eyes darted away, toward her notepad. "I took notes, up to a point, then the session kind of broke down."

She looked to Kaj, who quickly redirected Zoe's attention.

"Let's go. I've got a condo downtown."

He laughed when she looked at him in amazement. "You and your cop friends didn't know about that, right? There's a lot more you could learn."

"The only thing I want to know right now is why my muscles feel so beat up? How in the hell did that happen while I was dozing in an ergonomically correct chair?"

Kaj pulled her up, ignoring the question. "Let's go. Right now."

SHE ALLOWED HIM TO LEAD HER the several blocks toward his building. Risking nothing during the walk, she never spoke. And he didn't press. It told her that something terrible *had* happened. He was treating her as if she were fragile. She felt fragile, unsteady, and only wished for a distraction.

Arriving at their destination, he did distract . . . *it* distracted. The elevator opened up to the entire top floor, the penthouse . . . all his. She was drawn to the beautiful view of the river and bridges through floor-to-ceiling windows. There were no window treatments to block the vista.

"We didn't search this place, did we?" She smiled. "Your love shack on the river. Now that we're an item," she cocked one eyebrow, "I'll expect the full treatment here," she teased, then promptly wished she hadn't been careless in that way.

The open floor plan pulled her to the opposite side of the unit. The windows framed a glittering skyline. To Zoe, an architecture devotee, this was as compelling as the river view. All the windows, it tugged again.

She turned to find Kaj busy in the open kitchen. Already working at the stove, he waved her over to sit at the island counter. "Here, have a glass of wine while I fix us something. You must be starving."

She drew hard on the aroma of two sizzling steaks on the grill top, and watched him expertly work a knife around a ripe mango. His hands were beautiful. Strong, but not calloused. Perceptive and skilled. *Responsive*, she remembered, and smiled into her wine glass. The weight was lifting, at least temporarily. He couldn't possibly know how grateful she was at this moment.

She hopped off the stool and came around behind him. Running her hands around his waist, she leaned in to him. "Thank you." *Careless, but so very true.*

He pivoted to face her. Licking the mango off his fingers, he traced them over her lips and grabbed hold of her. Lifting, he spun her around and onto the counter. She wrapped her legs around his waist and arced her neck to his mouth while he unbuttoned her shirt, pulling it away from her.

And suddenly, it mattered very much what he thought of her. She'd never felt this way about someone. Surprised by the sense of vulnerability, Zoe brought a hand up to hide the scar at the base of her neck. Another thing she'd never felt moved to do before. And it didn't seem right to do it now. But she did anyway.

He gently took hold of her hand, guiding it away from the scar and leaving it to rest over his heart. She watched him, following his movements as he slowly lowered his mouth to find the scar, and kissed it. Not as a parent would kiss a child's wound to heal it, but as though he *loved* it . . . and wouldn't change it. Loved her scar, loved her every sharp edge, everything others might consider a flaw.

She'd never felt such a seduction. Something in her let go, something never before freed. Kaj turned off the flame, devoting his full attention to her . . . and bringing his own heat, they feasted on each other.

It was 1:00 a.m. when they finally gave in to food. They ate in bed, where Zoe was still awed by the view. In any direction she looked, there were either iconic buildings or the legendary river.

She marveled at the urban loft surroundings and the collection of abstract art. It was similar to her home, but raw, more industrial. Here the exposed structural elements were made of steel, and metal ductwork ran freely in all directions. Must have been for air-conditioning, as she'd noticed in-floor heat in the concrete under foot.

"I love this place. It's *absolutely* perfect." She leaned into him playfully, setting her empty plate aside. "I'm still hungry though," she teased.

"You want more? I've got plenty." He grabbed her, pulling her on top of him. "I'll never leave you wanting."

WHAT HE DIDN'T KNOW WAS THAT SHE would want him every time she thought of him. Feeling her legs go weak, she'd ache with the same need he felt for her. That they might share that impulse hadn't yet occurred to him. Despite what had just transpired in Camilla's office, *he* uncharacteristically felt like the needy one here. His overwhelming urge to please her, to protect her, felt like his own selfish need. His weakness.

CHAPTER THIRTY-SEVEN
DECEMBER 13 (EARLY)

THEY WOKE LAZILY AS LIGHT STREAMED IN through the windows. Zoe's head rested on Kaj's stomach.

Both shifted, propping up on elbows to survey the room. They were no longer in bed. Somehow they'd wound up on the floor amidst a tangle of sheets, pillows and interlocking body parts. The rug was askew beneath them and both the bedside table and at least one lamp were overturned. On the wall above them a painting hung at a dangerous angle, ready to drop. Turning back to look at each other, they laughed.

"It's a good thing you don't favor skirts. I'd be afraid for the others if you were ever to take up roller derby."

She elbowed him in the ribs.

"See?"

"Okay, well, this hobby is far more satisfying anyway. Did we break anything?"

Ignoring the upturned furniture and chaos around them, he ran a diagnostician's eye over both their bodies. "I don't think so. I'm feeling pretty good in my skin right now, how about you?"

"Very funny." Smiling, she leaned back down, her hair brushing over his stomach, and she kissed him there. "But, yes, I'm feeling more than good. How about a shower?" They both grinned and she stood, reaching down a hand to pull him up.

THE BATHROOM HADN'T BEEN NEGLECTED in the design. It was huge, and composed of concrete, tile and glass. A skylight spanned the entire ceiling of the spacious shower, which was more like its own separate room. Zoe opened a thick door to find a large cedar-lined sauna, with another showerhead inside. Next to the sauna, two large doors opened to a rooftop deck. The remaining walls of the bath mirrored the rest of the penthouse... floor to ceiling windows.

"Don't you feel a little exposed in this room? Can't people see in?"

"It would take a telescopic lens, but if they're that interested, let them look."

She smiled. "I see your point. I don't like feeling constrained either."

"Believe me, I noticed that. So did the bedroom." He smiled back, working his muscles with a massaging hand.

She rolled her eyes, but rose on tiptoes to kiss him.

"If you'll have me back sometime, I'd love to try the sauna."

"Sometime?" He laughed, "Of course. We'll enjoy it together."

THEY FINISHED WITH EACH OTHER up against the shower wall. A lot roomier than the call room shower, she'd thought when first seeing it. He'd washed her with his own hands, massaging her, relaxing each muscle before bringing every fiber back to attention. As her head fell back, and his into her neck, she squeezed her legs around his waist and fixed her eyes on the last remaining stars in the early morning sky before her vision clouded. She was happy at this moment. And it scared her.

She suddenly had a lot of questions about all of this, and *none* of them had mattered yesterday. How many other women had been through here? Nelson? Anders? She wouldn't have cared a day ago. This felt perilously close to needing promises, and she *hated* that insecure feeling.

Of course he had every right to wonder the same things about her. Mal even teased her once about all the balls hanging from her rear-view mirror. Told her to *leave some for the rest of us.* It was true. She'd collected them . . . and used them all.

And now Zoe felt guilty about that too. She suddenly understood their reluctance to share her. But it surprised her that she could feel possessive. That kind of nonsense never mattered before. *Oh, God, this is new.*

The shower reminded her, "So, I was wondering about something." She looked at him as she toweled off. "The other night, when you brought me home from the party?"

He waited. "Yes. What about it?"

"I still want to know what really happened." She smiled seductively, letting him know the truth would do.

"I already told you, and I'd never lie about that." He did his best to look offended, but was clearly amused.

"Yeah, but . . . how did you manage that shower?"

He laughed, pulling her to him. "Okay, you've got me there. I didn't lie exactly. I simply left out a few unimportant details. Of course I stripped and got in with you. It was the only way to get you clean, and I didn't want to put you to bed covered in vomit." He grew serious. "But nothing else happened, you weren't exactly in what might be called a consenting condition."

Her jaw dropped. "Do you have *any* idea what I was thinking? Or what *condition* you left me in the next morning? You are a sadistic tease."

He smiled, kissing her roughly, and took his own towel to dry her hair. Then he abruptly broke away. "We're going to be late for work."

He made a move toward the door but paused and turned back toward her stunned expression, "It took *every ounce* of my self-discipline."

She closed her eyes and smiled, rethinking that night.

THEY WALKED IN AND LOOKED AT THE BOARD, confirming a busy day ahead. The cases were all routine and minor. They'd clog things up for hours, but shouldn't have required the services of an ER, if only people had insurance.

Colds, rashes, sexually transmitted diseases, even head lice. But that was the routine at Minneapolis General. Zoe noticed the patient in cube three. Hemorrhoids, it said. She nudged Kaj and pointed. "Guy came in by ambulance. Can you believe that?"

Kaj shook his head. "Death by duck bites today."

She laughed, picturing the annoying day in store.

Ray called at 7:00 a.m. on the dot. "Did I catch you before you got too involved there? Got a minute?"

"Yeah, sure, Ray. What's up?"

"Got a hit on your idea. Showing Hanover's picture around at Lorna's Table. One of the cooks recognized her. She'd been there for a cooking class."

"Well, now at least we've got *something*. Listen, I realize it's probably a long shot, but I'll pick up the photos of Nelson's neighborhood contacts and show them around there for you. I know a lot of those people from work."

She elected not to say anything to Ray about her scheme and now wondered, as Kaj had warned her, just what the truth really was. It felt like they were for real. "Anything on Popeye?"

"What? Who?"

"Oh, sorry. Creepy radiologist. Mayhew. Popeye is what we've been calling him around here." She smiled into the phone.

Ray laughed. "I can see why. We're bringing him in again. Hoping to shake him up. I'm sure he'll have an *explanation* though." He paused, breathing deeply, "You okay, Zoe?"

It got to her. She felt love for Ray. But it wasn't the way she felt toward Kaj. Someone she'd only known for months.

"Yeah, I really am, Ray." She paused, listening to his breathing. He wanted more. "I'm sorry."

"Sorry for what?"

She wasn't sure herself. "I guess, for being such a jerk. Jack's probably right. I think I understand that now."

"Jack's way off base, Zoe."

"I just think I understand things a little better. I've yanked you around a lot, and I shouldn't have."

Ray laughed. "Have I ever complained?"

"No, but then again I've never let you. Like I said, a jerk."

A few moments of silence. "Just who are we talking about here, Zoe?"

"What do you mean?"

"Is it me you're worried about, or has something else happened? For you to understand means that you feel strongly about someone. Is it someone else, Zoe?"

"Aw, Christ, Ray. I'm sorry I even brought it up. Never mind. I'm not sure what's changed," she lied.

She was still being cruel. He deserved better. An answer at least. "I'll always be there for you, Ray. No matter what happens. Even after you've met your fantasy woman and had six kids." She smiled a warm smile she could only hoped he sensed.

She'd been closer to Ray than all the others. And he'd put up with her. It hurt, having to disappoint him in this way. But there... she'd given him his answer. Pretending wasn't right. And she'd never promised anything more than the friendship they had.

She could hear the catch in his voice. There were probably cops around, and here she was talking about this stuff, making it hard for him. "I understand, Zoe. I love you too."

Ray paused, and in that moment she realized he'd heard an 'I love you' in what she'd just said to him. He did understand.

"I always will. My dream wife will just have to deal with it." He teased, trying to make it easier on her, she knew. "How about your dream guy? Can he deal with me?"

She ducked into an empty cube before the tears came. "Ray, I do love you. And I'll make sure he knows you and I are non-negotiable. We'll always have each other's back, right?"

"It's okay, Zoe. I'll be fine. I just want you to be happy. You deserve that, you always have."

"I wish I'd have been able to give you as much. I don't understand any of this. Suddenly I feel as if I actually *do* have something to give. But why I'm telling you this, I don't know. It's cruel."

"You can tell me anything. Always."

Zoe settled down, and the tears stopped. "I believe you, Ray. Now please believe me. I never make promises, but I'm making one now. I will *always* be there for you. Guaranteed. And *everyone* in our lives will just have to deal with it."

"I'm counting on it."

"Thank you, Ray."

"Thank whoever brought about this change in you, Zoe. Guy must be a magician. This is the Zoe I always knew was there. I'm just happy you found her."

What was she doing? Jeopardizing a relationship she'd come to rely on, with a man who was accepting of her, demanding nothing . . . safe . . . in favor of an unknown. A man who'd made no promises, and if past behavior were any indication, he wouldn't last.

Her fidelity couldn't be counted on either. She had no experience in limiting herself to one man. But his pull was impossible to resist. Was this how all of his conquests felt at the beginning? *Oh, God.*

"Good-bye, Ray."

"Bye, Z."

ZOE WAS WIPING AT TEARS AS SHE STEPPED out of the cube. Kaj stopped her. "You okay? What's happened?"

"I just said a kind of goodbye to someone. Someone I care deeply about."

It had to be Ray. He remembered all the protective looks he'd gotten from Ray, whenever he'd been around Zoe. Ray had been important to her, and he couldn't expect that would change now.

"How did it go, Zoe?" He hoped Ray had handled it well.

"We're still friends." She looked defiantly at him. "And always will be."

Ray must have tried to make it easy on her. Even promised to stick with the friendship. It had to have been hard, unselfish and genuine. Mature was the word. He had a new respect for the guy . . . and wasn't sure he could have done the same.

"I'm glad, Zoe. I wouldn't want it any other way." He pulled her to him. Kissing the redness around her eyes. Tasting the salt. "I love you, Zoe." He needed to tell her that now, and she didn't pull away from it.

She was okay. It would be all right, he thought, as he watched her stride down the hall toward the waiting patients. And he thought about the sacrifice she'd just made for him.

CHAPTER THIRTY-EIGHT
DECEMBER 14 (EVENING)

THE SKATERS DID FAST LOOPS DURING warm-ups, trying to disperse the fog, but the thick blanket wouldn't lift. A sudden thaw had the rink manager struggling, and it was hard to see on the ice. They discussed calling it a night.

"Let's just go at it." Zoe was itching to play. She jumped off the bench and over the dasher boards, urging the others to follow. "Come on!"

"Zoe, you can't even see east to west, and I don't exactly feel like risking a bone. How about some common sense here, boys?"

"Come on. Short passes, no slap shots. No blind shots on goal out of the fog. Okay all around?"

She counted heads as she got the expected affirmatives. "We've got enough for two lines on each bench with the new player I brought. *Claims* he can play." She looked skeptically at Kaj, thinking it was probably just another ruse to stick with her. "We'll see I guess." She caught his smirk and had to wonder. He didn't look too worried.

"All right, Zoe, but Parker plays on the other team. We'll test his skills."

Zoe rolled her eyes at Ray. "Fine, we're wasting time. Trade jerseys if you have to."

The first lines off the bench were Ray, Zoe, and Anthony as forwards for the light jerseys and Kelly, Kaj, and Marty for the darks. Zoe loved the defensemen who joined her on the ice for the first shift. Gus and Dean were reliable, allowing her to go hard on offense and take longer shifts. With only two lines on each bench, no one would be squawking about ice time anyway. They'd all be gassed by the end.

They never hired refs, so there were no face-offs. Instead, Zoe tossed the puck onto the ice, with players jumping over the boards after it. Zoe and Kelly were the first to fight for it.

Zoe, having learned her brand of hockey at the hands of boys on the outdoor rinks in Canada, gave Kelly an illegal butt-end in the ribs and stole the puck. She quickly got rid of it, passing it over to Anthony. "Whoops, sorry, Kell, didn't mean it!"

"I'll get you for that!" He hollered after her as she sped down the ice to back up Anthony who was going in on goal.

"Only if you can catch me, old man!" she teased. Crashing the net, she picked up Anthony's rebound off the goalie and tucked it left upper shelf.

Zoe dug the puck out of the net and turned it over to Kelly as she and her team backed out of the zone to allow the dark jerseys their chance at a break out. Kaj's bemused look caught Kelly's eyes as he stood behind the net with the puck.

"What, you didn't know? She turns into a monster on the ice." Kelly then shouted to his team. "Let's get that one back, boys."

Kelly circled out from behind the net, moving the puck forward to Marty who shot hard up ice. His shoulder caught Zoe's as she moved to poke-check the puck away from him, sending her flying into the boards. "Ooops! Sorry, Zoe!"

Kelly laughed. "Can check 'Get Zoe' off my bucket list. Thanks, Marty!"

"Any time, Kelly!"

Ray appeared out of the fog, knocking Marty off the puck, but Kaj was ready and regained it, going in for a shot. Dean went down to block it, sending the puck into the corner, where Gus and Kelly now fought over it.

The puck popped out and up the sideboards. As Kaj went for it, Zoe was on him. She crosschecked him in the back, pinning him to the boards as she kicked at the puck to dislodge it from between his skates.

"You don't play fair on the ice, do you?" He managed to say through the pain of the stick digging into his ribs.

"Who says I ever play fair?" The sudden emptying of her lungs interrupted her laugh. He'd managed to quickly reverse positions and now had her pinned to the boards.

"You know everyone's talking about us don't you?" He whispered in her ear as she struggled to get free. A crunch of pads freed her, as Ray knocked Kaj onto the ice. Zoe spun away with the puck, leaving Ray to loom over Kaj alone.

"You hurt her, I'll kill you," he said before skating away.

Kaj jumped up to catch the players racing down the ice.

The fog turned out to be the extra player. Zoe collided with her own teammate as she raced over the blue line on goal. She and Anthony hadn't seen each other and went shoulder to shoulder in the slot. Zoe's helmet went flying in one direction and she in the other. A few drops of blood now marked her jersey. She finally slid to a stop at Kaj's feet.

"I know it's what you wanted, but guess what they're saying?" He smiled down at her.

"Same thing I'm *thinking*." She skated over to retrieve her helmet then jumped over the boards and onto the bench.

Both lines switched, and Ray sat next to Zoe, taking off his helmet. They leaned in to watch what they could see of the game, but the fog made it hard.

"Your boyfriend can skate. I wasn't expecting much. Where did he play before?" He reached over to wipe some blood off her lip.

"I had no idea he'd *ever* played before. But don't be too loose with the term *play*. All we know so far is that he can skate." She cast a glance at Kaj who was now on the other bench. "Be my guest and test him." Zoe grinned.

Ray smiled eagerly. "Will do. You don't know *much* about him do you? You two ever talk?"

"Talking's overrated." Zoe's satisfied smile answered the question.

"You're still bleeding."

"It's nothing. Just bit my lip in the collision." She wiped one arm over her mouth and looped the other around his neck to jostle him. He couldn't even force a smile.

"Zoe. I'm worried about him. I don't trust him."

"Well, since I'm the one who can't be trusted you *should* be worried about him."

His smiled this time, if only for a moment. "Well, I already know that. And I'm guessing he does too. But I don't give a rat's ass about his feelings. You on the other hand . . . mean the world to me."

Aw, shit. "I don't mean to hurt you. I really don't. But for right now I'm happy. Something's right about it. I just need to be honest . . . I owe you that."

"I know. And I am glad you told me. But I'm still skeptical about him, and I've got to be honest with you about *that*."

"Ray, I'm sleeping lately. Enough to dream."

"The last time you slept well enough to dream, it didn't turn out so well. I was there . . . remember? I still think about that."

"And I'm still sorry about that. But it wasn't that kind of dream. I was standing at the deep end of a swimming pool, and jumped in. I sank to the bottom and discovered that I couldn't swim ... I didn't know how."

"I'm sorry, Zoe." He put his arm around her, leaning in toward her face.

"No, Ray, no. It's not what you're thinking. After I found out that I couldn't swim I discovered something else ... I could breathe! I could breathe underwater! It didn't matter that I couldn't swim. It was the most amazing dream I've ever had. And it was so real that when I woke up I had to fight off the feeling that it might actually be possible. I even started thinking about super-oxygenated water and all that shit. Seriously. Crazy, eh?"

Zoe leaned her forehead against Ray's. "But it was beautiful, like a world I didn't know existed, and so real. It's somehow because of him. So go ahead and be skeptical, I am too I guess. But for now, I'm not fighting it, and that's *also* a new thing for me. I'm just sorry you know that all too well."

"You two, back on the ice!" The other shift had spent what they had.

They threw on their helmets and chased after Kaj who now had the puck. Going up against Dean and Gus on "D," he pulled the puck in close to carom off his skate blade, selling the deke and leaving Dean in a heap on the ice. Gus moved in, but with a spin move Kaj was around him. Crossing in front of the net, the goalie moved just as Kaj tucked the puck in easily through the five-hole.

Kelly and Marty mobbed him with hugs as the goalie dug the puck out of the net. Zoe breezed by him, tapping his shin pads with her stick. "Now we won't go so easy on you. Clear out."

She grabbed the puck from behind the net and building speed, maneuvered it easily past Kelly, who was already too slow at his age. Then she caught Marty leaning and left him looking like an orange pylon as she tucked the puck between his legs, only to pick it up at full speed on his other side. She topped out her speed going straight for the net. The defenseman swung toward her with a hip check, sending both Zoe and the puck into the net along with the goalie. But it counted.

Ray pulled her out of the pile, hugging her and laughing. "You know you skate like a girl, don't you?"

"Why thank you, Ray!"

KAJ'S STOP SPRAYED THEM BOTH with shaved ice, "Nice skating." And she was all the more appealing to him now, as if that were even possible. He grinned, grabbing the puck. "Clear out."

Zoe's team swung out across the blue line as Kaj built up his own momentum. Ray made straight for him, not expecting Kaj to give the check rather than take it.

Kaj left Ray stapled to the boards and then fended off the hook and hold of the defenseman.

Zoe went for the slue-foot, knocking Kaj off his skates. But not before he flipped the puck off the goalie's shoulder and into the net as he was going down. He landed on Zoe.

"It's true, you *are* cheap." Kaj pulled off his helmet and ran a hand over his bruised jaw.

"Puck hog."

He laughed. "Hey, I always win . . . by any means . . . get used to it." He wasn't letting her up off the ice just yet.

"Maybe what they're saying *is* right," she struggled.

"And what's that, Zoe?"

"That we won't last." It was turning into a wrestling match. He now had her arms trapped against her in a bear hug.

"And why do you say that?"

"Because I can't breathe, that's why! I won't survive it." She managed to get one arm free as he loosened his grip just slightly. "And because they say I'll be unfaithful, not having any experience with fidelity or self-control."

"Yep, that's what I've heard too." He released a hand to pull her helmet off. "They're also saying I won't be satisfied with *you* for long. You're too raw, and unrefined."

He smiled as her eyes narrowed on his, and interrupted her protest by taking her mouth in his. She sank back and quit struggling as he drew away the last of the blood. He pulled up, examining her. "There, that makes you a little more presentable. Not quite so unrefined. Now, what were you saying?"

"I forgot." Her look told him that after the kiss, it was *almost* true. He relaxed slightly and she maneuvered just enough to shift underneath him. "Oh, I remember now."

Then she kneed him, just enough to get free, and joined the group at the other end of the ice. Kaj looked toward the goalie, the only other player left on that end, and grunted painfully. "You saw that, right? You're a witness?"

The goalie laughed. "Could have told you that, man. Whatever has her pissed off; she gets rid of it on the ice. And I've *never* known her to play fair, only to win. Below the belt's nothing dude ... she's flat-out *cheap*.

"Hey, don't get me wrong. Nothin' against Zoe, she's tough both ways. Sure ain't no whiner. Even broke a bone out here once. But man can she skate. Got a helluva shot too."

"Well, she can definitely dish it. Good thing I'm wearing a cup." Kaj rose to rejoin the game.

"Yeah, but from the looks of the games you two play, you'll need your cup off-ice too." He called after him as Kaj sped away. "And, dude! You don't know what you're in for. She's been holding back!"

"Where'd you play before, Parker? Not many get by me like that." Dean's opponent clearly impressed him.

"A year of juniors then two years of college. WCHA."

"What made you quit? Injury?"

Zoe continued to undress; looking disinterested, but said to Kelly, "He's on my team next time."

"No, I'd finally decided on a career in medicine, and was also starting a business on the side. I had to pay my own way through school, and found myself saddled with a number of sudden expenses. While the athletic scholarship was great, it didn't pay all the bills and hockey just took up too much time. I never regretted leaving it ... in case you were wondering."

"Yeah, I kind of was. Seems like it would be hard to give up." Dean stopped unlacing his skates and leaned both elbows on his knees. "It was always a dream of mine, to play college hockey. I can't believe you'd walk away from it."

"Wasn't that hard really ... though that did sort of surprise me. Hell, it's only a game after all." He shrugged at their expressions, knowing he'd just said something sacrilegious. "Well, it is. Anyone else play juniors or college? Got a pretty high quality contest going here."

"Yeah, I carried a bag. Juniors ... out east. Then I played all four years at Harvard." Ray had them all laughing in disbelief. "Hey, I'm serious! Mine was an academic scholarship too. Ivy League doesn't hand out athletic scholarships you know. They want to make sure you can cut it. And I graduated, didn't I?" He wasn't giving up.

"I don't know, Ray, did you? If so, it was probably because you slept your way to graduation through the women professors." Zoe was laughing too, but said to the rest, "It might be true."

"How about you, Kelly?" Kaj elbowed him. "You play back in the day?" Kaj knew that the real Kelly hadn't played, but if his research was right, the man sitting beside him had.

"No, never played anything organized, just pond hockey. It was a pretty high caliber game though. 'Pick-up' is where guys experiment with their most creative moves. Some of them were college-bound. Held my own against them."

Zoe piped in. "Yeah, well, are they the ones who taught you how to slash like that?" She finished pulling off her elbow pads. "Kelly ... if you find anything left of my wrist on your stick, make sure I get it back, okay?"

"Zoe, you've given me more bruises than I can count. I'm currently multicolored." He threw his tape wad at her.

ZOE STOPPED UNDRESSING, now down to her athletic bra and her hockey boxers. There was no such thing as modesty among the medical profession *or* hockey players. She always enjoyed her own eyefuls of the men in the locker room ... bulging pecs and ripped abs. And she never tired of hockey players' tight rears. She knew of only two other activities that could give you that kind of muscular, well-defined ass ... biking and sex. So she figured she pretty much had her bases covered.

She looked over at Kaj ... definitely a hockey player. Definitely a player.

CHAPTER THIRTY-NINE
DECEMBER 15 (EVENING)

ZOE SAT WITH KAJ AT THE BAR, THINKING SHE might just be in love with the bartender at Lorna's Table. They were out of mint so she couldn't indulge in a Mojito, one of her favorites. He'd offered her a Caipirinha instead. It did the trick. Kaj was in the mood for beer and took his chances with a Moose Drool. A first time for everything, he'd said.

"So then you've been here before? With Anders?" Zoe downed the sweet drink too fast.

Kaj's eyes swept the dimly lit space, hiding his looking inward, Zoe thought. "Many times. Whenever there was a new installation at the Rosalux. Often after the theater." She saw him snap out of the past. "Great place, isn't it? Eclectic crowd. And I can tell you love the bartender." He smiled.

"Jealous?" she teased. "Think I'll have another. Get one more look at him."

"HE'S GAY." KAJ PAUSED LONG ENOUGH to enjoy the stunned look on her face. "And his boyfriend is *way* cuter than you."

"Isn't there a pill you can take for that? I want him." Zoe looked longingly down the bar. "That body, those drinks? I *definitely* want him. If there's no pill, I don't mind sharing."

Kaj grabbed her chin and redirected her gaze toward him. Laughing, "Well, I do. You're mine now."

Zoe returned a coquettish smile, and a long, slow kiss. She whispered as she kissed him, "I don't believe you. He's not gay."

He loved watching her eyes laugh. With every day, she let herself go more, trusted him more, enjoyed things more. It felt good to see.

He also saw mischief play across her face.

"Oh, I get it, any other man I look at is gay. Is that it?" She leaned back defiantly, "And what about all the women before me? Can I assume they go for the girls now?"

"I don't mind sharing either. I'm sure they'd like you." He held the poker face.

She laughed heartily, and then wrung her hands. "This is going to be so much fun."

"What exactly?"

"Teaching you that, like all good lovers . . . you should be just a little afraid of me."

"Afraid too? I was still at totally confused," he countered with his own smile.

"Okay, so maybe we should call Pete over here. I'll tell him you think he's gay and we're just checking. Hey, Pete!"

"Okay, okay! You win!" He leaned his forehead in his hands as Pete approached.

"I win? You sure?"

Kaj nodded, reluctantly.

"Two more here, Pete. Thanks."

Kaj peered out from between his fingers as he watched Pete walk away. He turned to Zoe, bringing his hands down from his face. "You're good."

"Remember, I used to be a cop . . . I know bluffs. But you made that far too easy." She grabbed the back of his head by a handful of hair and brought his mouth to hers."

He came up for air, "Well played. I guess I don't mind losing though." His mouth went back for another sweet lime kiss.

THE ITALIAN SAUSAGE PIZZA HAD THEM on their third drinks when the photos finally came back to their table.

"A couple guys thought they recognized this woman. If she were in here even once, she'd make an impression. Know what I mean?" Pete looked at the photo of Warren appreciatively.

"Yeah, Pete. She's a looker." Zoe looked triumphantly at Kaj and flashed him the winning grin, along with a kick under the bar.

"And these two—one of the servers says she's pretty sure they were in here. Separately. But she can't swear to it." He pointed to Mayhew's picture and to Marty.

"And this guy." He now pointed to the hospital administrator. "I recognize him. He hits the bar here fairly regularly. Does lunch. Usually comes in with a woman, but she's not in these photos."

Zoe hadn't brought a picture of Nelson along, and realized she should have.

"By the way, Pete, we were wondering…" Zoe looked at Kaj and paused just long enough for him to elbow her in the ribs. Satisfied, she continued, "Have you seen him in here lately?" She muffled a laugh at Kaj's clearly relieved expression.

"Depends on what you mean by lately. I guess the last time I saw him was maybe a couple weeks ago. But he could have come in when I wasn't working."

"How about the woman? She still coming in with him?"

"Yeah, last time she was."

That meant it wasn't Nelson.

Pete looked around uncomfortably. "Listen, I don't want to get anybody in trouble here. I don't think she's his wife."

"We don't want trouble either, Pete." She took the photos from him. "You've been a big help. What's for dessert?"

"Gotta recommend the cheesecake. It really *is* good."

"Make it one, with two forks."

Kaj called after Pete as he turned to walk down the bar. "Make it two. I want my own." His slightly angry eyes swung back to Zoe.

She leaned toward him, her head right next to his, and whispered in his ear. "Do you hear that? Listen carefully … it's the 'Rocky' theme song playing in my head. I land one more punch and I might just have to get up off this stool and do a victory dance."

He smiled at the image. "You really don't play fair do you?"

"Sorry. But you're so fun to play with I just couldn't help myself. Haven't you heard? They say I've no self-control."

"Promise?"

She smiled, and nodded appreciatively this time. "That's one to you."

WITH A GOOD BUZZ ON, they walked the several blocks to Kaj's penthouse.

"Nice meal and good company," she smiled, "but that information did basically nothing. It's fucking frustrating."

"You'll get him, Zoe." He supported her at the waist, and could feel her unsteadiness. Pete made them strong.

"I'm just pissed off about it … at myself."

"Hey, you've been working as hard as you can on this. Believe me, I've noticed."

"I have this weekend off. I need to focus on the case."

"That's fine, Zoe. I have to run up to the North Shore this weekend. I need some work done on my cabin there and have to get the place ready for the contractor. It's a good place to concentrate."

She pulled up short. "What? Another place? Bet we didn't search that one either, eh?"

Kaj grinned and urged her to keep walking. It was cold and he could feel her shivering. "That's right. But once again, I don't recall anyone asking me. I'd have told you." He leaned his face down in front of hers, smiling.

"You're too much. I expect to see the place, Kaj. But it's not going to be this weekend. I've got work."

"I was hoping we could throw your murder board in the car and you could come along. I don't want to leave you here. Maybe I won't go. The work up there can wait." He pulled her close, trying to warm her.

"Don't change your plans on my account. I'll be fine."

"Only if you agree to stay at my place. Otherwise I'm not going," he said firmly, and Zoe seemed to be considering it.

"Okay. You win. I'll spend some time there."

"With you, I'm seldom sure if I'm actually winning or not." They spilled into the elevator, already undressing. Kaj felt a little uneasy about their conversation, but with her naked body pressed up against the mirrored glass of the elevator, it only seemed like a distraction, and he left it to focus on her.

CHAPTER FORTY
DECEMBER 17 (EVENING)

SOMETHING WAS OFF. SHE WALKED EVERY room, stopping to inventory all she could recall about each space. Nothing seemed amiss. She looked especially hard at her den. The murder board and documents. Nothing different there except an odor in the air that didn't seem to belong. Maybe a mouse died in the wall.

If Kaj were the killer, his trip to the North Shore would be an opportunity to murder again. The North Shore was only a few hours from Minneapolis and a round trip back, including a murder, could be accomplished after having arrived there and using a credit card to make sure he was noticed. It would also be the perfect frame. A clever killer would notice that. But maybe it was all just wishful thinking.

She loaded her backpack. There was still the Thursday night graveyard shift to get through before the long weekend … probably a wasted one, she had to admit … but still worth a try.

Before leaving she trapped a barely perceptible scrap of paper between the jamb and door to the den before closing off the room, and dressed for the cold ride to work. The paper seemed to her like a slightly paranoid thing, but she always accounted for devious minds.

Zoe dressed for thirty-second frostbite cold. Black ice was forming at the intersections, requiring a slow and vigilant ride. Even so, her tire skidded at Franklin Avenue, and she barely got a boot down to catch herself before sliding through the red light. At this speed it was hardly a workout. Arriving in a bad mood, Zoe pounded down to Kelly's and used her key.

She parked the bike and peeled off her winter layers. Moisture rose from her skin. She'd worked up a sweat after all. The same cold-sweat odor you'd find at a hockey rink.

"Shep, what are *you* doing here? I thought you were done with your ER rotation." Zoe was still toweling off wet hair as she walked out of the call room to look at the board.

"Just covering for someone. Geir. He wanted this weekend off, and I offered to take a shift for him."

"Good to have you back for the night. How's it looking?" She tossed the towel over the back of a chair and hooked her hands behind her in the waist of her scrubs as she scanned the board. It was her usual "at ease" pose. Shep loved it, and wanted to grab her waist when she stood that way.

"I've got the guy in cube three. He's off getting films right now. Pneumonia versus bronchitis. I debated about even getting the chest x-ray, since I'd probably treat him the same either way, but he's homeless and coughing up a little blood. Smoker too. Was worried about TB or worse."

"Good move. Got a mask on him?"

"Sure thing."

"Sputum samples?"

"Working on it."

"Perfect." She grabbed a chart. "Looks like I get the drunk."

She headed for the "blue room." That her patient had been triaged into the room with a shower meant there was something that required sanitizing. She hated blue-room cases, and never felt even the least bit guilty about pawning them off on interns whenever she could. Shep was just lucky he'd already grabbed the other guy.

Zoe emerged from the blue-tiled room, heading straight for the sink when she noticed Kaj. "Just a second. I've got to wash up first. Desperately," she said through gritted teeth. She scrubbed her hands, arms and face before heading in his direction.

"As cold as it is, you'd think the homeless in this town wouldn't have to worry about bugs for at least a few months out of the year. Don't they die at these temperatures?"

"No, they'll be the last to survive." He embraced her.

"Hey, it's only three days." She grabbed his face and pulling his mouth to hers, she whispered, "Let's go up there together sometime though. I would like to see it. What's it like?"

"You'd love it. Twenty acres of forest and Lake Superior frontage. Good mountain biking. Also borders the outflow of an active river." He ran his hands through her hair. "Let's plan on it."

"It's a date. Now scram. My guy in the blue room needs delousing. I've also got to deal with his frostbite and the maggots making a home out of his groin. Once we get them cleaned out I'm sure I'll find the open wound they've been working on. Who knows, maybe the maggots kept him alive by preventing sepsis. He's a mess though."

She let out a long sigh. "Liver failure too. He's going to need a complete tune-up while he's here. Not to mention a vacation from alcohol. The internal medicine resident is going to want a piece of my ass after I chip this one up to him."

"Tell him your ass is all mine." He smiled. "Maggots, eh? Sounds like they found the one warm place. And you could very well be right, about doing the guy a favor. Remember … my place. Right?"

"Got the key in my jacket downstairs. It's in Kelly's office, with my bike."

"Good." He shook his head. "Wait a minute, you *biked* here tonight?"

She turned her palms up and shrugged. "What?"

"I should have known." He only shook his head. "I'll try to get back early. That's why I'm leaving tonight instead of tomorrow morning. I'll try to wrap things up quickly."

"Okay then, get going. I've got my hands full here anyway."

He left her with another dizzying kiss to remember him by. As he turned to leave she surprised herself … picturing this as the last time they'd see each other … and tensed at the parasitic thought. Where had that come from? There was no room for a lack of decisiveness.

She watched him walk out the door remembering that weeks ago, before him, she wouldn't have worried about her own safety. For so many years, it had just been her. But now there was this need to be there for him. It made her weak. She could feel it.

WATCHING ZOE AND PARKER TOGETHER, Shep's hopes had been temporarily dashed. He'd known all along that she was nothing more than a fantasy, but still … it's why he'd finagled the shift out of Geir. It gave him time with her, on a night when

Parker wasn't working. Seeing Parker leave had finally insured at least ten hours of watching her. Opportunities to brush up against her . . . to place his hand on her shoulder, and at the small of her back. All innocent interactions that no one thought twice about.

But the ten hours had turned out to be exhausting. There'd been no time for anything but work. Not even coffee, let alone food. They *had* gotten intimate though, as Shep considered being covered in the same blood an intimacy.

The local knife and gun club had been unusually active. Three shooting victims from one gunfight, a drive-by missing the target and hitting an innocent bystander, a dispute between teenagers at a party finally settled with a knife, and a DWI who'd crashed his car into a squad. Both the drunk and the officer needed attention. All that on top of the other bizarre nighttime ER activity.

SHE HADN'T THOUGHT ABOUT IT during the night, but now that it was over she realized how much the work had left her worn down and vulnerable going into the weekend. All she could focus on was food and sleep.

She rolled into her driveway after a tense ride home through morning rush hour traffic. All the car exhaust had worsened the black ice, causing two small falls that would leave bruises, but thankfully hadn't sent her into the path of any cars.

One fall must have looked worse than it was. Some construction workers had come at a dead run to help her, and she'd quickly waved them off. By now, all she could think about was sleep. She skipped breakfast and headed straight for bed.

LATELY, SHE'D BEEN DREAMING . . . through sweet, uninterrupted, restorative sleep. And to her great relief, she'd had no nightmares. The dreams had been at worst benign; at best . . . she'd wake Kaj, hoping to recreate the erotic imaginings.

But today's dream was different. She'd had a little trouble falling asleep at first, without Kaj's warmth. She was starting to rely on him, and fell asleep with that on her mind. The developing need for him, and the vulnerability that exposed.

Her brother, shaking in her arms, kept quiet. She'd covered his ears. Zoe heard everything though. The shouting, over and over . . . *where is she?* Even then she'd known he was talking about her.

She kept wanting to give herself up, and tell him to stop hurting her mum. She could hear that too. But her mother's eyes had communicated an absolute as she'd sent them running and then went to lock the door. Her command had been final. And there was her brother to think about.

Zoe heard her mother yelling at the man ... and at her. *The kids aren't here right now. They're at the neighbors' house, playing.* What Zoe heard was ... *keep hiding.*

When her mother finally fell silent, footsteps came up the stairs, and they weren't her mums. Someone else was below her, walking each room. Calling to her ... by name.

She closed her eyes and tried to slow her breathing ... pretending, for her brother's sake. Covering his ears and signaling quiet, she forced a smile and hoped that if he didn't hear, he wouldn't panic ... he wouldn't cry.

The man kept calling for her as they hid. Zoe figured either he was stupid or impatient. He may have been both, because he *was* fooled.

Zoe held them in the attic for a long time after she heard a car drive away, hoping her mother would come up. She tried to convince herself with a child's logic that if she hadn't seen it, it didn't happen. But really, she knew what she'd find. And it was finally her brother who couldn't hold still any longer. He complained loudly, and if anyone were still in the house, they'd have heard.

Zoe cautiously took her brother into the bathroom and went through their bedtime rituals. Making sure his teeth were brushed she tucked him in, read him a story, and turned the nightlight on. She told him he'd been good at hide-and-seek, mother couldn't even find them. That seemed to comfort him. She waited until he was asleep, and then slowly made her way toward the stairs. It all took forty minutes. Her childhood was over.

If she had truly been in denial about what she'd find downstairs, she wouldn't have bothered to put her brother to bed first. The therapist would later try to tell her that she'd been in shock. Going through the motions with her brother only kept her from facing what had happened. *Denying* it had happened. For forty fucking minutes ... yeah right.

She knew better, even then, and went through the motions because she *did* know what was waiting for her downstairs. That she didn't want to see it wasn't crazy. It was because she did know, and didn't want her brother to ever have to see it.

Standing at the top of the steps, wishing her father would get home and relieve her of the responsibility, she took her first cautious steps. Halfway down, she could see her mother's legs. One rested at an awkward angle. It looked like it would hurt, lying like that, and she rushed to her. Staying focused on the leg, she moved it to a more normal anatomic position, and then risked looking up . . . into her mother's eyes.

They were fixed, open in the same determined look she'd given Zoe when sending them fleeing to the attic. Zoe collapsed in the blood next to her, pulling her mum into her arms.

There was so much she wanted to tell her. Mostly that she loved her. She wanted to say it over and over again . . . loudly . . . until her mum would wake up and say, "Don't worry, dear, I know."

And that she'd done what she'd been told, and it had worked . . . that her mum was smarter than that man.

And that she was angry . . . at her mother for leaving her, at whoever had done this, and at her father for not being there. And angry with herself, for causing it all. She didn't know how or why, but somehow it was her fault. He'd been looking for her. It was the start of the clawing inside.

For a while, her child-like imagination pictured a wolverine, like the one she'd seen by the lakeshore. And from that moment on it used her. She was its malignant connection to a world where it wasn't welcomed. And she would spend years figuring out how to balance that . . . with living.

When her father finally arrived at the incomprehensible scene, he'd had to pry Zoe away from her mother, her arms refusing to let go. Dried blood glued the two together. Her dad would never know how that tight embrace was all that restrained her anger that night.

Tears weren't a problem then. She refused to reveal that weakness, to whoever he was. Anger made more sense, even then. It's one reason her dad felt she needed a therapist. Funny how that had worked out.

IT WAS HER STOMACH THAT FINALLY woke her, a mixture of hunger and clawing, and both required feeding. *Fucking therapist* was her first conscious thought. Drenched in sweat, the sheets were in tangles around her legs. Raking hands through damp hair and stretching, she decided to feed the beast first. She stripped to her bra and boxers and headed for the gym.

Her workout was hard. It had to be. The tension never gave itself up easily.

When done, and her appetite for violence at bay, Zoe concentrated on feeding a stomach that hadn't seen food in twenty-four hours. She headed straight to the kitchen and cracked some eggs. With the addition of bacon, toast, and strong coffee, she actually felt human again. After finishing a second cup of Peets, Zoe put her feet up and watched the runners across the street. No sign of the two men it was her hobby to lust after. They were morning runners. It just felt like morning to her now.

She relaxed with the coffee and a beautiful sunset. At least there'd been no sleepwalking. Maybe it was only the tangled sheets around her feet, but somehow she'd ridden it out in bed.

She made herself get up, stripping her bra and boxers as she moved. Turning the water temperature up, she let it cascade over her, and washed off the last of the hospital, the sweat, and the intolerable scent of fear.

It wasn't just a nightmare. Weren't nightmares supposed to be odd, distorted versions of reality? This was a memory. It had happened. She sucked in the clean smell of shampoo, rinsing off just in time to hear the phone ring. Dripping, she wrapped herself in a towel and ran for her cell.

"Where are you, Zoe?" It was Kaj.

She was too off guard to lie. "Still at my place, eating and showering. Had a rough night at work and I fell asleep. Just woke up a little while ago." She did her best to sound relaxed. There'd been no problem. "What time is it?"

"Six. And you just woke up?"

"Yeah, a little while ago."

"My place, Zoe. No messing around here."

"I said I would, didn't I? Give me a chance. I'm not completely staying away from my house *all* weekend. I've got things to do, remember? All the documents are here."

The back of her neck feathered as she remembered the door to the den. She hadn't even bothered to check it when she arrived at home. Starting down the hallway as they talked, she tried to hide the sharp intake of air as she found the tiny scrap of paper on the floor.

"You okay, Zoe? What happened?"

"Nothing. Just stubbed my toe as I was heading for my clothes. I'm still dripping wet. How about if I ring you back later?"

"Wish I was there."

She could picture him smiling.

"I wish you were too." She had to get him off the phone . . . and find her gun. "Listen, I'm freezing. I've got to get dressed. I'll call you back in a few minutes, I promise."

"Okay, but the signal isn't very good here. Don't be surprised if you can't reach me."

"I won't. And don't worry if I can't. Promise?"

"No. But with you I'm getting used to worrying."

"Sorry." And she truly was. Her resolve to avoid attachments had always been in anticipation of a tragic end. Tragedy really happened, and not just to other people. She knew that, she'd lived it after all, and just didn't want to drag anyone else into it with her. "Okay then? I'll call you?"

"Yeah, Zoe. Love you."

"Later Kaj."

"Have I got any choice? Go get dried off. Bye."

She threw the phone down and ran to the closet, grabbing her weapon. Readying it, she held it down at her side as she made her way first for any rooms she hadn't been in yet since getting home that morning, saving the den for last.

She was cold, the moisture still evaporating from her skin and she started to shake. It felt too much like fear. *Settle down.* No sign of anyone.

She returned to the den, and slowly opened the door part way. The room looked empty. She took one cautious step to enter the room after noticing the cold air and open window. She pushed to open the door all the way but it came crashing back at her, knocking the gun from her hand and bloodying her nose.

He was on her before she could roll or reach for her gun. Two gloved hands held tight around her neck. Her right hand pinned awkwardly beneath her, she punched at his jaw with the heel of the other. But without enough momentum, it only made him angry. She could feel the pressure move front and center on her neck.

At first he seemed to be holding back, just trying to subdue her by pressing on her carotid arteries to black her out. But now she truly struggled for air, and pictured the kind of death a fractured larynx could cause.

He curled at the serious knee to the groin and let go, seeming surprised by the fight in her. Zoe rolled and grabbed for her gun, rising and swinging it up as he jumped out the open window. His ability to bolt after the blow surprised her too. She managed to get one shot off as he disappeared into the darkness, but knew that she'd missed. Not having clear confirmation of her target, and with neighboring homes in line, she'd instinctively cheated low, and knew she probably shouldn't have fired at all.

She ran to the window and looked out... nothing but footprints leading toward the alley. She turned to pick up the landline in the den.

Sirens came for her out of the darkness. A squad slid to a stop first. Then they called Ray, and got to work.

SEEING HER, ALIVE AND BLOODIED, "I'm hoping like hell for a body somewhere. Where is he, Zoe?"

She closed her eyes against the failure.

"He's gone. I let him get away." Her eyes spilled as she looked up at Ray. "Bloody fucking hell!"

"Zoe?" He approached her carefully.

"Unfortunately, all this blood is mine. I couldn't even make him bleed. You'll probably find a slug in the windowsill. I blew it, Ray."

"Well who was it?"

Her eyes went flat, and stared out the window. "He was dressed in black. Had a ski mask on, and gloves."

"You're kidding, right? You can't make him?"

"I wish I were. He never said anything either. If it was Popeye, that's all I would have needed. Only got a grunt out of him with the knee to the groin. The hit to the jaw didn't even get a reaction, except to make him squeeze harder." She pointed to her neck.

The reddened impressions were obvious.

"Where else are you hurt?"

"Bloody nose is all. Looks worse than it is."

"Where's lover boy?"

"At his cabin on the North Shore."

"Want me to call him?"

"No. I don't want to worry him. I'll be fine. I just can't fucking believe it. I had him and I let him go."

"Zoe, for Christ's sake! He could have killed you. You did what was necessary to stay alive. You couldn't have expected this."

She brought her eyes slowly to his, along with the same dead-eyed look that would always turn Jack's stomach. "You don't think so?"

"What are you saying Zoe? That you knew he was coming?"

"It was a long shot. I figured he'd targeted Anders to frame Kaj. I just hoped that with any luck he might come for me too." She looked away, back toward the window.

"Wait, I can't fucking believe this! You set yourself up with Parker to lure this guy? It's all a lie? You and Parker? Nothing but bait? What the hell, Zoe!" He got up to pace.

"I won't apologize for that. Only that I didn't kill him. And with Kaj, yes, it started as a lie ... for me anyhow. But now it's the truth." She slowly got up, testing her own stability, and felt a little light-headed.

"I was expecting him. This weekend. I'd set it up that way. I was ready ... but so very, very tired. And in the back of my head, I think I figured it was a hopeless long shot. So he still managed to surprise me. Of all the stupid things."

"And you couldn't tell me about this?"

"Like I said, it was such a long shot. And I figured if it was going to work, the odds were better if few people knew. He's crazy smart, Ray. You know that. I didn't want to spook him and waste this opportunity. I figured I could handle it ... if only I hadn't been so fucking tired when I got home."

Ray spun and punched the wall. Red erupted from his knuckles. "Fuck!"

Zoe flinched.

"Ray. It's just now sinking in. Something's off about this. It doesn't fit."

"How's that? That he might have killed you right away and not set things up like the others?" Zoe watched him shudder.

She only shrugged. "Yeah, I guess there's that. But it's something else. It's as if he was up to something different this time. It bothers me that he wore a ski mask. If he'd had to wait outside long, it's below zero; he might have actually needed it. But if he used it to hide his face, that doesn't make sense. Sticking to pattern, he'd have planned on killing me. Why would it matter if I saw his face? In fact he'd have wanted me to. I'd lay money on that.

"The other thing is, it seemed like such an amateur attempt. I think he was even surprised that I fought back. Breaking free of him was too easy. I'd have expected more."

Ray raked the bloodied hand through his hair. "I'm going to get the techs in here. They'll want to get what they can off you too. Stay right where you are. I'll be back after I talk with the troops and see what they've found."

ON HIS WAY DOWN THE HALL he spotted Zoe's cell phone on the floor, found Parker's number and hit send.

"Hi, Zoe. Heading over to my place now?"

Ray paused. "It's not Zoe, and I hope you can prove where you were tonight."

"Ray? Is that you? Where's Zoe? What's going on?"

"You're going to want to get back here right away."

"Ray! Tell me what happened? Is Zoe all right?"

"Did you know what she was planning? You fucking son of a bitch! You knew! And you let her do this!"

"Is she all right? Ray! Tell me!"

"Yeah, she's not hurt too bad. But how in the hell could you have let her do this? She never told me, you know! She was on her own with that maniac, no backup."

"Damn it! I made her promise to stay at my place. What do you mean not hurt *too* bad?" Kaj jumped through the gears.

"You don't deserve…"

"What happened there? Ray?…Ray!"

No signal.

CHAPTER FORTY-ONE
DECEMBER 18 (EVENING)

"FOOTPRINTS TO AND FROM THE DEN window." Ray had little else to report. The gunshot brought people to their windows, but apparently too late. No sign of a running man, a masked man, any man.

"There's no telling how long he was in here." She sickened to think of him watching her... the gym, the shower, sleeping even? Wouldn't she have noticed? No, probably not... she'd been so tired.

"Well, hell. I'm no good now. I'm burned. He won't come for me again... at least not here. He's too smart for... but... wait, this doesn't fit."

"He'd couldn't have been here long when you surprised him. You probably just caught him off guard."

"Afraid not, Ray. When I left for work last night, I had a feeling, you know like the house felt different? Anyway, I sensed it, maybe even smelled it, in the den. So when I left, I put a give-away in the door. It'd already fallen out before I ever opened the door to the den. I think he'd been through the house before I surprised him."

Ray winced as he fisted the injured hand. "You mean you thought someone had already been in your house, and yet you came back to it and... *fell*... *asleep?* Didn't tell me, or anyone? What the *hell* were you thinking?"

Zoe's head fell back against the wall. "Can we let that go now, Ray? I was just thinking that it was a paranoid thing to do, and that it was all a freaking long shot anyway. And then when I got home I was so tired and forgot. I mean *really* dead on my feet. Okay? The answer to that question isn't going to change the more you keep asking it. It may have been *stupid*, but it's the answer. Now, let's focus on what it all means."

Ray blew out a long breath and narrowed his eyes on her. "All right. So maybe it does give us some insight into how he operates. He may have been in your house before and felt comfortable moving through it while you slept. Could have been getting things ready I suppose."

"Okay, two problems with that. First, if he'd been in my house before, I think I'd have noticed it, when I wasn't so tired. Secondly, what exactly was he getting ready? We found nothing. Not a thing disturbed other than the mess from the confrontation in the den. And third…"

"You said two things."

"Ray!"

"I'm still pissed. Go on."

"Third, why did he wear a mask? If he'd planned on killing me, what difference would it make if I saw him? In fact, I'd have bet a month's salary he would *want* me to see him. And fourth," she shot Ray a warning glance, "why didn't he say anything?"

"Well, that one I do have a theory about. Maybe it *is* Popeye. His voice is as good as a fingerprint." He stopped at the look on Zoe's face and just waited. It seemed like several minutes before she spoke.

"Okay, now that was weird. I'm sitting here thinking of all the reasons this is different from the others, and there it is. That same feeling I've been getting at the crime scenes. Something to do with the guy not speaking, or at least that's when it hit me." Zoe went to the kitchen and poured several painkillers into her palm, downing them dry. Ray followed. "I've got to think about that."

"What are your plans for tonight Zoe? Maybe you should come home with me. You definitely shouldn't stay here. And we should get you looked at."

"I'm not hurt. I'm just angry with myself. And you and I both know he's not coming back here. Damn it! We could have had him tonight. I used up my chance. It's as bloody simple as that."

She raked both hands through her hair and looked around. "But you're right. I don't think I could relax here tonight. I promised Kaj I'd stay at his place, so I think that's exactly what I'll do. When he called…" she suddenly remembered she hadn't called him back. "Shit. I was telling him I was heading over there as soon as I finished up here."

"Your phone's on your bed. I silenced it after I lost the signal with Parker. He's probably been trying to call you."

"What? You answered it?"

"No, I called him. Thought he might want to get back here." He grabbed Zoe by the shoulders, turning her to face him squarely. "He should never have left you alone. And he knew all along what you were trying to do? Guy's a piece of shit if you ask me."

"He knew I'd do it no matter what. He only agreed to go along when he thought it would keep him closer to me. Took me a while to finally shake him. I think he and I both started to fatigue though, figured the idea was off, that I'd read more into the guy than I had a right to. After all, messing with a cop *is* a pretty bold thing to do.

"And that brings me to the fifth thing that's off about this. He wasn't that hard to fight, and seemed surprised by the fight in me. That doesn't fit if he thinks he's coming after a cop. He should have come loaded for bear, don't you think?"

"Yeah, I'd have to admit that is strange. Of course most people *would* be surprised by your strength. Ask anyone who plays hockey with you."

"I'm just cheap. Everyone knows that too. Anyhow, sure I'm stronger than most women, and I've got skills, but still . . . it's as if he thought I'd just roll over for him. And! He never showed me a weapon!"

"Okay, you're up to six now."

"Well think about it, Ray. I suppose I *could* have surprised him enough that he didn't have time to get it out of a jacket pocket, or wherever. I mean I had a loaded gun leading me into the room and all. But he was hiding behind the door. He must have figured I might walk in. So where was his weapon? And if he'd dropped it in the scuffle, I guarantee he didn't have time to find it before he left. I kneed him hard and was back on him fast with my gun. Yet somehow he managed to get out that window. If he'd had a weapon he would have had to make the choice between retrieving it and facing me or jumping out. There wasn't time for both. I'm sure of that."

Zoe walked to the bedroom and retrieved her phone. Several missed calls from Kaj. She came back to the kitchen table to join Ray. "Hardly any of this matches what we've seen from him before. I don't get it."

"Yeah. That makes two of us."

Chapter Forty-Two
December 18 (Late Evening)

H ER HAIR POOLED OVER HIS PILLOW, still wet from the shower. He wanted to wake her, but she looked deep, and needed the rest.

Instead he visually inspected every inch of her, inventorying the bruises and the raccoon eyes from where the door had struck her face. After noticing the marks at her throat, he turned out the lights and watched her. The rise and fall of her breasts as she pulled deeply. The curve of her hip illuminated by the skyline lights. A place she loved to be touched. Her legs, muscular when called upon, but now soft and smooth in their flaccid state.

She jumped, her hands reaching for her throat. As her eyes shot open, he was at her side. He could see the initial terror give way to what he'd hoped for. She relaxed, her eyes softening this time, and she focused on his face. Her body followed, curving into him.

"Glad you're back." Her head fell back, and he cushioned it with his hand.

"Sorry I left." Her neck was so thin. He watched the pulse at her carotids. Remembering how he'd admired the curve of her neck so long ago, he leaned down to kiss the bruises . . . and kissed her scar.

She smiled. "I think that's when I knew I was recklessly in love with you. That you weren't just . . ." her eyes smiled now too, "my weakness."

His hair swept over her neck as he moved up to connect with her. His eyes . . . questioning . . . smiling . . . sometimes full of an animal aggression . . . but always focused on her. He hoped she no longer doubted that.

"And when would that be?"

"It was when you brought me back here after my session with Camilla. You probably don't remember, but you kissed the scar on my neck."

"Oh, but I do remember, Zoe. I remember everything about that night." He didn't break away from her gaze. Instead he leaned down to gently kiss the purple margins of her facial wounds, keeping his eyes locked on hers.

"Do you remember what you were thinking?" She chuckled at the thought. "Well, now that's just silly isn't it? Thinking you'd remember."

"How could I forget? I know exactly what I was thinking. The same thing I'm thinking right now." He gave her the smile he knew she craved.

"That I love every inch of you, everything about you. Love how you think, the way you make love. Your physicality and strength. I love your long, lean legs, the soft curve of your hip, and the feel of your hair over my skin. I love your long, slender neck. And I love your scar. Everything that makes you who you are. Everything."

ALL AIR ESCAPED HER, and she drew hard to refill. She wanted to tell him. Tell him what she really was made of. That to love her scar was to accept her anger, and to understand her past. She wanted to trust him.

But she was tired. So very, very tired. She closed her eyes as he continued to kiss her . . . softly over her bruises, teasing across her stomach, her hip.

He took his time, blowing on embers, moving in only when she was ready to catch fire. She was at the precipice, holding her breath for that one moment, waiting for the tipping point, the fall.

And then it pounded through her as if she were falling down a staircase. Her breath freed itself on an uncensored moan, and she fell loose onto the sheets, as though there was nothing left to feel. But he was only starting.

HE SMILED AT THE PLEASURE he'd given, and moved back to kiss her neck again. This time, he rose to use his hands. Slowly he massaged her shoulders, her breasts, and then worked down over her thighs. Taking the time, focused only on her, he worked his way back up until he felt it build in her again. Her body started to meet his in anticipation of each stroke.

He threw her arms above her head, kneading her muscles, and trapping her wrists. Feeling her yield to the vulnerable position, he drove. Thrusting, slowly at first, teasing, then deeper and harder, but still slow.

He sensed the desperation in her, begging him to a release. His pace quickened, until her cascading cry accompanied his pained, throaty moan as he threw his head back and buried himself in her.

He dropped softly into her neck…kissing her again…back to where they'd started, and rose to look in her eyes. She could only manage a smile, and to murmur his name. Leaning down to kiss her above her eyes, he gently worked his way around the bruise, and then fell to her side, still holding her. Until her eyes shot wide open.

"It's important!"

"What? What is it Zoe?" He could feel her tense, everything undone in an instant.

"When we make love, we make noise. Doesn't everybody? The disc, of you and Nelson…there was no sound." She propped up on an elbow, pushing him down on his back.

"So, it was only video. Why is that important?"

"Maybe she didn't make it." Zoe was looking out the window now.

"I don't see how that follows. And *I* certainly didn't make it!" He pushed back, both sitting up now.

"I'm not saying *you* did. But maybe it was someone else. And it ties to what's been bothering me about the scenes too."

"I'm still not following you. How does a lack of sound imply that someone else made the disc?"

"I have to call, Ray. I need to get in Nelson's house. Now."

He jumped up to throw Zoe her clothes and quickly zipped, belted and adjusted his own. He'd seduced her while fully clothed. It had to have made her feel even more vulnerable, and yet she'd trusted him. Knowing what he knew of her past, it amazed him that she was capable of any kind of trust at all.

Chapter Forty-Three
December 18 (Midnight)

THE "FOR SALE" SIGN REMAINED, AND SO did the snow. No one had bothered to shovel the walk… at least since the blizzard. They stomped off their shoes as they entered and let Zoe lead.

She headed straight for the bedroom, the site of both the murder and the video. Ray knocked shoulders with Kaj as they followed her up the stairs. It wasn't an accidental bump. Rather, more like a hockey check. Kaj stopped and grabbed his arm, jerking him back. Ray's hand paused reflexively at his weapon. Kaj shoved his arm as he let it go.

"Do we have a problem?"

"What the fuck do you think, Parker?"

ZOE WAS SITTING ON THE BED, where Nelson's body had been found. A new mattress replaced the bloodstained one, put there by a realtor staging the house for potential buyers. The wall had been scrubbed and painted. The carpet replaced. But very little else had changed.

Zoe recalled the photo of Nelson in this very spot. She tried to look in the direction that Nelson had been looking, then scanned back to gauge the camera angle. "The photo had to have been taken from over there. Did you bring the photos?"

"Yeah, everything you asked for. They're right here."

She hastily spread them out on the comforter, searching for the right one. It was a photo of Nelson sitting on the bed. "Yeah, this picture had to have been taken from over there." She rose to stand in that spot, and looked back at the bed. She studied the picture again.

"Ray, you've got the disc?"

"Right here."

"Load it."

As the disc began, her focus broke for only a moment as she looked at Kaj. She let the disc run, then paused it and dove for the pile of photos on the bed, locating the ones she recalled from Hanover's and Anders'. She hadn't consciously acknowledged the one from Anders', but it must have registered in her somewhere, because she knew exactly what she was looking for.

In both photos there was a framed picture of the victim displayed prominently on a shelf. Each was a candid shot, as if the subject had been taken off-guard. Actually . . . she reconsidered . . . as if they'd never known they were being photographed at all. None were looking directly *at* the camera.

Then she returned to the scene of Mickman's murder. Zoe scoured the photos, finally finding what she was looking for. There was a framed picture of Mickman, seemingly unaware, looking past the camera. It was assumed to have been a promotional photo placed there by Mickman herself, next to the pile of head shots and resumes. It looked to have been taken outside somewhere, her hair lifted on a breeze.

Zoe shoved the crime scene photos into Ray's hands. She fixed her eyes on his and impatiently pushed his hands up toward his face, "Look at them! What do you see?"

Ray shook his head, looking back at her. "Walk me through it, Zoe. I don't know."

"I almost missed it. He's been taunting us all along. Look closely. Look at the photos I gave you. *What* do you see?"

"Zoe, please. I'm not following you. I've looked at these photos a million times. I get nothing from them."

"The pictures *in* the photos," she pointed to the candid shots at each of the crime scenes.

"What about them?" Ray appeared to be lost, and Kaj came to look over his shoulder.

"Kaj, do you recognize the photo of Anders raking leaves?" Zoe pressed.

He studied it for a moment. "No, but that doesn't mean much. Like I said, I didn't spend much time there. And it's something I could have missed."

"Missed that photo? I don't think so. She's beautiful in that shot. Radiant. The yellow and gold of the leaves, a backdrop for an almost dance-like pose. *You* wouldn't have missed that, even though I did at first." She saw the sadness in his eyes. "But my guess is that you never saw it. It was placed there by her killer."

Ray started to look closely at the other photos. "What about these? Same thing?"

"I think so, Ray. If it hadn't been for the disc, I might not have stumbled onto this. Look at them. He was smart enough not to use the same type of frame in any of them. But there were three things bothering me about those photos... Nelson's really. The others just confirmed it. First, the frame he used for the photo of her on the bed. It just doesn't fit this place. *She* wouldn't have chosen it."

Zoe drew close to Kaj. "Did you take this photo of her?" She hoped like hell he hadn't.

"I can't remember ever even seeing that photo. I'm *sure* I didn't take it. I never took any picture of her, for any reason."

Zoe grabbed for the disc and restarted it. She paused it at just the right spot and shoved it at both Kaj and Ray. Compare this with the photo.

Zoe walked over to the window and looked out. Then turning back to look at the bed she shoved both fisted hands in her pockets. "We've got him."

Seeing Ray and Kaj study the two images in apparent confusion, she redirected their attention to the similarities. It was the second thing.

"Consider where the camera had to have been to take either of those images."

"Probably right where you're standing." Ray looked like he was just starting to process things.

Kaj came over to join her at the window. "The photo maybe, but I guarantee no one else was in this room when I was. There was also no camera where you're standing now." He looked around. "And I don't see where she would have hidden one."

"The window, Kaj. I'm backed right up to the window. He wasn't in the room when he took it."

"How could anyone have taken pictures through this window?" He looked out at the distance to the ground.

Ray jumped up. "Holy shit."

"That's right Ray. It would be easy if you lived next door."

Ray visibly paled. His jaw dropped slightly as he stared back at Zoe.

"Both images were taken on the same tripod would be my guess. In fact, the still photo could have been taken directly from the disc, or at least on the same night. She looks like she's talking to someone. You?" She looked at Kaj.

"It could have been. I do recall her sitting on the bed in that way as she removed her stockings."

"Right. She's looking lovingly at someone to the side of the camera. More specifically, *talking* to someone. Joking? Flirting maybe? Looks happy. Who else would be present at a time like that? We're looking at the beginning of a seduction here. That's the third thing. You might miss it in the other photos, but not in this one. It's the photo itself. It didn't make sense to me. No one else should have been in that room but the two of you."

Ray looked across at the window directly opposite Nelson's. "Oh, my God, Zoe."

"Guess your instincts about Mayhew were right. It broke loose in me when I thought about there being no sound on the disc. One reason for it could be that the recording hadn't been done from within the room itself, but remotely. Then all the rest of it tumbled into place. It made sense. He *had* been taunting us, right from the beginning. Clever maybe, but *always* a mistake."

"Zoe, you've got it all wrong."

"What? C'mon, Ray, *maybe*, but I like it. This works. We get a warrant to go in next door. And get some tech guys to look at the images. It also fits with my strong belief that the first kill was close to home. It was just *really* close. That's all."

"Mayhew doesn't live there, Zoe."

She backed up to the edge of the bed and dropped. The men waited out her full minute of stunned silence while she stared at the window, deep in thought.

"All the signs were there. He's a friend for God's sake. I didn't even consider him. It wasn't Warren who approached him with the idea of an alibi. It must have been the other way around. Why wouldn't I think of that?"

She looked back up at Ray. "What did Mayhew say about the conversation with Marty when you brought him in again?"

"Yep. He denied it. Said it was his word against Marty's. That Marty must have been confused, or mixed him up with someone else."

"Marty was good. He got all chatty and led me along. Really had me fooled when I talked to him that day in the ER. He had to have made it all up on the spot too. Creative guy."

"Marty? He lives next door?" Kaj looked across the night at the window.

"Afraid so." Ray was still looking at Zoe. "Listen, I didn't see it either. I had access to the same information, and I just didn't figure the guy for it."

"It's not the same. I'm around him a lot. I should have picked up on it." She grimaced and closed her eyes. "And me of all people, letting a fucking relationship get in the way. If this wasn't so damn serious..." She felt sick. And to the men...she looked sick.

"You can't blame yourself, Zoe. You've done the best you can. He's been clever..."

She interrupted him. "Is that supposed to be some sort of consolation? It's only well-intentioned crap. I fucked up here...again. It's that simple. Bloody hell! There are people who might not be dead if I'd been clear on this."

Ray pulled hard for some air and straightened up. "Well, I wasn't clear on this either." He looked at Kaj. "But we've got him now. I'm going to get things rolling. I'll call Jack and get him working on a warrant. I don't want to spook this guy without a way to get inside though. The lights are all out over there. Hard to tell if he's home or not."

"Let's hope not. If he saw any of this...he might have left." Kaj started toward the steps. "Let's go." As they walked down he added, "Marty would have had access to my schedule, as well as all the rumors. And he could easily have *seen* me with Julia if he lived right next door. Of course my relationship with Liv wasn't exactly a mystery among those at the hospital either."

"I'll be putting someone on his house. We'll keep an eye on the place until I get a warrant. Meanwhile, if he tries to leave, we can bring him in for an interview and buy time that way. If he arrives at home, we'll just keep watching and assume that he didn't see any of this. Now let's get out of here. I'll let you know when the warrant comes through."

Chapter Forty-Four
December 19 (1:00 AM)

I WAS THINKING LIKE HIM . . . IN HIS HEAD for a while. But that lame attack at my place threw me off. Now I feel like I don't know anything anymore."

Zoe blew out a long foggy breath in the cold. At these temperatures, even Kaj's luxury SUV took a while to warm up.

They pulled up to a stoplight, and Zoe felt his gaze. "What else?"

"How do you know these things?" She turned toward him. "It was a nightmare. Something I rarely have. Why it happened then, I don't know. But it distracted me so badly that when I woke up it was all I could think about."

He punched the gas at the green light. "Take a guess. Why did it happen then?"

"I dunno, probably because I was so tired, and because lately I'm finally sleeping well enough to get to a dream stage. But . . . it wasn't a nightmare the way I picture most people having them. It wasn't some distorted, loosely linked series of images. It was an accurate memory. Almost as if . . ."

She shook her head sharply. "I'm not used to dreams. I need to pay closer attention to them I think."

"Zoe, what was it about?" At her hesitation, he pulled the car over and parked. "You owe me some honesty, Zoe."

She shifted in her seat, and turned to face him. "So do you. How much do you already know? What did I say to Camilla?"

"Are you sure you're ready to hear it?"

Zoe laughed. "Do you think this stuff is subconscious? That I actually have a hard time remembering it? These are no gradually recovered memories. They're vivid, and I've lived with them for years. It's you I'm worried about."

"Me?" He reached out to take her hand.

"Yes. How much did you hear, and are you ready to understand it? It must have been bad. Camilla's still having a hard time holding eye contact with me. I'll have to deal with that too eventually. But, Kaj, there's a *lot* that's bad. You may never look at me in the same way if I tell you. And I don't think I could handle that."

"You want me to be honest, so I'll tell you. I didn't say anything because I was afraid these memories were explosive to you, and that you'd push me away if I pressed the matter. That I might even harm you by bringing them up."

"That may have been true... *before.*"

"But I know some of what happened in Canada. I did some digging."

Her eyes darkened. He tightened his grip on her hand as she tried to pull away.

"I was worried, and I did what I had to. You'd have done the same, and I won't apologize for it.

"As far as your session with Camilla, it had to do with your being held captive. Camilla had no clue. I could tell she was shocked, and I think now that some time has passed she's hoping you'll talk to her. But I told her nothing more than what she heard in the session. The rest is up to you, when you're ready."

He apparently knew so much, yet from him Zoe hadn't felt either revulsion or pity. His acceptance was unexpected, and she clearly had it. But his understanding? She didn't have that yet.

She recalled Ray's uneasiness after the episode with the knife. Would Kaj have reacted in the same way? Would he understand that she'd thought of a million ways to kill the man? And could he still love her knowing she was capable of it?

"Well then it appears you know some of it... but not what's important."

"I realize that, Zoe. But I haven't wanted to push you. And it won't matter. It won't change a thing between us."

"Just so you understand... I *will* kill him, Kaj." She said it with certainty.

"Not if I get to him first." He didn't even blink. Didn't hesitate.

It chilled her, seeing what her own anger looked like in someone else's eyes. Perhaps there were some things he did understand.

"But that's exactly what I've been trying to avoid all these years. I don't want anyone else involved, or hurt again because of me."

"I am involved. With you and everything about you. That won't change, and it's what I want."

"But what *I* want is for you to be safe."

He laughed now. "Safe? How is that ever possible? I want to *live*. And living means having you in my life."

Zoe paused to study his face, to think about letting herself love him. Letting *him* love her.

"You know, something happened the other day that still haunts me. I saw a man in the ER, an Ojibwe elder ... very strong, stoic guy, not much for talking."

He nodded.

"His family came in with him, and they were frantic. Telling me he needed to see a psychiatrist right away. I *certainly* didn't expect that."

She smiled as she recalled the scene. "They were convinced that something was terribly wrong with him, because all of the sudden he was actually *talking*!"

But her face quickly sobered. "He was talking about fear. They took me aside and told me they were worried about suicide.

"So I got him alone, and sure enough ... he talked."

"What was his problem?"

"He was a dialysis patient, with kidney failure from long-standing diabetes. What had him terrified was that his diabetes was robbing him of his eyesight."

"Doesn't surprise me. I'd be terrified too."

"Of course, that's what I thought at first. So we talked about his hobbies, what he liked to do. You know, to see how much losing his vision was going to limit his quality of life. But he dismissed everything. Said it would be hard and all, but that I was missing the point."

Kaj leaned in, "What exactly was the point?"

"I asked him about his thoughts, when he felt overwhelmed and afraid. I was amazed the guy even admitted to it. He was old, and ill, but sturdy, you know? The kind of guy you never expect has a doubt or fear about anything.

"But eventually he started telling me about the war. He'd been young at the time, but his recollection was so vivid. The firefight he described caused him to visibly cringe when recounting the explosions. His body reacted to the narrative with a visceral fear you could actually see. He was sweating, shaking, and hyperventilating. I even had to silence his cardiac monitor as it annoyed us both with a faster rate.

"He described it as though he had every detail memorized, like a movie he'd seen a million times. And that was precisely the point. He had seen it a million times and never told *anyone* about. I was the first."

He smiled sadly, and nodded. "PTSD?"

"Whatever name you apply, he was just desperate for a way not to think about it." Zoe shook her head in resignation. "It's how I've felt replaying my own memories. But I'm beginning to look at things differently. I wonder if one should think about a traumatic memory, and rethink it, over and over again, until you change the memory itself, or at least change how you look at it. You can't change facts, of course, but you can change the meaning they have in your life. Unfortunately this poor guy thought it was too late."

"How's that? What made it too late?"

"His eyesight. Kaj, when you close your eyes, you see primarily blackness don't you?"

"Well, yes. I suppose. Perhaps a little glimmer of light, but mainly darkness."

"Not him. He could never count on the safety of darkness. Instead, whenever his eyes closed, hoping for sleep, he'd see the same graphic war scene, over and over. And he just fucking suffered with it. Even convinced himself for a while that it was his penance ... for surviving." Zoe had to pause and slow her breathing.

"For a while he drank, until his kidneys failed. Then he sobered and used the TV to fall asleep to. Always found some way to cope, but never *once* sought help.

"Until finally he was terrified by the prospect that with nothing else to look at, going blind, all he'd have left was that movie inside his head. There'd be no escape from it. With no vision, he'd have nothing else to look at ... even when awake."

Kaj reached out to wipe her face.

"And his silence wasn't just a cultural stoicism, it was a misguided idea of victory. I've always thought that by trying to ignore those memories I take away their power, because I feel like such a victim when I think back, and I don't like feeling weak. So I simply try not to think about them. Besides, it's as if he wins every time I replay them, or attach any importance to them. But they are important.

"This patient, he viewed his memories through a prism that emphasized the horror and loss, rather than his personal heroism. I get that too. It's hard to put any positive spin on events where those close to you die."

Zoe paused, and looked out the window. Kaj waited.

"Sometimes I think there are a lot of people who are in love with the *idea* of being damaged. To them it's a romantic fantasy. And they seem to be the ones who consume everyone's attention.

"But then there's this guy, a guy who's for real, and he never talked once. It's the *taking* it that's misguided. You make yourself into a victim that way. *Give* away your power for Christ's sake. Yes, I understood him.

"And it made me think. I may never have a chance to confront my abductor … in fact it's quite possible that he's dead. But even if so, by *not* confronting him, he still stays in control. I have to get free. Don't get me wrong, if he's alive and I had the chance to kill him now, I'd take it." She paused, debating whether to say it. "And I have killed before Kaj, I know I'd do it." She saw the recognition on his face.

"While you were a cop."

"No, a different time … a time when killing felt good. It was *my choice* to kill, and I'll never apologize for it."

"Zoe, of course I have questions, but I'm still here. You can't say anything to push me away."

"I'm all too aware of what I'm capable of, and I *would* kill. The way I feel now, I'd *have* to. But honest to God I wish … I really wish … that I didn't feel that way."

"Well then, that's a start isn't it?" He smiled.

If she wasn't sure before, she was now … God she loved him. But she only returned a sad smile.

"I used to think it would be weak to let go of the anger." She looked down at her lap. "But I worry now that it's really a reluctance to let go of him." She looked back up, turning to Kaj. "Why? Why should I feel that way?" She stopped, embarrassed at having said so much. It wasn't like her.

He leaned in to embrace her, but she pushed him away. "Let's go." She looked straight ahead, waiting for Kaj to make up his mind. It took awhile.

Kaj worked the car back into traffic. They headed for his downtown place, passing the hospital on the way. In the after-bar rush most drivers were drunk, plain and simple. Not a good time to be on the street.

They both saw it come peripherally. A flash of orange, an old Camaro, speeding through the intersection. Kaj swerved to avoid the car running the red, but the pedestrian left lying at the curb hadn't been so lucky. Zoe jumped out the door at full speed toward the young man on the ground.

Carmen was leaning over him, frantically tying her scarf around his thigh just above the pulsing opened artery. Kaj followed at a sprint.

"It wasn't me this time! Honestly! I was about to walk across the street and he pushed me back! But I didn't plan this! It just happened!" She looked at Shep, bleeding through the torn femoral artery. "Please help him!"

They worked fast, and were only a half-block from the ER doors.

Once inside, Kaj took over with Shep and Zoe moved her attention to Carmen in a different room. "Are you hurt anywhere Carmen? Did the car hit you? Did you fall?"

"No, no, I'm not hurt at all. Not a bit, just worried sick about Shep. He saved me you know. He *really* did. I'd have walked right in front of that car. I didn't see it!"

Zoe did a quick exam anyway, and found Carmen to be completely unscathed. They talked a while more, and then Zoe left her with a cup of coffee and a nurse while she went to check in with Kaj.

"How is he?"

"Stable. Surgical team is looking at him now. Vascular is assessing the degree of damage to the artery. But I think he'll be fine."

"The limb?"

"It's badly broken, but I've seen far worse. As we expected, everything else looks fine. No other serious injuries. How's Carmen?"

"Physically okay, but she's pretty shook up about it. Get close to her and you can tell she'd had a bit to drink tonight. Thought I'd take your car and bring her home, or even to your place if that's okay with you?"

"Of course. Whatever she prefers. I'll be home as soon as I wrap things up here. It won't be long. They're almost ready to take him. Lucky for Carmen he was just getting off his shift . . . and not so good for Shep. Call me if Ray phones before I get back."

"Sure, but I doubt it. The warrant's going to take time."

"Zoe? I hope Carmen was leveling with us, that she didn't plan this. I've never known her to put someone else in any real physical danger before, but if she did, I can't let that go."

"Oh, I believe her. She wouldn't do that. She's too careful. But I think maybe she should rethink her strategy anyway. I don't like that she sometimes puts *herself* in harm's way."

"Agreed. I'll talk with her." He held Zoe's eyes. "Zoe? Before you go . . . what was she doing out this late?"

"Don't laugh." But Zoe did. "Kilt Night at Keegan's Pub. She and some lady friends go there to admire the men. Says it's great fun, Irish drinking songs . . . the works. Maybe we should try it sometime." Her smile widened as she looked down at his legs, long and lean in his jeans.

"Don't think for one minute you're getting me in a kilt. I've no Irish heritage that I'm aware of. Only bloodthirsty Vikings. And I don't think they wore skirts. If they did, I don't even want to know about it," and he threw up his hands.

"You know it's not just legs they admire." She moved her eyes from Kaj's face down his body.

"Let's put it this way, the ladies hope for windy conditions when it's warm enough to open the patio." She reached out, pulling him toward her by his belt.

"The day I see *you* in a dress, we'll talk." He fisted his hand in her hair, bringing her lips to his. "It's something I've yet to experience."

"I don't do well in heels. So don't get your hopes up."

"Oh, but I am." He grinned and pulled her close.

CHAPTER FORTY-FIVE
DECEMBER 19 (3:00 AM)

M AL." IT SUDDENLY OCCURRED TO HER.

"What dear?"

"It's nothing, Carmen. I just remembered something I have to do. Sure you're going to be okay?"

"Of course, dear."

"Kelly will be here any minute. I'll meet him downstairs and let him in before I leave. Sure you don't want to stay at Kaj's place?" Zoe looked around the small apartment.

"Nonsense, dear. I'm fine. Just worried about Shep."

"He'll be fine, he's in good hands. Minneapolis General is exactly where you want to be in your time of need." Zoe gently pushed Carmen's hair back out of her eyes. "You going to hold up?"

Carmen closed her eyes briefly, savoring the warmth of human touch. It had been so long. "I'll be fine. Kelly doesn't have to come. It's silly to bother him."

"He wanted to come, Carmen. He's concerned. Now I need to go. If Kaj stops by, let him know I took his car and I'll be back soon."

Zoe struggled to extricate herself from the well-used sofa she'd sunk into. Then she waited for Kelly in the lobby, and gave him a quick version of the news. All of it. Carmen, Shep, and Marty.

"Gotta run. There's something I need to do fast."

"Zoe, what is it that you have to do in the middle of the night?"

"Obviously something that can't wait."

SHE PUSHED OUT THE DOOR into the cold and felt her lungs seize up with the first deep breath. Her throat instantly went sore as the cold, dry air passed through. But the car hadn't lost all of its heat yet, and she was able to take off her gloves.

It wasn't a great distance, but in other respects it was a world away. She crossed the Hennepin Avenue Bridge, taking her through the Northeast Riverside neighborhood, then swung onto Central Avenue, continuing until she found Mal's sorry excuse for a neighborhood.

Mal claimed it sucked, and she was right. Zoe hadn't paid that much attention to it before. Yet now, she needed to notice everything. Another charming old neighborhood, redeveloped. But here there was no reclamation of the past, no respectfully restored architecture. This was urban renewal at its worst.

At some point several decades ago, the entire area had been razed. In place of closely spaced urban bungalows now stood the mutant version of a suburb, an attempt to deny the city surrounding it. The homes were now larger, yet fewer people occupied them... the lawns bigger, but untended, and somehow filled with junk. The workmanship was shoddy and the architecture... well there was only one word—nondescript.

Garages dominated the facades yet, as Mal had pointed out, cars were parked on almost every lawn at skewed and careless angles. Exteriors were in desperate need of maintenance. Walkways weren't shoveled, just walked through and padded down. In this neighborhood it looked like nobody cared.

It gave Zoe the creeps. She thought back to the party at Mal's. It hadn't seemed quite so bad then. Maybe that was the story in this neighborhood. You had to be shit-faced to stand it.

She found the house. Lights were still on upstairs, but there were no cars on the lawn or in the driveway. Zoe flipped off her lights and quietly rolled to a stop a few houses down.

She didn't have her weapon; it was still a home. *Note to self: go back there and get the damn thing before morning.* Despite her attempts to reassure everyone, she knew she was still a priority for the killer. He'd be angry, and wouldn't let it go. The upside though, was that it would influence his decisions. He could be expected to make bad ones now.

She silenced her phone, trotted up to the garage, and looked in... only Mal's car. She scanned the street. If it was there, he'd hidden it.

She looked toward the light upstairs. No one at the window. Zoe let herself into the unlocked garage and quickly found the tools. Palming a box cutter, she called Mal from inside the garage.

"Hello? Zoe? What are you doing up at this hour?"

"I could ask the same thing of you Mal. You okay?"

"I guess so. I am now anyway. How did you know I'd be up?"

"I didn't. Just guessing."

"Zoe. How did you know? How did you know I needed to talk to someone?"

"Like I said, just guessing. Want me to come over? You alone?"

"I am now. I don't want to bother you though. We can just talk on the phone."

"I'm right outside, Mal. Why don't you come down and let me in."

"Looks like you're a good guesser. I'll be right down."

Zoe met Mal at the front door and moved quickly to get inside, shutting and locking the door behind her. She rapidly surveyed the room.

"No one's here with you?" Zoe looked at Mal for any sign of dishonesty. Mal could be hiding him, or he could be in the house, threatening violence if she didn't go along with him.

"No, there was, but he left."

"Who was here, Mal?"

"Zoe, you're scaring me. What's going on?" Not something she'd say if he was behind the door with a knife, or if she was trying to convince Zoe that everything was normal. Zoe decided Mal was telling the truth.

"I'm sorry, Mal. I'm not trying to scare you, but there's something you need to know. It couldn't wait till morning. Now who was here?"

Mal looked at Zoe's shoes. "It was Marty. We broke up tonight."

"When did he leave?"

"It was well before midnight, but I can't get to sleep."

Before midnight meant he'd had time to get home and could have seen them at Nelson's. It would also have given him time to slip out of his house without being noticed. The fact that she hadn't heard anything from Ray had her concerned. "What happened?"

"Zoe ... he was so nice at first." She looked away. "But he didn't treat me so good." Mal started to cry.

Zoe grabbed Mal's hand and pulled up the sleeve of her nightgown revealing the purple impressions of fingers around her upper arm. "Oh, God, Mal, where else are you hurt?"

She knew. He was good, leaving bruises only on places that wouldn't show. Mal pulled up her nightgown to reveal massive bruises in all colors.

Zoe could tell from the pattern of bruising there'd been some serious non-consensual sex. She'd seen it far too many times. Working in an ER, Mal had too. There was no explaining it.

"He's been at this a while hasn't he Mal?" Zoe carefully helped Mal to the couch and sat her down. "Mal, wait, before you answer, I need to ask you about any other doors or access to your house. Is everything locked?"

"I think so, Zoe. There's a back door, and all the windows."

"No trellises? No way to reach the second floor windows from outside?"

"No. Nothing like that."

"Okay, I'm going to walk the entire first floor and check every door and window. How about the basement?"

"Oh, I almost forgot, because I never go down there. Two windows."

"Okay, where's your cell phone?"

"Upstairs."

"Here, take mine. You stay put and don't let go of the phone. I'll walk the first floor and then the basement. If you hear anything from me, anything bad, call 911 and get out of here. Run to a neighbor's house. Is there someone you trust?"

"Yeah, but Zoe, I'm afraid."

"It's probably nothing, Mal. I don't want to scare you. I'm just being *very* cautious right now. We'll talk when I'm done. Okay?"

"Okay, Zoe."

"Now stay right here, near the door. And Mal? It goes without saying… don't let anyone in, okay?"

"Yeah, Zoe. Got it."

Zoe started with the room they were in and carefully inspected every window. All locked. Nothing appeared tampered with. The kitchen door was also locked. So was the kitchen window. She was beginning to feel better.

When she finished with the first floor she started cautiously toward the basement, unable to find the light till the stringed pull brushed her head at the bottom of the stairs. At that same moment she alarmed at something, and engaged the blade of the box cutter with one hand as she pulled on the light with the other.

She stiffened, and listened carefully. Mal said she never came down here, but someone must have. There was an odor. It smelled like grease.

Hearing nothing, she walked across the basement toward the aroma ... a half-eaten hamburger and some fries had been tossed into a small wastebasket at the far end. She needed to think quickly. Someone had been down here very recently.

Trying to appear unconcerned she turned slowly, looking at all the potential hiding places. There were too many between her and the stairs. She gauged the odds of a run for it. Not good, her trek toward the wastebasket had brought her across the entire basement. If he were down here and hiding, he'd get to her. And after the attack in her home, she counted on him using deadly force this time.

In the instant it took to assess the situation she decided to continue with what she'd come down to do, or he'd know that she felt him in the room.

Muttering, but just loud enough, "Wish Mal hadn't tossed that food. I'm freaking starving." A reason for being interested in the food.

She kept the box cutter hidden in her palm, partially up her sleeve, and casually went to the windows.

"Mal, you should always keep these windows locked, girl. This is not the best neighborhood." Not something she'd say if she thought a killer was listening in.

"Did you say something, Zoe?" Mal yelled down the stairs.

"No, Mal, it's okay. Just talking to myself. I'm almost finished. Just a sec."

Zoe found both windows unlocked. She shook her head and muttered some more under her breath, locking them both. She hoped she'd given nothing away when she noticed little dust left except at the margins on one of the windowsills. It had clearly been used recently, and repeatedly.

Appearing unconcerned, and looking casually around the room, she walked the distance to the stairs ... forcing a normal pace, not too slow or too fast.

Her eyes missed nothing though. Every step was calculated, her muscles taut below her clothing. She was ready for him and could see each potential place of attack. Her adrenaline prepared her, but also made it hard to appear unafraid.

By the time she got to the bottom of the stairs, her back was turned to the one last hiding place. She reached to turn off the light, but listened as intently as she could. She'd have to sense him without seeing. There was no other way without giving herself away and precipitating a confrontation now, at a time of clear disadvantage to her.

She pulled on the light cord, shutting it off, and forced an easy pace up the steps. No one followed. When she got upstairs, she made a quick decision. Noticing there was no way of locking the basement door she felt the beginnings of a plan and left the door wide open.

She joined Mal in the living room. Now came the hard part. Was he in the house or had he left? He could be anywhere. He might have been in the basement, or he could be hiding upstairs. They could call for back up, but Zoe didn't want to be a sitting duck while they waited. There was Mal to think about here. They simply needed to get the hell out. But then what if he was outside? Waiting for them. And what was she going to say to Mal? If he was in the house, he might hear her and force the issue. *He might hear.* She decided.

"Mal, everything's fine. Your house is locked now. But why don't you come and stay with me for the rest of the night?"

"Zoe, that's really nice of you, but I couldn't. Really I'll be fine. I'm feeling better. Maybe we can just talk a while and then both call it a night. Can I get you a drink or something?"

"Mal, why don't you stay at my place tonight?" It was said slowly and forcefully, with the same tone they frequently used in the ER when talking code. Usually around a ramped up patient . . . someone high, drunk, or off psych meds . . . and prone to violence.

Mal stared at Zoe, then said in a flat tone, "Should I get my things?"

"No need, Mal. Let's just go, and I'll get you back here by noon tomorrow. Meanwhile you can get some sleep." Zoe said it so casually she was afraid she'd fooled even Mal.

Mal smiled tentatively and took a deep breath. Zoe knew she too recognized this as a dangerous moment . . . the exit. "I'll just grab my shoes and coat on the way out, okay?" It was truly a question, one that Mal was expecting an answer to.

Zoe hesitated for only a second, before noticing that the door to the entry closet was open, the interior visible. "Sure Mal. Let's go."

Zoe didn't move to help Mal with her coat, not wanting to reveal the box cutter still in her hand. For the same reason, she didn't pull her gloves out of her pocket and put them on.

They moved toward the door, and Zoe did what she could to look out at the front entry without sending any alarms. Zoe purposefully left the door unlocked, even while pretending to lock it behind her.

They went down the few stairs and onto the walkway. Zoe led Mal with her free hand through pressure on her back, guiding her in the direction of the car. She was ready at any moment to shove her to the ground if she had to, out of the way of an attacker or gunshots. Zoe would absorb that herself.

With each step Zoe felt more convinced that if he were outside, he'd have acted already. As they approached the car, she used the remote to unlock it.

"Get in quick, Mal."

Zoe jumped behind the wheel, started the engine, locked the doors and threw snow as she peeled out.

"Hand me the phone."

"Crap! I set it down when I put my coat on. Oh, Zoe, I'm sorry."

"No time for sorry. Let's find a phone." As they drove out of the neighborhood, Zoe scanned the street. "Look quick. Do you see his car?"

"Marty's? No, I don't think so. But you're going so fast I can't tell."

"It'll have to do."

They pulled into a 24/7 and Zoe dialed Ray while Mal waited in the car with the doors locked. She gave him the short version and asked him to get people over there right away.

"We left the front door unlocked. Mal's with me. I'm going to bring her to Kaj's for now. She gives the go-ahead. Do what you need to."

"Right. But Zoe, you shouldn't have gone over there alone."

"You know what? I'm getting that shit from all sides, and I'm tired of it. In fact, I'm tired period. I'll do what I need to do. We'll talk later." She hung up on him.

He tried a call back on her cell, but her silenced phone was already on its way through the streets without her.

Chapter Forty-Six
December 19 (4:00 AM)

"OKAY MAL. *NOW* WE TALK." ZOE kept her eyes looking back and forth from the road to the mirrors. "You buckled in?"

"Yeah, Zoe. But now I'm really scared. What was all that about?"

"Mal, you meant it when you said you never go into your basement, right?"

"Yeah, almost literally. The last time I was down there was when the furnace broke, probably a year ago. I hate basements."

"Well, someone's been down there, and very recently. Point of entry was a window that looked to have been used more than once. In fact he may have been down there while I was. I didn't want to precipitate a confrontation, but I thought if I could sell it . . . that I didn't suspect he was in the house . . . then we could slip out. Either he wasn't there, or it worked."

"I don't get this, Zoe. Why would he have been sneaking in and out of my house? I hadn't threatened to leave him before. I hadn't pushed back until tonight."

"It's more than just you, Mal. I don't know how to say this other than to level with you, the way I'd want to be told. You're just going to have to be strong. Ready?"

Mal looked scared, but "Ready."

"We suspect Marty of the recent killings. Nelson, Hanover, Mickman, and the Ander's mother and daughter."

Zoe paused, letting it sink in.

"What? That can't be. How do you know?"

"We don't know, not for sure, but it's pretty solid. He's a watcher, Mal. He looks through windows. Takes pictures. Then he recreates some scenario that's of importance to him when he kills. I'm sorry to say this, Mal, but you might have been part of his cover . . . or maybe his longterm plans. Were things off? Things you might have missed?"

Mal took a deep breath and stared out the front window. "There was a lot that was off about him, Zoe. I just didn't want to see it. I liked him, you know? And for a while, the sex was good. I mean really good." She thought awhile.

Zoe stayed quiet.

"Not emotionally good, just physically. But *you* know … you're a woman. We like physically good too."

Zoe smiled at her. Yeah, she knew. Why it seemed to be such a secret, she didn't know. Zoe let her go on.

"But there were other things. I mean, yeah, the sex was good, but it was always like … aggressive. You know how it goes, sometimes we *like* it aggressive too, right? It makes us feel how much we're wanted."

Zoe nodded, and waited.

"But other times … well you need someone who can match your moods and needs. But it was always just one way with him." She stopped and pulled at the shoulder harness.

"Oh, fuck, that's just bullshit. I know the difference between aggressive and violent. And it only got worse. You know?"

Zoe nodded again. "I understand the difference, Mal. I know what you mean." Zoe was all too familiar with the difference between satisfying an urgent, aggressive need and the horror of rape. She'd experienced both.

At times it surprised her that she found any pleasure at all in sex after what had happened. She thought she could see that same question in Kaj's eyes the way he looked at her sometimes. Must have been after he'd done his digging.

She even used to wonder if maybe her desire for sex had started out as a defiant behavior, but now found that she didn't really care anymore. Eventually she *had* grown to enjoy it, as one of the few pleasures she allowed herself, and it made one less thing her abductor had stolen. Mal was quiet, and Zoe waited.

"Aw, hell. He got weird on me in other ways too, always wanting to control everything.

"It started out so mild that it didn't seem like such a stretch at first. And when it got worse, it was so gradual. I hoped he would change." She glanced at Zoe.

"Yeah, I know how lame that sounds. It always sounds stupid from an abused patient. But it was so damned gradual. God, how did I let it get so out of hand? It's just that the line started out kind of fuzzy with him, and it got *so* blurry that he was able to keep moving it without me recognizing what was happening."

"Don't be too hard on yourself, Mal. You can do that later if you want, and maybe you should," Zoe hoped Mal *would* go through a serious gut check over this, "but right now let's just get you somewhere safe."

Zoe was suddenly very tired. The sun would rise soon and she was already hitting the wall. She decided to tuck Mal in at Kaj's, then go to her house and hopefully keep an appointment with Marty . . . if she could just stay awake that long.

"Mal, I'm going to key you in. If Kaj's home, just tell him what happened, that I don't have my phone back yet, and after I handle one more thing I'll be back. He'll take good care of you."

Mal held back at the elevator door.

"Come on, Mal. Are you still worried about the disc? Guess who made it?"

"It wasn't Kaj?"

"Nope. And it wasn't Nelson. It was Marty. Neither of them had any idea they were being recorded. Does that help?"

"Yes and no. But it *will* help me face, Parker."

"Then we're good?"

"Yeah." Her eyes filled.

"Okay, up you go." Zoe handed Mal the key and pushed the elevator buttons. "It'll open directly into his unit on the top floor. If he's not home, just make yourself comfortable. There's food, whatever you need. I'll see you shortly." She backed out of the elevator.

"Yeah, Zoe. Thanks." Zoe watched Mal disappear behind the closing doors. She felt guilty about not trying harder to talk with Kaj. He'd worry . . . but at least he wouldn't be in the way, trying to stop her. Same thing with Ray. She pulled into another 24/7 to call him back.

"Sorry I had to hang up before," she lied. "I was with Mal. It's complicated."

"Oh, I doubt it's all that complicated, Zoe." Apparently she wasn't fooling him. "But I'll let it go this time. I tried to reach you on your phone though, more than once. You could have picked up."

"That's what I'm calling about. I don't have my phone. It was left at Mal's. Did you find it?"

"There was one upstairs, but it looked to be hers. I'll check with them again. Where are you? How can I get word to you?"

"I'm on the road right now, calling from a pay phone, but I'll be back at Kaj's shortly. Just call his number if you need to reach me."

"Okay. And where can I find Mal?"

"Kaj's downtown place." She gave him the landline number. "What did you find at the house?"

"Like you said, clear evidence of someone having been in the basement recently. Bet it made her easier to control when he knew her every move. Should have the warrant by noon. I'll find you then. No sign of him at his house though."

"Okay, thanks, Ray. I've got to get going. One more thing to do, then I'm going to get some sleep before that warrant comes through." She hung up on him again. Not finding the phone was valuable information. She was back to thinking that she knew him.

CHAPTER FORTY-SEVEN
DECEMBER 19 (5:00 AM)

KAJ MADE SURE MAL WAS FED AND tucked into the spare bedroom...sleeping. He understood the mindset of someone who'd just broken free of an abuser as well as it was possible to. It was a frequent ER situation. But there was a part of him that would never understand it. And it was always complicated.

He tried not to pressure her with too many questions, only enough to find out where Zoe was. Unfortunately, Mal didn't have a clue. He called Ray.

"Where's Zoe? I've been trying to call her, but Mal tells me Zoe left her phone at Mal's."

"Christ, Parker, you want I should hold your dick for you too?"

Kaj paused, realizing that Zoe had left them both behind. "You and I both know she won't stand for much interference. I mean, would you?"

"Listen, so you can't be with her every second, but can't you at least know *where* she is? Is that too much to ask?"

"Yeah, Ray, it *is* too much. Trust isn't exactly her strong suit...and you know that. Now where could she be?"

"No idea. But I will give you something to think about. There was no sign of her cell at Mal's. You know what that means don't you?"

"He *was* there? While they were?"

"Probably. My guess is the whole time. Close call."

"Too close. Why didn't he act?"

"Probably because he has other plans and because Zoe was careful. Might also have figured I was on her heels. This is a guy who plans, and wants things done his way."

"I can't sit around waiting for her."

"Well, you're going to have to for now. I'm coming over to interview Mal."

"She took my car, does that help?"

"Yeah. I'll put the word out on it."

"I guess that's something. Without my car, I'm stuck here." He let out a laugh.
"What's so funny?"

"She's good."

"How's that?"

"Without her cell, and with my car, she's managed to get rid of both of us for a while. No interference." Kaj blew out a long breath.

"Listen we've got cops stationed at any place we think Marty might show, his house, Mal's, the hospital. They're even doing regular drive-bys at Zoe's, just to make sure. I'll be over in a few minutes."

Kaj gently woke Mal, and handed her some of Zoe's clothing. "Detective Perry will be here any minute. I'll have coffee and food waiting when you come out."

SHE WAS SITTING AT THE KITCHEN counter. Ray recognized the clothing. A reminder that lately, Zoe spent most of her nights at Parker's. The two men sat down on either side of her.

"Coffee, detective?"

"No thanks." Ray jumped right in. "Mal, I'm going to have to ask you quite a few questions about Marty. It may be hard, but just do your best to remember. We'll start with what's fresh . . . last night."

"Zoe knows this stuff, we talked."

"Yes, and that will help. But we need to get some specifics. Not only what happened, but when. Things like that. Okay?"

"Sure." She only picked at her food. "I guess it could have been worse."

"Yes. You're lucky Zoe was there to help you get away." He heard himself say it, but all he could think was . . . *what in the hell were you doing with that guy? Why did you put up with his crap? Could have gotten one of your best friends killed over it too. Someone I care about. Good thing there wasn't a kid in the house. Should have your fucking head examined* . . . all the things he thought of whenever he encountered a domestic situation. No, he really didn't understand it.

The only person he had any less understanding for was the abuser. Guy like that was off the chart. If it was true that she should have her head examined, it also followed that this piece-of-shit Marty should be strung up by his pea-sized balls. At least Ray had some control over that part.

Mal did her best to recall everything, but the interview was taking too long. Her tears were just below the surface and kept erupting. Ray would always pause, while she composed herself, but he never once suggested they resume the interview later. He needed this information now. And as far as he was concerned, she owed it to Zoe. Mal could just damn well suck it up.

It wasn't till she spoke of Zoe's journey to the basement that she was able to manage some degree of detachment. *That* hadn't happened to her.

"What time did he leave last night?"

"If he left, it was before midnight. I've thought about it and it was probably more like eleven."

Ray silently did the math.

Kaj confirmed it. "That would have been plenty of time, wouldn't it?"

"Yeah, I'd say so. Mal, how long was he there with you? What time did he come over?"

"Oh…Zoe didn't ask me that. Let's see. I think it must have been about 5:00. We were going to eat at my place then take in a movie. It all went to hell though." She started crying again.

Ray and Kaj exchanged a look of alarm.

"Mal, you sure about the time?"

"Let me think." She stared at the wall, at nothing. "Yep. Absolutely."

End of interview.

Kaj spoke. "One more thing, Mal. Your car, do you have the key with you?"

"Yeah, it's in my coat pocket."

"Can I use it?"

"Sure, Kaj. Anything I can do to help. I can't thank you enough you know. Both you and Zoe."

"Don't worry about that, Mal." He kissed her on the forehead and it looked like she might cry again. "We're glad to do it."

"Let's go." Ray was already walking out.

"Start by dropping me off at Mal's. I'm going to use her car. Then we can spread out."

"How could we have gotten this so wrong? What really bothers me is that she doesn't know. Mal never told her…and Zoe never asked."

CHAPTER FORTY-EIGHT
DECEMBER 19 (EARLY MORNING)

ZOE RAN REDS AND FISHTAILED TURNS, trying to beat him there. She could handle it either way, but getting there first would be to her advantage. It made sense he'd be flying under the radar, driving the speed limit and parking some distance from her house. If she hurried, she'd have time.

Zoe drove the block around her house. No sign of his car. She skidded into her driveway, got out to enter her code, and immediately hid the car in the garage. Scanning her surroundings, she saw no evidence of an intrusion there.

Working fast, she located her tools and hid a box cutter in her pocket. Then she grabbed a hammer and hid it under her coat as she walked into the house.

No one in the kitchen. She grabbed one of her largest kitchen knives and a small paring knife, adding them to the collection of weapons she had under her coat, then took another large kitchen knife and placed it under a newspaper on the counter.

Moving through the house, she convinced herself she was alone and picked up her pace. She strategically placed a weapon in each room, hidden under expected objects. Nothing would be obvious, but they would all be easily accessible. Then she went for her gun. It was still where she'd hidden it. She kept it with her as she finished her preparations.

Starting with the spare bedroom, she arranged the pillows and blankets so it would appear that Mal was sleeping, then closed the blinds. She did the same with her own room, again closing the blackout blinds she used when she needed to sleep during the day. It would be hard for him to make anything out in the darkness. In the bathroom, she ran the shower over some shampoo and dampened two towels, tossing them carelessly on the floor. Finally she threw her coat over the couch, then went to the entry closet and found another coat to toss over a chair.

It would now look as though two women had arrived, freshened up and collapsed in bed, just like she'd told him they were going to . . . if he'd been within earshot. For good measure she got two beers out of the fridge and poured them down the drain, then set the bottles on the kitchen table. Now he could assume they were not only tired, but had also been drinking… deeply asleep and more vulnerable.

Zoe settled on a centrally located hiding place. After all, she didn't know how he'd come in, what he'd be armed with, or what his plan would be. She chose a place that would allow for good auditory and visual coverage of her house … a loft-like area in the living room. There were sculptural pieces displayed on the front edge, but if she rolled to the back even an extremely tall person wouldn't see her. She used the stone and metal of the fireplace hearth to boost herself up. If she had to get down quickly and quietly, she could lower herself enough for a short drop onto the couch. And if she needed to bolt, she could swing herself over a smaller opening on the other side, and drop next to the side door.

But that was another thing that made the spot desirable; if she chose not to confront him, he might *never* discover her unless he was absolutely convinced she was home and did a thorough search. It was like the attic in that respect, except for one thing … she wouldn't be trapped if he did find her.

She also realized that as tired as she was, if she had to wait long, she might fall asleep. The way she felt, it would be hard not to. And if that did happen, he still wouldn't be able to surprise her. It might occur to him to look there eventually, but it certainly wouldn't be the first place he'd consider. She'd have time to hear him and wake up. And if he never showed, she'd simply get the sleep she needed.

She thought of her clothing. Did any of it make noise when she moved? She took off her shoes. Her pants were corduroy. Pulling them off as she lay there, she changed the box cutter to the pocket of her sweatshirt, shoved the shoes into the back corner of the space and rolled up her pants to use as a pillow. She was now as silent as she could be, and nothing could be seen. She waited.

Lying down felt good. Too good. She continued to listen, but felt herself drift … back to Canada. Hiding again. Afraid. The gunshot caused her to twitch. She listened very carefully, not sure if it was the gun in her memory or if it had been something in the house.

She never did hear a car. As predicted, he must have walked. But she did hear *him* … quiet though, and if she'd been truly sleeping she might not have heard.

It sounded like he was on the roof, easily accessed by climbing up the tiered planters in the backyard. You could step directly onto the roof that way, no ladder required. Trees rattled in the wind, and the entire house creaked, making his movements harder to identify, but his progress sounded slow and deliberate. She imagined the ice on the roof, and the skylight, which would lift easily. She listened for it.

She only heard his feet touchdown. Hanging from the skylight opening it would have been a very short drop, then there was nothing. She suddenly alarmed at the possibility that he'd been in the attic all along. That drop would make the same sound. But of course it didn't matter anymore.

He would be pausing to listen for any signs that he'd been heard. Zoe barely breathed.

There were areas of her floor she knew would yield, and she listened for the familiar sounds. But he was very good, or he wasn't moving yet.

He would have seen into the bathroom from where he'd dropped, even without moving.

She thought she heard the movement of clothing, perhaps the nylon shell of a jacket. Then there was one small squeak, interrupted. He would have stopped immediately. She imagined he was now the one listening again. Wondering if anyone had heard. Zoe stayed still.

He started again but must have been walking against a wall, avoiding spans that might creak under foot, because she couldn't localize him. Then there was a small click. He probably hadn't completely turned the doorknob before he'd pushed on it. It sounded like the guest bedroom.

She still couldn't see him directly from where she was, but noticed that he was vaguely visible in a reflection off the window above the entry. It faced the hallway to the bedrooms. But it meant there was a chance he could see her too. She stayed completely still, offering him no peripheral movement. She could make out that he was leaning into the guest bedroom. He closed the door, silently this time, and moved toward the master bedroom…he'd been in the house before. It seemed like he was buying it. Zoe figured he'd want to come for her first, viewing Mal as the weak one here.

Zoe saw in the reflection that he was looking in her room, and had the weapon pointed toward her bed. She waited as he slowly entered. This was her chance, before he discovered the ruse. She hopped onto the couch and with her weapon ready she made fast and smooth for the bedroom.

"Fuck!" Her own voice made her jump. It echoed in the forced and artificial silence. She saw that the pillows and sheets had been hastily torn apart and the window thrown open. He'd left. Apparently she'd been too slow and he'd spooked.

Zoe raced to look out the window and felt her adrenaline surge at the sight. No footprints in the snow. Realizing how easily she'd made the mistake, there wouldn't even be time to turn and face it. The blow came from behind and slapped her forehead into the top half of the open window. Glass shattered, and fell along with her into the blood.

SHE WOKE TO A PAIN SPREADING from her forehead down her neck, and found that she couldn't move. Her shoulders burned.

As her vision cleared she saw that her arms were spread above her and secured as Nelson and Anders had been, with leather hospital restraints.

"Rise and shine, bitch." He slapped at her face and she felt the taste of fresh blood . . . then looked Marty squarely in the eyes.

"Nice of you to get ready." He pointed to her legs, no pants.

She probably hadn't been out long. The rest of the blood covering her face hadn't dried completely. He'd only had time to carry her to the basement and secure her wrists to a wooden ceiling beam.

"You stupid, fuck, I *will* kill you this time." She tugged against the shackles.

"This time? There's been no other. If there had been, *you'd* be dead." He laughed when he saw her struggle.

Zoe wasn't ready for the pain in her shoulders as she dropped against the restraints. She moaned and met his eyes as he stepped closer. He was clearly enjoying it.

"And from the looks of things, you're in no position to kill anyone, are you?" He smiled triumphantly.

She struggled to get her legs to work. Stretched out fully, she could just barely touch the ground flat-footed. It meant she could get footing for a maneuver if she had an opportunity. He'd have to get close at some point.

She managed to support her weight and take some of the tension off her shoulders. Looking around she saw the weapon she'd hidden, hopelessly out of reach. She couldn't tell if the box cutter was still in her sweatshirt pocket, but knew it didn't matter. He'd have her clothing off soon.

She tried to think, should she play up her vulnerability, or resist? Which way would he like it? Which way would buy her time? She decided to test it.

"I felt something tear. It's bad. Can't you take me down? I'll do whatever you say." It sounded lame even to her, but she had to start somewhere, try anything.

He laughed and then pivoted quickly, backhanding her in the face. "Bitch, you might not want to fuck with *me*." It sent her head snapping back and into darkness for a moment.

"Sure, I'll make it easier for you … you won't have to *pretend* to be hurt much longer."

Zoe waited for her head to clear. She wasn't sure she'd gotten her answer. She struggled against the restraints, wincing and grunting in pain at every tug on her shoulders.

He stopped and casually watched as she kept dropping her weight against the leather straps. He grinned and leaned against a support pole, looking disappointed when she finally stopped. "What? Giving up? Poor shoulders can't take it anymore?"

"Fuck you." She spat in his direction. "I *will* kill you, and they'll be thrilled to find your bones … the fucking missing link they've been looking for."

He only chuckled.

"On second thought, you're nothing but a dickless evolutionary dead-end."

His eyes flashed, then quickly reset, and he laughed again.

"That's more like it." He turned to a duffle bag and began removing things. His back was to her, but too far away. No obvious move she could make. She struggled weakly while looking around the room. There was nothing. It would all depend on him and what he brought to her.

"What are you doing?" Zoe was hoping that whatever it was would take time. Eventually someone would think to check for her here. She was looking toward a small basement window when he turned to face her.

He looked quickly toward the window, appearing to doubt himself for a moment, then turned back to her and smiled. "I wouldn't want you to die thinking someone was about to find you. Remember this?" He held up her cell phone.

Her heart dropped.

He seemed amused by her expression. "That's right. You've had some incoming texts, wondering if you've found your missing cell," his smile broadened, "and just where in the hell are you anyway?" He roared with laughter. "You made this so easy. I took the liberty of texting back. As you. Told them you found it on the floor of your car.

"Your cop thinks you're on your way to Parker's, planning to get some sleep. Sound about right?" He grinned.

"Parker thinks you're on your way to his place too, and you want him to wait for you there. Your phone battery is low and you're turning it off. But soon, when you don't show and he starts to get antsy, he'll get another text with a change of plans. You'll want him to come here. But he won't get here before I've left. And when he does, he'll find you dead. He'll move to cut you down. You picturing this with me? Meanwhile, the cops will have gotten their 911 call from a payphone. Should put them here just in time to find Parker with your blood on his hands and no alibi. And when they finally get around to searching his penthouse, they'll find Mal . . . dead. That should pretty much seal the deal against Parker."

Her stunned expression only made him grin. "Oh, you don't see that happening?" He reached into his pocket and pulled out a key. "Key to Parker's place. He'll have some explaining to do, don't you think? No one else would have had access or opportunity."

She looked toward the cell phone and felt a touch of hope, letting it play across her face. "Don't worry, we won't be interrupted. I turned it off, no GPS. Saving the battery, remember? They wouldn't think of using the signal anyway. After all, you just told them you're fine. Why should they?" He laughed, turning to the duffle bag, but then paused and looked back at her. "And if you're wondering about the texts? Planted . . . by Parker, to throw off the police." He laughed. "I thought of everything."

That might be true. And she'd always been ready to die. You didn't become a cop if you hadn't thought that through. But dying wasn't what scared her.

She allowed herself to consider her death, and it's aftermath. Leaving Kaj alone to face this, that's what frightened her. If there was any hope, it was to buy time. She let a small smile play across her face when she realized what her fears meant. She had a reason to live.

He noticed. "What's so funny, bitch?"

She looked past him, not wanting to share the moment. "It's something you'd never understand." There *was* something separating her soul from the man who'd controlled her all these years. And in this moment, restrained and facing death … she was for the first time, free.

"Whatever. You're crazier than I thought."

That might be true too. She still hadn't ruled that out. "How did you get the key?"

He grinned. "Interested? I was originally going to use it to take you at Parker's, and then frame him that way. I simply took an impression at the hockey rink. Just slipped into the locker room between shifts. No one noticed. Remember the fog? Got his credit card number at the same time."

"How did you know I was alone here? Were you watching me all along?"

He smiled at her. "It's something I'm very good at." It was a non-answer. He turned back to the duffle bag. "I plan on getting away with this, you know. There's no hard evidence of my involvement. In fact there's far more pointing to Parker, even now." He set up the tripod and attached the video recorder, taking time to get the camera angle just right.

"How do you expect to get away with it if you record yourself in the act?"

"You'll see." He didn't start the camera, but came toward Zoe. Reaching into his pocket, he pulled out the box cutter. "I always find it best to use the victim's own weapons when possible."

As he drew close Zoe kicked at his knee. If she could bring him down, his head might be within reach of another well-placed blow. And if he were out for even a minute, she'd be able to flip her legs around the beam and use her teeth on a restraint.

Her heel only partially connected, but did bring him down. Unfortunately he fell to the side instead of toward her, out of range. She hadn't even been able to hobble him by caving the knee.

"Glad this is going to be a challenge." He rose smiling again. "Too bad I'm going to have to tie your legs too, I rather liked watching them flail about."

He went to the duffle bag and brought back two lengths of rope. But this time he landed an uppercut to her jaw. Her head snapped back in a flash of light, and then darkness. She fought back the heave in her stomach after the blow. When her head cleared and the retching stopped, she found her full weight hanging from both arms, her legs limp and ankles tied to support posts off to each side. Zoe's head throbbed and her stomach threatened with every movement.

He came back toward her and engaged the blade of the box cutter. Zoe closed her eyes and braced for the pain. But it didn't come. She slowly opened her eyes to find him smiling at her, less than a foot from her face, the box cutter held up in his hand. "Where should I cut first?"

Zoe spat at him again, the bloody foam hitting its mark this time. His smile only widened. "Do you know what I'm going to do?" He reached out, cutting off her panties and sweatshirt in careless strokes that nicked her in several places. She tried not to let the pain show, but it wasn't the flesh wounds that hurt. She could barely feel them over the explosion inside. It was a familiar pain—this clawing at the question ... *do you know what I'm going to do?* She *did* know. Could imagine it as if she'd planned it herself. That she could think like him ... it made her wretch again.

He nodded appreciatively and walked toward the camera. "I think that maybe you do. And I know exactly what *you're* going to do. How you're going to respond, even what you'll say to try and make me stop. And yet you'll say all of it, and do all of it, even though I'm telling you right now that it won't help. You have no control. That belongs to me now."

He ramped up.

"But before you *beg* me to kill you, I'll make you do things simply because I want you to, and because it pleases me. Because I can." He waited for her stomach to settle, looking relieved that nothing had come up, "and because it hurts you."

He stopped himself, letting out a sharp breath, and went behind the tripod.

"Smile for the camera. It'll be your last one." He ran off a few frames ... restrained, bloody and naked. As humiliating as it got. Zoe's heart sank at the pain this would cause others after she was gone.

It was clear to her that he was setting up for a snuff film. She craned her neck to watch him as he put on a ski mask, a hooded sweatshirt and sweatpants. If his back were to the camera, it would be impossible to identify him. He and Kaj were about the same height and build too.

Shit.

He came toward her with a ball gag. She wouldn't be able to reveal anything during the ordeal either. Her focus was now starting to move away from saving herself and toward how she might trip him up so they'd catch him later. Could she still send some sort of signal? Or trick *him* into talking?

"You know what? This little video is going to wind up all over the Internet."

She struggled harder against her restraints, seeing the whole thing now. She was about to give him everything he wanted. With one kill, not only would he further implicate Kaj . . . and she was sure he'd already prepared an airtight alibi for himself . . . but he was going to raise the stakes. All just as she'd predicted.

She stopped struggling when she realized the camera was running, and stared at him, reading the dark amusement in his eyes. He turned it off.

"That's right. Young people are on the Internet 24/7. A lot of them will see this before anyone catches on. In fact I'll upload it before I go, and leave the laptop and video equipment here. My prints aren't on anything." He raised his latex-gloved hands. Hospital issue.

"And I'll leave an extra set of leather gloves here . . . the ones that Parker used when he was making this video and killing you. The ones I took from his closet when I tried out the key. The ones I'll make sure to dip in your blood. And this electronic equipment? Just purchased using one of Parker's credit cards. Remember? Hockey rink? Fog?"

He clearly wanted her to know how clever he was, even if she had to die afterward. He started to laugh, but stopped when she resumed struggling in favor of running off some more frames.

She noticed that her hands were gradually coming closer together as she pulled on the restraints. The knots were tight along the beam, but they were held in position only by the friction of rope along splintered wood. *Buy time*, she thought. If she could keep his attention on her face, on her body, and away from the beam, she could bring her hands together and undo the restraints. As long as her shoulders didn't give out.

Her muffled screams were unintelligible through the gag, but she continued acting, giving him what he wanted. He was enjoying her pulls against the leather and rope, the movement of her breasts, the terror in her eyes . . . and she knew that he would let this go on for a while.

Her hands were within range … if he would only turn away for a moment.

But he kept staring. So she stopped moving, thinking that she did have one more weapon, and dropped her head in resignation. As she slowly lifted her eyes to look at him through sweaty, blood-soaked hair, he held the camera on her for a few more moments, and then turned it off.

"You're a good actor, Zoe. But I won't be mocked. Real terror, Zoe … you *will* give it to me."

He turned the camera back on and came toward her, his back to the lens. This time he grabbed her breasts roughly until he got the scream he wanted, the one fighting real pain. She could see him stifle a laugh, and he was close enough now. She reared back and came forward with her head.

"Bitch!" She'd drawn blood, including his this time. But with the layer of fabric absorbing some of the blow, it hadn't been enough to knock him out. She on the other hand, was close to losing consciousness and her head wound gaped even further, spraying them both with fresh blood.

As she fought to stay awake she considered that he wanted her that way … because it hurts *you*. Maybe she should pretend a blackout. But it would be impossible to fake when someone was willing to test your level of consciousness through serious physical pain.

The good thing was that she'd connected with his forehead, and scalp wounds bled like crazy. Some of his blood dripped to the floor along with hers. It could be evidence, and at the very least would require time in dealing with it. In the process, he might also make a mistake.

He backed up toward the camera and shut it off. But he didn't rewind it. He was thrown off by her maneuver and his voice was on that tape, perhaps enough for identification or at least to eliminate Kaj. It appeared he didn't realize it. He ran for a towel. Mopping up the blood from around his eyes. He reached for his gun. Guess they were done playing around.

"Know what, Zoe? This towel, and these clothes I'm wearing … they're going to burn in your fireplace. Looks like Parker was trying to get rid of evidence, don't you think? Sure, that must be it."

His grin disappeared when he raised the gun to her head and shouted, "Do you think I'm fucking stupid? I was going to burn them anyway, you moronic cunt."

She kept her eyes on his, and didn't flinch. He would need more from her, she thought. He hadn't worked his way up to this plan only to quit now, without getting everything. He lowered the gun. She was right. "But whore, they don't burn until you die." He reached into the duffle bag for a length of pipe, and then turned the camera back on.

He approached her slowly, his back to the lens, from an angle that afforded the camera a good view of her. It captured her face as it registered that her death wouldn't be as simple as a gunshot. She wished for a moment that he'd just given her that bullet.

But facing him squarely, she refused all emotion as she watched him manipulate the pipe in his hands, taunting her. It was the only thing she could deny him now. She kept working the restraint as he came toward her. One hand was now free, and he hadn't noticed. Almost, she thought. She started working the other with her free hand, making it look like she was struggling against them, and gave him the terrified expression he wanted to see. *Keep looking at my face.*

Her eyes were fixed on his when she jumped involuntarily at the concussive sound and the spray of warm blood. His head had exploded in red and tan, across her face.

The shot came from the far window, fired through glass. She couldn't see through the blood and tissue in her eyes to make out the shooter. But he yelled something, just before the start of a police siren nearby.

She closed her eyes against the rush of cold air through the broken window and allowed herself a moment of regret, followed by a moment of thanks. And within seconds she fell hard against the remaining restraint, darkness a welcome retreat.

CHAPTER FORTY-NINE
DECEMBER 21 (MORNING)

ROUTINE SOUNDS OF A HOSPITAL WARD greeted Zoe when she woke. Kaj gently stroked her head.

"Who shot him? Which cop? Who should I thank?" She tried sitting up, but the leaden feel of her head stopped her.

"It wasn't a cop, Zoe. Hold still and try to rest. You were in pretty bad shape when we found you."

"Who was it then? A neighbor? I heard a siren just after the gunshot. That's the last thing I remember clearly."

"You do remember. I was sort of hoping you wouldn't. They're not sure, Zoe."

"He fired through the window, and yelled something. I couldn't make it out. But it had to be a cop."

"There were footprints to and from the window, but even the dog couldn't track him. The trail disappeared at a sidewalk, and Ray figures he got into a car. Dog lost him there."

"I don't get it, why would someone save my life and then run?" She was suddenly aware of the pain in her shoulders too, and tried to bring back what had happened after the shot. She remembered the rush of cold air through the shattered window, and shivering . . . then a vague image of someone cutting her down and throwing a blanket over her.

"We don't know that either, but the sequence on the video was as you remember. The siren started right after the gunshot, probably scared him off."

She stiffened. "I'm sorry, Kaj. Why did you have to see it?"

"So that I'd know how to help you. Ray recognized that."

"Kaj, his blood was all over me, and all I can remember thinking at that moment was that I wish it had been me who'd shot him . . . and that he'd seen his goddamn death coming. The way it happened, he died thinking he'd won."

"In his hell . . . he knows, Zoe. He knows he failed."

"I was almost free, you know. He didn't notice I'd already gotten one hand out. And I was so close with the other one. I would have had him then, when he came close to me. But someone beat me to it."

"A lot of that blood was yours, Zoe. But yeah, you'd have had him."

"How did you know to go to my house?"

"Both Ray and I separated to look for you. I was about to drive by your house when I got your text asking me to wait at my place. So I drove back, but I didn't like it. Something seemed off."

"I guess you *can* think like a cop after all. Maybe I need to give you more credit."

"So I talked to Mal one more time, and got every detail. She remembered what you'd said when she sensed that you were trying to talk to her without someone else catching on, like in the ER."

Zoe smiled. "I knew she'd understand."

"Well, you'd said that the two of you were going to your house to rest for a while." He leaned down to kiss her mouth softly, tenderly. "I'm getting to know you pretty well, Zoe. If you dropped Mal off at my place, that meant you were going back to yours. And once again, you were right. I'm just sorry we didn't get there sooner. We must have just missed the shooter, or the siren scared him off. The squad pulled up on my heels, and Ray within five minutes of that."

"It was you? You cut me down?"

He nodded, and she locked on the sadness in his eyes. It went deep.

"I'm sorry, Kaj."

He blew out a long breath. "You were in bad shape. It looked like you'd taken a severe beating to your head, and there were multiple lacerations." He reached up and touched the bandage above her forehead. "The big ones right there.

"Though you don't care much about scars, I took the liberty of getting a plastic surgeon to sew you up. Hopefully there'll be no permanent reminder. Your hair will cover it if there is."

She smiled weakly. "Thank you. But I'm afraid I'll never forget it."

"I know." His eyes focused on hers, concerned. "I called in a clean-up crew too, after the cops were finished. You love that place ... I didn't want any reminder left there either."

"Thanks. Really. How's Mal?"

"She went home after we identified him. The large exit wound came through his face. We weren't sure at first."

"I know. There wasn't much left to identify. I can still see it. I was staring right at him when it happened." She watched his jaw clench. "Is she okay?"

"Yes. Once we confirmed the danger to her was past she just wanted to get home. It's over." He looked away from her. "Zoe?"

"Yeah?"

"Are you sure about the timing of that first attack? Could you have been off about it?" Then he kissed her.

It was a distraction. "Not a chance, Kaj. Why?" She tried to rise up on one arm. It was her shoulder that stopped her this time.

"Nothing important. Ray is going to ask you to work through a timeline. Just wondering."

"That's bullshit, Kaj. What's up?"

"It's just that Mal says Marty was at her place during your first attack. But maybe she's the one who has it wrong." He shrugged.

"I don't like inconsistencies, Kaj. It's no different than medicine. And you know how that works. What does Ray think? I need to talk to him."

"Sure, Zoe. We'll call him. But he's not too worried. You were right about who the killer was, and what he'd do. You were right all along, according to Ray."

"I never made Marty for this. I didn't know."

"But you were convinced it was someone from Julia's neighborhood."

"I don't like this. If it wasn't Marty that first time, then who?"

"Ray thinks it *was* Marty. He figures Mal got the time wrong. Anyway it's over now." He looked away again.

"You're not a very good liar, Kaj. And Ray wouldn't let that go so easily. *I* certainly wouldn't."

"Zoe, when you're able, we'll go through it together. But not now." He gently stroked her face, on the few places that didn't appear bruised and sore.

Zoe was quiet for a while. Thinking. Finally she pulled her head off his shoulder. "He would have gotten away with it you know... if he'd killed me."

"Maybe... but he didn't. It's over."

"He was going to plant evidence against you. The cell phone message you got . . . it never came from me. He used it to keep you at your place. Then he was going to switch places with you and make fast work of Mal. Pin that one on you too. He had it all worked out."

She squeezed him, though the pain in her shoulders flared. "He was ready to take the wrap for the domestic, but that's it. He figured there was no good evidence tying him to any of the murders. And you know what? I think he might have pulled it off."

Kaj stayed quiet.

"You know, when I got home from work yesterday morning" . . . She looked at him, confused. "It *was* yesterday morning, wasn't it? How long have I been out?"

"You're missing a day, Zoe. It was the day before."

"No kidding?" She laughed. "Ouch."

"Careful, Zoe. What about that morning?"

"Actually, it was before I left for work the night before. I'd noticed something was off. As I remember, it was an odor. Barely perceptible, but you know how sensitive some people are to odors? That's me." She paused to look at him.

"Yes. Aromas can be strongly associated with memories."

"Anyway, it makes me wonder if he *was* in the house then." She thought about it. "Well if he was, at least he didn't kill anyone after I let him get away that time.

"But none of that makes sense either. Despite all the stupid mistakes I'd made the first time, I could have had the *flu* and still handled him. He wasn't that hard. The second time, he was like a different person. Prepared." She stared past Kaj at nothing in particular. Kaj waited. "He said it wasn't him. He told me that . . . I remember now."

"What? Who?"

"Marty. When he was getting ready to do me. I mouthed off to him about it and he said he hadn't had a go at me yet, that if he had I'd already be dead. I remember it now. I didn't think too much of it under the circumstances. Figured it was just bullshit. But he did say it. Maybe it was true. Could there have been two different men going in and out of my house?" She felt a tremor in her gut.

Kaj held tighter. "We'll check the timeline with Ray. But it doesn't matter Zoe. It's over."

And when Zoe looked into his eyes, she saw that it wasn't.

CHAPTER FIFTY

DECEMBER 21 (MIDDAY)

KELLY WAS IN HIS OFFICE WHEN KAJ found him.

"What's the matter? Is she all right?"

"She's awake now. Improving."

Kelly beamed. "Tough isn't she? I knew she'd come around soon."

"Kelly, what is she to you?" Kaj moved to lock the door behind him.

"Hey, Parker, what's up with this? I'm her friend. She's like a daughter. I told you all that before."

"That's right, you did, and that was before." Kaj came toward Kelly.

Kelly backed up. "Before what exactly?"

"Before I figured out who you really are."

"Hey, we're on the same side here, Parker. It doesn't matter who I am. All you need to know is that I care about her. Same as you."

"You care enough to set her up?"

"Th'hell are you talking about?"

"That monster, from her past, you've been trying to lure him here, haven't you? It was you. You planted that story in the paper last year, saying the police had lost interest. You knew he'd be looking for her." Kaj continued toward him.

"Wait a minute. I don't know what you're talking about. This whole 'monster' thing, what the hell is that?" Kelly felt the wall behind his back.

Kaj's hands now rested on Kelly's shoulders.

"Wait! Even if I said I knew about the guy . . . from her past, and the article, why would I do that? And just how would I pull it off?"

"Gee I don't know, Scotty, but you implied in the article that you were dead. Suicide, wasn't it?" He saw surprise turn to anger on Kelly's face, and knew that he was right. "Could it be that you have connections? And strong motive. I know what happened to your family."

"Damn it, Parker! You can't interfere now. I'm close. He's here, somewhere. I've been trying to warn Zoe to keep alert, but I can only say so much. She doesn't know who I am . . . and she's not strong enough yet."

261

Kaj pushed hard against Kelly's shoulders, pinning him to the wall, but let go when he showed no fight in return. "So instead you deliberately put her in harm's way, perhaps even risking a repeat of what she went through before, without her knowledge? You fucking piece of shit! Do you have any idea what might have happened?"

Kelly moved and Kaj stopped him with an uppercut to the jaw.

Blood foamed at the corner of Kelly's mouth as he slipped along the wall, coming to rest on the floor. His eyes followed, landing vacantly at Kaj's feet.

"I'll wait it out, Kelly, or I'll beat it out. Your choice. But we're not leaving this room until you talk."

Kelly made a move toward the door, but Kaj sent him over the table with another blow.

"I've got nothing to say!"

"I've never been more serious in my life, Kelly. I'd do anything. Do you understand yet?"

Kelly rubbed his jaw, appearing to consider the threat. Kaj waited.

"Maybe I do understand. Okay. Then I'll have to trust you to give a shit." He sat upright on the floor. "I thought I could bring her along faster, get her to open up so we could actually talk about it, and plan. But she's damaged, Parker. Worse than I thought. She'd never let me get that close."

"But she'd slipped away from him! She'd managed to do that much. He didn't know where she was, did he?"

He risked looking up at Kaj. "I don't think so. I don't think he thought to look in the States. For a while he didn't have time to. I had him on the run. Tracked him through Canada. Had tips from local cops all over. The best tip was the one I scared out of that fucking therapist's wife."

Kaj looked back at him in disgust.

"Yeah, that's right, it was me. She knew more than she was letting on, and I didn't have time to coax it out of her. That information brought me out to Medicine Hat. Put me on a good trail. But he was always ahead of me. I needed him to relax and get sloppy.

"So I thought up this idea of finding Zoe and sticking to her . . . maybe he'd come. I'd protect her if he did, and nail him in the process. I had no other option Parker! And I swore I'd find that son-of-a-bitch.

"The cops back home, they helped me when I needed a new identity, or an in for a job. Even money now and then. They kept an eye on Pender's wife too. I mentioned her in the article, figuring she might be the one other person he'd want to come for. So you're right ... I do have connections."

"What about the cops here? Anyone know? What about Ray?"

"One guy knows. Won't say who. But it's not Ray. He'd be the last one I'd tell. He's in the dark, same as everyone else. She didn't want anyone to know, I could tell that about her right away. And Ray would have said something."

"So instead you fucking laid it on her doorstep all over again? Risking her like that! What kind of man are you?" Kaj was ready to pick Kelly up off the floor and force him to fight this time.

But Kelly visibly slumped. "I've become a man who *wouldn't* do that ... that's the problem. I started this whole thing in motion before I knew Zoe well enough to love her, and to realize how hurt she is." He lowered his voice to a whisper. "Before I quit blaming her."

Kaj stiffened.

"She's so bad off she's never talked about it with anyone. Wants to leave it all behind, that's all. She sold the farm, left Canada ... that was it. No word, and no family to wonder about her. It didn't take long for me to find her though, and I'm sure eventually he would have too. She never changed her name."

Kaj softened only a little. "You should have spoken with her first." But he could see how it might have happened. The guy had lost his entire family. And Zoe didn't talk. But 'blaming' her?

"I shouldn't have done it at all." He raked both hands through his thick gray hair and stared at the floor. "But I just couldn't get over it. My whole family was gone. Zoe was my only hope of finding the bastard. She's the only one with a visual on him. Pender's wife claimed not to have seen him, and I tend to believe her seeing as how she's still alive. So I had no sketch, nothing to go on. He'd been like a ghost I kept chasing. The only way I could think to find him was to stick close to the one person he was after. She's still all I've got." He paused to look directly at Kaj. "Problem is, now I see her as my only *family* too."

Kaj let his fists relax. "You can't wait any longer, she has to be told. Kelly, the man who broke in and tried for her the first time ... it wasn't Marty."

Kelly jumped to his feet. "I knew it! I knew he was here. I'd been working to bring her along, trying to get her to realize that she might be a target, without alarming her too much. But she just told me I was being paranoid. And I couldn't let her know who I was."

"Why, Kelly? Would that really have been so bad?"

Kelly laughed. "You don't know how she was before you came along. If I'd even tried to bring up her past, she would have had nothing more to do with me. And if she knew that I'd been lying to her ... well that would have been the end of it. The more I grew to love her, the less I was willing to risk that."

Kaj sucked in hard. "Yeah. I suppose I *can* see that." He thought about his own reluctance to bring it up.

"And it wasn't until just recently that I thought he might *actually* be here, in Minneapolis, that the whole thing had finally produced results. I mean why put her through it all again if he wasn't going to show anyway? We're talking *years* here Parker. Years I either tracked him or waited.

"I'd begun to think he'd never show ... that I'd lost him. Or maybe that he was already dead. So why dredge it up?"

Kaj sat down on the couch. The standoff appeared to be over. He leaned back on the couch and closed his eyes for a moment.

"You built a new life here, faked your own death, and assumed a different identity ... so he wouldn't know you were here, close to her, and waiting. And all of that on the theory he'd come for her again. How were you so certain that he *would*?"

"He came for her twice already didn't he?" Kelly looked away.

"Kelly, the guy yelled something after he blew Marty's head off. It's on the tape. 'She belongs to me' is what he said. Zoe doesn't know it yet. And I don't want to tell her until I figure out what it means." He waited until Kelly looked back at him. "I think *you* know. Now open a vein, Kelly. Spill it ... everything."

The threat was back. And Kelly looked stunned. "Holy shit. Okay, I'll tell you what I know, what *we* know, the cops that is. But I'm not sure it qualifies as *everything*. And if you think what she's gone through already is explosive ... well this tops it. I don't even want to say it, because I'm not sure it's true. But it *does* make some kind of sense."

"I don't see how it can get much worse, but okay, I'll think of it that way ... as a theory."

"In that light, you might not want to tell her."

"Kelly, I'm not a patient man. I said I'd *think* about it. Now tell me." He tensed and leaned in, as they sat across from each other.

Kelly leaned forward too, puffing his cheeks out through a long breath. "Okay. It's about Zoe's mother. There was this rumor... of a rape about nine months before Zoe was born. Her parents didn't marry until about a month after that. There are some who think this monster is actually her biological father. How much of this Zoe's father knew, I don't know. He might not have known any of it. The rumors didn't start until he was dead... after Zoe had left town."

Kaj's eyes darkened on Kelly, who looked a little afraid. "That's why I want you to think long and hard before you tell her this. I mean... what is she supposed to do with that? And does it even matter? It only mattered to me because it pointed to a motive for his apparent obsession with her. Other than that, why pursue it? We could *disprove* I suppose, with DNA samples; dig up her dad if she'd let us. But again, why risk it? It might only hurt. What if it's true? She could wind up blaming herself more than she already does. Maybe even think less of herself. And that's just about the last thing she needs. Am I right?"

Kaj's teeth clenched, starting a headache that was going to take off on him. He could think of one good reason she should be told, or at least a reason to make damn sure someone else got to the guy first. He looked hard at Kelly.

"Do you know what you're saying? Do you have any idea of the position you've put her in? If this rumor is true, it's not just about your guilt over hiding it from her, or about protecting her feelings, it's about setting her up to kill her own father. You had to *know* that she might be the one who'd have to take him down if he surfaced. And even if he does deserve a fast track to hell, she shouldn't have to be the one who sends him there!" He watched Kelly's eyes shift away.

He grabbed Kelly's shirt. "Look at me, you bastard! You even counted on it didn't you? She was a cop then. You figured she could handle herself. You were going to *use* her to do it."

Kelly nodded, keeping his eyes where Kaj wanted them. "That was then, and it seemed fitting. I'm a cop too, and if it were me I'd want the chance at him."

Kaj jumped up to pace and shoved Kelly away as he rose, wishing he could put him through the wall. "That's the problem! She *does* want a chance at him. Acts like she *needs* it!" He pushed at the locked door. "Christ, you've got us all trapped in this, haven't you?" He kept pacing, thinking.

"Why the hell didn't you tell the cops?"

"Like I said, same reason I didn't tell Ray. Someone might say something to her. When I came to town she was still a cop! She was one of them. She'd have heard things."

"It was more than just about her finding out, wasn't it Kelly?"

Kelly finally looked down.

"Your plan was more important than she was, you just didn't want it to fall apart did you?"

"I couldn't let it leak. If word got out we'd drive him even farther underground."

"Okay, then that's what we need to do. Make it known loud and clear that we're onto him. Spook him. Drive him away. Do it through the police. I can't risk her in a confrontation with him now. Despite what she's been through lately, she's actually making some progress with all of this. And *fucking A*, Kelly, that's more important than finding this guy."

Kelly shook his head. "I don't know, Parker. It's damn important. Not just to me, but to her. We're so close . . . if I could just get to him first. Do you know what it would mean if he were out of her life for good?"

Kaj's shoulders knotted up and his fists clenched again, ready for a fight with someone they couldn't find. "I know. And I know what I'll do if *I* get to him first. But, Kelly, what if it's her? How is she supposed to live with that? It almost happened for Christ sake! And it's not just about her killing him. What if she finds him and he catches her off guard with a confession that he's her father? Would she hesitate? Would she forget to protect herself?"

"Just give me a chance at him before you say anything."

Kaj pictured it either way. Protecting Zoe from a knowledge that might destroy her and a man who might do the same.

"I'm not making any guarantees, Kelly. And when I figure out how I want to handle this, I'm not waiting for your approval either. She needs to be told about the first attack . . . only that it wasn't Marty . . . for her own safety. She already suspects something. But I won't say anything about the possibility that it might have been her real father."

"Deal then?"

It didn't feel right to hide *anything* from her, but at the moment it seemed better than the alternative. And maybe Kelly *could* find him. Reluctantly, he agreed. "Deal."

Chapter Fifty-One
December 22 (Evening)

S HE THOUGHT ABOUT WHAT KAJ HAD just told her, and what was on the tape
… she belongs to me. It meant any man who touched her might be in danger.
She moved to separate herself from Kaj, looking out a window.

The idea of losing Kaj, *either* way, scared her. But there were only two accept-
able outcomes to her way of thinking. Both options required ending their relationship and taking this on alone. Either she would kill the bastard, or he'd kill her. In
both scenarios, Kaj would live.

Her soul was her own. She'd convinced herself of that now. But he'd left her with
an open wound that refused to scar. She felt infected through it, contagious even, and
wasn't sure his death could change that. Damaged goods. Kaj didn't need that either.

Zoe's eyes filled at her memories of Dan and all they'd gone through together.
She thought she'd saved him, and had clung to that idea as she struggled to heal after
the violent loss of their mother … only to become the ultimate cause of his death too.

Her body jerked visibly, remembering the feel of rough hands pushing her
onto the floor of a car. She hadn't the strength then … but she did now.

When Kaj moved toward her, she straightened herself and breathed deeply.
He stopped.

She'd always taken comfort in remembering that she *had* eventually managed
to kill one of them … the one she was *supposed* to kill … the one he'd counted on
her to kill. He'd actually laughed at how clever he was, and how easily manipulated
he'd found her to be. Even that one act of resolve, an act she thought took back at
least some control, he'd spun into his own intention. He'd told her that for her it
had only been an act of weakness, of malleability, and tried to convince her that it
was part of his plan all along.

And while she saw the truth in it, he *had* indeed planned it; she would never
believe that he'd *made* her do it. Needing to own that one act of violence, to Zoe,
didn't seem at all odd.

She also told herself that she'd do it over again, in exactly the same way…but again, the proximity of his way of thinking and hers, the blurring of the lines between them, had her shoving the heels of her hands against her eyes. "No."

Kaj moved closer.

She'd learned from the beast after all. But the question still remained…would the rage leave, along with him? How thoroughly had that anger woven its way into the person she'd become?

She chilled at the very real probability that it was an essential part of her now, that to a large degree she depended on it. And just what in the hell was she supposed to do with that? Accept it? It somehow tied her to him … or did it? Did it define her? She was visibly falling apart.

"Zoe, please talk to me. I know this is hard to hear, but you *have* to hear it, for your own safety."

And still she didn't turn to him.

He surprised Zoe by bringing his hands down hard onto the table, immediately apologizing when Zoe flinched. "I'm sorry." He grabbed hold and spun her to face him, but was met with both fists.

Zoe struck him in the side of the head with one hand, followed by a jab to his sternum with the other. The act caused her to grimace in pain, as her own wounds flared. He reached around her, trapping her arms, only to be kicked at. She resisted violently, with everything … as if back in the attic.

"Zoe, you don't really want to do this, not to me … not to anyone."

"I have to!" She quit struggling, and finally looked at the flesh and blood she was fighting. "Don't you see that? I'm dangerous to you. We're dangerous."

"We?"

"That man and me!"

"Oh, God, Zoe. You're not him. You've nothing to do with him."

"I can't let what happened to Marty happen to you. Now that he's back, any man in my life is in danger. We have to hold off until he's found."

"You mean until *you* find him. Good God, Zoe, don't you hear yourself? How long has it been? How many years have you been waiting to find him? And what if you don't? Do we go on waiting for life to start? For our lives *together*?"

"But we know he's close now."

"He's *been* close, probably for a long time! He's obsessed. He only shot Marty because he thinks you're his to torture, and *kill*. I'm not that kind of threat to him Zoe. You're giving in!"

He pulled her tight. "I know you've felt it. It's freedom. You even spoke of the need to take back your life, with or without a confrontation. With or without *revenge*, Zoe. Don't you see that it's what makes sense here? Don't give him this power!"

"You don't understand. He'll go through anyone who dares to stand in his way. And that's what you'd do. Don't you see? That's what got my family killed? It was *because* of me! I can't let that happen to you."

"You also can't go on blaming yourself for the actions of a madman. I don't know how you've survived that all these years. Your anger, it's divided, between him ... and you. *Wrongly!*"

"Sometimes people *are* to blame. They screw up. They're responsible! And even if you could convince me that what happened back then wasn't my fault, if anything happened to you now ... it *would* be. I can't live with that."

"Zoe." He brushed her hair away from her eyes, and kissed her forehead. "*My* Zoe, I'll never again call you a victim, as I don't think of you that way and I know you don't like the idea of *feeling* like one. But just this once, we're going to discuss the fact that you *were* victimized.

"You were young, and they were evil. It wasn't your doing. All you did was manage to survive it.

"Zoe, I couldn't be more proud of who you are, but you *were* a victim ..." he gently placed a finger over her mouth as she started to protest, "... *then*. Don't let him victimize you now."

She pulled his hand away. "Well, if you understand everything so well, then tell me this ... what am I supposed to do with the knowledge that a man who killed my family, and raped me ... a monster ... might have just saved my life? Where in the hell does *that* go?" She struck his chest again. "How do I make it fit with *anything*? With any way of thinking, or feeling?" She felt the persistent headache worsen.

"Zoe, he was manipulative. He enjoyed it. I can only guess where it was leading. But you got away." He paused and took her face in his hands.

"Shooting Marty ... Zoe, it wasn't your *life* he was saving. I think you know that. But in any event, you'd almost gotten free. You didn't need him.

"And we both know it would have ended very badly for Marty once you were loose. His minutes were numbered either way." He risked a smile.

She smiled back. And because they could smile at each other, she allowed herself a moment to feel safe. To feel that if they were talking like this, holding each other, so beautifully in love, nothing bad *could* happen.

The look in his eyes, the urgent need... what every woman wanted. And what she felt toward him. She needed him too much. *Loved* him too much... she could say that now. And it weakened her again, the passion they were both fighting against. She released them both. "Help me."

Unrestrained, he backed her up to the window, her clothes disappearing in ripped pieces as she worked to free him of his. His mouth came down over hers with a violent force, claiming her with an appetite she hoped he would never sate. Tilting her head, she revealed the smooth curve of her neck for him to take as he picked her up, her legs wrapping around his waist. She had it in her ... to love that much. "Now. Please, now." *Before I change my mind.*

He boosted her higher, carrying her to the bed. Her hair spilled over eyes that were closing around a building climax at the feel of his strength. She craved it.

His eyes flared, and she felt his acute need as he lowered himself over her. *Ignore the bruises, the wounds. Please... don't hold back.*

And for her, all else blurred too. There was nothing now, except him. She could feel his grip tighten as the first release shuddered through her. As always, he wouldn't be satisfied with that. He pulled back to kiss the sheen on her face, her shoulders, and her breasts. Allowed her the moment, and then moved to ready her again.

But this time she would be the one to give. She pushed to roll him over and straddled him, moving to bring him into rhythm with her. His eyes remained fixed on hers, penetrating, as she brought him closer, until in one violent move, he had her on her back again, driving hard and deep, both releasing at his almost anguished moan. Zoe fought for air as he emptied himself into her, the warmth washing over her again.

CHAPTER FIFTY-TWO
DECEMBER 27 (EVENING)

DESPITE THE ARCTIC FRONT PULLED OVER Minnesota by the jet stream, Zoe's house was overheating. It was all the people...and all her idea. She needed new memories in the place, because...as she'd told everyone who'd expressed doubts...she sure as hell wasn't going to let Marty *or anyone else* chase her away from the home she loved. *Never again,* she told herself.

So instead, they were celebrating. Another small victory, Zoe thought. The party was meant for Shep, temporarily confined to a wheelchair...and Carmen...but it marked a number of things worth celebrating. As such, it drew a huge crowd.

A small circle had gathered around Kelly as they timed him doing a crossword puzzle Zoe had given him. It was a difficult one...the payback she'd promised after he'd trounced her at Scrabble. But he was uncharacteristically struggling with one of the clues and the small crowd had immediately turned it into a party game, complete with bets. The two camps...either heckling or cheering...were making it hard on his powers of concentration. Zoe started to worry that she'd made it *too* hard.

The landline telephone rang, and Zoe answered. A telemarketer. She was about to hang up when she considered the bet she'd placed on Kelly and changed her mind. Time was running out. And the caller was from the University of Minnesota, her alma mater, a good cause, a smart bunch, and they wanted a donation. *How convenient.*

As she did the math, weighing what she stood to rake in if Kelly could wrap up the puzzle in the next few minutes against the sum 'Cyrus', from the university, was hoping to milk out of her...she decided.

"Okay on one condition, as you claim to represent an institution of higher education, I'm going to need you to *prove it.* Answer one question first. If you get it right...you get your donation. Deal?"

"Why not? I'm sitting in a room full of students, from all different departments. Okay if I use them?"

"I was counting on it, Cy. Okay, here we go."

Zoe gave him the crossword clue and waited for Cyrus to check with his peers. When he came back with an answer, Zoe asked him to hang on. She picked up her cell and texted the answer to Kelly.

She watched from across the room as he glanced at the display, quickly shut it, and looked up at her. He returned the grin and promptly finished off the annoying puzzle.

As the room erupted in a combination of cheers and boos, Zoe returned to her phone call. "Nice work Cy old man. That was just ... *swell*. I'll even throw in an extra hundred, as this was just too amusing. Not to mention profitable." And she was feeling about a hundred dollars worth of guilt.

"Hey, it was nothing. Thanks, Dr. Lawrence."

Zoe wandered over to where Landon, Camilla's husband, was telling tales that revolved around Camilla's wilder days. He started to bring up the story of how the two of them had met, but at Camilla's silent admonition, detoured to the story of her "escape from the closet."

Camilla was no longer silent, "You tell that story, Lan ... I swear ... I'll withhold sex for a year."

"Darling, you don't let me tell that story, and *I'll* withhold sex for a *week*. You'll never last."

Zoe was about to laugh, but seeing Camilla ramp up for a fight, she quickly bit the inside of her cheek.

"Just what are you implying, Lan?"

Zoe was really having trouble now. *Don't do it, Lanny. It's a trap. She's a psychiatrist. You can't possibly win.* Withholding sex on the other hand ... yeah, he had her there. Zoe thought he might actually win that battle.

He was about to speak when Zoe jumped in. "How 'bout I tell the closet story? After all it was *entirely* my fault." She looked pointedly at Camilla. "Yes, it was me, I dragged Camilla into the whole thing ... *kicking and screaming*," she lied through a plastic smile.

"Besides, Cam, you can't exactly withhold sex from *me* now, can you?" This time she looked conspiratorially at Landon, hoping he'd give her the reins. He did.

"Well, then I'll talk Kaj into taking care of that for me." She stared at Zoe.

"Can I get that in writing, Cam? Cuz I'll start another pool. And I'd lay serious money against that happening," Zoe replied with an easy and alluring confidence that had Kaj wrapping an arm around her waist and leaning down to kiss the now genuine smile.

"So help me God, Zoe..."

Zoe interrupted her. "Don't worry, Cam. This story turns out all right. And once the baby comes, we can't tell it again for what...probably twenty years? Let's enjoy it now."

"Zoe, what little I remember of that night...I'm still trying to forget."

"That's not what it seemed like at the time. You said, and I quote...*I've never laughed so hard, been so hung over, or had so much fun in my life*...end quote."

It was, by a considerable margin, a cleaner version of what Camilla had really said...and Zoe watched her relax.

Zoe skipped over how they'd wound up in the closet in the first place...she wasn't sure her imaginative and creative powers were up to the task...and went straight to the escape, hoping no one would ask the obvious question. As the story went, she'd woken up and then shaken Camilla awake. She made sure to leave out the part where Camilla had then retched into a corner of the closet, and noticed her relax even more.

Zoe amused the crowd at her own expense with the account of her naked foray out of the closet to scope out the house. She couldn't find their clothes...and they weren't alone. She'd returned to the closet to report on her findings.

"There were two men...two incredibly handsome men," Zoe looked sharply at Landon, "sitting at the bottom of the steps leading to the only exits." *Be careful what you wish for, Lanny old man.*

"Excuse me while I go find something to kick," Landon countered.

Camilla smiled.

Zoe noticed that everyone was leaning forward, mouths ajar, as if listening to a scary story around a campfire. *This had better be good, they have high expectations.*

"I'll jump to the chase...literally. There was only one way out of that place without going through those men." She smirked at Kaj who seemed to be listening intently.

"So, using the good judgment that had gotten us into that situation in the first place," she paused for the laughter, "we put on men's sweatpants and t-shirts which we found in the closet and we ... I mean *I* ... grabbed Camilla by the hand and ... *dragged her* over to a window.

"We quietly and cleverly," she looked at Camilla's amused eyes and read *more like drunkenly and stupidly,* "climbed out onto a small roof overhang. Pushing off hard ... while *pulling* Camilla with me ... I jumped into the deep end of the backyard swimming pool.

"So there you have it ... the two of us, running through the streets of downtown Minneapolis looking like wet t-shirt contest escapees." Zoe leaned over to whisper in Camilla's ear. "I had to give them something."

"That was you guys?" Carmen looked stunned.

"You saw us?" Zoe looked a little worried. Camilla sat bolt upright.

Carmen smiled. "Oh, my ... I'm sure countless people did. There would have been very little left to the imagination. Isn't that so?"

Camilla and Zoe exchanged a look of sheer terror.

"Well, there had to have been witnesses to your little escapade. Surely you'd thought of that?"

"So ... ah ... how, what," Zoe and Camilla stumbled over the words together, until Carmen interrupted them both.

"You know ... I've been meaning to speak to you ... *both* of you ... about making a donation to Dr. Nelson's charity. It's a good cause. Health care for homeless teens. I'm quite *sure* you'll both want to contribute," she smiled, "now ... and yearly."

Kelly laughed so hard you would have thought it was the last laugh.

But when Zoe and Camilla joined in, it was clear they had far more to laugh about. Small price to pay, well worth it, Zoe thought.

KAJ MOVED CLOSER TO CARMEN and whispered into her ear. "You never saw anything did you?"

She smiled and whispered back. "Never said I did."

"Well played. What was it that you used to do for a living? *C.I.A. maybe?*"

HAVING HAD HER POCKET PICKED FOR TWO donations already, the sound of the doorbell had her practicing the word "no" in her head. She wasn't in the mood for a snotty-nosed kid selling discount books. She took her time in reaching the door; secretly hoping the kid would give up and leave.

When she finally opened the door and looked out, no one was there. *Yes, kids . . . predictably impatient.* But there *was* an envelope at her feet.

She looked into the dark, scanning the street and the trees beyond. Pausing for a long time, she noticed no movement, not even peripherally.

She stooped to pick it up, keeping her eyes on the street, and decided to read it right there.

The envelope hadn't been sealed, just tucked in. No saliva. She grew even more suspicious. It was addressed to Dr. Lawrence in a messy, almost childlike script.

The text of the letter was in line with what was on the envelope. From what little she knew of handwriting analysis, it looked real. No hesitation, no inconsistencies.

As she read, she had to shut the door behind her and take a seat on the stoop.

Dr. Lawrence,
I saw you on the news, and tried to see you in the hospital. I left the disc. I was never in her house. I thought you knew that, but I guess not. I got the disc out of the computer I stole from the house next door. I sold it. If I hadn't, and would've brought it in with the disc, maybe you would have figured that all out. But I needed the money bad, because I left all the jewelry. When I ran through our dive and out the back door, I dropped the jewelry so he'd stop for it and quit chasing me. But Andi was there. I didn't know, I swear. I thought she was at work. Of all the nights to let her go home early. He killed her on July 4th. Her last name was Stafford. I think her parents live in Elk River. You might want to tell them. That's all.
Lucy

ZOE NOW HELD THE LETTER BY ITS EDGE, thinking they might be able to process for trace. But as it hadn't been sealed, this Lucy kid had probably thought of that too.

Zoe stared into the blackness across the street.

The door behind her opened. "You okay? Who was it?"

"Who was it? Interesting you should ask. It was an answer to something that's been bugging me . . . why the description of the kid in the ER didn't match that of the missing kid."

She held up the letter for him to read without giving it to him. "Take a look before I bag it and give it to Ray. Apparently there was a witness after all, and you'd have been off the hook if Marty *had* succeeded in killing me."

She watched him tense at her words, and then read the letter.

"We'll process it, but I'd win another bet on that one. There'll be nothing."

"So we had the wrong kid identified as dead?"

"Apparently. There were no fingerprints left on the body. No dental history. Not even a face remaining to identify. No parents on record, and no matching missing person report . . . what parents there were probably didn't give a shit. And of course no sign of either kid since July 4th. No one really knew either of these kids, only enough to describe." She looked thoughtfully across the street. "But Lucy tried to get word to us."

"Let's get you out of the cold. Give it to Ray, and then we're going to forget about it. It's over anyway. My guess is the kid just needed to clear her conscience and find a way to get word to Andi's parents."

"Yeah . . . probably." She thought awhile and then smiled. "Want a cocktail? I was just getting ready to take orders for another round."

"Yeah, surprise me." He pulled her up. "I'll give you a hand. Let's go in."

Zoe paused just before they opened the door. "Kaj, this kid could have . . ."

He put a hand up to her mouth and softly pressed against her lips. "Please, don't say it. I know. Why now? Why not before all the others had to die? I'd like to believe that it's because this Lucy is no more than a kid. That she's been scared and hiding. Probably worried the guy would come after her. And now that he's dead, she felt safer. But we'll probably never *know* why. And it's too late anyway. It's over. Over, Zoe."

"Kid seems to have a problem with adults. I remember feeling that way."

He squeezed her tighter.

"But now that I am one, it's appears to be kids I dislike."

"Yeah, well, we'll work that out later too." He smiled.

"Ha! I don't see that happening. But, Kaj, this kid is only a few years away from being a grown-up. Seems to me it's time for her decide just what kind of an adult she wants to be. Kid's got a decision to make."

"Yes, she does. And she still has time to work it out. I say we don't give up on her. We find her. She needs help with that decision, and a lot of other things. But for right now...I simply forgive her, Zoe. You need to as well. I forgive her for being afraid. And I admire her for surviving. As I admire you. We're not hanging onto anything from this case. Is that clear? Because it has to be clear."

Zoe looked into the cool blue of his eyes, and then at his angular jaw. She reached up to touch the roughened shadows on his face, in need of a razor. Sharpness and coarseness everywhere, yet all she sensed at that moment was tenderness.

Such a thoughtful and kind man she had. A man who actually understands people, yet somehow still manages to think the best of them. A man not looking to blame anyone, not comforted by that. A man who knows how to put reason and logic to work, and yet lives with a fiery passion. A brilliant and loving man ... *her* man.

LUCY EDGED BEHIND THE TREE WHEN ZOE stared in her direction. She had a flashback to the last time she'd worried about being seen. That hadn't turned out so well for Andi.

She recalculated her escape route again, just in case they fanned out to find her. They'd never catch her though. The asshole that killed Andi never had.

If she *had* known, had *seen* Andi, she told herself she would have stayed and fought, tried to protect her. Or made Andi run with her.

But whenever she thought about it, she wound up breathing too fast again. It was easy to think things like that about yourself, when you didn't have to prove it. Being a kid was no excuse. It wasn't right to fool yourself about stuff like that.

Lucy really had meant well with Andi though. In fact she'd viewed taking Andi under her wing as the one truly unselfish thing she'd done while on the streets. She taught her everything she knew, but still tried to keep her out of it. Lucy had even encouraged her to find a real job. That's where Lucy thought she was that July 4th night.

That Andi was dead bothered her, but she'd watched other friends die, and knew that dwelling on things that couldn't be changed was a waste. No, it was two other things that dogged her, and both gave her a headache. She was learning to pay attention to those headaches.

First, that Andi's parents didn't know where she was. That was one thing Lucy could fix.

She'd worked it out... if they were good people, and actually cared, it might give them some peace. If not, and they didn't give a shit, at least it might make Lucy's headache better.

The second thing was harder to figure. It had to do with Lucy's own need to count for *something*. Sure, she was a runaway thief, but she was also a good and loyal friend. She'd mattered to Andi... and wanted someone else to know it, now that Andi was gone. So at least this Doctor Lawrence would know. An actual good person would know... and know what she'd done. It felt kind of like a confession. She wanted badly to feel good about herself again.

But there was more. And not wanting to fool herself, she'd begun dwelling on a thing she couldn't change. It wasn't a good sign, she knew, and it weighed her down in a world where she had to stay swift... and not care too much about anything.

She'd spent months running from that man, not sure if she could believe that Andi wouldn't talk. But with each day that went by, each day he never came, she had to face the truth... and it haunted her.

The killer mistook Andi for the thief... and Andi let him believe it. She'd sacrificed herself. It was the reason Lucy was still alive. People were always underestimating them. Even Lucy. And it was too late to fix that.

EPILOGUE
JANUARY 1

ONE SIDE OF HIS FACE WAS A NEW color. The same color as the tire iron that broke through the bones. The metal that shattered his arm and ruptured his kidney when he'd curled to protect what was left of his face. That same unyielding rod had swung through his ribs, collapsing his lung and bruising his heart. It now raced and skipped beats. He could feel it.

Blood oozed from jagged edges where the skull and crossbones of an onyx ring had split the skin around his eye. He couldn't move that eye anymore, and saw double. It felt like his eyeball was stuck, caught on something maybe. When he breathed, red foam rattled in and out of his mouth.

It was a sucker punch. He hadn't been ready. And after that, there was nothing he could do. Funny, he thought, as the ambulance screamed it's way through the intersections ... he was still the one people stepped back to avoid.

As he rocked from side to side, feeling the ambulance slow, swerve and speed up again, it started to eat at him. The idea that he could be fucked with like that made him retch. The EMT pushed away.

He flashed back to the last time that had happened. He must have been what ... twelve? He wasn't sure. It was so long ago. But he'd toughened up in a hurry. Got his hate on. He thought about the kid who'd done a disappearing act after that.

Those two guys were going to die.

They may not have been the reason he'd come to this town, but they were two more reasons why he would stay. Too bad the people who'd watched him getting rolled wouldn't know about it. But he'd make sure *they* knew ... before they died ... the guy with no neck and the guy with the ring.

They wheeled him directly into a room with lots of equipment and bright lights. No waiting this time. There were blue scrubs and white coats everywhere. Maybe he was hurt worse than he thought. They worked fast.

He heard someone say that *whoever this guy is, his own mother wouldn't recognize him anymore.* Another one said *he has an entirely new architecture to most of his face.* They must have thought he couldn't hear them.

Then he noticed it. Most of them probably *didn't* know he was aware. It was because of his face. They looked only as much as was required, and then redirected their gaze.

The one person who did look at him...looked at him hard...she seemed to be in charge. She probably *had* to look at him.

But she was also the one person who should have recognized him. And she didn't. Why not? Maybe it was because all she saw was the deformity, the misshapen part of his face, and not the whole thing. Or maybe it was because one eye looked in a different direction from the other, and she didn't know *where* to look.

He must be frightening, hard to look at, and unrecognizable to anyone who'd known him before. He would be someone you would turn away from. Avoid eye contact with. It gave him an idea.

The walls were changing color...they were blue before...now gray.

It was getting harder to breathe, and his chest felt heavy.

The walls that had paled to gray now darkened from the edges.

He felt hands on his chest. It was the doctor who'd looked hard at him.

He heard her yell *clear!* And then the lights went out on his idea.

ZOE AND KAJ RECLINED ON THE COUCH, feet propped up on an ottoman, looking out over the city lights. Zoe pulled from her bottle of beer. "The mugging. What did you make of that guy?"

"What do you mean?"

"I don't know exactly. It was weird." She shook her head, and took another long drink. "Just felt like I was missing something there."

"I can't imagine what. He's alive because of you. They won't be able to put him back together exactly the way he was before he got the crap beat out of him, but he'll be passable. Nothing more you could have done on your end. It's up to plastics to see how pretty they can make him. That is if he wants them to."

"Now what do *you* mean?"

"Just that a lot of guys who come in like that, they don't have the patience to cooperate through a lot of surgeries and rehab. You know that. You've seen it. They want to be patched up and cut loose, especially if they have a bottle to get back to. And as much as you and I would like to strap them down and do what's right, it's still up to them."

Zoe sighed. "Yeah, I know that." She took another drink.

"Listen, if you're feeling off about it, and I honestly can't imagine why you would, just remember that you saved his life. That was your job today, and you did it. Handling the airway issues with his degree of facial damage, well . . . that was tricky. I don't know how you could have done a better job.

"Besides, the extent of his injuries went far beyond his face. If he'd been brought to any other ER, maybe even to any other doctor, he wouldn't have made it. You had to work fast . . . you did . . . and he's alive because of it. What he does next is up to him. You have to let it go at that."

She chuckled at the long speech. "I guess that's what I'd be telling Shep right now. Am I really such a pain in the ass?"

"You *are* high maintenance my dear," his eyes sparkled. "But not too loud, he's down for the count in the next room. Took a sleeping pill."

He pulled her into an embrace.

"How long?"

"About a week, then he'll be ambulatory. You know he hinted that he'd have preferred to stay with you," he grinned.

"And?"

"That's when I asked him if you needed to take out a restraining order against him."

Zoe laughed. "Go on."

"He said no, but added 'not anymore.'"

She grinned. "He's over it. Besides, with Carmen making the case for him, the female interns all think he's some kind of a hero." She rolled her eyes. "And all the time I put into convincing him that he's not."

"He was a little obsessed, you know."

"Apparently. I guess that's easy to see now. But come on, haven't you ever felt that way about someone?"

"Yes, of course . . . as a twelve-year old. But anyway, I told him to consider him-self lucky . . . it was Carmen who really wanted to take care of him."

"Hey now! That wouldn't have been so bad."

"No. It wouldn't. But he doesn't know that."

They tapped beers in a toast. "To Carmen . . . and heroes everywhere."

"Let's go to bed, Zoe. This day tried it's best to beat us up. I think it's time we healed our wounds."

She was in need of a lot of healing. But the high maintenance comment couldn't go unanswered. "Our? If there's going to be an 'us,' let's get one thing straight," she teased, "I have very high expectations."

He lifted a brow. "Have you now?"

She worked to look serious. "And when it comes to lovemaking . . . you'll find that I *am* very high maintenance."

He was fighting for control of his smile, and kissed her as she kept talking.

"And do you have any idea what that makes you?"

He lifted his head eagerly, and looked into her eyes. "Your sex slave?"

She couldn't help it any more. She laughed. "I was thinking more like my side-kick, but that'll do."

"Promise?"

"Without a doubt. You'll be putting out."

His head angled and he smiled in appreciation. "I happen to like that idea very much."

And when he smiled, she thought she might just dive into the cool blue of his eyes, and still be able to breathe. His love . . . their love . . . it was like oxygen.

"But you know what else it makes me?" He started to undress her.

"No, tell me." She closed her eyes at his touch.

"A very lucky man."

"Oh, yes, I promise you that too."

ONE EYE SNAPPED OPEN, THE OTHER remained covered. He felt his heart race as he pulled on the restraints. A nurse flew to his bedside to calm him down, and turned the alarm off on the monitor.

"Easy there, sir. You've just come out of surgery. Do you have any pain?"

"He moved his mouth to speak, but realized that although there was no tube there, he couldn't move it, and he was somehow attached to a ventilator. His eyes flashed in terror.

"You can't speak sir, because your jaw is wired and you have a tube that enters at your neck to help you breathe. I'll ask you yes or no questions and you can squeeze my hand in response.

"Do you have pain? Squeeze if the answer is yes."

The nurse jumped at the strength of his grip. "Okay, then. Let's figure out where. Is it pain around your face and head?"

Squeeze. *Yes!*

Again the nurse jumped. "Okay. How about your chest?" She braced herself this time.

Squeeze. *Yes!*

"And what about your arms?"

Squeeze. Squeeze. *Yes! Yes! Yes! Everywhere!*

"Don't worry sir. We'll fix that." The nurse pulled her hand from his, and went to get the morphine.

The ventilator filled his chest. *Yes. We'll fix that.*